WINDS OF WAR

OF

A *Buried Goddess Saga* NOVEL
II

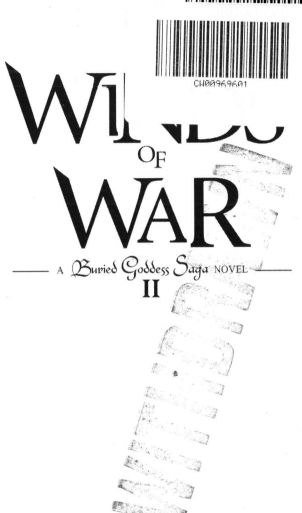

RHETT C.
BRUNO

JAIME
CASTLE

JOIN THE KING'S SHIELD

S ign up to the *free* and exclusive King's Shield Newsletter to receive early looks and new novels, peeks at conceptual art that breathes life into Pantego as well as exclusive access to short stories called "Legends of Pantego." Learn more about the characters and the world you love.

ALSO IN THE SERIES

Web of Eyes

Winds of War

Will of Fire (Coming January 2019)

LINCOLNSHIRE
COUNCIL

Library items can be renewed online 24/7, you will need your library card number and PIN.

Avoid library overdue charges by signing up to receive email preoverdue reminders at

http://www.opac.northlincs.gov.uk/

Follow us on Facebook
www.facebook.com/northlincolnshirelibraries

www.northlincs.gov.uk/libraries

Robyn—more beautiful than Oleander and far less cruel.

DRAV CRA

BROTLEBIR

THE DRAGON'S TAIL

hornsheim

crowfall

THE
GLASS KINGDOM

west vale

fittingborough

YARRINGTON

grumbling

troborough

THE
TORRENTIAL
SEA

bridleton

FORT
MARIMOUNT

winde port

oxgate

TRADER'S
BAY

THE
BLACK SANDS

nahanni

saujiban

L'ATIAPUR

fellwater swamp

THE
WEBBED WOODS

THE BOILING WATERS

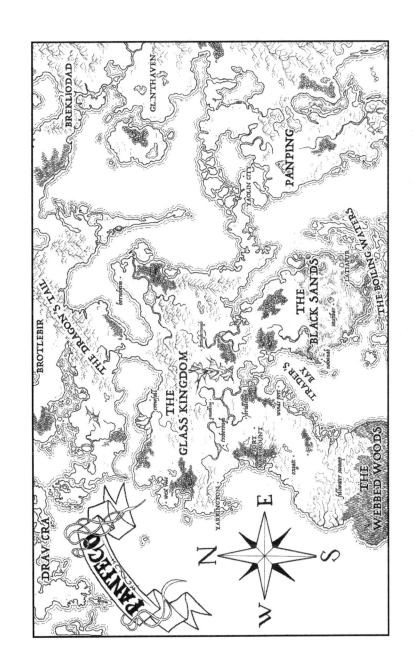

PROLOGUE

Wooden planks coated in a thick layer of moss creaked under Bartholomew Darkings' heavy boots. He closed the paint cracked and weather-worn doors behind him. The Church of Iam was enveloped by darkness but for a faint light filtered in through a circular stained-glass window, so covered in dirt the imagery was impossible to distinguish. A long aisle separating the pews was abandoned. The pews themselves were askew, and the gilded Eye of Iam had fallen from its perch over the altar. Shards of its glass core lay scattered across the floor, coated in dust.

"Hello?" Darkings called out, crossing the threshold. Only his echo answered.

He brushed a string of cobwebs from his hair, yelping like a man on fire, flailing to break free. He struggled to dignify himself, catching his breath and straightening his silk tunic. He removed a note from his pocket. On one side was a red hand and on the other, an unsigned invitation to the church with a time and day scrawled beneath.

"Another one of your made-up stories, isn't it father?" Darkings said to nobody. "The Dom Nohzi... I should have known better."

He crumpled up the note and tossed it aside, then turned toward the door. Just as his fingers wrapped the handle, he heard rustling behind him. He whipped around to find a man shrouded in a dark cloak holding the note. The man drew back the hood, revealing hair as white as the snow sprinkling the streets just beyond the doors. His pale skin didn't show even the slightest wrinkle, not even at the corners of his eyes which were so dark it was as if they had no whites at all.

"What resolve you show, Bartholomew Darkings of Winde Port," the man said. "Waiting all of three minutes?"

Darkings had met men from Brekliodad before, but none with accents so harsh.

"Th... there was no one here," Darkings said. He wasn't sure what to expect when he used his father's contact to reach out to the Dom Nohzi, but just the sight of the man made him feel like his heart had stopped. "Where did you come from?"

"You called for us. You do not get to ask the questions here, Southerner."

"Yes, I..." Darkings drew a deep breath so he'd stop coming off like a blathering fool. His was one of the wealthiest families in Pantego, he could deal with a glorified hitman. "I have heard when it comes to eliminating enemies, your order is the best there is."

"What do you seek? And I warn you, waste my time, and you will leave here without a tongue."

Darkings swallowed the lump in his throat. "I need you to kill a man."

"Every poor soul stuck on this plane wants a man dead. The Sanguine Lords are neither man nor god, and we are their silent hand. If he is worthy of their judgment, then it will be so. If he is not, then yours will be the life forfeited. Do you accept?"

"You'll kill me? That wasn't part of my fath—"

"A man who marks the death of an innocent deserves not to live."

Now Darkings' throat went dry. He knew he should have further studied his father's notes about this ancient order of killers, but he was in such a rush. After what happened in Bridleton, losing everything he'd worked so hard to build, he'd been desperate. He pictured the flames devouring his home, all thanks to that damnable thief. He was through waiting.

"The man posed as a priest of Iam to rob me of my mother's last remaining memory. Then, he used a Panpingese witch to burn everything I loved to the ground. He is the foulest, most inso—"

The cloaked man raised a finger to silence him again. "A mystic?" he said.

"I suppose. You can kill them both if you want, but all I ask for is her companion, Whitney Fierstown. I want him delivered to me. Alive, so that I may see the life flee from his eyes."

The man inhaled through his nose and closed his eyes as if someone had just laid before him the most delectable meal imaginable. He looked at the ceiling and smiled. "The Sanguine Lords accept this offering."

Before Darkings could get out another word, the man was less than an arm span away, closing the long distance in a second. He pulled a knife from his cloak and slashed Darkings across the arm.

Darkings howled in pain. "You said they accept!"

The man raised Darkings' arm. He held a vial between two fingers and allowed the blood to trickle into it until it was full.

"Blood given, for blood required," he said. "This is our pact. If you fail to fulfill your end of the arrangement, my order will hunt you to the ends of the world. They will find you anywhere with this." He plugged the vial, then shook it in front of Darkings' face before stowing it.

"Clearly, you have never heard of my family. Whatever you ask for will be paid in full and then some for every minute you add to that bastard thief's suffering. Gold, gems, anything."

"I have no need for riches."

"Then what do you want?"

The man leaned forward, allowing Darkings to see beneath the folds of his cloak. A row of knives was strapped to his chest, sharp as galler talons. He raised Darkings' chin with a single finger, so their eyes met, then answered.

"Power."

I

THE KNIGHT

Torsten knelt atop Mount Lister, flattened centuries ago in the God Feud. Ice and snow gathered within the Eye of Iam carved into the plain, shimmering like glass when the clouds broke. White flakes danced down from a blanket of gray that hadn't waned in weeks. King Liam Nothhelm the Conqueror had ruled over the Glass Kingdom for all those years, yet now Pi stood in the center of the plateau, his mother Oleander beside him in a blue, velvet dress. Lush, white furs draped over her shoulders to fight the cold wind. She'd been unable to take her eyes off her beloved child since the moment he awoke from death. Unable to stop smiling, even though he hadn't muttered a single word since.

The boy was twelve years old, but he didn't look it. Even weeks later, the color hadn't returned to his gaunt cheeks. But it was his hazel eyes, so much like his father's, that made him seem so much older. They bore the struggle of a whole lifetime. Dark bags hung from them like sacks of wheat, and crow's feet jutted from the sides as pronounced as a man five times his age.

Wren the Holy, the blind High Priest of Iam, held a newly

crafted Glass Crown above the boy's head. It was even grander than Liam's had been. An Eye of Iam in the center was set with a large diamond gleaming as a pupil. By Oleander's demand, there was a thin line of glaruium laced around it, ensuring that her son's crown not suffer a similar fate as her late husband's.

Wren spoke, but Torsten couldn't focus enough to hear the words. He could only think of how much had been lost since Liam's illness and subsequent death. Uriah Davies, Torsten's true predecessor as Wearer of White and Commander of the Glass Army, had been lost at the hand of the Queen's traitorous brother. Without Liam on the throne, an insurgency the likes of which Torsten hadn't imagined possible had arisen. A rebel Shesaitju force had even sprung up in the south, waiting to strike, ready to take back what they felt was theirs.

And the Queen... that stunning, proud woman standing beside her miracle son, she had left a swathe of death amongst her own people under the guise of trying to save Pi. Even if Torsten understood how the love of her son could drive her to such awful things, he knew the kingdom would never be the same.

He could feel it in his bones as he watched the coronation. He expected more enthusiasm—a fraction of joy, even. This was the day a new king was formally recognized; the king of the most vast and wealthy kingdom Pantego had ever known. But as Wren lowered the Glass Crown over the Miracle Prince's head, properly declaring him king beneath Iam, people cheered in presentation only. Torsten could see it in their faces; they were doing so out of fear and not love. And for all the realms Liam had brought under the rule of the Glass, no foreign dignitaries showed.

The Queen embraced her son when the ceremony was through, and then Torsten. She whispered something in his ear that he missed. The new king offered nothing, just received the crown and left wordlessly, leaving Torsten and Oleander behind to catch up.

The boy was now king, both legally and in the eyes of the Holy Lord. A boy Torsten knew little about beyond his having spent the last year cursed by Redstar to see nothing but the horrors of the Buried Goddess, Nesilia.

It all felt like a bad dream.

Once they made it back to Yarrington and returned the boy safely to the castle, Torsten left his white armor behind and found himself wandering the streets as he'd so often done as of late. He listened to the people as he walked, how they talked about the Crown now compared to when Liam was king, or more unsettling, avoided talking about it. They were scared. All of them.

His stroll took him to a tavern he'd been frequenting down in Dockside, not far from the spot in South Corner where he'd grown up. The Maiden's Mugs was like any other tavern in the area—dark, dank, and filled with the kind of riffraff with which the King's Shield was above dealing. Tired old men drinking until their vision went blurry, grasping at barmaidens, cursing their rotten luck.

It was the kind of place Torsten's father loved. A godless place smelling of sweat and sorrow. And every time he visited, he couldn't help but imagine how his life might have turned out had Liam not raised him from the muck.

He was just happy to get out of the snow. Winter had fallen upon the Glass Kingdom in a way not seen in a decade. It was as if Pantego still wept frozen tears for the greatest king Pantego had ever known instead of celebrating the newly crowned Miracle King.

Torsten supposed that's how Pi would be named: King Pi the Miraculous. It brought a shiver not caused by the cold.

The Maiden's Mugs was raucous as usual, but as the weeks went on, more and more were driven in at night to escape the weather. Torsten wasn't concerned. Even without his armor, he outmatched any dozen men in the bar twice over.

The hearth was warm, and beside it sat a cross-eyed bard strumming a lute, keeping the myriad conversations private. A sign hung on the wall and read, Order any drink ye like, so long as it's ale. But Torsten wasn't here for that. He'd seen so many soldiers turn to drink to drive out their demons, but Torsten could thank his wretch of a father at least for teaching him the evils of alcohol.

He sat in a corner booth and watched the staircase leading to the apartments upstairs, waiting for Sigrid Langley to come down. When she finally did, he sank further into shadow. Skulking wasn't like him. In fact, it reminded him too much of that rotten scoundrel, Whitney.

A drunkard grasped at Sigrid's behind and earned her elbow to his gut. She flashed him a forced grin on her way by, then slid behind the bar to start her shift serving the dregs of Yarrington. Torsten shimmied out from his seat and tried to blend in. Not an easy task for a man his size.

He was mere paces away from the stairs when he heard her voice. "My Lord, Wearer, I can't imagine what ye could be doing here."

Torsten stopped. His gaze drooped slightly, but he recovered before he spun to greet her with his best smile. She held a tray of sloshing mugs for eager customers. She was well-kept, fiery-red hair in a bun, face clean. Her beer-stained dress, however, was cut so low Torsten felt he was sinning just by looking. His father had his mother do work like this to earn autlas before she passed from fever. Dressing like that was the best way to get tips in a place like Dockside.

"My lady," Torsten bowed his head, "the pleasure is—"

"He don't wanna see ye," she interrupted. "How many times ye gonna come around?"

"Until you allow me to pass."

"Ye expecting me to be believing I'm stopping ye?"

"Your brother took an oath. I'm already ignoring the law by not dragging him before the throne, so if you'd please just—"

"Dragging him before the throne to see who? The true king is dead, Wearer, and there ain't no one fit to rule in that castle. Rand told me all that went on in that Iam-forsaken—"

Torsten placed his palm over her mouth. He must have moved too hastily, or maybe it was just his size, because she flinched in terror, tray nearly toppling.

He was always shocked at how openly Dockside folks would speak ill of the Crown—as if they didn't realize they were committing treason. Maybe they just didn't care. Dungeons had food after all, and they were warmer than wooden shacks rattled daily by the bitter, oceanside breeze.

"Ye know what?" she continued. "Be my guest. Go on. See what ye sorry old lot did to my dear brother. Don't come back down here looking to wash yer regret in a pint though."

Torsten held his tongue and turned to climb the rickety old flight, the wood groaning. He rounded a corner to a corridor of tightly clustered doors. The housing above the tavern was cheap, and rightly so. Cobwebs lined the planked ceiling and the floor sagged in the corners. To Torsten, it wasn't worth a single autla to live in such a place. Maybe he had forgotten his roots.

The door to Rand Langley's apartment was a few planks of wood poorly fit together. If the purpose of a door was to maintain privacy, his failed on every account. Through the large cracks, Torsten could see Rand sitting at the table, staring into a withering flame, hand wrapped around a mug of ale, but Torsten knocked anyway.

When no answer came, he drew a deep breath and pushed the door open. His hand clutched the Eye of Iam pendant hanging from his neck.

It was the sight, not the smell that made his stomach turn.

Torsten's quarters in the castle were far from opulent, but

Rand's home could fit in one corner of it. A candle flickered on a table cramped against a mattress stuffed with hay. The whole of it was nearly a thick pool of wax, cooling quickly as a cold draft poured in from a frost-coated, cracked, glass window.

"Rand," Torsten said softly from the entrance. "It's good to see you again."

"Torsten?" The young man broke from his daze. "Torsten!" He jumped up from his chair, then toppled backward, knocking it over. He burped as bent to pick it up. "Forgive me," he said, speech slurred. "I wasn't expecting such a noble guest."

"I'm far from noble."

"Nonsense! You're the Wearer of White again." He extended his arms wide and banged his knee on the table, then stumbled a few more paces and placed his hand on Torsten's shoulder for balance. His breath reeked of ale. The stuff in Dockside was so strong it masked the ocean stench. Torsten remembered stealing a sip when he was a child and nearly vomiting. Even before he took the Shield vow, he never touched it again.

"Come, let's sit," Torsten said. "I have an important matter to discuss with you." Torsten wrapped him and guided him back to his seat. It was only in the candlelight he noticed a few stale shreds of bread, thick with mold, in the basket near the window.

Rand plopped down. His eyes lit up at the sight of his ale as if only just realizing it was there. He pawed at it a few times before gaining purchase and raising it to his lips. He took a long sip, then stopped, peering at Torsten over the rim.

"Will you have a drink with me, sir?" he asked. "I think I have another mug around here some…" His words trailed off as he reached out and rifled through an open cabinet.

"That's okay, I'm here on behalf of the Crown." It wasn't strictly forbidden by the King's Shield for a man to drink, assuming it didn't grow into a vice. So long as they remained true to Iam and the Glass, and put duty above all things, even themselves, their oath was upheld.

"Oh." Rand burped. He clanged his mug down hard on the table, spilling some all over his hand. He slurped it up and reached for his basket of bread with his dry hand.

"Bread?" he asked, tearing a piece off the stale loaf with his teeth. A small puff of mold rose, but Rand didn't seem to notice.

Torsten shook his head. He considered sitting across from him, but the rickety wooden chair looked like it'd crumble beneath the weight of him.

"I'd like you to consider returning to your post," Torsten said. "The King's Shield needs its best men for the days ahead."

Rand laughed. "Then it doesn't need me."

"No, you're exactly who we need. It was Liam who decided our order needn't have armigers of noble knights and gentlemen, but the best men the Glass Kingdom had to offer. The most loyal. This is no place for a man of your quality to live."

"Why not? I like it." He laughed again and took another swig. "The best part of living above a tavern." He raised the mug.

Maybe Rand was permitted to drink, but Torsten knew a dangerous vice when he saw one. He only hoped he wasn't too late. "I haven't been Wearer long," he said, "but you were the finest of the few recruits I trained myself."

"And my sister is the finest barmaiden this side of the gorge." He snickered and went to take another drink. Torsten ripped the mug out of his hands and flung it against the door.

"Would you listen to me, Rand!" he shouted. "You took an oath. To shield Iam's chosen king and Country from whatever evils would seek to undo them. Until your dying breath, it cannot be broken."

"Then hang me!" Rand snapped. His grin faded and his face contorted with anger that instantly rendered Torsten silent. Beyond his training, Torsten didn't know the young man personally, but he'd always been restrained, disciplined. Always followed orders.

"Do you know what I did when I was Wearer?" Rand whispered, lips trembling. A tear rolled down his flushed cheek. "I hanged them all. Everyone who disagreed with *her*. Everyone who couldn't save her precious boy. Because that's what we're supposed to do, isn't it? Serve the Crown? I wasn't the Wearer; I was a gods-damned executioner!"

"Rand, I..."

"You're what? You're what!" He slammed the table. That was when Torsten realized his hand was quaking as well. "You're sorry you weren't there?"

"You weren't ready."

"And you are? Ready to hang men simply for doing their jobs? Then you might as well do the same to me because I'm not coming back."

"The Queen was grieving," Torsten argued.

"The Queen deserved to be strung up over that wall with the rest of them."

"By Iam, keep your voice down! That's treason."

"Iam turned his back on us, Torsten. Don't you see that?"

"No, he is still with us. I saw it with my own eyes, Rand. He sent the prince back to us. Offered us all a second chance."

Rand scoffed. He leaned back in his chair, eying the bit of spilled ale pooling across the floor. "Did you visit their graves?"

"Pi's? I was there, Rand! I saw the miracle of his rebirth with my very eyes."

"Not him," Rand whispered. "All the people she hanged—I hanged. Deturo, and Holgrass, and Tessa...If Iam is with us, why didn't he bring them back, too? Why only bring back a mad prince who mutters evil in the dark."

Torsten's heart leaped into his throat.

"You thought you were the only one who ever heard him?" Rand asked, clearly noticing the change in Torsten's expression. "It was the curse of Redstar that made him do such things," Torsten offered. "No, that boy is cursed. Everyone who goes near him... they... they end up dead. I'm never going back to that place. I don't care what you do to me." He swung his hand as if shoeing Torsten but fell off his chair.

Torsten's fist clenched, but he bit back his response. Instead, he watched as Rand pawed at the cabinets again, searching for something else to drink on his hands and knees like an animal.

Torsten wasn't sure why he kept returning to this tavern. Perhaps it was because he too had risen from the shog of Yarrington's poor to the height of King's Shieldsman, But the boy he helped train was clearly gone—deader even than King Pi ever was. In some ways, deader than King Liam. Only a sniveling coward remained.

Without royal edict stating that one was no longer fit, either by age, injury, or worse, serving the King's Shield was a lifelong vocation. Deserting the post, as Rand had, was punishable by death. Had he cursed the Crown so profusely in public, Torsten would've had no other choice but to drag him to the dungeons. But they were alone, with only the soft whistling of wind through the cracked window and the sizzle of a candle nearing wick's end for company.

Torsten couldn't help but pity him. He knew Rand never should have been left alone to deal with Oleander's unhinged fury, and if Torsten hadn't chased Redstar to the Webbed Woods, perhaps he could have kept her from killing so many. It was only that guilt which prevented him from turning Rand in.

"The light of Iam is with you, brother, whether you feel it or not," Torsten said as he backed away. "Should you ever find the strength to hold it again, there will always be a shield waiting for you in the Glass Castle."

Rand grunted an unintelligible response without looking back. His tear-filled eyes went wide as he found another jug of ale.

The young man looked much like Pi had when Torsten found him pacing his room, muttering madness, thanks to Redstar's curse. As Torsten backed out of the tiny apartment in the shog-end of Yarrington, he couldn't help but trace a circle around his eyes and ask Iam to forgive the boy.

The worst curses come from within.

He could imagine no worse fate than having his faith shattered. He'd rather deal with twisted Arch Warlocks like Redstar any day. Because, try as they might to break him and the faithful masses, he knew they would always fail as Redstar had. The man who tried to unravel the Glass Kingdom now sat chained beneath the castle awaiting execution. And now that the coronation had passed, the time had come to rid the world of him and turn the pages on a new chapter.

II

THE MYSTIC

"This is a stupid idea," Sora said.

"Just trust me for once?" Whitney groaned. "'World's Greatest Thief' twice over, remember?"

"That's great, except I feel like I am doing all the real work."

"You're right, looking pretty must be really difficult for you."

Sora punched Whitney in the arm. "No, but acting helpless is. Why are we targeting these men again?"

"Because," Whitney said, feigning exasperation, "they have a horse and a wagon, and I'd rather not walk the rest of the way to Winde Port. I'm tired from slaying monster-gods."

She punched him again, harder this time. "And what, we just leave them stranded in a gorge? I told you, we're only going after people who deserve to lose what they've got. Like Darkings."

"But where's the fun in that?" Whitney smirked.

Every time Sora saw that look on his face, she wanted to slap it right off, but the next thing she knew she was knee-deep into one of his asinine plans.

"I don't like it," she said.

"Trust me, Sora. I've dealt with a million caravans like that."

Sora raised an eyebrow. "They stop in small towns like Trobor-ough and swindle everyone with worthless 'trinkets.' They can keep their wagon and trash if it makes you happy. All we need is one horse, they have two. Would you rather steal one from some poor stableman?"

"If you didn't toss all our gold onto the streets of Yarrington we could have just bought one."

"Sora!" he playfully shook his head. "I never thought you'd be so against my autlas-giving nature."

"I... You are the most maddening person I've ever met. A single gold autla, that's all we'd have needed."

Whitney crossed his arms. "There's no lesson in that! I promised to help you become the second best thief in Pantego, and that's what I plan to do."

"I don't remember that promise."

"It was something like that."

Sora sighed. "Fine, but this better be worth tearing my tunic. I liked this one."

"There she is!" Whitney clapped his hands, then wrapped his arm around her. "Now, do you remember the plan?"

"Of course. 'Use my assets,' as you so eloquently put it."

It was lesson number who knows how many since she found Whitney in that dwarven ruin, kidnapped by Redstar's Drav Cra followers posing as cultists. When she decided to go with him to steal the Prince's lost doll, she didn't think he'd treat it like a real apprenticeship. But his 'lessons' were endless—and endlessly obnoxious—as if thieving were some great art.

Back in Grambling, the last town they passed through, he'd swindled a drunken tailor out of boots. Played him in a game of gems, even though he'd swiped all the good cards before and hid them up his sleeve. Sora asked what the lesson was in that and he might as well have shrugged when he said, "Always check your stack before you deal."

It wasn't that he'd changed terribly since their time together as children in Troborough, but now, he had a one-track mind. In her experience, all young men had one track minds, but Whitney's was different. All he seemed to care about was stealing and making a name for himself. And none of what he took even mattered, he was happy just to throw it away. It was an obsession.

What's worse, in the thrill of their few jobs together she'd forgotten herself, but afterward, she always questioned if Wetzel had spent the final years of his life training her so she could become a thief. She'd grit her teeth and look up to the sky, then sigh and follow along behind Whitney. Because she cared about exactly one person in the world, and as incredibly irritating as he could be, he now stood right beside her wearing that goofy smile he always did when he thought he had a bright idea.

She had nowhere else to go. Nobody else to be with. No home.

"Sora." Whitney snapped his fingers in front of her face to get her attention.

"What?" she asked.

"I'm going to be just over there." He pointed to a large boulder dotting the side of the dirt trail where the path fell off down a sharp slope into the Jarein Gorge. The rift in the land was massive and deep, a canvas of red and russet rock where snow didn't cover it. At the far bottom, a river connected Winde Port with the Walled Lake which was half frozen by winter's touch, and eventually through tributaries to Yarrington or east into the Panping Region.

"If they try anything—"

"I won't be far," Whitney interrupted.

"I was going to say I'm going to roast you alive." She smiled. She couldn't help it around him, even when he was being a pest.

"I'd expect nothing less from the great and mighty Sora. We need to get you a name."

"Can we steal that next?" she joked before realizing he might take her seriously. She had no interest in being ennobled. She had no parents that she knew of, no family connections, and she'd been fine living that way her whole life.

"It's on my list. And don't worry, this is a merchant caravan with a guard or two. No way they're going to try anything too nefarious."

"Easy for you to think while hiding behind a rock."

"You'll be fine," Whitney assured her. "When the time is right, you know the plan."

Sora took a deep breath and let it out. She could take care of herself. She drew a thin line of blood along her leg with her knife which once belonged to her late teacher Wetzel.

Then she slapped it into Whitney's waiting hand, harder than she needed to. Not only would the cut help with the illusion of being a damsel in distress, along with her purposefully ripped clothes, but it provided ready access to a font of sacrifice which would allow her to tap into the magic of Elsewhere.

Blood drawn is never wasted, she told herself. *Power from sacrifice.* That was the main lesson Wetzel imparted in his teachings. The image of him crushed and charred under the roof of his shack after the Shesaitju raided Troborough flashed through her mind. She did her best to force it away.

She stepped out onto the Glass Road which connected Yarrington, the capital of The Glass Kingdom, and Yaolin City in the eastern region. The further from the capital they got, the less impressive the road grew until it was just a narrow line of dirt skirting the cliffs and a peppering of gravel for footing. She scraped away the thin layer of snow with her hands, always gloved when in public to cover her blood mage scars, then lay across the road as if she'd been beaten and left for dead. She tore the shoulder of her tunic a bit more after she got comfortable, just in case, then closed her eyes.

A few minutes later she was shivering. As she lay there, alone and vulnerable, she realized how much a gamble this was so far out in the middle of nowhere. The Jarein Gorge wasn't safe territory for anyone, let alone a young lady. It was the quickest route to Winde Port by land and Sora remembered talk back in Grambling about bandits who nestled up in caverns along the bluff.

She thought about building a tiny fire in her palm for both warmth and protection when she heard the creaking of wagon wheels and the thumping hooves of the leading horses.

A harsh voice cried out. "Whoa!"

The wagon rumbled to a stop. The horses snorted in protest, metal clanked, and footsteps approached.

"She dead?" one voice asked.

"She's a pretty little thing," said another, then added, "for a knife-ear."

"Knife-ears shag as well as the next, I say," said a third.

She could imagine the disgusting man's grin as he spoke, but she held her tongue. Although she'd only been outside of Troborough a few times, she wasn't naive. Her small village had its fair share of traveling bands and troupes passing through the Twilight Manor over the years, the kind of people who thought they were better because they'd seen things, who thought every woman in town was theirs, ripe for the plucking.

Sora much preferred stealing herself away into the hollow below Wetzel's shack, reading the dusty old tomes on magic he'd gathered throughout his long, friendless life.

"She dead?" repeated the first one.

"Dun't think so. She's breathing."

Sora moaned, putting as much desperation into it as she could muster.

"Well, don't just stand there, help her into the wagon!" Hands fell upon her, sliding and groping around unnecessarily. Her muscles tensed involuntarily but she relaxed them and stuck to the plan.

She cried out in mock pain. The men backed off. "Don't move me, p-please. I-I think I've broken s-som-something."

She made believe the noon sun was blinding her like it'd been ages since she'd opened her eyes.

"What happened, my dear?" asked a portly fellow in orange silks. He had the look of a trader—combed gray hair under a feathered cap and a calming smile. His accent reeked of Old Yarrington arrogance as he annunciated each syllable of every word.

Two hunks of muscle and armor stood off to the side, whispering and grinning with one another. They were nearly identical. One made crude gestures toward Sora, the other snickered. Another man with ash-colored skin and a scaled leather cuirass knelt beside her. A Shesaitju... a Black Sandsmen like the ones who had ravaged her hometown.

The sight of him made her lose her train of thought. She could feel the cut on her leg burning as if Elsewhere were begging her to draw on it and turn the man into crispy flesh like his kind had done to Troborough.

Stick to the plan, she told herself. She'd felt terrible about robbing a group she knew nothing of, but a part of her now considered how nice it would be to ride south on two horses instead of one.

"My wagon's h-horse got sp-spooked," she said. "Drove off the ledge. I-I barely... I barely j-jumped in time." She eyed each one, in turn, looking for signs of suspicion but found none.

"Over there?" asked the old man in silks, pointing toward the ledge which emptied into the gorge.

Sora let out a soft moan and nodded.

The twin brutes stopped joking long enough to walk with their leader toward the ledge. Their plate armor was impressive, but unmarked, meaning they were swords for hire keeping the wagon and its owner safe. Which also meant there might be something worth taking inside.

Sora cursed herself for thinking like Whitney.

The Shesaitju stayed by her side. He inspected her, eyes pale and gray like the sky after a rain shower. He said nothing, but Sora nearly shuddered under his gaze.

"I see nothing at the bottom!" one of the mercenaries called back. "Nothing at all."

"H-how could you?" she asked. "'Tis only shadow down there."

"Oi, you know what it looks like down there? What'd you first crawl to the ledge to see the remains of your cart before you flopped over, girl?"

The big men laughed.

"And pray tell, what was a knife-ear wench like you doing out here all alone so far from your home?"

"Looking for a real man, I say," said one of the guards with a grunt.

"Pick her up," the trader ordered. "We can't leave her here in this state."

Sora began to sweat more than she already was. The Shesaitju continued to stare, silent.

The armored men grabbed her and yanked her to her feet about as gently as if they were hefting a dead warthog. She maintained her composure and groaned, even though her blood was beginning to boil.

She could hear Whitney's voice in the back of her mind, "Lesson three: never give up the grift until the grift is done!"

She swore silently, wondering what he was waiting for.

"Another member of our merry band?" one of the mercenaries said to the trader.

A large hand slid over her breast and squeezed hard. She

whimpered, experiencing real pain this time. Her eyes fell toward the cut on her leg. She imagined what it would be like to light the man on fire starting from his boots.

"Something funny, girl?"

She hadn't realized she'd been grinning at the thought.

"P-please," she begged, "I'm just trying to get to Winde Port. M-my cart went over—"

The mercenary squeezed her jaw and tilted her head up to get a better look at her like she was a prized steed. "You already said that."

"Enough," the trader said.

"Why? You think a pretty little thing like this wound up out here alone? What's your game knife-ear?" He turned her head again, this time more forcefully. Instinct kicked in, and Sora bit down on the soft bit of flesh between his thumb and forefinger. He howled, and she broke free.

"You wench!"

The other twin grabbed her and threw her down near the wagon. Her head bounced off dirt and gravel and had her seeing stars.

"Stop this, now," the trader said.

"You hired us to protect you. The way I see it, knife-ears on the road are nothing but trouble."

One of the twins placed a knee against the small of her back to hold her down. She heard the other's belt clasp come undone. The trader protested but neither listened. A familiar tingle ran through her spirit as she felt a hand against her thigh. The area around the cut went simultaneously cold and hot. The rest of her was disembodied. Numb. She felt fire crackling on the tips of her fingertips when the cart shook and down stepped a stocky, little, red-haired dwarf. He held a mug in one hand, ale dripping down his scraggly beard.

"What in Meungor's Axe is goin on out here?" He looked at

Sora, his eyes each looking in different directions, then at the mercenaries. "Pull yer pants up, animal."

He shoved the mercenary in the chest, and even though the man towered over the dwarf, he backed down. As Sora rolled over, she noticed a strange sort of a hat topping the dwarf's shaggy hair. When he got closer, she realized it wasn't a hat, but a half-broken circlet made of blown glass.

"I was not going to allow it, Grint." The voice came from beside Sora. She hadn't even noticed the soft-spoken Shesaitju standing beside her with his scimitar drawn in defense of her. She instantly felt sorry for wanting to torch him.

"By the look of it, ye were outnumbered."

The twin mercenaries had their hands hovering over the grips of their weapons. Grint and the Shesaitju stepped in front of her.

"Fellows, I do believe it's time we moved along," the trader said.

"Just leave her be an' get yer horny hinds back aboard," Grint growled. "Ain't helpin her, nor hurtin her. Just move along."

"We're tired of listening to you, dwarf," one of the mercenaries said, his belt still undone.

"Too bad. I made better men shut their traps than ye, *Dorblo*." He spat the name like it was an insult. "And I be in charge of keeping this here caravan safe."

Grint grabbed Sora by her ripped tunic and shoved her aside without even an attempt to be careful. So much for her savior.

"Get inside!" he barked.

"You're not paying me," Dorblo said. "He is."

The old trader stammered over a response.

"Plenty more gold to go round if we lose the two of ye." Grint stroked the battle axe hanging from his belt.

"I dare you," Dorblo said.

"What ye be, is needin to get in the wagon." They stood face to face, the dwarf up on the balls of his feet. To his credit, he made himself nearly as tall as the man, but Sora hadn't seen a battle of testosterone like this in her entire life.

"You ain't worth my time," Dorblo huffed, finally backing down. He nudged his twin, and they stormed off together toward the ledge and away from the dwarf. The old trader dripped with sweat, eyes darting back and forth between them. By the looks of his carefully manicured fingers, he'd never been in a scrap in his life.

Sora went from wanting to burn them all, to feeling like she was watching a play performed by the school children in Troborough.

Whitney where the yig are you?

"She needs help, Grint," the Shesaitju said, his sword still drawn.

"We ain't a charity," Grint said.

"We aren't monsters either."

"We got no room for another. 'Specially not her kind."

"You know it's not safe here after dark. That's why we were hired."

"I said, there ain't room. Ye be wantin to walk all the way to Winde Port?" The dwarf gave the gray man a shove.

"Do not strike me," the Shesaitju man said.

"Don't make me, then."

The dwarf shoved him again, and the Shesaitju retaliated.

Sora crawled back slowly and was about to run when she heard someone whisper her name.

The horses snorted, and the wagon creaked as it lurched forward, causing Sora, and all five men to stop bickering to look over. Whitney Blisslayer sat at the reins of the wagon. The armored twins and the trader were far enough to be of no concern, but the dwarf, nose now bloody and probably broken, and the Shesaitju, in far worse shape, were both close enough to be trouble.

Sora scrambled to her feet. Whitney grabbed hold of her hand and yanked her up beside him.

"Took you long enough," Sora bristled.

"Take the reins!"

"What?"

"Just take the reins!" Whitney said as he gave them a vigorous snap and the horses shot forward. He let go, and Sora fumbled to grab them. Heavy flakes of snow stung at her cheeks and arms as the carriage was pulled along.

Whitney rose and leaned over the side of the carriage. The dwarf took a swing at him with his battle axe but, dizzy from his fight, missed. Whitney reached out, plucked the half-crown from the dwarf's head and pulled himself back up.

"All right, on the horse and we'll cut the carriage free," Whitney said. Sora glanced back at the men chasing after them and remembered how they'd treated her—a lost soul on the road in need of help. Even if her state was a ruse, she couldn't believe strangers would treat a person in such a way.

She said nothing, only snapped the reins and propelled the entire carriage around a sharp turn on the cliff-side trail. It tilted onto one wheel and drifted on the icy, slick path. Sora closed her eyes, fearing they would suffer the fate of her own lie, sliding off the edge and into the canyon below, but the horse whipped around the corner and yanked the carriage down so hard Whitney almost lost his Glass Crown.

"Thanks for the carriage!" Whitney shouted. "And Grint, Whitney Blisslayer thanks you for the crown!"

Sora tightened her grip on the reins as if somehow she knew he'd take his attention off the road to offer his usual bow and flourish. One hard bump or sharp turn would have sent him flying off the cliffside. And after leaving her with those rotten men, a part of her wanted to pull back on the reins.

"I thought you just wanted to take a horse?" Whitney said as he climbed back to sit beside her. She squeezed the reins so hard her knuckles went white as a corpse. "What? I'm not complaining."

"You're a bloody pile of shog, you know that?" Sora snapped. "How long were you going to wait? Those men were about to..." She couldn't even get the word out.

Whitney, on the other hand, grinned ear to ear. He had the broken circlet in his hands and marveled at it. Now that the dwarf's messy hair didn't cover it, she realized it was much more than a circlet. It was a crown—half of one—with flawlessly cut gems set into every point. The glass was so pure it caught the high sun and painted an area of his leg with a prism.

"Are you even listening?" Sora said.

"Of course, I am," Whitney replied. "I knew you had nothing to worry about."

"No, *you* had nothing to worry about, watching me get tossed around from five hundred paces away." Now that enough distance had been put between them, Sora allowed herself to take her heated glare off the bumpy road and back on Whitney.

"I watched you single-handedly stop one of the most powerful warlocks in the known world. You know what that makes you?"

She didn't answer.

"The most powerful blood mage in the whole world. Huh, how about that? 'The World's Greatest Thief' and the 'World's Most Powerful Blood Mage' riding together into the sunset."

"It's noon, you fool."

"It's a figure of speech." Whitney placed the half-crown over his head and leaned in front of her. He bobbed back and forth, trying to get her to say something.

"You should be grateful you know," he said.

"Are you serious?" she asked, incredulous. "For what exactly? You using me as bait? Forcing me to play along with the stupid games of a child looking to prove himself greater than a father long past? What? Tell me."

"Wow, that hurt," Whitney said, but his smile told a different story. "Look, we just scored something big. Really big. And what's best about it is who we stole it from."

"They were just a couple of… of… there's not a harsh enough word for them."

"Except the Black Sandsman, he looked like he had a little crush on you. First, they destroy your town, now you're falling in love with one." Whitney shook his head in mock disappointment.

Sora's cheeks went hot. She wished Whitney wouldn't have noticed even though she could tell he did. It wasn't that she found the ash-skinned man attractive. She just felt terrible for grouping him in with others who looked like him, like all the sorry men who'd cursed her simply for being a knife-ear since she left home.

"At least *he* was willing to stand up for me," she said.

"Like he stood up for Troborough?"

"What?"

"That sorry lot. They were there in Troborough the day it was burned down."

Her brow furrowed and for an instant, curiosity replaced her anger, then a sharp turn in the road drew her attention back to the horses. The way grew so narrow that there wasn't half a meter alongside the carriage separating them from certain doom. And on the other side was a sheer cliff, the rock as red as blood. She was grateful the horses seemed to know the way.

"That's how the dwarf had what's left of the King's crown I stole." Whitney pointed to his head. "They *all* fled the place when the Shesaitju attacked, including your would-be-savior. I think I remember seeing him kick a helpless woman begging for a ride so they could speed away."

"And you knew about this?"

"Came up with the plan the moment I spotted their wagon

across the gorge. I never forget a group that deserves to be robbed."

She took her hands off the reins to slap him on the arm with the back of her bandaged hand. "This partnership isn't going to work if you don't trust me."

A thousand different answers flickered across his face, all of them probably warranting another slap. Sora was glad he took his time. "You're right," he said, finally. "I'm sorry. I thought it would be better if you thought it was just another mark. I didn't want you to go all, you know, explody because these men might have been responsible for…"

His words trailed off. She knew what he was about to say. He'd been good about not bringing up Troborough too much. The wound was still too fresh for her. A mercenary group like that one might have been able to save dozens of townsfolk if they hadn't run. *They might have been able to keep Wetzel from being…*

"I wouldn't have killed them all," she mumbled. She wasn't sure if she believed those words, which frightened her. She could feel that tingle of energy on her arm and hand again, pulsing in her blood. Even the Shesaitju who came to her defense. She wasn't sure what she would have done.

"I'll believe that when you tell me how you beat Redstar," Whitney said.

She had no response. Torsten thought what happened when she released enough energy to stop the Arch Warlock was the work of Iam. She thought maybe she'd drawn on Bliss' godly blood. But the spider's corpse had been meters away from her, and neither she nor Wetzel had ever been able to draw on any blood but their own before.

"Exactly," Whitney said.

"Did you know?"

"Know what?"

"That they were the kind of men who'd do… that… to me."

Whitney swallowed the lump in his throat. "All I knew was that they were thieves and cowards," he said.

A smirk played at the corners of her lips. "You're a thief, and if I remember the woods correctly, you yelp like a coward."

"But I do it with style! That bastard dwarf challenged me to steal the crown, then swiped it during the attack and fled. I am many things Sora, but you should have seen me fighting off Black Sandsmen until the Glass soldiers arrived to save the day."

"Didn't they arrest you?"

"Which time?"

They shared a laugh, and Sora felt the itch of tension fading. It was the same every time he did something wrong. She'd scold him, and then a few wisecracks later and he'd have her smiling and forgetting why exactly she'd been so angry. Not this time.

She leveled her gaze at him until he had no choice but to make eye contact. "If you ever lay me out like fresh meat again, Whitney Fierstown—"

"Blisslayer," he corrected. Her scowl stole the color from his cheeks.

"If you ever do that again, I'll burn your hands so deep you'd never steal another thing. Do you hear me?"

"I hear you."

"I'm serious."

Whitney circled his eye with one finger. "I swear to Iam and all the fallen gods. Never again." She kept her lips straight and continued staring until finally, he frowned. "I didn't think it would go that far. I promise."

Sora exhaled through her teeth. "It's okay. We'll consider using my assets one of your more forgettable lessons."

"You just have to keep working at it."

"Forget it."

He smirked, then leaned back and made himself comfortable. "Oh, Sora, we'll make a thief out of you yet."

"Yeah…"

She stared off into the distance where a watchtower rose over an outcrop of rock, and the road twisted back around toward a colossal stone bridge crossing the gorge. The columns and arches supporting it sank into the shadow of the rift. Others sprung out from anchors in the snow-covered rock. It made the old wooden bridge crossing Troborough's portion of the Shellnak River seem like a plaything. She didn't even know man could build such a wonder, yet here she was, growing further and further from the home she knew with every second.

"So, that's the bridge to Panping?"

"Yeah. Older than the Glass Kingdom itself. Dwarves built it… I think."

"And why aren't we crossing it?"

"It's a long way to Yaolin City and the roads are filled with things worse than Grint Strongiron. Like I've said, it'll be a quick ride down to Winde Port. We'll sell the silks and whatever else is back there, buy passage on the first ship to Yaolin City, and be there in half the time."

"What about the crown? I bet we could purchase our own ship with that."

He looked at her, appalled. The last time she'd seen him appear so concerned about anything was right before he delved into Bliss' lair, which meant this wasn't just one of his games.

"So, that really did belong to the late king?" she said.

"Plucked it off his holy head."

"Then you might want to consider hiding it." She gestured to the watchtower standing proudly on their side of the bridge where the road bent south. Another waited on the other side, blue and white banners of the Glass Kingdom draped from the tops. Archers waited on the walls, and more soldiers stood at the base. They searched another wagon waiting to pass.

Whitney sprung upright. He yanked the crown from his head, looked at her, then back at it.

"You're right," he said. "If they recognize this we're dead."

"Recognize what? I've never seen it before in my life."

"Very funny. Slow down." Whitney crawled into the wagon and dug through a pile of fine silk blankets, wrapping the half-crown in one.

"You better hurry up!"

Sora snapped on the reins, and the jolt sent him tumbling into the back of the carriage.

"Sora!" he yelped. He lost the crown in the pile of sheets and scrambled to find it. She couldn't help but chuckle as she noticed the great Whitney Blisslayer beginning to sweat. It was the least he deserved for almost getting her killed just to get the relic back, after all. And if she was stuck with him on this journey to see the world and the home of her ancestors for the very first time, she was done doing everything on his terms.

III

THE KNIGHT

I t was no easy task, repairing the Royal Crypt after an earthquake split the ceiling, leaving a zigzagging gash down the base of Mount Lister. Canvas and wooden scaffolding covered it, but snow flurries still found their way in where pilgrims and worshippers tried to peak in at the site of Iam's latest miracle.

The entire wall, which once housed the caskets of Liam Nothhelm and his son, Pi, had ruptured. And so, Liam's corpse was placed off to the side, coin-covered eyes staring up through the lid of his glass sarcophagus. The casket beside his was empty, fractured by the quake before Pi stumbled out that fateful night.

"Lord Wearer?" the dwarven foreman said.

Dwarven artisans were summoned to perform the repairs, for they alone possessed the skills to undertake such a task quickly. The tunnels were older than the castle, older even than the Glass itself having been dug thousands of Dawnings before humans migrated south from the Drav Cra tundra.

Torsten's focus was so lost between the remains of his great king and the site of Pi's rebirth, he barely registered the dwarf's words. As a Hand of Iam, he was not one to question the one true God, but he couldn't stifle the questions echoing around in his head over the last weeks.

Why not Liam? Why not both of them? *Why him? Only him?*

He knew how horrid it was to think. No father should be forced to live in a world where his son had already passed, but the Glass Kingdom needed a leader—a true leader—now more than ever. The wolves were waiting to pounce, and once the wonder of Pi's triumphant return to the realm of the living and subsequent coronation wore off, Torsten knew they would.

The dwarf shook Torsten's arm. "Me Lord."

"What?" Torsten snapped, too late to adjust his tone. He breathed deeply. "Apologies."

"Ain't no matter, me Lord." The dwarf pointed toward the heaviest bit of construction. The burly little dwarf's beard drooped down to his belt, and his biceps were as wide as Torsten's, even though he was a third his height. "Just lettin ye know we're gonna need a bit of extra support in that sector. Struts be makin things uneven—"

"Do what you must," Torsten interrupted. "I just want this place closed in so nobody can disturb them."

"Aye. Bad luck disturbing the buried and the dead."

Torsten nodded.

The dwarf didn't leave, only shifted his weight to the other foot and scratched his head.

"Was there something else?" Torsten asked.

"It's uh…. All this work's gonna take longer than expected."

"How much longer?"

"A fortnight? Maybe three."

"If you need more men, there are plenty of folk in South Corner who can use the coin. Trust me."

"Won't help. With the mountain so damaged, we gotta work slow or risk cavin the whole yigging thing—excuse me words, Lord."

Torsten motioned for him to continue.

"Then there's matchin the architecture, and I tell ye, even we dwarves don't build em like this no more. The stonework's impeccable."

Torsten ground his teeth. "The Crown hired your crew because you're one of the best in the Dragon's Tail."

The dwarf clicked his tongue. "The best willin to travel so far south to work on a crypt. Ye humans do love yer dead. We burn ours and give em to the air. Fires keep us warm and the demons away. Just bein round em gives me the willies."

Torsten bent to meet him face to face, knowing how much the dwarves hated being reminded of their stature. He grabbed him by the collar. "I don't want to hear your excuses," he bristled. "You're being paid handsomely. Get it done or we'll find someone else who can."

The dwarf didn't back down. "Ain't no one better than dwarves, Glassman. And ain't none of em other than me who'd be wantin to risk bein slung over a wall by the throat by the Queen Mother."

Torsten squeezed tighter, then decided better of it. He shoved him away. "Just get it done."

The dwarf bowed excessively low. "O'course, yer Highness. We won't stop til the job's done or yer coffers be dry."

"Dwarves," Torsten grumbled. As he turned to leave, he thought he heard the foreman mutter something about 'flower-pickers' under his breath.

The new Master of Masons, Leuvero Messier was instructed to find the best and Icarus deToit, the new Master of Coin, to pay whatever it took, but the new Royal Council lacked experience, among other necessary virtues. Of all those who'd served directly under Liam, only Torsten remained. The others had been dismissed, executed, or fled the Queen's rage while he was off to the Webbed Woods.

Even Uriah had to start somewhere, Torsten told himself.

Being the Wearer wasn't an easy job, and it wasn't his place to question his station. Still, he longed for the days when Uriah wore the white helm, and the only worry was if news of the late king's condition would leak beyond the castle walls. Things were simpler then.

Instead, he now had business in the dungeons, facing one of those Royal Council members who'd fled and now returned. The warren of dwarven-built tunnels deepened and grew less ornately carved until it was no more than plain, efficiently stacked blocks of stone. Somehow, even the room full of corpses found a way to smell more pleasing.

Torsten turned into the lower dungeons. Sir Nikserof stood with a torch before one of the cells. He noticed Torsten and struck his chestplate in salute.

"Wearer, he's in here," he said. "They say he strolled right into the prefect's estate in Winde Port, begging for his old station back." Torsten returned the salute. He wasn't sure of the soldier's name as he had traveled all the way from Winde Port.

In the cell sat an older gentleman wearing fat mustache. He dressed like a noble because he was one.

"Sir Unger!" the prisoner exclaimed. He jumped at the bars and poked his head into the opening. "There's been some sort of mistake."

"No, Lord Darkings, there hasn't been," Torsten said. Yuri Darkings was the former royal Master of Coin, handler of finances. He had the tanned skin of a man from the great port city to the southeast, and no man knew more about the Yarrington coffers than he. "You abandoned your kingdom in its time of need."

"Oh please, Shieldsman," he countered, his sense of nobility returning. "It was a matter of survival. Oh wait, you wouldn't know. You were sent away before she'd really lost it."

"I did what I had to for the Glass."

"So did I. You think it would have helped anybody had I stayed and wound up hanged like Deturo and the others? Now we have some pimple-faced Master Physician no good to anyone. Now let me out, and we can put all this behind us."

"Your role has already been filled."

"What, by some pup from the market district? One of my assistants? I was hand-picked by King Liam before his body failed. I never imagined how much I'd miss him being around."

Torsten didn't want to voice his agreement, but his expression betrayed his thoughts. Yuri seemed to gain confidence in seeing he was getting through.

"He kept me too busy to breathe with all his conquests," Yuri said, "but at least those made sense."

"King Pi has returned," Torsten said, mustering his most authoritative tone. "Everything is as it should be, yet I'm told you were in no rush to return. You would have been in Winde Port for a week or two before Prefect Calhoun says you walked through his doors."

"Would you have been scrambling to return here?"

"Am I not here now?"

Yuri sighed and backed away. "You've made your point, locking me away down here. But be smart, Sir Unger. I know what it takes to fund a war. I hear the rumors. I know what's coming."

"I am merely a member of the Royal Council," Torsten said. "I don't decide who sits on it."

"Ah, but you have her ear."

"There is a new king now."

"Please, I may have just returned, but I have ears all over the city. I know the 'Miracle King' hasn't spoken a word since he was returned to life, if that's even what happened."

"It was. I was there."

"Relax. I'm not questioning anything these days. All I know is that everyone who disappointed Oleander wound up dead or down here, but all she did was kick you from the castle and onto some insane quest. Don't be a fool, Unger. I can help, just as I have for decades."

"I'm sure you could. But how could we ever trust a man who'd abandoned his post?"

"I hear the Caleef is visiting soon. I know exactly how much they owe us in delinquent taxes, how much they've been skimping since the late king's condition became public. Down to the autla. And I know how much it costs to arm a Glass Soldier for war. Who is in charge now, deToit, my apprentice?" He laughed when Torsten's face betrayed the answer. "He can barely grow a beard. You need me."

Torsten wanted to curse the man, but he knew he was right. As much as he loathed merchant-types with all their scheming and counting coins, men like Yuri were all that kept the Crown from drowning in debt. War was expensive, if it came to that, and another loan from the Iron Bank in Brotlebir was out of the question. Liam funded more than half his campaigns through them, paying the dwarves back when another foreign city was sacked and absorbed by the kingdom.

Investing in Liam had been a smart decision, and his ability to settle debts had forged strong alliances with the dwarven kings, especially King Cragrock of Brike's Hollow. Investing in the unpredictable Queen and a child, however; that was far riskier. The fact ever more proved by the quality of artisans willing to travel to Yarrington. In the days of Liam, dwarves would have fought one another for the chance to build something for him. Now they sent their leftovers.

"Your reinstatement is not for me to decide," Torsten said. "But I'll speak with her."

"I suggest you do it fast. It's never a good idea to be in a castle surrounded by strangers. You know me at least, and you know I know what I'm doing. Can you say the same for anyone else in the new Council?"

"I said I'd talk to her." He turned to Sir Nikserof. "See to it he is fed well and made comfortable during his time here."

"Sir." Nikserof saluted.

"We're all that's left, Torsten," Yuri said as Torsten turned to leave. "We can't let her mar Liam's legacy any further before the boy is even old enough to lead."

Torsten grunted a response, then continued along. He knew Yuri only as well as he needed to, being that they served on the same Council for the last year, but he also knew the old dwarven saying that the demon you know is better than the demon you don't. And Yuri was right. There was nobody in Yarrington better with money.

Torsten reached the other end of the dungeons when he heard a cackle. The sound of it made his blood boil and his heart race.

"My, my. My dear sister really has made a mess of things," Redstar said through the metal mask covering his face to keep him from drawing blood with his teeth. All that was visible beyond it were his dark eyes. It was the playfulness in them Torsten found most unnerving. Locked in the deepest dungeon, to be executed any day now, yet everything seemed like a game to him.

"Quiet!" one of the two guards posted outside his cell snapped.

Torsten stopped and bit his lip. He told himself not to turn and face the manipulating heathen. It never led to anything good.

"Why don't you let me out and I'll talk with her? I can join the fair prince. Miraculous, what happened to him, wouldn't you say? It is like he has some strong tie to the Lady. Two souls beneath this mountain were once buried but not dead, not really. How... poetic."

Torsten couldn't hold it in. He turned to engage when Sir Wardric Jolly arrived and slammed on the bars in front of him. The gray-haired Shieldsman was the unofficial second in the King's Shield, having served since before Torsten was born.

"You'll hang soon enough, knave," Wardric said. He turned to Torsten and saluted. "Sir, I need to talk with you."

Torsten held Redstar's gaze for a moment longer.

"Buried, not dead. Buried, not dead," Redstar sang, snickering.

"Torsten," Wardric said, finally earning Torsten's focus. He guided him around the corner. "When are you going to get rid of him already?"

"The Queen did not wish to besmirch the miracle of Pi's rebirth by spilling the blood of her brother before the coronation," Torsten replied.

"Well, that's done with now, and nothing boosts the people's spirits like a good execution."

Torsten smiled and patted him on the back. "His time will come. Now, you seemed in a hurry. Is everything all right?" He'd become used to things going awry. When someone of any stature approached him, he assumed the worst. However, the old, weathered Shieldsman appeared calm.

Wardric led the way through the labyrinthine tunnels beneath the Glass Castle. "Queen Oleander is requesting your presence in the Throne Room," he said. "He's arrived. A day late and with no notice."

"Naturally. The Black Sands want to see Yarrington as it is, not as we would present it to be for the coronation. Afhem Muskigo tested us with fire, and now Caleef Sidar Rakun will test us with his eyes."

"*If* they're working together," Wardric offered.

"If Muskigo truly did attack without blessing, Caleef Sidar will have no choice but to align with us."

Wardric sighed. "I tire of these games."

"Brace yourself, my friend. I fear the games have only just begun."

"Iam save us all."

"So, you have faith He's with us again?" Torsten asked.

"The only legitimate heir of Liam Nothhelm rose from the dead. Wren the Holy believes it a miracle, why shouldn't I?"

"A miracle, indeed," Torsten said.

But whose?

He couldn't keep the thought from popping into his mind. Every time he pictured Pi standing in the Royal Crypt, crown and bloody Drav Cra orepul in hand, Torsten thought of those last words he'd heard the boy whispering in darkness—Redstar's words.

Buried, not dead... buried, not dead.

"You went to see him again?" Wardric asked as they rounded a corner into the castle's east wing. Tall, pointed-arched windows lined the hall, stained glass shining like precious gems beneath the winter sun.

"See who?" Torsten asked, happy to be stirred from impure thoughts.

"The boy, Rand."

"He's a boy no longer."

"You're wasting your time, Torsten."

"I refuse to let another worthy soul abandon his post."

"Then consider the reason he left," Wardric pleaded. "Consider the reason the Royal Council is sparse, and those who remain are grossly under-qualified whelps."

Torsten shot a glower his way. Wardric took him by the shoulders and stopped him outside the door to the Throne Room. "How long will the miracle steal everyone's attention? Eventually, we have to address what happened while you were gone. How can the people trust leaders who hang physicians and servants for merely speaking truth? Our dungeons still overflow, and we don't even know who really belongs there."

Torsten lightly shrugged Wardric off. They'd grown closer in the weeks since he'd returned from the Webbed Woods. Of all the Shieldsmen, Wardric had given Torsten the hardest time after he'd taken over for Uriah Davies, his long-time predecessor. It took horrid times, but Torsten now knew that if he could trust anyone throughout the kingdom, it was the gray-haired Shieldsman standing before him.

"Let us deal with one problem at a time," he said. "We were all lost after Liam passed. A new king doesn't change that. None of what happened was right, but we can only look forward now. Agreed?"

Wardric drew a deep breath, then backed away. "Agreed. Now, go make sure the Caleef answers for what was done."

"He will, my friend. You have my word."

Torsten turned, but Wardric grabbed his arm. "Don't let her cause a war we cannot win. We've lost enough already."

Torsten nodded, then stepped into the Throne Room. Pantego's ultimate seat of power, a Glass Throne possessed by a juvenile king, towered over the room. By the new king's side stood Queen Oleander, and behind her the Council of nobodies her unbridled rage had left them with. Torsten was the only among them who'd seen war while serving under Liam. For Iam's sake, he was the only one who'd ever even held a sword.

Glass Soldiers lined the hall along with a handful of Shields-men. The former remained at attention, stoic, disciplined. The latter saluted Torsten, fists against their chests as he passed. Torsten recognized only a few of the Shieldsman beyond Nikserof who remained downstairs. Sir Mulliner, Reginald, a few more faces he couldn't put to names.

His own fingerprints upon the Shield, compared to Uriah's, were nearly imperceptible after he spent so much time catering to the Queen's will and sending others to their deaths at the hands of Bliss. And now there were fewer within the walls of Yarrington than ever before. Following the death of Liam, dozens had been dispatched to strongholds throughout the kingdom by Wardric when Oleander wasn't looking. All across the southern reach, they trained the Glass armies and fortified, preparing for another attack by the Black Sands. Then there were those like Rand and Lord Yuri Darkings who had fled Oleander's wrath and deserted their post.

"You're late," Oleander said from beside the throne. She was easily one hundred paces away, but her voice carried down the vaulted ceiling like a galler in flight.

Torsten bowed low. "I had some affairs of the state to address, Your Grace."

She slowly shook her head. "You know I don't like waiting when I call."

"Apologies, Your Grace. It won't happen again."

"You always say that." She held her stern glare for a few seconds before it gave way to a smile.

Just the sight of it gave Torsten pause. Her late husband had named her the Flower of Drav Cra, and never had an epithet been apter. A month had passed since Pi was reborn, and since that day she was as confident as ever, never leaving her quarters without a veritable army of handmaidens preening her.

Presently, she wore a blue gown—always blue—more extravagant than any Torsten remembered having seen her in. It was cut low—always low cut—revealing the lines of her collarbone, then sweeping up around her slender shoulders like peacock feathers. The bottom cascaded down the throne's dais. With Tessa dead at the hands of her wrath, Oleander's new favored handmaiden—he wasn't sure of her name—was busy unfurling the ends, so it appeared like a waterfall cascading down glass steps.

Torsten couldn't help but remember when he found Oleander at Pi's bedside, shattered by grief after the boy died. It was as if she too had experienced a rebirth through his resurrection, the whole castle even. The court went from cowering from her grief-stricken wrath, to impossibly busy with the coronation and other affairs. And now, the royal entourage of the Shesaitju Caleef was arriving in the heart of Pantego. On the surface, everything seemed back to normal, but one look around, and it was painfully clear how much it wasn't.

As Torsten took his position to the left of the throne, he realized he'd never attended an audience with any but Liam seated upon it—even when the King was sick and his body rendered useless, it was him.

As usual, Pi slumped to one side of the glass seat three sizes too big for him. The chair's arm was so high it could have served as a headrest. He dressed in an elegant satin tunic, his long, dark hair combed as his mother spent so much time doing every night. Torsten found himself growing angry at the sight of the boy's beautiful crown, so much more extravagant than Liam's but fought it off.

"The Shesaitju are a proud people," Torsten whispered to Pi while they watched the main doors of the castle. "Choose your words carefully, but do not give an inch."

King Pi half-turned his head to regard Torsten with a single eye. Torsten averted his gaze. The boy's expression didn't change. Not a word. Not even a nod. His mother would tell him to take his time finding his voice again as she stroked his hair every night. But Torsten remembered his voice—the voice which whispered to the Buried Goddess in the night; thanks to Redstar.

"The Shesaitju will learn humility," Oleander said, standing on the opposite side of the throne. "Don't worry, my precious child, they are here to grovel and apologize to their new king, nothing more."

"We must distill more information about the attacks," Torsten implored. "Find out if that afhem was acting alone so we can pit them against one another."

"Nothing more." Oleander shot Torsten a cold glare he knew was meant to silence him. As beautiful as she was, even Liam the Conqueror couldn't wield a glower with such vinegar.

Torsten swallowed the lump forming in his throat, but didn't back down. He couldn't. The Miracle King didn't talk, and so the Queen Mother had been his mouthpiece. When Rand Langley failed to contest during his short run as Wearer, all who spoke ill in her presence found themselves on the wrong end of a noose.

"He will declare his fealty," Torsten said, "but first, please consider a tactful approach. The caleefs once fancied themselves living gods. Appeal to their dignity and we can use the truth to our advantage."

"Weren't you there when Sidar Rakun bent the knee to Liam and renounced his deification?"

"I was," Torsten said proudly.

"The *greatest* warlords in the world, and we crushed them. The Caleef knows his place, unlike some of us."

"My Queen… I—"

Before Torsten could finish, the double doors opened. Light poured in, shimmering off the gold clothing and beads of the Caleef's entourage. Wardric arrived to greet them and disarm the guards. When he was finished, he nodded at Torsten, who waved them to approach.

Torsten glanced at King Pi who didn't even budge at the sight of them. Oleander, however, grinned wide, her lips a dark shade of violet. Torsten turned back to the hall to watch the entourage of dignitaries and shirtless servants approaching. A handful of them carried the Caleef on a golden platform, plumed at the back with broad palm leaves, the veins painted gold.

Unlike the rest of his people, Sidar Rakun wore all-black, head to toe. Even his dark gray skin had two bars of paint, black as the beaches his people came from, running down from his eyes to his chin. And though Liam's longtime, defeated rival was as old as he had been, his dark hair didn't show a touch of gray.

They stopped in the middle of the hall. An afhem barked something in Saitjuese. From behind the Caleef's chair, his Serpent Guard—the elite defenders of the Caleef and his afhems, masters of the Black Fist combat technique—silently fanned out to form a line on either side of him.

Their name was well-earned. According to legend, they were just as slippery and impossible to strike as snakes—though Liam had little trouble. Golden leather armor covered them head to toe. Gilded masks, bearing the shape of a snake's head, hid their faces from their hairlines to the tips of their noses. Rumor had it they filed their teeth into fangs, though their mouths remained closed.

Servants lowered the Caleef's platform. Two took his hands and helped him down. Torsten struggled not to roll his eyes. Last time he saw Sidar Rakun, more than a decade ago, he groveled on the floor and declared his mortality. Liam never needed a servant to hold his hand when he could still walk. Even after his legs failed him, he never needed to be carried or fanned. The man had dignity unto death.

"So, it's true," Sidar said as he approached, staring at King Pi. His voice was deep and full of timbre, but Torsten knew it was all bravado. He'd heard his true voice when he'd surrendered the first time.

Sidar stopped before the dais and stood tall. Oleander's face twisted with rage.

"You stand before Pi Nothhelm," Torsten said. "Son of Liam Nothhelm, first of his name, the Miracle of Iam, and High King and Lord of the Glass Kingdom."

"'The Miracle King,'" Sidar said as if imitating someone. He remained standing straight.

Torsten coughed and looked toward the Caleef's legs.

"Ah, yes, my apologies." The Caleef bent his knee, though never allowed it to touch the floor before standing proud again. "I am so very pleased to see you well again, King Pi."

"Turns out no one believes in punctuality," Oleander said, eyeing Torsten.

"Your Grace?" Sidar said.

"We expected you here yesterday on the day of my son's coronation under Iam."

"We set out from Latiapur the moment we received Sir Unger's galler bird. We ran into a few delays at Marimount, however. I wish I could have been here, but your son wears the crown of his father proudly."

"The crown is his own," Oleander corrected.

"Yes, it is, isn't it? It is a great pleasure to see you again as well, Your Grace," he addressed Oleander. "I believe the last time I saw King Pi, he was this tall." He held his hand just under his kneecap.

Oleander stepped forward, her hand falling upon the arm of the throne. "Yes, I believe it was the day you wore the white of surrender to these very halls and cowered before my husband."

Torsten coughed from shock.

"Your Grace, today is a day of celebration," Sidar said.

"No, yesterday was a day of celebration," Oleander interrupted.

"Ah, yes," Sidar said, tipping his head slightly. "But Liam's great son has returned to us. Iam smiles upon you again. Must we dwell on a bitter past?"

"Iam smiles upon us all," Oleander said. For once, Torsten agreed with her. Showing the godless Shesaitju the way of Iam after they were conquered wasn't easy. Many of them still clung to their old ways of worshipping their ancestors and warlords.

"Yes, of course. I will admit, I have struggled to feel his light since my heart was opened to him, but seeing your son alive and well, sitting right in front of me after hearing of his unfortunate fate…. It truly is a blessing."

"Enough pandering, Sidar. You are going to make me sick. Do not pretend you were only invited here to share a feast in the name of our new king. The Wearer of White sent for you because your people raided villages under the protection of the Crown."

"When I heard what happened, I prayed for the well-being of your people. Whoever raided your lands did so without my knowing."

"Ah, of course. Then who should I blame for killing my people?"

One of Sidar's afhems whispered something into the ear of another. They smirked.

"I do not see the humor in this," Oleander snapped at them. "What did they say?"

"I didn't hear, Your Grace," Sidar said. "But my people would be wise to remain silent whilst I converse with their queen." He glared back at his entourage, and they immediately fell silent.

Torsten's understanding of Saitjuese was rough, but it was enough for him to put together the comment. *"I hear she kills her own,"* they said. Torsten decided it was better not to translate.

"Your Grace, have I done something to offend the young

king?" Sidar asked, clearly in an effort to change the subject. "He has avoided looking at me since I entered."

Oleander wrapped her way around the throne and sat on the armrest. She ran her fingers through Pi's hair, then stroked the crown. Pi continued staring blankly at the wall.

"My son, your King, does not wish to look upon you until you swear fealty to him," she said.

"I do not understand your meaning, Your Grace."

"'Your Grace.' 'Your Grace,'" she mocked. "Are you so kind to all your friends before you stab them in the back?"

"Your Gr—Queen Oleander. The Kingdom of the Black Sands remains loyal to Yarrington. Our lands have prospered under the rule of your late husband."

"Torsten?" the Queen said. He preferred Sir Unger in such a public setting, but she never was one for the ceremonial.

"Yes, my Queen?" Torsten replied.

"In your vast experience, do loyalists delay tax payment and then burn a handful of innocent farming villages to the ground, destroying crops that would help this city... oh, how did he put it... 'prosper' through the winter."

Torsten feared where her bluntness would lead, but there was only one clear answer: "No."

"Then you see why I hesitate to believe a word out of your mouth, Sidar." She turned back to him, and Torsten saw him shudder slightly. "Perhaps you came here to discuss the weather, but you were summoned here to answer for your transgressions."

"Your Grace, you must understand," Sidar said. "Storms in the Boiling Waters ravaged us this year and cost us greatly."

"How convenient."

"If the Master of Coin lists all discrepancies we will fulfill our obligations as we are able."

"You think I care about a few loose coins? You walk up to this throne, up to your holy King, as if nothing is wrong. You wear black when white is more appropriate. The smelting of your little platform would pay for all your *discrepancies.* But would payment and apologies put those villages back together?"

"As I said, the perpetrator of those attacks is unknown to me."

"So, it is a mystery to you that one of your afhems is secretly raising a vast army west of the bay? What did you hear them call him, Torsten? Mosquito was it?"

"Muskigo, Your Grace," Torsten said.

"Indeed."

A flicker of emotion passed over Sidar's face. Whether it was confusion, guilt, or surprise the Queen knew, Torsten wasn't sure. There was a reason Muskigo raised his army in the fog of the Fellwater Swamp. He didn't want to be known.

"My Queen," Sidar whispered, "perhaps we should continue this conversation in private."

"Anything you want to say, you can say here in front of my son, your King, and his Royal Council. Do you admit the afhem called Muskigo was acting on his own authority when he attacked my lands?"

"I was not aware of his intentions. I was led to believe he raised a fleet to answer the call of the Breklians who have been under the heavy hand of pirates."

Torsten studied his face as he talked. Either Sidar was the best liar he'd ever met, or Torsten had his answer. Muskigo was acting entirely of his own accord, and Sidar Rakun was as shocked as Torsten had been when he stumbled upon the army.

"Strange, we've heard nothing of the plight of the Breklians," the Queen sneered. "Unless my loyal Wearer and scouts are lying, he is camped in the Fellwater, preparing to ravage my kingdom even further."

"I swear to you in the name of Iam, this news comes as a surprise to me."

"Then, do you renounce him as one of your own? Will you

raise your forces with us and remove the stain of his being from Pantego?"

Sidar exhaled. "It is more complicated than you might think, Your Grace. His is a respected family that has walked the black sands for centuries."

"Then you endorse his slaughtering of innocents while my people mourned the loss of my husband?"

"No, never, my Queen, but if I raise arms against an afhem I—"

"Enough," Pi said softly.

Torsten thought himself hallucinating, but the Queen spun a full circle toward her son. Even the nearest guards broke their discipline and turned their heads.

Sidar too was stunned speechless. Even had he not known of the boy's lingering silence, for a ruler of Sidar's age and stature to be addressed so boldly by a child was a rare thing.

"Excuse me, Highness?" Sidar asked.

Pi placed his feet beneath him and rose to a standing position on the throne. Torsten felt a chill so cold it was as if the doors had been opened and Winter's Thumb had migrated south. The King's eyes had been little more than a blank stare for months, but now they glinted with the same passion and vigor his father's once did.

"I said, that's enough. Your queen asked a simple question. Will you declare the traitor an enemy and stand with us, or are you our enemy as well?" Even his voice had changed. It was smooth and confident, carrying across the hall like a practiced orator. He sounded like his father.

Sidar stuttered over a response.

"My Queen, perhaps the Caleef was right and we should proceed privately," Torsten tried to whisper to her behind the throne, but she was too preoccupied staring at the hard features of her baby boy to hear him.

"It isn't difficult," Pi said.

"I can strip Muskigo of his title and demand he surrender," Sidar said. "But I cannot order my people to stand against one of their own. You must understand."

"I understand that Afhem Muskigo is an enemy of the Crown, and unless you lie, a traitor to you as well."

"And he will be given the chance to remedy his mistakes. Please, Your Grace, I beg you not to act rashly. Be reasonable. Let us address this misunderstanding diplomatically before resorting to war."

"An act of war has already been committed," Pi declared. "My foolish mother was merely too distracted to notice."

For the first time since he spoke, Oleander stopped marveling and winced, shaken by the harshness of his words.

"My precious boy, certainly you don't—"

Pi held out a hand to silence her. Her lips sealed immediately, something Torsten thought was impossible.

"Sir Unger," Pi said. He turned to face Torsten.

"My King?" Torsten could barely get the words out. A year as Wearer of White and he'd never actually had a conversation with the boy.

"Until the Caleef reconsiders, he and his followers are to be confined to this castle. As of this moment, I declare the Kingdom of the Black Sands enemies of the Crown."

Sidar staggered back a few steps, then looked to the Queen. "Your Grace, I was invited here to celebrate your son's coronation. This revelation complicates things, but I am prepared to discuss the situation peaceably. However, we will not stay here as prisoners."

Pi stepped to the edge of the seat where he stood a good head taller than Sidar and stared down his nose at him. "You will proceed to your quarters, or you will be forced there."

Torsten was busy thinking of how to de-escalate the situation when he felt suddenly compelled to reach for his sword. It was like he wasn't even in control of his own body, years of service instinctually willing his muscles to serve his king.

He removed it a few inches from his back scabbard, and every Glass soldier and Shieldsman present followed his lead. The sharp rasp of metal hummed through the hall.

A Serpent Guard sprang into action, hurried to the Caleef, pulling him down from the dais to be surrounded by his men. They were unarmed, but as the Serpent Guards dropped into fighting stances, Torsten knew they needed no weapons to be a threat.

Torsten fully drew his claymore. His men did the same, surrounding the Shesaitju entourage with halberds and longswords. One young, overeager soldier stomped hard toward them. A Serpent Guard disarmed and turned his own weapon on him in a single motion.

"Stop this!" Torsten barked. He moved before Pi and the Queen and lowered his voice. "Your Graces, I do not think this wise. He tells the truth about Muskigo, I am sure of it. Perhaps he can talk the rogue afhem down, but if we do this, war is certain."

The Queen remained too consumed with her son to answer. Pi, on the other hand, reached out and laid both his hands on Torsten's shoulders. He may have appeared frail, but Torsten felt unexpected pressure from them, felt small beneath them.

"Sir Unger," Pi said. "Your name was featured in many great tales my father told me before his days of illness. I would hate to see one of our finest commanders exiled again for defying orders."

Torsten's heart sank. The boy had been in a deep sleep when Torsten had been sent away by the Queen on a fool's errand, yet somehow he knew. And to retrieve his worthless doll nonetheless. Now, as Torsten stared upon Pi's face, despite the boy's size, he saw a child no longer. The boy didn't just sound like Liam, it was there in his eyes, too.

Torsten turned to face the Shesaitju Caleef, unable to deny his new king. He could barely control his own breathing he was so overwhelmed, so confused.

"Caleef Rakun, your king has spoken," he said. "Order them to stand down, and there will be no bloodshed."

Sidar glanced back and forth. His men formed a wall around him, but halberds closed in from every side. Wardric had taken up position with a contingent of Shieldsmen at the Throne Room's entry. His sword was drawn, but he looked as tentative as Torsten knew he should be.

Taking the Shesaitju leader captive—a man many of them still believed to be a living god—was an unsound decision only a fledgling king would make, one he knew he should counsel more vehemently against.

"Stand down and come with me," Torsten demanded.

"It's not too late to stop this, Oleander," Sidar said. "He's just a child; you are a queen."

Torsten felt a sudden surge of rage and energy. He stormed forward. One of the Serpent Guards went to impede him, but he grabbed the man's arm before it struck his throat, snapped it at the elbow, and flung him into the others. Then he hefted his heavy claymore with one hand, extending it toward the Caleef's neck.

"He is your King," he bellowed. "And you will stand down."

Sidar raised his hands in surrender and nodded for his followers to do the same. His men obeyed without question. Glass soldiers promptly aimed their halberds at the gray men's chests and directed them toward the exit.

"Are you all insane?" Sidar shouted. "My people will not forgive this!"

Unable to control himself, Torsten grabbed the Caleef by the arm and yanked him along more roughly then he'd intended to. It wasn't until they were nearly out of the room that his anger subsided enough for him to breathe again.

Sidar continued protesting, cursing in common and Saitjuese. Pi remained standing on the throne. His mother stood to his left, stunned into silence, staring as blankly as her son had been only minutes earlier. But Pi looked to his right, smiling as if someone were standing in the empty space beside him telling a hilarious joke.

IV

THE THIEF

"This is Winde Port?" Sora asked, clearly unimpressed.

"Oh, I've missed this place," Whitney drew a deep breath. He could smell the salt of Trader's Bay even from the other side of the city. They were on the main road heading in, Merchants Row. It was dotted with mobile trading posts and merchant caravans, not unlike the one they'd stolen.

The city itself was built on a small peninsula jutting out into the mouth of the bay where it narrowed to Winder's River. Northerly, it cut up to the Jarein Gorge, through the Great Ravine. A web of manmade canals ran through a hodgepodge of buildings. Unlike Yarrington, where all the stone matched, or in the Dragon's Tail where everything was undeniably dwarven, Winde Port was just stone, clay, and wood—some from the North on Winter's Thumb, Crowfall, Fessix and the like, and some black, like the trees of the Shesaitju lands. Thatched roofs and Panping tile. In fact, the only thing that gave the place even the slightest resemblance to a city of the Glass Kingdom was the tremendous cathedral standing proudly in the skyline, its Eye of Iam glistening under the morning sun.

Whitney leaned over the side of the wagon and snagged a large chunk of meat skewered on a stick from a vending cart whose owner's back was turned. He held it out, offering Sora a bite. She recoiled in disgust.

"Don't know what you're missing," he said with a full mouth.

"This place is disgusting," she bristled.

"This place is freedom."

Whitney meant what he said, but saw her point. It wasn't Old Yarrington—it was hardly South Corner—but it was the one place in the Kingdom where race and heritage didn't matter. Everyone was welcome so long as they had a few autlas and a dream.

"You should love this place," Whitney said. "No difference between me and you here."

"So what? Here nobody will call me *knife-ear*?"

"Well, I wouldn't say that, but they won't say it with such… I don't know… scorn."

Sora rolled her pretty, amber-colored eyes and reached out for the stick.

"I knew you'd come around," he said.

She took a bite and juice dribbled down her chin. "Oh, by Iam, that is delicious," she garbled.

Whitney just smiled and turned back to the road. She reached for it again, but he pulled it away. "Get your own."

He waited a few seconds for good measure, then offered the stick again only to find that she was no longer next to him.

"Sora?"

He spun until he saw her walking toward the meat vendor. He clicked the horses to a stop, and hopped down, hastily looped the reins around a post.

"Wait up!" he shouted, running to catch up. "I was kidding. Have a bite."

"No, you're right. I want my own."

She reached into a small bag they'd found in the carriage and pulled out a silver autla. "One, please."

The vendor, talking and chiding with another customer, turned only a little faster than it had seemingly taken Whitney and Sora to get to Winde Port in the first place. His face scrunched up at the silver, and then, Sora.

"Ain't from round here?" the vendor asked.

"Just rolled into town," Whitney pointed at their caravan.

"Oh, you picked a bad time to visit Winde Port. Glass transferred a bunch of soldiers just last week. Been rounding up all the *rainclouds*."

"Rainclouds?" Sora asked.

"Ya know, the Shesaitju, gray skin and all." He laughed, then said, "Been a mess, so, price is twice that until the threat dies down. Just not enough people buying any more."

Whitney and Sora exchanged a sidelong glare.

"What threat might that be?" Whitney asked.

The man laughed again. "Where you been, in the woods?"

"Actually—" Whitney started, but Sora slapped him in the arm. "That spot is getting sore!" he snapped under his breath, rubbing it.

"Please, continue," Sora said.

"You ain't heard about the Black Sands rebel army mounting?" the trader asked as he lifted a butcher knife and sliced a chunk of carcass—looked like deer. "There's been attacks. Towns burned to the ground."

Whitney couldn't believe they'd somehow forgotten what Torsten said about a giant army of Shesaitju gathering in the swamp. Of course, Winde Port would be feeling the consequences of the Black Sands attacks. It was the largest trading hub in Southern Pantego, along Trader's Bay, with tributary access into Eastern, Western, and even Central Pantego through Winder's River and the Walled Lake.

"Rumor was some noble from Bridleton came to the city since his estate was turned to ash," the trader went on before turning to grab another piece of meat.

Whitney swallowed hard, then mouthed the name, "Darkings," to Sora.

She nodded.

"Anyway, do yourselves a favor and leave town. Especially you." He pointed to Sora with his cleaver. "When people get scared of one foreign face—they get scared of all of 'em."

Sora's features darkened. Whitney imagined after the bigots she'd endured in Bridleton and beyond, she was a bit more wary of warnings such as that. She feigned a smile, and turning to Whitney said, "You're right. I *should* love this place."

Whitney thought he saw her eyes begin to water as she pulled up her hood and walked a few steps back to their carriage. He brushed flecks of swiftly accumulating snow off the carriage bench as he climbed. He'd spent many a winter month in Winde Port and couldn't remember another so cold. At least there was one thing to be thankful for—in the snow, Sora's drawn cloak would look less conspicuous.

After a few moments of silence, Whitney leaned in and said, "Look, let's just get to the harbor and charter a boat. We'll be out on the open sea and away from all this in no time at all."

"Fine," Sora said, offering no argument.

Their wagon rolled down Merchants Row toward the city proper. Winde Port might have been part of the Glass Kingdom, but it had always been far from the grasp of the law. It was never uncommon to find a table where dwarf, Shesaitju, Panpingese, and regular old Glass folk like him could sit down and enjoy a game of gems.

It appeared all that had changed.

A palisade wall now wrapped the city all the way to the coast on either side. The northern end was still under construction. It covered one of the canals that ran out alongside Merchants Row to make transport easy, and he only then realized the water on their side was dried out by a makeshift dam.

The wooden walls boasted blue and white standards, and soldiers from Yarrington were everywhere. It made Whitney queasy. He wondered if Torsten might be fumbling around in his bright white armor, ruining yet another thing Whitney loved.

Ahead, several Glass Soldiers gathered at a gateway. *A gateway in Winde Port.* Whitney scooted closer and put his arm around Sora, slowing their pace so as not to draw attention.

"Aye!" one of the soldiers shouted. He was more decorated than the others, with a feathered helm and shiny, King's Shield armor. And Whitney knew, when Shieldsmen were watching the gates, that was when things in the kingdom were about to run afoul. "Stop the cart."

Whitney exhaled. "Another one of these," he mumbled, remembering how impossible Torsten could be. "What can I do for you today, Sir Knight?" he asked, bowing his head with a flourish.

"Commander Citravan of the Winde Port legion," the man corrected. "You heading in?"

"No, we're g…" Whitney cut off his sarcasm before getting them into trouble. "Yes, sir," he said instead. "Silk traders on our way to Yaolin City."

"Don't care where you're going." The commander signaled to one of his men, and a soldier hopped up onto their wagon without even asking. He peeled open the canvas and rifled through some of the goods inside. Sora seemed nervous, but Whitney wasn't sure why. He'd already stashed his half of the Glass Crown somewhere nobody would ever think to look.

The guard stepped out and nodded to the commander.

"All right, move along," Commander Citravan said.

"Thank you, Sir," Whitney replied. "Keeping the Realm safe. There's no higher calling under Iam's Eye."

"Move along."

Whitney bit down hard, forcing himself to not test the man. He looked to Sora as their wagon rolled forward, expecting her to be joining him in frustration. Instead, she stared off to the left.

Another shorter, spiked barricade bowed away from the main wall on the opposite side of the city. Pikemen stood guard at every entrance into a vast camp filled with gray-skinned Shesaitju. Men, women, and children all huddled together in wooden shacks and tents, despite the cold. No warm hearths, just fire pits out in the open to keep warm.

"So much for freedom," Whitney said.

Sora didn't answer. She simply stared, expressionless.

"Serves them right for what they did," Whitney said, thinking of the day they'd burned Troborough and taken from Sora everyone she'd ever known and loved—though he wasn't sure he meant it.

He locked eyes with one of them, a little gray-skinned girl of about five years, eating scraps of rotten meat by a dwindling fire. That little girl had done less to Troborough than he had.

"Yeah..." Sora said softly.

"By all the fallen gods, what did you do with my Sora? You're supposed to be telling me we should abandon all our plans and try to help them."

Sora was silent, again.

Shesaitju were led in a long single-file line through the gate and toward the detainment camp. Rusty, silver chains strung them together at the wrists and feet. The sound was horrifying, like they were all being led to execution. Behind the line, a soldier of the Glass poked and prodded them.

"In you go, rainclouds," he chortled. One of the Shesaitju cursed at him in his native tongue and earned a club to the stomach. The guard reached down and wrenched the man's hair back as he heaved for breath, and spoke directly into his ear loud enough for Whitney to hear. "My sister died in Oxgate, you swine. You'll rot in here."

"Aye!" Commander Citravan shouted. "I said, move along."

"Sorry, sir," Whitney said. "It's just... my wife is from around here and she's never seen the city... well... like this."

"All Shesaitju west of the Great Ravine are to be detained until the rebel Afhem Muskigo surrenders," he explained. "It's for their own good. They'd get torn to pieces otherwise. Now, I said move along. I won't ask again."

Whitney got the wagon rolling, but Sora didn't stop staring at the sad state of the Shesaitju until they were beyond the palisade.

"Just forget about it, Sora," Whitney said once they were in.

She glared at him. "Typical Whitney Fierstown—"

"Blisslayer."

"Would you shut up with that already! Just because you got some letter sealed by the Crown doesn't mean you can just throw away who you've always been."

"Technically, it does, but that's beside the point. I—we—worked hard for that name. You can't just go forgetting it."

"Well, it's not right, locking them out there. It's cold."

Whitney sighed. "There she is. A second ago you wanted to burn their whole camp to the ground."

"It wasn't their fault."

"No, it wasn't. But out in the world, it starts to get hard telling, doesn't it, knife-ear?"

He winced impulsively, but she didn't strike him. Instead, she shot a glower his way that made him feel like shriveling into a cocoon.

"I'm just making a point," he said. "Out in the world, if you stay somewhere too long you'll wind up wrapped up in the affairs of lords and ladies. It's the same thing I told you back in Yarrington."

"What, and there are no lords in Panping? What'll we do when we get there and my people are locked up thanks to some rebel warlord thinking about no one but himself?"

"We move on to the next place." He placed his arm around her, knowing full well the risk he was taking considering her mood. "You think I fancy myself a Glassman because I was born outside Yarrington? I'm as much one as you are Panpingese."

"Not according to that piece of paper in your pocket." Sora either cleared her throat or chuckled, Whitney wasn't sure which.

"All I'm saying is that in our line of work, we're all on our own. Yeah, make that lesson number... whatever number we're on: it's us against the world."

"And what exactly would you call our line of work?" Sora asked. He could tell by her tone she was starting to cheer up. Which was good, because a month-long voyage across the Boiling Waters to the land of her ancestors would be worse than Elsewhere if she was in a sour mood. And if seeing a group of Shesaitju forced to live in a camp, thanks to a possible rebellion, was the worst she'd ever seen... she had no idea what she was in for if pirates attacked.

"Thieving?" she went on. "That's too simple. We did burn down Darkings' mansion. What about scoundreling. Is that a word?"

"We're beyond description."

"Scoundreling it is, then," she said.

He slowed the wagon down beside an amassed crowd watching a street performer—a Panpingese kid juggling torches. He let the fire come as close to his face as possible, egging on a crowd of wealthy Glassmen in the merchant district. After he finished and earned a chorus of applause, he pointed to Sora.

"You!" he called. He had the voice of a proper showman,

booming, yet inviting all at the same time. Impressive for his age. Whitney had run with a few performing troupes in his time. The acting was fun, but distracting a whole crowd of men and women with full pockets was even better.

Sora glanced between Whitney and the kid, then laughing, stopped the wagon.

"Go on," Whitney said. "You're part of the act now."

The crowd parted to let Sora pass. Whitney heard a few lewd comments about her looks. Lucky for them, he couldn't see who'd said them. He hopped down and watched from the back.

"I uh... wow.... she's gorgeous enough to be Empress of Panping, isn't she?" the kid asked, earning a mixture of laughter and cheers. Sora's cheeks went as red as the walls of the Jarein Gorge. Whitney gave a nod of approval, even though he knew the kid wasn't watching him. He was probably half her age, he was so young, but he was good.

"Now, stand right here." The kid took her by both hands and led her to a tiny stand.

"Here?" she asked, so embarrassed she could barely get the words out.

He gave her one last adjustment. "Right here." He bent down, and from beneath the stand, drew two curved daggers. They looked Shesaitju in design.

Only in Winde Port, Whitney thought, smirking.

Sora's face drained of color. Two Glintish women dressed in feathery gowns yelped.

"Now, whatever you do," the kid said, "just don't move."

Sora looked to Whitney, but there was nothing he could do. The performer began juggling the blades all around her. She closed her eyes as one twirled up over her head, the kid catching it on the other side. *Ooos* and *ahhhs* filled the air as he danced with blades, each one closer to cutting her than the next. Until one sliced her arm. Just barely, but enough to make her howl. Half the crowd lunged forward to help her, but Whitney didn't budge. He waited patiently until he felt the faintest pressure against his side. Reaching back with cat-like speed, he caught the hand of a pickpocket.

He shook his head in disapproval as he looked down at the performer's younger running mate. The boy looked like he was going to fill his trousers with shog. It was probably his first time getting caught. Whitney remembered his younger days of honing his quick fingers on the streets of Winde Port. Traders and wealthy shoppers were the easiest targets around—easily distracted and usually with too many things on them to notice if something went missing.

Whitney however, was neither. "C'mon kid, oldest trick in the book. Never go for the man at the very back of the crowd because he clearly has trust issues." He released the boy's arm and gave him a light shove. "Now scram."

Whitney continued watching for a moment, then bulled his way through the crowd toward Sora. She was hunched over, holding her arm while the performer tried to assess the damage. He looked nervous too, and Whitney could see why. A stream of blood ran from the cut down her arm, trickling over the hem of her glove. He'd nicked her far deeper than was planned.

Whitney wanted to smack the kid upside the head, but his attention was drawn elsewhere. Smoke poured out of Sora's clenched fists. It was faint, but there was no question it came from her.

Within her?

He still barely understood how magic worked, blood-based or not, only that it drew on Elsewhere, the realm of banished gods and demons created by Iam after the God Feud.

The fabric over her fingertips began to sear. Whitney quickly hooked his arm around her and rushed her back through the crowd. The performer grabbed at Whitney's arm, asking if she was okay.

"You juggle knives like my grandmother," Whitney said, then added. "And your little brother has fingers as light as a zhulong. I sent him running that way if you're looking."

The performer looked both ways, then snagged his tin of autlas donated by the gathered crowd and bolted. Whitney leaned Sora against the carriage.

"You okay?" Whitney asked. "You need me to chase down the knife-ear?"

She managed to break her grimace for a second and smirk. Then shook out her arm. There was a long cut across her forearm over a row of ghosted scars he'd never noticed before.

"Seriously though," Whitney said. "You're not going to explode again, are you?"

"I'm fine. That area is just tender from… growing up."

She flexed her arm and a bit more blood oozed out. Whitney had to turn away to avoid gagging. He made it look like he was just getting one of the silk blankets from their wagon. He wrapped it tight around her arm.

"There you go..." He coughed, again to cover for the sick feeling in his stomach. "Most expensive bandage ever." Blood soaked through the fabric quickly. "Those scars—"

"Are where Wetzel used to cut me to help me tap into my abilities. It brings up bad memories."

"Of him dying?"

She nodded. "And living. Unlocking a link to Elsewhere isn't easy. I hated him every day until it worked and then even still, for a while."

"Well, let's make sure and leave these fine folk intact. Using blood magic in public in the Glass Kingdom is a one-way ticket to the gallows, even here."

She groaned. "I'm starting to hate this place, too."

"Oh c'mon." Whitney pulled her in tighter and pointed over her shoulder at Winder's Wharf where the tops of masts soared high over the city skyline like tree trunks stripped of their boughs.

"We're in paradise," he said as he took a great big whiff of the salty air. To him, it was the smell of freedom and relaxation. There was nothing in the world further from the worthless town he grew up in than sailing upon open seas.

V

THE KNIGHT

"Well, that was certainly unexpected," Wardric said. They stood in the Shield Hall. Snowflakes swirled in through an open, arched aperture overlooking Mount Lister and the Torrential Sea, carried by an icy breeze.

"I'm still trying to understand," Torsten said.

"What's there to understand?" Wardric walked toward the opening. "Apparently, our timid prince wasn't so shy after all."

Torsten gripped the railing. His eyes fell on Mount Lister. The top of the mountain was a mere silhouette through the low clouds but the area at its base where the earth crumbled into the Royal Crypt below, remained visible. The tarpaulin covering it flapped, and he could imagine the tiny dots of dwarven artisans flitting about inside.

"I know," Torsten said. "It was like Liam was alive all over again. I swear to you Wardric, I could literally feel him next to me. Before I knew it, my sword was drawn…"

"You won't see me complaining about the new king growing up fast. I haven't seen anyone put her in her place like that since

Liam. Apparently, Pi was paying attention all those many years ago."

"He declared war. There's no question of the state of the kingdom now."

"Like the boy said, they acted first. The last time we stood in this chamber I told you we had to teach the Shesaitju a lesson in force. You were wise to delay that while the Queen Mother was unstable, but we can't be cautious forever."

"It won't just be Muskigo. He'll rouse more afhems seeking to 'free' their Caleef."

"Good, let all the traitors show their colors so that we may put them in their places."

"You did not see Muskigo fight. Nor did you see his innumerable army."

"Are you losing your faith, Sir Unger?"

Torsten sighed and turned away from the overlook toward a large, slate table. Eyes of Iam, spiked flames, and other sculptures covered the slate table like the parts of some elaborate game. Each blown-glass figure represented an army, thousands of young men whose lives were now in jeopardy thanks to the impulsiveness of a twelve-year-old.

Torsten reminded himself that Liam too had been stubborn in his youth. He wouldn't have conquered the world, wouldn't have brought glory to the name of Iam if he hadn't been. Like Pi, Liam's father had died when he was still young, leaving Liam as king at only sixteen. Though four years might as well be a lifetime that early on.

"How long do you suppose we have until word gets out?" Wardric asked.

"Days," Torsten said. "Maybe less. I trust the Shield, but our numbers are thin, and I don't recognize half the people in the castle anymore."

"Another thing for which to thank our lovely Queen Mother."

"And what thanks is that, Sir..." Oleander appeared in the entry. Pi stood in front of her, barely reaching her waist with the top of his moppy hair. The fire in his eyes was gone, and he looked every bit as tired and disinterested as he once had.

"Sir Wardric Jolly, Your Grace." He bowed low, but Torsten could sense the bitterness in his tone. He'd been a pillar of the King's Shield for longer than she'd been queen and she still didn't know his name.

"Your Grace." Torsten bowed. "We were discussing the potential... consequences of the King's decision."

"He was brilliant, wasn't he?" She smiled and patted his head. He didn't react in the slightest. "Why should we have to play coy with those who should be kissing our feet?" She led Pi to the stone seat at the head of the table and helped him onto it. He slumped back, barely able to see the map.

"We must consider the implications carefully." Torsten turned to the map. "From my scouts, we know that Afhem Muskigo remains in the Fellwater with his army. They have completed numerous siege engines—"

"Breaching towers, catapults," Wardric explained.

"I know what that means," Oleander snapped. She took a step toward Wardric, her tall, Drav Cra frame looming over him. All the confidence Pi had stripped from her when he scolded her seemed to have returned in full. "Torsten, who is this man who addresses me as if I need his explanations?"

"He has served the King's Shield for decades, Your Grace," Torsten said. "Longer even than I. He fought faithfully by your husband-King. He's the most loyal sword in the Glass."

"Well, tell him to keep his tongue sheathed in my presence."

Torsten grabbed the back of Wardric's armor and guided him away. If fury could manifest in flames, the room would be ablaze.

"Muskigo's army seems prepared to march at his command," Torsten said, refocusing the conversation. "News of their Caleef's detainment will most certainly expedite things. We can only guess at his exact numbers since they are hidden by the swamp's fog, but it's enough to know Muskigo has been preparing this coup since the moment Liam fell ill."

"Oh, Torsten. Sweet, loyal… *gullible* Torsten," Oleander said. "You really believe the lies spun by Sidar Rakun?"

She positioned herself before him. They were the same height, but they rarely saw eye to eye. He couldn't help but be rapt by her lips, glistening a deep indigo that matched her dress, by her long blonde hair, so fair it shone silver under a certain light.

Torsten took a moment to gather his breath. "It doesn't matter what I think, Your Grace. The King's decision will inspire others to the rogue afhem's call." He gestured to the area on the map where Pantego forked off into the rocky and black sand-ridden beaches of the Shesaitju. "These cities southeast of the Walled Lake have large, concentrated Shesaitju populations. When word—"

"The Master of Rolls has already sent word across the kingdom that all gray-folk are to be placed under armed watch," Oleander interrupted.

"I'm not sure…" His voice trailed off. He shook his head, frustrated. "How? The audience only just concluded."

"Don't look at me," she said. "Your king gave the order the moment we stepped out."

"Taking such a harsh stance will only encourage revolts, Your Grace." Torsten regarded the boy, but Pi remained emotionless. "We must focus on the true enemy south of us."

"Better to root out all insurgents now than wait until the army is nearer," Wardric said. "Why don't we sail a fleet down from Winde Port, catch them napping in Fellwater?" He smiled proudly like he expected Oleander's approval. Instead, she ignored him.

"The Shesaitju have been fighting within their islands for centuries," Torsten argued. "They are renowned for their naval combat. In that shallow water and fog, so far from home, we would be at a great disadvantage, especially if their scouts see us coming."

"And how could anyone miss a mass of ships sailing down Trader's Bay?" Oleander remarked.

Wardric bit his lip. Torsten could tell he was growing frustrated and tried to urge him with his expression to relax. Nobody knew better than Torsten how hard it was to get and stay on Oleander's good side.

"Does it benefit you, keeping fools around, Torsten?" Oleander asked.

Wardric was squeezing the table now. But before he said anything stupid, King Pi said, "Excuse me, Mother, but why exactly are you here?"

Torsten glanced up and saw that the boy now stood and stared down at the map. That fierce look in his eyes had returned.

"What was that, my dear?" Oleander asked.

"I said, I'm curious why you are here? You are not king and have no experience with war, yet you insult this soldier who served beneath Father in numerous campaigns."

Her whole body tensed but she maintained a calm expression.

"As Queen Mother, it is my duty to help look after your kingdom. I learned a lot watching your father, Iam rest his soul."

Torsten traced his eyes in prayer to Iam. Wardric did the same, though there was no missing the mirth tugging on the corners of his mouth. Pi did not—Torsten noted.

"If you paid attention to Father," Pi said, "you would know the best course of action is to rely on the expertise of the Royal Council when its outside your own specialties. Of course, because of your actions, Sir Unger is the only man of proper resource who remains on *my* council."

"Pi..." Oleander's lips started to tremble. The muscles on her long, slender throat contracted as she fought back tears.

"Now, please," he lifted a hand, palm out, "allow them to continue without interruption."

Oleander stared at her son a few seconds longer, her eyes welling. His façade didn't falter, stern, cold, the way Liam was with irritators. Torsten wasn't Wearer when the man could still walk, so he didn't have as much insight into how he was with Oleander, but Uriah had always said how rigid he could be when she spoke out of turn.

Oleander stood and curtsied. She didn't weep aloud, but Torsten noticed her shoulders bobbing on her way out of the room. He couldn't help but feel sorry for her despite everything she'd done, despite turning Yarrington into Elsewhere while he was gone. She'd done it all for Pi.

"So, attacking them first is out of the question," Wardric said. He lifted a statue of a zhulong—the pig-dragon beasts the Shesaitju were so fond of—which represented Muskigo's army then placed it back down.

Torsten forced himself to return his focus to what was important. "Agreed. Only zhulong would be able to handle mud that deep, and he has many."

"You told me that the afhem seemed brash, proud," Wardric stated.

"He is bent on revenge for the wars their fathers lost."

"Then he won't sit idly after he learns of the Caleef's imprisonment."

"No," Torsten said. "He'll seek to destroy the seat of Liam." He looked to Pi, who remained attentive. "I understand the choice you made in light of their attacks, my King, but you have to understand how so many of them view their Caleef. You are the Word of Iam. For many of them, he remains a living god."

"Then they must be shown the error of their ways," Pi said. "There is only one true God."

Torsten nodded, smiled. It wasn't long ago that the boy had

been cursed by his uncle with thoughts of the Buried Goddess, yet now he sounded like a true king of the Glass.

"We will do everything in our power to prepare," Torsten continued. "Muskigo will have two choices." He stretched across the table and tapped two Eyes of Iam. "He can head straight north and take Fort Marimount."

"It is a mighty fortress, Your Grace," Wardric explained. "Half-built by the ancient dwarves themselves."

"And it's all that stands between him and a full-scale invasion of Yarrington. If he takes it, they can dig in and reinforce themselves. With your edict against the Shesaitju enacted, they won't be difficult to find."

"You did not approve of my decision, did you?" Pi stopped him.

"Your Grace?"

"You can be completely honest with me without fear of hanging, Sir Unger."

Torsten drew a deep breath. He'd never known what it was like to serve someone he didn't have to walk on eggshells around. "I would have appeased and distracted the Caleef with finery while we first handled Muskigo. Then reprimanded Sidar Rakun for such loose control of his people."

"Feigned complacency before striking like a snake in the weeds? Careful, tricks are the craft of the fallen gods."

Torsten's brow raised. Pi was smirking now, and Torsten realized it was the first time he'd ever seen the boy do it. He didn't sound like he was only twelve, and just like in the Throne Room, he barely looked it.

"That is true, Your Grace," Torsten said. "But Liam taught us to learn from our enemies in defense of the faithful. First, we win, and then, beg Iam for forgiveness."

"Then I do apologize for my reaction, Sir Unger."

"You need never apologize to me, Your Grace. The Black

Sands had to be dealt with, one way or another." Torsten's gaze jumped between the young King and the map a few times before he was able to gather his thoughts.

"Marimount would be option one," Torsten continued, "or turn his army along the bay and sail for Winde Port."

Wardric nodded in agreement, running his finger along the river running north from the trade port. "It's not as defensible as the Fort, but the winters aren't so harsh there, and it would allow him easier access to Eastern and Western Pantego."

"It's exactly halfway between here and Latiapur, and it would provide him with a port to the West."

"A strategic location, sure, but they'd sacrifice a lot of men taking a city so far from Yarrington when they could close the distance better at Marimount. You said it yourself, the afhem was brash and confident."

"Brash, confident, and willing to have his men train in the wet and the cold until they could be called ready."

Wardric scratched his chin. "We don't possess the men to properly reinforce both potential targets."

"We don't have the men to meet Muskigo's army in open battle at all. Our legions in the East must remain to ensure a similar situation doesn't evolve in the Panping Region—Governor Nantby has already begun building defenses against such an attack, however unlikely. In the North, they defend against Drav Cra marauders who don't believe in allegiance. In the Northeast, we continue to honor contracts with the dwarven King, Cragrock, assisting with the grimuar scourge and to secure the borders with the Breklians."

"You just named our only forces with any experience in battle. We've been sitting on our fat asses ever since Liam got sick." Wardric laughed a mirthless laugh.

"It's time to consider a conscription. Bolster our numbers."

Torsten could see Pi listening, but the boy remained quiet.

"More untested men to join an army that hadn't been tested in a decade?"

"Muskigo's men are angry, loyal, and worthy, but only a small percentage of them probably ever served as mercenaries, and none of them are used to our winters. If he cuts a straight line for Yarrington, we should be able to defend Fort Marimount against whatever he throws at us."

"And if he heads northeast to Winde port?"

"Then I pray to Iam we can overwhelm him with numbers. The King's miracle has the people in good spirits after all the foulness that preceded. If we issue a call now and focus on a chance for vengeance for the villages Muskigo slaughtered, we should have success."

"It's winter, and grain stores throughout the region are low. People might eagerly take up the sword knowing they'll get their bellies filled in the legion."

"Then it is decided?" Torsten asked. "I'll have scouts watch for the first sign of movement from Muskigo's forces so we can reinforce his target. Galleys will be sent out into Trader's Bay in case he does move by water. Perhaps they can slow down his much larger fleet to buy us time. Frederick Holgrass will issue a conscription edict from here to Westvale, and then again to Hornsheim."

"Holgrass the new Master of Rolls?" Wardric asked.

Torsten sighed, they were all new. "Yes. All men of proper age and health will be beckoned to the call of their king. Are you in agreement, Your Grace?"

Torsten and Wardric both turned their attention back to Pi, but found that he no longer stood at the table. He was sunken back into his chair, half-asleep. He nodded his head listlessly but said nothing.

"It's settled then," Torsten said. "I'll bring word to the Royal Council and have the proclamation prepared immediately."

Wardric nodded in agreement. Torsten, however, couldn't stop staring at the young king who looked so dejected.

Now he sees how many more lives might be lost in war because he was too eager.

Oleander never learned from or admitted her mistakes, but Liam never forgot his. He used that knowledge to crush his enemies. It was then that Torsten realized he may have underestimated Pi, that there may have been even more of Liam the Conqueror in him than he'd ever imagined.

VI

THE THIEF

Whitney pulled the wagon over at the edge of Winder's Wharf and took in the sight. Like the rest of Winde Port, nothing in the place matched. It stretched the whole of the peninsula, from a stone platform carved into the low bluffs to the north down to creaking wooden planks atop the sandy, southern beachfront. Canals branched off at random intervals like fingers stretching out into the city. They alternated with paved roadways, making it simple to ferry supplies. The locals even traversed them with gondolas during warmer months when they weren't frozen over.

Ships of all sizes, from every corner of Pantego, moored in the harbor. He even spotted a Breklian corsair vessel, its fanning sails like a stack of daggers from his angle. Brekliodad was one of the few places the Glass Kingdom's influence didn't reach, yet here they were in Winde Port.

Everything looked as it had the last time he'd visited, except one new addition: three Glass Kingdom warships floating out in the bay, keeping watch.

"So, which one should we steal?" Whitney asked.

Sora snorted. "Don't be ridiculous."

"What? We just stole the caravan and that was easy enough. A ship can't be much harder. My eye's on that one." He gestured to the small, agile ship from Brekliodad.

"You can't sail a ship with two people."

"Says the woman who can summon fire."

"How about for once we just pay for something? It's not like we can't get the autlas." She looked back into the wagon at all their stolen goods. "If we sell it all we could probably buy a small ship. If you let us sell that yigging crown, we could probably get a galley and a crew."

"Don't even look at it." Whitney lunged forward and reached under one of their horses. He had the crown pinned under its stomach using the strap from the saddle. He removed it, wrapped it in a silk blanket, and stuffed it into a fold in his clothing. The points poked into his ribs but he didn't care.

"What do you even plan on doing with that thing?" Sora asked.

"I'm not sure yet, but I'll know it when the time comes."

"Well, I still say we sell off all of this stuff and get out of here before those monsters we stole it from come back."

"You know, you're no fun at all. This wouldn't be the first time I've stolen a ship."

"Oh boy, here we go. Please, Whitney, oh glorious and grand-master thief, tell me the story I know you'll tell me no matter what." Sora folded her arms across her chest.

"Many moons ago I found myself first mate to Grisham 'Gold Grin' Gale, king of the pirates and master of the seas. But he knew as well as I did that he wouldn't even have a ship had it not been for me."

"And where is this ship now?"

He rolled his shoulders. "Who can say? Likely at the bottom of the Torrential Sea."

"You know you're not old enough to have done everything you say you've done, right?"

"Age is but a number." He sighed and looked at the ground.

"Fine, let's see if we can't go charter a ship." Whitney grabbed one of the horses by the lead and started off toward the docks.

"Charter is a strange way to say steal."

"Nope, this time you're right. I may be many things, but I'm not the one to try sailing a ship through the Boiling Waters. It would be tough to teach you any more all-important lessons if we're stranded on a rock."

"No more lessons." Sora closed her eyes, smiled, and let out an exaggerated breath. "Almost sounds like paradise."

Whitney ignored her and led the wagon to a tailor at the end of the docks. There wasn't a type of trade hard to find in Winde Port. They rifled through Grint's gang's belongings. Mostly it was silks, but there were a few other trinkets as well. Nothing so opulent as the Glass Crown, but Sora seemed eager to add it all in as a bonus. They threw in the horses as well. The portly merchant looked like his eyes were going to bulge out of his head as he took in his haul. Whitney knew they were getting an awful deal, but it would be more than enough to catch a ride like royalty aboard the finest ship sailing east. They'd leave nothing but an empty, horseless carriage for Grint and the others to find.

When they reached the harbor, the wind and cold had hulls groaning, and that was as close to the sound of waves as there was in Trader's Bay. The water was like a sheet of glass, with portions of the coast so still, they might have been frozen. Whitney couldn't remember the last time it got cold enough to turn the bay half-solid. It was such a harsh juxtaposition to the murky waters of the Torrential Sea bordering Yarrington where massive waves pommeled into Mount Lister and towering sea walls.

Down by the beach, along the splintering deck, stood Whitney's favorite watering hole in all Pantego, Winder's Dwarf. He stopped outside and looked to Sora.

"All right, if there's anyone I trust to get us to the Panping Region in one piece, they're in this room," he said. "I know these people. Just stand there and look pretty and the deal will keep getting sweeter."

Sora groaned and rubbed her temples between her index finger and thumb. "You have a strange way of complimenting a lady."

"Oh, you're a lady now?" Whitney then flung the door open and shouted, "Tum Tum!"

Everyone in the tavern repeated the words and slammed their tankards twice on the bar or tables. Raucous laughter followed.

"I thought we were here to charter a ship?" Sora whispered after she took a good look around the place.

Like most of Winde Port, the bar's interior was unimpressive. But like any good tavern, it was crammed with sloppy drunks. But unlike most, Winder's Dwarf had no need for a bard. Those slovenly, unassuming men were from every corner of Pantego, even beyond the Glass—well, except the Shesaitju, Whitney noticed. Which was fine with him, he'd always found their culture to be incredibly formal and drab.

But there were Dwarves and Panpingese, men from Brekliodad and the far north. There was even a half-giant hunched over in the back of the room with women draped all over him, though it wasn't clear how he even got through the front door.

"No better place to strike a deal than within these walls," Whitney said. "Plus, Tum Tum is a stand-up dwarf. Nothing like Grint. You'll love him."

"Tum Tum is a name?" she asked, incredulous.

Whitney parked himself on a stool furthest from the door and Tum Tum waddled over. He was so short and his belly so round that he looked like a pufferfish. His coal-black beard grew in patchy, with whiskers sticking out from his nose and ears that he never cared to trim. Grint Strongiron made all dwarves seem like thieving, backstabbing cowards, but Whitney had known Dwotratum "Tum Tum" Goodbrew for years and he was the finest dwarf there was.

"Whitney Fierstown!" Tum Tum said. "Thought ye were dead."

"Not dead. Reborn!" Whitney exclaimed. "Whitney Blisslayer now. First of my name."

"Yer yanking me beard."

"Nope." Whitney reached into his pocket and slapped down the writ given to him by Torsten himself. Tum Tum leaned up over the bar and scoured the paper. "Got the seal of the Crown and everything."

"By Meungor's axe it does! How in Elsewhere did ye manage a thing like that?"

"If I started that story we'd be here all night."

"That's for sure," Sora mumbled.

"Let's just say a member of the Royal Council owed me big time."

"Well, I'll be." Tum Tum folded the writ up and handed it back to Whitney, then stepped onto a low stool that helped him see over the bar.

"Aye! Everyone!" he shouted. "We got ourselves a noble in the house!" More laughter rose and tankards slammed. "I suppose that means ye can pay double now?"

"You should be paying me to drink in this shoghole you call a tavern," Whitney said.

"Watch yer mouth. There's a lady present."

"Finally, someone notices," Sora said, deciding to take a seat.

Tum Tum reached out and took her hand between his chubby fingers. "And what may I have the pleasure of callin ye, my lady?"

"Sora."

"Blisslayer?" Tum Tum finished for her. The look on her face made him question what he said before he even finished. "You two aren't?"

"Married? Gods no!" Whitney burst out laughing and earned a well-deserved elbow into his ribs.

"He should be so lucky," Sora said through clenched teeth. "We're friends from childhood, catching up on old times. Sora, with no other name and proud of it."

"Well, any friend of Whitney the Filcher Fantastic is a friend of mine. First round's on me." Tum Tum opened a tap and ale poured freely into a couple of earthenware mugs.

"Afraid there'll only be time for one round, my friend," Whitney said. "We're hoping to catch passage to Panping— Yaolin City, in fact—before things around here heat up any more."

Tum Tum threw his head back and released a hearty laugh from deep in his belly. "Ye ain't goin nowhere without a temporary trader's license issued by the prefect. All ships be grounded, as ye can right see. Only ones leavin be those tradin essential goods and able to prove it."

"Well then, a second round it is!" Whitney said, slapping the bar.

"That's it?" Sora asked. "You give up?"

"If you call a night in the best pub in Pantego 'giving up,' then we really need to reconsider my lessons."

Sora slid her ale away and said, "Tum Tum, why are all ships grounded? Any word on when things might let up?"

"Just got into town I be guessin? Saw the Black Sandsmen in lock up on the way through? Rumor is there be a war brewin and the Boilin Waters ain't safe, that there be some group of rebels waitin out there, wantin vengeance for the new king lockin up Caleef Rakun."

"So, we're stuck here?" Sora asked.

"As a pickaxe in mud."

Whitney threw his mug back. Half the ale wound up dribbling down his chin. "Very simple really," Whitney said between swigs. "Just gotta find someone with papers heading that way who wouldn't mind a couple of fine-looking stowaways."

"Are you confused about what simple means?" Sora asked.

"Ye might be in a bit of luck," Tum Tum said.

"Why's that?"

"That there's Tayvada Bokeo. Not likely many be crazy enough to risk both the Boilin Waters and gettin shredded by a Shesaitju fleet, but he be a member of the Winde Traders Guild. And nobles always be welcome at the guild. Tayvada!" the dwarf called to him even before Whitney could respond.

A thin, Panpingese man sauntered over, smiling and shaking hands with all those he passed. His hair was the color of a Dawning midnight, and he wore it pulled back so that his pointed ears were unmistakable.

"Tum Tum, the place is lively as ever," he said. "Good fortune to you."

"Aye. Here's someone I'd be wantin you to meet." He put an ale down in front of Tayvada and continued. "Whitney Blisslayer, first of his name."

"Ah, Mr. Blisslayer, a pleasure. Tayvada Bokeo at your service." He bowed, then turned to Sora, took her hand, and kissed it. She seemed so stunned by what he was, she barely reacted. "And your wife? Stunning! So good to see a Lord of the Glass and a Lady of the East in matrimony together."

"Oh, she ain't—"

"It's an honor to meet you as well, Lord Bokeo," Whitney interrupted Tum Tum. He bowed low in return, sneaking a glance over at Sora. Her glower looked like it could slice through glaruium.

"What brings you both to town?" Tayvada asked.

"I've—*we've* heard great things about your guild and hoped to enter the fold," Whitney lied.

"So good to know our reputation has carried all the way to… Yarrington raised I'd say?"

"So right you are!" Whitney forced a nauseating laugh. Sora tittered and smiled with the grace of a proper lady. He had to give her credit. If he didn't know any better, he'd have thought she hadn't grown up in a crummy shack on a dried-up river.

"And you, my dear, when did you leave our beloved Panping?"

"Actually—" Sora started, but Whitney cut in.

"Actually, we were planning to catch a ship there before hearing of the horrible things happening in your fine city and the slowdown in the harbor. We have business in Yaolin City. A potential import deal with her family. We grow barley on a plantation north of the city, you see."

"An exceptional crop," the man remarked.

"But it appears we are without the temporary license needed to charter passage. And to travel by land, at this point, would delay things beyond what we can afford."

"I see. Prefect Calhoun issued the edict shortly after the new king declared war against the Black Sands."

"So we heard. I attempted to meet with the prefect and get all this sorted out, but all this has him too busy for unexpected audiences and we're not from around here."

Tayvada shook his head. "Of course. In general, that man is notoriously hard to meet with and these are rough times here in Winde Port. Haven't seen everyone up in arms like this since the Panping Wars. What was that… has to be more than twenty years ago?"

"And some change now," Whitney said as if the man didn't know. Liam's War, which brought down their Council of Mystics and absorbed all the Panping Region under the Glass, had been two-and-a-half decades ago. He knew because that was when Sora arrived in Troborough on a caravan finding homes for children orphaned by the fighting.

"Such a shame. Normally it wouldn't have mattered at all. Would have merely cost you a few more autlas to charter east as passengers."

"Which is what I told my wife on the ride here. Much safer sailing to Yaolin City from here then all the way around by way of the Torrential Sea. Alas, it seems that was the better option."

Tayvada scratched his chin and took a look around the room. Then, he leaned in closer and lowered his voice. "I'll tell you what, I like a couple that proves our peoples can live harmoniously after so much bloodshed. These days, that's more important than ever."

"There's no one in the world I'd rather be with." Whitney took Sora's arm and gave it a loving squeeze. Her false smile deepened while she returned the gesture, but she dug her nails into his back at the same time.

"Well, why don't you come by the Guild Hall later this evening. Find me and I'll see what can be done to get you to Yaolin City in fair time—short of hitching a wagon—yes?"

"That would be superb, Lord Bokeo."

"Please, call me Tayvada."

A soft purring sound emanated from the man. Whitney nearly let a laugh sneak out at the thought of a man as proper as Tayvada gassing up the place. Then a pair of reptilian wings flapped behind him. Whitney didn't even try to hide his surprise.

"Whoa!" he shouted, taking a step back and bumping into the bar. A few glasses rattled as he looked to Sora, whose jaw dropped.

"I am so sorry," Tayvada said. "I sometimes forget she is there." A dark brown creature about the size of a large sack landed on his padded shoulder. Scales covered every bit of its body, with frills around its head plate. A pair of small wings stretched out acting also as front legs, claws serving both as joints and feet.

"Is that… a dragon?" Sora stammered. The creature blinked at her inquisitively. Its piercing, snake-like, yellow eyes had two sets of eyelids. A thin, translucent layer which closed sideways beneath a normal, vertical pair.

The man laughed. "Dragons are long gone, my dear. This here is Aquira. She's a wyvern—a distant relative of the dragon found in the Pikeback Mountains. She is nearly full-grown and mighty friendly… unless she considers you dangerous. You're not dangerous, are you Lord Blisslayer?"

"Not toward a beauty like her," Whitney said. "That's for sure." He grinned and again glanced toward Sora. Her face was like stone, unmoving from awe. He'd seen a few wyverns before in Panping whereas, she'd clearly never seen anything like it. They were extremely rare and valuable. They didn't, however, burn down villages and eat men as they couldn't sustain flight for long with their small wings.

After a long moment, she finally whispered, "May I touch her?"

"It is doubtful she'll let you. She may be friendly, however, wyverns are notoriously proud. But by all means, try. She won't bite."

Sora reached out. Aquira backed away and stuck out her serpentine tongue. Whitney was about to tease Sora when the wyvern suddenly leaned back in and nuzzled her head against Sora's outstretched hand.

"Bravo!" Tayvada said, giddy.

"Her scales are so dry!" she exclaimed.

"Let me see. A friend of mine had one and he loved me." Whitney went to pet Aquira, but the wyvern hissed at him before flying back and hovering behind Tayvada. Her breath was hot, like the hazy air just above a roaring fire.

"Don't fret, my friend." Tayvada lay his hand on Whitney's shoulder. "She has a soft spot for women."

"She just has good taste," Sora said.

Whitney crossed his arms, then plopped back down on his stool. "So, the Guild Hall, tonight?" he asked.

"Yes, tonight," Tayvada said. "I shall see you there. And do wear something... fitting?"

Whitney looked down at his tattered cloak. "My apologies. It has been a long journey."

"I understand. Until tonight, my Lord and Lady." He bowed, then nodded Tum Tum's way. "Come Aquira!"

Whitney turned to Sora as the man walked away, Aquira flapping to keep up with him. Sora was finally able to turn off her smile, but Whitney's remained ear to ear. He raised a fresh tankard of ale to both her and Tum Tum.

"See?" he said. "Simple."

VII

THE KNIGHT

Torsten could almost taste the energy in the air the night of Pi's declaration. A flurry of genuine activity passed through Yarrington the likes of which not seen since the passing of King Liam. People active not because they felt they had to be, such as had been for his coronation, but out of true desire.

He could hear the great King Liam's voice imparting wisdom before yet another war, "Common people don't revel in the fear of the royals behind walls," he said. "They crave an enemy they can reach. Villains that breathe their air, walk their dirt... spill their blood."

It was a simple concept, but as Torsten looked out upon Yarrington, he understood better than ever. For months, the city had been obsessed with things they couldn't control; a dying king, a queen driven to the brink of madness, unprovoked raids, hunger, a miracle—but now the taverns bustled. Together, young men and fathers drank and cursed the Shesaitju. They flooded the barracks across the kingdom, volunteers on top of conscripts.

All that time, trying to avoid war and Torsten forgot what the

Glass Kingdom was founded on. Half a century ago, they were just another kingdom in the corner of Pantego. Then a young king was called on by Iam to take up the sword, to bear His name, to bring greater Pantego under a single crown.

Liam had been older than Pi, yet Torsten couldn't help but wonder if history would repeat itself, would give a second chance, granted by Iam, to stay true, to keep spreading his light.

"Shouldn't you be planning?"

Torsten whipped around to see Oleander in the doorway of his chambers. It was neither modest like Rand's apartment nor luxurious like the King and Queen's, but it suited him. Instead of paintings and sculptures, the flawlessly cut stone walls were covered in weaponry. The shield of Sir Roderich of Cornhovel—a city no longer on the map thanks to so many battles, the Spear of Sir Von the Valiant—relics of great Shieldsmen he could aspire to.

It was, however, no place fit for the Queen Mother.

"Your Grace." Torsten bowed. "I wasn't expecting you."

"At least someone still bows to their queen."

She entered the room, her long legs carrying her to Torsten's bedside in only a few strides. She sat on the edge and her handmaiden made sure her dress didn't bunch—not a dress, Torsten realized. She wore a negligee as extravagant as any gown in Pantego. The frills were woven with gold, and the blue fabric was stitched in a tight floral pattern. The light of the moons poured through Torsten's window and caught it, allowing him to clearly see the silhouette of the lithe figure beneath.

Torsten averted his eyes, wondering if she knew. Then, he realized that he too was out of uniform, wearing only the sweat-laden, baggy tunic worn beneath his armor. He could only imagine the stench. The audience with the Caleef had every ounce of perspiration rolling down his back and from his shaven head.

"Forgive me," Torsten said. "If I knew you were coming I would be dressed appropriately."

"Can you stop being such an insufferably honorable man for once?" she groaned.

"And you..." She spun on her handmaiden. "If I wanted you to follow me in here I would have asked."

The young woman froze and stuttered, "Your Grace, I—"

"Get out!"

The young handmaiden scurried out of the room like a rat caught foraging at a banquet. Torsten watched the young lady's retreat and caught a glimpse of the Queen making herself more comfortable. His heart raced. There had never been a woman on his bed, let alone her.

"Your Grace, is there anything you need..." His words trailed off when he heard her snivel. His eyes lifted and found her face buried in her palms, crying.

Torsten rushed to her side. "What happened?"

"He's so... cruel," she whimpered.

"Who?"

"He wasn't like this when he was younger. Before everything. He was a sweet, kind boy. Uriah always said so, too. Now, I... I don't even know him."

Torsten sat beside her. He was a hair's breadth from laying his hand over hers but thought better of it. He slid away a bit, where the overpowering scent of her flower-blossom perfume wasn't so intoxicating.

"Oh, him," he said. "He's been through a lot, Your Grace. He's just figuring things out."

"I should've never let Redstar anywhere near him."

"None of us should have, but he can't poison Pi's mind any longer. He's locked up and won't be seeing day's light anytime soon."

"Don't you see, Torsten? I've been caring for a stranger ever since that day." She turned to him, tears causing her makeup to run. The last time he saw her so affected was when he found her cradling Pi's corpse. Now the boy was alive, yet she cried all the same.

"I only knew him from afar before then, so I cannot say."

"He loved to read. I'm not sure where he got it from. His father was a man of action, and I... I didn't learn to read until Liam brought me here. There's no reason for a woman to study in the far North."

"Then I'm glad you're here, Your Grace."

"Do not spin lies. Do you think I've not heard the whispers all these years? About the 'foreign whore Queen.' Do you think I don't know how they talk about me now? The murderous witch who lost her mind. I was only trying to save him."

"And Iam heard your prayers and returned him to us," Torsten said before thinking. He didn't believe that. The people prayed, maybe, but Iam didn't reward senseless killing. In the corner of his mind, ever since that day, Torsten always wondered if he'd been the one who'd caused the miracle. If it had been his unwavering faith that broke whatever curse Redstar had laid upon Pi and inspired Iam to return him to the realm of the living.

He never presumed to know the machinations of Iam. All he knew for sure was Oleander's rampage wasn't the cause of it. It couldn't have been.

"I thought everything would be back to normal when you found him in the crypt," Oleander said. "But now, when he starts talking, all I see in him is his father."

"Liam was a great man."

"He was. From the moment I saw him in the tundra, I knew he had no equal. Redstar couldn't understand why I left without a fuss. He still doesn't."

"I remember."

"You were there?"

Torsten nodded. "I was Uriah's squire."

How could he forget that day? Liam sought to conquer the

Drav Cra before he realized he never could. The land beyond Winter's Thumb was wild and always would be. But then Liam saw the stunning daughter of a chieftain, barely of proper age. She stuck out like a flower growing through the ice.

Oleander ran her fingers along her tear-covered cheeks. "Oh, how time has ravaged me since then."

"You are more radiant than ever, Your Grace." That, he meant. How Liam fell for someone so young, he would never understand, but the man had an eye for seeing beyond what others could. Somehow, he knew the marvel Oleander would blossom into. A fierce queen and the greatest beauty in Pantego... now sitting on Torsten's bed.

"How in Iam's name are you not betrothed, Torsten?" She smiled, though her swollen eyes made it pitiable, and sidled closer.

"The Crown is a Shieldsman's only love, Your Grace."

"Right, of course. You're not still chaste though, are you?"

"My Queen?"

"A virgin, Torsten."

"I know what it means, Your Grace. I just—"

"You are, aren't you!" Oleander said, seemingly forgetting about her tears.

"Of course not!" Torsten exclaimed, cheeks red as cherry plums.

"No, how could you be? Conquering all those foreign lands with my husband. I'm sure you were treated like a king by all the whores he brought in."

Torsten choked on his next breath.

"What? You think I don't know?" She laughed. "He had enough mistresses to fill the Great Hall."

"I... the King kept to his tent...."

"My sweet Torsten, you don't have to lie to me. I know who my husband was. Within these walls, I was the love of his life, but out there? Every time he returned from some great battle, it wasn't blood I smelled on him."

"He loved you, my Queen," Torsten said softly. He could think of nothing else, and even those words barely managed past his lips.

"I know he did. And I loved him when I could. But the others were all beautiful, faultless and fleeting loves. Only *I* suffered under the weight of his honesty. As I now suffer under the weight of my own son's—his son."

"For a boy his age to have been through so much... I can't even imagine. I truly believe he's simply still figuring things out, Your Grace."

"Torsten, please do away with the formalities. We are alone in this room."

"Of course, Your Gr—Oleander." He didn't need the reminder of their solitude, it was all he could think of.

She rested her head against Torsten's shoulder. He quaked with conflicting emotions. He had never—could never—deny how stunning she was, how powerful, but he'd been on the receiving end of her wrath far too many times.

"I did it all for him," she said quietly after some time had passed.

"I know."

"No, you don't!" She removed her head from his shoulder, but her anger quickly subsided and she returned it again. "How could you?" she continued, calmly this time. "You have no child of your own. You're like all the rest. You think I'm some crazy, murderous shrew."

This time, Torsten was the one to break the connection. He stood, hands balled into tight fists. "I think you were broken by grief and made mistakes. And I may not have a child, but my quest to bring young Pi back to this realm showed me terrors no man should see. Included are your brother's torments, masquerading as a man I respected, and a beast so grotesque her visage assaults me in my dreams."

He stared off into the shadow of his room and imagined her there. The Spider Queen Bliss, her eyes like amethysts staring back at him, wanting to devour him.

"Torsten." The Queen took his hand, pulled him toward her. When he drew his gaze away from the shadows and back toward her, he found her solemn again. Bliss was said to be a goddess, and at that moment Oleander seemed her equal.

Before he knew it, they were sitting so near one another, their legs touched. Her long, painted nails ran up his arm and along the bare flesh of his neck. All the tiny hairs on his body rose with it.

"My greatest mistake was losing faith in you. Sending you away," she said softly, leaning in. Her perfume wafted around his nostrils, making it impossible to retreat.

"I'm here now," he said, voice quavering.

"Of course you are, my loyal, handsome, knight. I never properly thanked you for stopping my brother." Her other hand gripped the back of his neck. Her fingers were cold, but her breath was warm.

"You can start by finally executing the bastard." His voice shook and his breath came in spirts. "The coronation is over now. I cannot bear another day knowing his shadow looms over us. Especially with war to come."

"Tonight, then? I'll let you hold the sword." She drew herself closer, throwing one leg over his, her knee resting between his thighs. Her negligee stretched, falling off one of her slender shoulders as her body contorted. "I've heard Pantego has no finer swordsman. Surely, you could *handle* it."

Torsten knew he should back away, but he'd never seen her so intimately. Her milky skin was supple, without blemish. Her eyes bore so many different shades of blue it made the summer sky seem dreary. There wasn't a man in all the Glass and beyond who hadn't dreamed of this. He wasn't sure what Oleander was up to —she was always up to something—but he couldn't stop. His heart beat so fast he felt like it would drive him to an early grave. Her lips fell upon his. They tasted as wonderful as her perfume smelled.

He didn't lean into it. He couldn't even move. But she did all the work. One of her long legs wound its way around him and squeezed until their chests pressed together.

He could deny her no longer.

He kissed her hard in return. His hand found its way to the small of her back, and as he prepared to lay her down and give into the silent, sinful cravings that had been building in him for so long, out of the corner of his eye, he saw someone familiar pass by his chamber. Realizing the door was still open made his eyes go wide, but the man he thought he saw caused him to release the Queen.

"My Queen, stop," he panted. He tried to remove her leg, but she only stretched the other around him, laid back on the bed, and tried to reel him in again. "Oleander, stop."

Hearing her name gave her pause enough for Torsten to break free without having to lay his hands on her.

"What?" she said. "Liam can have all the fun in the world but his sweet, widowed queen can't?"

"No… I… it's him."

Torsten sprinted to one of many racks filled with various arms. He grabbed his most trusted claymore, then swept out into the corridor.

"Redstar!" he bellowed.

He wasn't sure he was right until halfway down the passage, the man stopped and turned. It was Redstar no doubt, free of chains. A luxurious robe now fell around his feet, the same color crimson as the birthmark covering his face. A mischievous grin split Redstar's face. If he feared being caught, it didn't show. By the looks of him, he'd even found time to have a bath.

"Torsten, my old friend!" he exclaimed. "I was hoping to stumble upon you first."

"Show me your hands, now."

Redstar raised them without protest, not even a spot of blood on his scarred palms.

Torsten rushed him, pressing his sword to his throat. "On your knees." He advanced the blade, pulling it back before drawing blood, only just realizing how dangerous that could be. "If you try anything, I swear to Iam I will—"

"Torsten what is the meaning of this?" Oleander called from his room.

He glanced back just long enough to see her features darken as she realized the situation. Her negligee was still askew, her hair as wild as the land from whence she came.

"Redstar?" she whispered.

Redstar's brow furrowed. "Oh, now this is interesting."

"Quiet!" Torsten growled. He extended the sword further, until the tip put an indent in Redstar's skin. "How did you escape?"

"Escape?" he cackled. "I was set free."

"On whose word?"

"Mine."

Torsten whipped around. Further down the hall, past the entrance to his room, stood Pi. Oleander straightened her clothing before turning to see him as well. His frame was cloaked in darkness. What was easy to see, however, was how serious he was—as stern as Liam Nothhelm on the eve of battle.

VIII

THE MYSTIC

Sora couldn't remember her long trek from the Panping Region to Troborough. She was far too young all those years ago. However, she'd been told she was a part a large group of refugees, orphans, mostly, whose parents were slaughtered in the Third Panping War. Somehow, she'd never been angry with the Glass, not really. Maybe it was Wetzel's influence and teaching, but she understood war. She realized the Glass wasn't really the enemy any more than her own people. Besides, had it not been for Wetzel, a Glassman, she'd likely have died, starved and exposed to the elements.

Her childhood was pleasant, but in light of recent events, she started to see how she'd been treated differently from the rest of the children. She'd thought it was just because of weird, old Wetzel. But now she knew it was more. An inherent distrust of her kind by nearly everybody in the western Glass Kingdom, whether they realized it or not.

The only times she'd really felt normal was when she was with Whitney. He didn't look at her like she was a great, big mistake. Whether they were splashing in the Shellnak, or nabbing little cakes from the baker—that was Whitney's favorite. Sora's favorite was sneaking into the Twilight Manor to listen to the traveling bards spin melodic yarns about far-away places, but that was hers alone. Whitney never believed her when she said she'd done it and she'd never showed him how, even though he practically begged her. To Whitney, she was just Sora, the girl from downstream with funny ears.

Music always had a way of making Sora feel comfortable when she was among all the older folk of Troborough. Some people had long walks in the fields, or riding horses, or thieving, but for Sora, it was the sweet tones of a lute expertly plucked. She didn't play an instrument, but always wished she had.

Standing there in the entrance to the Winde Traders Guild Hall, Sora realized that all the best bards who came through Troborough—Fabian "Feel Good" Saravia, Dudley "Dreamboat" Blanco—they'd all been nothing compared to what Winde Port had to offer. As she listened to the notes, she felt like she really stood before the golden arches of Glinthaven, birthplace of the bardsong.

"Sora!" Whitney's voice snapped her back to reality. "Let's go see what fortune holds for us!"

Whitney tapped his foot, waiting for her, clutching his letters patent, the document the Glass Master of Rolls had drafted for him. They somehow proved him nobility, even though she knew his parents were simple farmers. The stupidity of the entire situation constantly astounded her.

She knew from Wetzel's dusty, but limited library that in the land of her ancestors, there weren't any papers to prove a person was of worth. *They* proved it. From great mystics to great minds, any man or woman could rise… at least until the King of Glass took hold.

She sighed.

At least these papers might help get them to Panping faster.

She tried not to show it around Whitney, but she'd never been so anxious to get anywhere in her life. Something had awakened in her when she defeated Redstar. Torsten thought it was Iam, she'd said it was the blood of Bliss, but somehow, she knew there was more to it. And she knew the answers had to be somewhere in Yaolin City, a land where mystics once freely drew on the powers of Elsewhere without blood sacrifice or condemnation.

For now, she needed to play the role of Mrs. Whitney Bliss-layer. She certainly looked the part of nobility. They'd received quite a handsome sum from the goods in Grint's wagon. Enough to buy her a sparkling gown with lace trim fit for the Queen of Glass herself. Long, fingerless silk gloves covered her up to her elbows, assuring no one would discover her dark secrets by spying the many scars crisscrossing her hands and forearms.

Had she been wearing the Glass Crown, she could have passed for royalty. She hated to admit to herself that Whitney could as well. High, leather boots met his green, silk tights at the knee. He wore an exquisite doublet marked with intricately embroidered filigree. The whole ensemble was inexplicably both dashing and ridiculous all at once, much like the man who wore it.

But that was nothing compared to the others eating and drinking within the guild. Ladies wore unnaturally-colored hair high in plumule fashion, layer upon layer. Their faces were masked by makeup worthy of a masquerade. And the men looked no better, wearing puffy white wigs and collars so thick and ruffled they looked like they were being strangled by fluffy kittens.

Whitney had told her on the way over that the longstanding merchant families of Winde Port put the nobles of Yarrington to shame with their pomp and circumstance. The real thing made her feel more out of place than ever before, regardless of what she wore.

Whitney, on the other hand, sniggered as they passed by a table of four men all wearing puffy, patterned shirts.

"Hush, Whit," Sora warned. "You'll embarrass us."

"Yeah, because we're the ones who should be embarrassed."

"For once in your irreverent life, would you just try and behave yourself?"

Whitney stopped at a table in the corner, bent at the waist, and beckoned her forth. "Why, of course. Right this way, milady."

"Better than knife-ear," she grumbled.

They sat down and ordered drinks. It was such a normal-seeming thing, yet Sora realized she'd never been waited on before. In all the taverns she'd ever visited—a total of two—she had to carry herself up to the bar.

Presently, the server returned carrying oddly-shaped glasses filled with violet liquid.

"This is no ale I've ever seen," Sora said.

"It's a Winde Port delicacy called a cocktail," Whitney said. "Ridiculous name, I know, but it's fruity. You'll love it."

Sora lifted it and studied the liquid. It looked like poison out of some fairy tales she'd found on Wetzel's bookshelf. But all around the room, nobles were throwing them back. She gave it a whiff. It smelled like the first lavender blossoms of spring.

"Would you just try it already?" Whitney griped.

Sora brought it to her lips and took the tiniest sip imaginable. Her eyes went wide. She tilted the glass and downed half in a single gulp.

"It tastes like the plums Farmer Branson grew in the fields across from my house!" she exclaimed. "I can't wait to have another..." Her voice trailed off. Sadness came like a deluge at the thought of that field, now black and burnt at the hands of the Shesaitju.

"Enough of that look in your eyes, Sora. This is about trying something fresh and new. Drink up. The bottom of that glass is the start of a new one."

Sora forced a smile. "Are you trying to get me drunk, *husband*?"

"Never." Whitney laughed. "So, do you see Tayvada anywhere?"

"No," Sora answered. "But I hope his drag... wyvern is here. I've never seen anything like it."

"I have," Whitney said, finishing his drink in one mouthful. He raised a finger for the waiter to bring more.

"Is this another of your tall tales?" Sora asked.

"I don't tell tall tales. I speak history."

Sora rolled her eyes before she too finished the rest of her drink. Whitney went to request another, but she waved him down. She'd never drank much more than a single ale or a sip of honeyed wine from Wetzel's cupboard. The old badger didn't like her losing control when she was still getting a handle on her abilities. And after what happened in the Webbed Woods, she wasn't too keen on it either. One "cocktail" and her head was already feeling light.

"I wonder where Tayvada is," she said while Whitney tried another beverage, this one, a sickeningly bright shade of orange. "We need to get going."

"What's the rush?" Whitney asked. "Look at this place, it's beautiful. I used to have to sneak into places like this, come up with a whole elaborate backstory and name. If only Torsten could see me now." He kicked his feet up on the bench across from him.

"He'd probably want to burn those as much as me," she said, referring to his boots she'd just shoved off the bench. "Now c'mon, we should find him."

"You need to learn to relax. Oh, shog..."

"What?"

"Don't turn around," Whitney said. "I said *don't* turn around!"

It was too late. She was already craning her neck to see behind her. She cursed herself for not listening to him, but it was his fault for making it so impossible.

"Darkings…" She whipped her head back around. The sight of him stole the breath from her lungs. "Did he see you? I think he saw you. He did. He's coming this way."

"What do we do?" Sora whispered.

The man sauntered over, eyes poring over Whitney and then, Sora. He carried himself like one who'd never done an honest day's work, and he likely hadn't. His face and hands were smooth as a man half his age. There was so little grit in his voice, Sora could imagine the demon ears of Elsewhere perking up when he spoke. Her hand instinctually fell toward the handle of the knife in her belt.

"Father Gorenheimer, wasn't it?" he said. "Oh wait, Whitney Fierstown, that's right. Though, now I hear it's Lord Blisslayer. How many names can one man have?"

In the weeks since they'd last seen him, he'd grown bushy mustache which looked like a fuzzy caterpillar resting on his upper lip. Chest hairs poked out from beneath an expensive looking tunic, and when he smiled, Sora recoiled. Yellowing teeth poked out over his bottom lip.

"Constable Darkings!" Whitney exclaimed. "How's your daughter?"

Sora felt all the color drain from her cheeks. She couldn't believe that after they robbed and burned down the Constable of Bridleton's home, that was the first thing Whitney would say. Then Sora remembered how she hit the poor girl to keep their flirting from getting everyone killed.

It wasn't her finest moment.

"I've shipped Nauriyal to a convent in Hornsheim," Darkings said. "Turns out she played not-so-small a role in the destruction of my home—but you already knew that, didn't you? Maybe a little hard work in the bitter cold will teach her to respect her elders."

Whitney's beaming smile didn't fade in the least, but his eye twitched.

"No matter," Darkings continued. "I promised you last time I saw you that I'd have my revenge."

"And here you are! Should I expect you'll gut us, here and now?" Whitney asked.

"This is a room for gentlemen. I would never tarnish the good name of Darkings. Not here in the very guild my grandparents helped build so many Dawnings ago. You see, Darkings is not a name you should have meddled with. Do you even realize the enemies you've made?"

"What do you want, Constable?" Sora asked, exasperated.

He slid into the booth next to them and his face turned deadly serious. "Do not speak to me in such a flippant manner, *knife-ear*!" he hissed. Now her fingers wrapped firmly around the wooden grip of her knife.

Darkings faced Whitney. "You burned everything I built to the ground," he said. "My father served as Master of Coin to the Crown for twenty years, and he will be reinstated under the new king in short time. If I even breathed word of this to him, the King's Shield would have your heads on pikes."

Sora looked to Whitney. She didn't have to ask out loud if he knew that Darkings was the son of a member of the Royal Council. She did it with her eyes, and his said, "no."

The worldliest thief in Pantego and he doesn't know a thing!

She wanted to explode at him but somehow kept quiet.

"If I were you, I wouldn't bother daddy," Whitney said calmly. "Turns out, people thought it was another act of the Black Sands. Sounds more plausible to me than a couple of nobles rolling into Bridleton for a bit of respite, no? Plus, the Wearer of White already *is* reinstated, and he's a good friend of m—"

"You are no more noble than the shog on my boot!" Darkings spat.

"I have papers saying otherwise. Bearing the royal seal itself."

"A piece of paper won't keep you…" He cleared his throat and stroked his mustache. "Are you a gems playing man, Mr. Fierstown?"

"*Lord* Blisslayer. And, yes I fancy myself rather good at all games of chance. Up for a game or two?"

Darkings scoffed and leaned in. "You have shown your hand, boy, and it is not a winner. I, on the other hand, keep mine close to my chest. When you are least expecting it, you and your Panping witch will find yourselves drowning in your own blood and piss."

Whitney brought his drink to his lips and before taking a sip, said, "I've always enjoyed a swim. I'll be looking forward to it."

"Don't you worry. You'll be seeing me again soon enough."

Whitney opened his mouth to speak but a server approached the table.

"I'm sorry, I didn't know it would be a party of three," he said. "Can I get you something, Lord Darkings?"

"No, thank you. I was just leaving. Please, get this special couple a round of your finest Breklian brandy, on me. It might be their last," he paused, "in Winde Port."

Darkings stood, grinned, and walked away.

"Was that a threat?" Sora asked, finally feeling like she could breathe. She didn't release her weapon until he was completely out of sight.

"An ominous warning, I'd say," Whitney said, taking another sip of his drink.

"This isn't funny, Whit. We are on lockdown in an unfamiliar city with an apparently powerful family after us."

"This city isn't unfamiliar to me. We're going to be absolutely fine."

"How in Elsewhere did you not know who his father was!"

"I'm supposed to keep track of every twit on the Royal Council? They're in and out like flies, and with the mad Queen, I barely know who's king anymore."

"Why am I not surprised?"

Whitney didn't answer. He leaned over the table, tilted one of his empty glasses and watched it sway back upright. "You hungry?" Whitney asked.

"You're thinking about food at a time like this?"

"You're not? We haven't had a decent meal since Grambling, back at the Walled Lake."

"Aren't we here just to get some papers from Tayvada?" she asked.

"Do you see Tayvada?"

"No." Sora's face scrunched. "Should we ask someone?"

Whitney sighed, then rose. "I'll be right back."

Sora sidled a little further into the booth, wary of leaving her back exposed. Darkings was an obtuse fool but he wasn't accepting like the rest of the people here. And he didn't seem to care about all the fineries. She glanced over each shoulder and saw plenty of others like her—*knife-ears*. She tried to just relax and enjoy the music. After a few tunes went by without him returning, she started to worry that Darkings had exacted his revenge on Whitney already and she'd be next.

A sudden movement made her yelp. Whitney slid back into the booth from the other direction, carrying what looked like a leg of lamb. He stretched it toward her but she declined.

"You had me worried sick and you were getting food?" she asked.

"Sora, you've gotta learn to relax a little. Take it all in. We are exploring the wide world together. No agenda. No worries!"

"Except the little bit about a man wanting us dead. Oh, and the mounting army. Oh, and—"

Whitney groaned. "Do you want to know what I found out about Tayvada or not?"

"Fine."

"Turns out one of his servants came about an hour ago to leave message that he fell ill and wouldn't be..." Whitney puffed out his chest and put on a distinguished effect, "'...attending any of his appointments this evening.'"

Sora threw her hands up in frustration. "Great. Now we have to wait for him?"

Whitney took a bite of lamb, then with his mouth still full said, "Nope. I got his home address."

IX

THE KNIGHT

"**Y**our Grace, please help me understand," Torsten said to Pi, keeping his voice low. "Why would you free him?"

They were in Pi's old chambers now, high up in the Glass Castle's West Tower. He hadn't yet found reason to move to his father's quarters—besides, Oleander still occupied them. There were bars on the window, an unpleasant reminder of Pi's fall.

"You could just ask me," Redstar said. He sat at Pi's desk, the same smug grin plastered on his face that he'd worn when revealing his true self in the Webbed Woods.

"Silence!" Torsten snapped. He stood behind him, claymore in both hands, the tip grinding into the stone floor.

"Pi, my precious boy, don't you remember what he did to you?" Oleander sat beside him on a bed two sizes too large for him, stroking his hair.

He remained indifferent.

"I forget, sister, which of us has more of your people's blood on our hands?" Redstar remarked.

"Sir Davies was worth a thousand of any of us!" Torsten said. "He died because of you."

"Just kill him, Torsten," Oleander spat. "I will not have him poison these halls any further."

"You will do no such thing, Wearer," Pi said, calm and collected. He turned to face them, head and neck only. "No harm will befall my uncle."

"He tried to kill you! To destroy everything inside of you."

"What, with this?" Pi reached across his bed and lifted the tiny, Drav Cra effigy sewn for him by Oleander at his birth. By the ancient customs of her former people, an orepul was said to bear a piece of its owner's soul.

The young King lifted it, then without a second of hesitation, ripped the head from its stitches. The Queen gasped as it fell to the floor in two pieces. Torsten's heart sank with it. Not that he believed it wielded any power—such would be heresy—but he'd been through exile and back to retrieve it for the Queen.

"Not with that, Your Grace," Torsten said after a brief silence. His fingers squeezed so tight around the handle of his sword it hurt. "He put a spell on you with blood magic. A spell that had you seeing awful visions of darkness and terror and the Buried Goddess. I know because I felt them too shortly after you fell from this very window."

"Excuse me for trying to open his eyes by showing him the truth," Redstar said. "How was I to know that children grow up so soft here in the capital that he wouldn't be able to handle it?" He walked across the room as he spoke and lifted the two pieces of the orepul to study them more closely. Torsten imagined seeing an effigy supposedly holding a piece of Pi's soul would unnerve him, but he didn't seem so in the slightest.

"Because of your dark magic, my son, your king, leaped from that window!" Oleander shouted. She tried to stand, but Pi extended one of his short arms in front of her.

"My uncle acted vindictively because *you* refused him," Pi said. "Because you forgot that the ice of the Drav Cra runs through your veins, as it does mine. I may not approve of what he did to me, but I do understand."

"What have you done, Brother?" Oleander asked. "How have you twisted his mind this time?"

"Oleander, I'm hurt." Redstar stuffed the orepul into a pouch, then placed his hand over his heart in mock-surprise. "I've been locked away safe and sound. Pi came to me."

"You don't deserve to breathe the same air as him!" Oleander grabbed a small letter opener off the bedside table, sprung to her feet, and charged him. Torsten caught her just in time, the blade only inches away from Redstar's eye. A heartbeat later, he wondered what in Elsewhere he was thinking by stopping her.

Redstar didn't even flinch. "Now we both owe each other, Sir Unger," he said. His grin deepened as he stood and patted Torsten's back.

"Torsten, don't let him do this," Oleander said. "He can't be trusted. He tried to kill my son." She tried to squirm free, but Torsten's brawny arms didn't give. "He tried to kill my son!"

"I know, Your Grace," Torsten whispered. "But not like this."

"Guards!" Pi called. Not a second later, the door flew open and two members of the King's Shield entered, weapons drawn. "Please remove my mother to her chambers until I see fit. She is feeling ill again and I worry what she might do."

The guards glanced between the King and Torsten.

"You will not lay a hand on me," Oleander hissed. "I am your Queen."

"They will do as their king asks, *Mother*, and so will you," Pi said, a man's timbre in his tone. "When I met with Redstar, he called on the names of Iam and his goddess in heartfelt apology. He has repented for what was done out of spite and anger." He lowered his voice and said, "When will you?"

Torsten felt all the fight leave Oleander. Her arms went slack. The words were harsh, yet partially true. An apology from a deceiver like Redstar meant as little as one made in the name of the Buried Goddess, but Oleander too had acted from a dangerous place.

"Pi…" Oleander's voice cracked. "He's a monster. You have to trust me."

"Our weakness after Father grew ill has emboldened our enemies," Pi said. "Perhaps monsters are exactly what we need now."

Torsten regarded Redstar. He'd manipulated the entire kingdom to help him destroy Bliss, the apparent enemy of his people's own fallen deity, but doing that didn't even seem to compare to how self-satisfied he now appeared.

"Just go, Your Grace," Torsten whispered in Oleander's ear. "I'll make sure he never sees daylight again."

She turned and took Torsten's hands. Hers were quaking.

"Oh, Torsten," she sniveled. "Loyal, Torsten. Show him the light of Iam that breathed life into him again." Her fingers slid apart from his, then she slowly backed away between the two guards.

Torsten nodded the Shieldsmen along but didn't break eye contact with Oleander until she was through the door. She'd been a terrible queen when she was in charge, one who had senselessly murdered so many of her loyal servants. But at least Torsten knew why. Perhaps she was a monster too, but if that were true, there was no term foul enough to describe her brother.

Redstar sighed. "Perhaps now we can discuss how to handle the Shesaitju situation in peace and quiet, Nephew."

Torsten lashed out and grabbed him by the collar. He pulled him close. The Drav Cra were inherently tall, but Redstar was the runt of his family. Torsten towered over him.

"You will address him as your King," Torsten growled, then shoved him back into the chair.

"Relax, Sir Unger." Pi stood and paced in front of his window. His head barely reached over the sill, but Torsten wasn't foolish enough to believe he was a child anymore, even if he looked it. Whatever had happened between his death and rebirth, he was as much a man as they were.

"I understand your hesitance to trust my uncle," Pi said.

"Beyond being a murderer, he is a heretic and practitioner of blood magic," Torsten said. "He is the enemy of the faithful and the scorn of Iam's vigilant Eye."

"And he is not only one of the most respected leaders in Drav Cra as dradinengor of the Ruuhar Clan, but also named High Warlock by the rest of his order."

"Arch Warlock," Redstar corrected.

Torsten scowled his way. "That is not a title we of the Glass should abide."

"Maybe so, but it is a title which allowed him to gather thousands of capable warriors to our cause in only a month. My father turned from their lands because he knew they were a hard, unconquerable people. Yet the tomes of history teach us that all men descended from the tundra. Drav Cra is in all our blood, and it is half of mine."

"Liam knew they couldn't be trusted. He knew how far Iam was from their hearts."

"Yet he brought one home. Made her queen. Because my father knew that worth could be found in the strangest of places. He knew that the wild tribes of the North would have bowed to my mother if only she remembered them. That was how he planned to conquer them. Through blood, not by blood."

"How do you know that's what he planned?" he asked, even though it sounded exactly like something Liam would do. He hadn't only been a fearless commander who charged into battle and inspired his own men, but a tactician without equal.

"Sir Davies said as much when I was very young," Pi said. "But then Father grew too ill and our borders stopped expanding. My mother could have been useful to him then. Instead, she remained a cruel, foreign treasure locked up in this castle scaring everyone away."

"Your Grace, she gave birth to you. She sat at your side every night while you were ill."

"And she let the kingdom crumble. You said it yourself, our armies are weaker than ever. We don't trust any of our allies in Panping or Brotlebir to come to our aid. Instead, we're calling on conscripts who've done nothing but plow fields for a decade."

"And drink," Redstar added. "For centuries, my people have been battling cold that makes this seem like summer. Scraping and clawing for leftovers of the few beasts that still roam the tundra."

"After two decades as queen, my mother's failure will be rectified," Pi declared. "The mighty warriors of the Drav Cra will march at our side."

"The heathens should never be allowed into this city," Torsten bristled.

"I sent for them weeks ago." Pi stopped at the window and had to lean up on the balls of his feet to look down over the sill.

Torsten rushed to his side and threw open the window. Cold air and flurries blasted his cheeks but he craned his neck over the edge so he could see the castle's entry bailey. Snow and clouds dulled the light of the twin moons but there was no mistaking the gathering. Hundreds of tall, pale Drav Cra men wearing heavy furs and axes stood waiting. Enough of them to slaughter everyone inside, King and Queen Mother as well.

Among them were others dressed in ragged robes of layered animal furs, wearing necklaces festooned with strange totems and bones—true Drav Cra warlocks, not just in the capital, but within the walls of the castle. They didn't even bother to pretend they were cultists to the Buried Goddess or cover their faces with hoods and white masks like the ones who followed Redstar in the Webbed Woods. They let their faces show, black paint covering their eyes with a line of red over the lids. Cracking, white paint covered the rest of their faces and ran down their necks as if they needed to make their pale skin paler.

"By Iam, what have you done?" Torsten's voice shook.

"I'm finally using every advantage at our disposal," Pi said.

"Had I known how wise the young King was, I would have come straight to him a year ago and skipped all the nonsense," Redstar said.

"You call that nonsense?" Torsten growled as he whipped back around. "Your Grace, I am your Wearer of White, commander of your armies. Why wasn't I told about this?"

"You are loyal and you are respected, Sir Unger," Pi said. "But I knew your piety would hinder your ability to see the benefit of this alliance."

"And the only pay they require is food," Redstar said, grinning so wide Torsten wanted to slap it off his face with his spiked, glaruium gauntlet.

"You expect my men—you expect *me* to march beside these heathens? Those are warlocks of the Buried Goddess down there." Torsten took Pi by the arm and the glare he received sent him reeling back. "If my men cannot trust their brothers in arms, I cannot lead them effectively."

"And you will not have to," Pi said. "As part of this arrangement, I have named my uncle Emissary of Drav Cra. You will command the armies, but he will lead his people under you. You will work together to bring this Shesaitju rebellion to an end. Then, my father's blessed work will be continued."

Torsten fell to his knees. "My King, I beg you, don't trust this man. The things he's done. The things he can do. He is a snake in the flesh of a man."

"'Iam is mercy. Iam is compassion. Light.' All my life I've heard this, yet all those who love gods of other names are ridiculed and condemned. I spent a great deal of time reading as a child. The holy texts beg for peace in Pantego. And here, those of Nesilia stand ready to fight by our side. Wren the Holy speaks of her evil. Redstar however, says that she was as close to Iam as skin to bone."

"Lies from the mouth of a deceiver."

"Possibly. Yet the God Feud teaches us that fighting amongst each other helps no one. And so, Torsten Unger, you will find a way to work with my uncle for the good of the kingdom, or you will find yourself exiled again."

Torsten glanced back at Redstar, at a man so wicked Iam sought to mark him eternally with the red of blood. A man who wore the guise of Sir Uriah Davies after luring him to his death. A man who'd been willing to risk everything to vanquish the Spider Queen Bliss, and for what?

Now he had the ear of the young, impressionable king after he drove the boy mad with dark magic. Torsten's fists clenched. He knew he could take Redstar down right then, ending whatever game he played. But as he looked back to Pi, he also knew that wasn't the way of Iam.

Perhaps Pi wasn't as ready for rule as Torsten had thought earlier that day, but he was right about what Iam stood for. And Torsten would be there when Redstar's true nature was revealed to him again. As he always would be.

He bowed his head. "I will serve in whatever way you see fit, Your Grace. But I will never trust him after what he did to you and neither should you."

"That is why I have a Shieldsman who served my father for so long at my side." Pi laid a hand on Torsten's shoulder.

For a moment, Torsten felt silly being so proud of receiving the praises of a small boy. Then Pi's arm fell away and he longed for it to return. The young king lay back onto his bed, all energy seeming to fade in an instant as the color drained from his face. It might have been the light, but Torsten thought the dark rings around his eyes seemed more pronounced than ever.

"Now leave me," Pi said weakly. "Both of you."

"Of course, Your Grace," Torsten said, rising. "You must be exhausted."

"Yes, seeing reason can be so tiring." Redstar bowed exceedingly low.

It reminded Torsten of the way the thief, Whitney, used to praise him in jest. Just the sight of it had him nearly swinging his sword in a wide arc across Redstar's neck. He controlled himself for Pi's sake.

They started off out of the room, side by side until Redstar stopped. "Ah, Your Grace, before I forget," he said. "I spoke with Yuri Darkings in the dungeon—the former Master of Coin who fled your mother's scorn. He is eager to return to his post, and in this time of war and uncertainty, it seems wise to have an experienced hand in charge of finances."

"You eavesdropped on my—" Torsten was cut off by the gentle voice of the King. He remained staring up at the ceiling with his limbs stretched out, now totally drained.

"Excellent idea, Uncle," he groaned. "Have him reinstated immediately."

"At once." Redstar bowed again and hurried out of the room.

Torsten seized him the moment they got outside and slammed him against the wall. His nostrils flared. His blood felt like it was on fire. It took all his willpower not to crush the traitor's neck.

"'Excellent idea,'" Redstar gurgled, repeating Pi's words. "Thank you for shedding light on the Council's needs. I needed to build a little faith."

"I don't know what you're up to, but I swore to you I wouldn't let you hurt him again," Torsten snarled, squeezing tighter.

"Can't…" he gurgled again, "…can't a loving uncle do what's best for his nephew?"

"Every word out of your mouth is poison." Torsten released him. Redstar fell to the floor, coughing and rubbing his neck. Once able to breathe again, he looked up, wearing that same annoying smirk.

"As I told you in the dungeon the day you brought me back, my work is already complete. Nesilia smiles upon me, and now she wants me here, serving my new king. Who are we to question her?"

"The name of the Buried Goddess will never be uttered here with impunity."

"I believe I just heard Pi *utter* it in the same sentence as your loving, wonderful Iam."

Torsten shoved a boot against his chest and pinned him back against the wall. "Don't you dare use His name."

"Or what?"

"Or I will do what I should've done in the Webbed Woods."

Redstar grinned through the pain of Torsten's full weight. "You can try," he said.

Suddenly, Torsten felt heat on his shin and looked down at a smear of blood on Redstar's hand. A glimmer of fire swirled around it. Blood magic, being used in the very halls of the Glass Castle.

Torsten's grip on his sword tightened. He couldn't stop it. A moment of weakness washed over him, or perhaps it was Iam guiding his hand. The King might banish him, or worse, but at least they'd be free.

Redstar grabbed Torsten's leg with his fire-wreathed hand. His pants burned away and his skin blistered. He didn't care.

"Iam forgive me for what I must do," he whispered under his breath. Then, he raised his blade.

At the same time, Redstar bit his other hand, drawing fresh blood. He raised his palm and Torsten felt all his muscles tense. He remembered the woods, how Redstar flung him and his companions around like rag dolls.

The Arch Warlock was clearly weakened from his time in a cell since Torsten still felt a twinge of control. It stung as much as the fire on his leg to try and move his muscles against the magic but he gritted his teeth and fought to try and break free.

"Sir Unger!" someone hollered from down the hall.

Torsten couldn't turn his head but he peered over with his eyes. Wardric stood in the corridor, fully armed. Beside him was a female Drav Cra warlock, her wild hair threaded with jagged beads made of bone. She sliced her hand and raised it. Her power, combined with that of Redstar, flung Torsten back, slamming him hard against the wall. His claymore clattered to the floor.

"Release him!" Wardric drew his sword and raised it to the warlock's neck.

"He assaulted Drad Redstar," the woman hissed.

Torsten's entire body seized. His back was crushed against the stone so hard he felt his ribs beginning to snap inward. A scream bubbled in his throat, one that would certainly rouse Pi if he hadn't been already.

Redstar stood, then dusted off his clothes. "Ah, my dear Freydis," he addressed her. "I was wondering when you and the others would arrive."

"Shall we send him to the goddess, Drad Redstar?" she asked.

"No, my over-eager friend. Release him. They're our allies now." Redstar lowered his own hand.

Torsten crumpled to the floor. Somehow, he'd forgotten what it felt like to be manipulated by blood magic—like an infant in the arms of its mother. It was a feeling he'd hoped never to experience again.

"My apologies, fair Shieldsman," Redstar said. "It was only a misunderstanding."

Freydis lowered her bloody hand as well, but Wardric still wielded his blade.

"It didn't look like it," Wardric said. "Why does that monster walk free?"

Torsten tried to stand but his muscles were as sore as they'd been on his first day of King's Shield training. He stared ahead at Pi's chambers. In a moment of weakness and fear, he had nearly broken the oath he made to the boy beyond its finely carved door.

"It's fine," Torsten said, panting. "Stand down, Wardric."

The Shieldsman didn't listen, only extended the blade further underneath the flaking white paint on Freydis' slender neck.

"What is the meaning of this, Torsten?" he asked. "I rode to bring you urgent news from the Southern Reach and find a barbarian horde camping at our doorsteps. This woman claimed to have been invited."

"By the King himself," Redstar pronounced with a flourish.

"Don't speak, knave!"

It took all the energy Torsten had to gesture to Wardric to lower his weapon. "It's true," he began through labored breaths. "Our young king has decided to free Redstar and make an alliance through him with the Drav Cra."

"That's madness," Wardric said.

"But true."

"You see? Just a squabble amongst new friends," Redstar said. He sauntered over, abounding confidence in every stride, then hoisted Torsten up by the shoulders. He brushed his own shoulder, and gave Torsten a playful slap on the cheek. "Good as new."

Torsten's stomach churned at his touch but he was too exhausted to push him away.

"Now, Sir… Jolly, I believe?" Redstar said. "What news do you bring from the South?"

Wardric slowly lowered his blade, but didn't drop his guard. Freydis on the other hand remained still and silent, her pale, gray eyes seeming to glow from the black paint smeared across the top half of her face.

"I bring news for the Wearer, and him alone," Wardric said.

"It's fine," Torsten grumbled, rubbing his temples. Now that the dominating magic had worn off, his head was starting to ache. "What is it?"

Wardric's gaze darted nervously between Freydis and Redstar until eventually, he took a step forward. Disgust contorted his features but he continued anyway.

"Muskigo's army is on the move," he said. "They've left their ships to drift into the swamp's fog and march north under the light of nigh'jels, straight toward Fort Marimount."

"And then Yarrington," Torsten finished.

Muskigo had made the first move, and if he took the ancient dwarven fortress, he'd have a stronghold within direct reach of Yarrington. The villages he'd already raided would be nothing compared to the slaughter he could unleash around the capital.

Torsten wasn't sure what to say next. He'd fought in many wars, but never at the helm. His mind was racing when Redstar clapped loudly.

"Looks like we won't have to wait to test the King's brilliant plan," he said. He turned to Torsten. "I so look forward to getting to know you better."

The crimson half of his face creased like parchment as his smile formed, deeper and more gleefully than ever before. And it was then that Torsten knew he'd missed his best chance. Because now, he truly did need the traitorous leech.

"Come Freydis. We have much to catch up on since I left for the Woods." Redstar went to Freydis' side, and she sneered at

Wardric before they continued on down the hall together. Two warlocks, free in the Glass Castle, yet somehow that wasn't Torsten's biggest problem.

In only days, Muskigo had apparently learned of his Caleef's detainment and was on the march. There was no time for conscriptions to be filled out or properly trained, unlike the throng of hunters and heathens at the castle gates who were already prepared for battle. Now there was no way out of it. Torsten would have to march beside the man whose curse had once killed Pi only for him to breathe again; the man whose actions led to Uriah Davies' death, Oleander's breakdown, and Torsten to experience fear at the hands of Bliss like he'd never imagined before.

X

THE THIEF

I t was dark by the time they'd left the Guild Hall. The moons, Celeste and Loutis, hung high above the city. Celeste shone orange and bright through a thick fog, but Loutis could barely be seen peeking through. Whitney still couldn't believe how chilly it was so far south. He saw Sora shiver out of the corner of his eye and absent-mindedly shed his cloak to wrap around her.

She smiled, then asked, "You know where we're going?"

"Yeah, I've never been to the Panping District, but it's not far from the bay."

"The Panping District?"

"I'm sure there's another name for it, but that's what I've always called it. C'mon this way."

They passed shops and houses all locked up for the evening. Some still had wares up for display and Whitney had to keep his hands in his pockets to control himself. Furs from Hornsheim, globes from Yaolin City, and a suit of armor forged from dwarven bronze that might have made even Torsten jealous. Nigh'jel lanterns from Latiapur hung from posts along the way, the tentacles of the amorphous creatures within pulsing a soft green light. The Shesaitju may have been locked up, but apparently, the people of Winde Port were happy to keep using those.

Whitney followed the lights to a rickety bridge crossing over a canal. Beyond, the light grew scant with only a candle here or there glowing in windows rotting off their hinges. Women dressed in clothing far too slight for the weather beckoned Whitney and Sora toward dark alleys. A portly Northern merchant chatted with one down on a gondola docked in the freezing water.

"His place should be just around the corner," Whitney said.

"Good, I don't like this side of town."

Wharf Street and Delanie Road crossed at a lightless church. It seemed all but abandoned. Snow covered the carved, wooden gates. Nobody even bothering to have swept it away. The stone was chipped, and the stained glass along the façade and up the spire was so dusty, the design was indecipherable. It was always unusual to see a Church of Iam be so forgotten in the Glass Kingdom. But Whitney had seen it before, and he knew that although they'd pledged themselves to Liam and the Vigilant Eye, the Panpingese people it was constructed for simply never showed up.

"Come on," Sora said. "I'm cold."

"Light a fire." Whitney began walking again but stopped when he saw Sora standing at the end of the street, staring.

"What is this?" she asked.

Ramshackle, wooden row houses were crammed along a narrow street that, beyond the church, cheapened to dirt. Ropes covered in drying clothes were hung from one window to the next, some hanging lower than Whitney's head, barely able to dry in the cold. A few Panpingese men and women lay huddled in a structure that didn't look like it'd had a roof for a century.

The air reeked of smoke from the chimneys so tightly

clumped together they created a thick cloud. Beneath the scent of burning wood was something else less pleasing.

"It smells like shog and piss," Whitney said.

"Looks like it too." She scanned from one side of the street to the other, incredulous. "This is the Panping District?"

Whitney knew what to expect. There were certain... amenities... that could only be found in a place like this, and he'd spent plenty of drunken nights in Winde Port. He didn't have the heart to tell her that the real name of the place was the Panping Ghetto.

"According to the city map," he said.

"I don't understand," Sora said. "Tayvada was dressed nicely. He is a trader in the guild. Surely he has enough money..." Her voice trailed off before she said, "He *has* to live here, doesn't he? They make all of my people live in this... this filth."

"I'm sure he's just a man of the people." Whitney took a few steps and Sora followed. A man bundled beneath a stack of furs groaned and rolled over onto the path. As they went around him, another woman in a candlelit window stared at Whitney, her almond-shaped eyes unflinching.

"Supposedly, he lives just over there." Whitney pointed to a larger row house at the end of the street. It was in much better shape than the buildings flanking it, with patterned wood panels at the second story, but it was still far from luxurious.

"Sora?" Whitney asked.

He looked back and noticed that she'd fallen behind. She kneeled in front of a pair of skinny children. The older of them coughed while the other leaned against him, wrapped in a ratty blanket. Whitney couldn't tell if they were faking. Begging was a full-time occupation in some parts of the world, and nobody earned better than children.

"Sora," Whitney said. "Leave them be."

She ignored him, and instead, opened one of the full coin purses they'd earned for selling Grint's stuff. She placed a gold autla in each of their hands and smiled, watching as their eyes went wide. They'd probably seen bronzers or even silver before, but never gold.

They said something to Sora in Panpingese, the words rattling off their tongues so choppy and fast that Whitney didn't pick up any of it. He knew a bit of the language from his travels, but Sora, on the other hand, knew none.

Whitney took her arm and gently guided her away. "C'mon, Sora. Tayvada's house is right up here."

She shook him off. "Are you heartless? No one should have to live like this."

"We can't help them all."

"Oh?" She lifted the purse, removed a coin, and flung it up through an open window. "Are the people of Yarrington more deserving of our riches?" She took another and flicked it onto the ground.

"No, but we didn't need money then."

"We don't *need* all of this." She went to dump out more coins, but Whitney grabbed her arm. He could see the rage in her amber eyes, that same rage she used to release an explosion of light and energy that defeated Redstar. He was just glad she wasn't bleeding.

"We don't know that. It won't be cheap if we need to purchase passage at a time like this. And if we need to buy a ship ourselves, it'll be even more."

"We can go by land," she said softly.

"War's coming. There's a merry band of mercenaries on the road back that likely want us dead, plus an incredibly wealthy ex-constable who definitely wants us dead. We need to leave here as fast as possible, and nobody can touch us on a boat. We'll go see your homeland and maybe after, you can come back here and we'll load up as many children as you want, bring them to Panping so they can starve there instead."

Sora was stunned by his words. He wasn't sure if it was because of the harshness, or because she'd become accustomed to him joking, but he was an expert on the ugly truth of the world. It was never an easy thing to realize.

"You give one coin to each of them, and they'll eat for a week," he said. "Then we'll be long gone, and it'll be back to normal for them. Some people are just plain unlucky, Sora. But we're living, breathing proof that it doesn't have to be that way. It's all up to them to fight for more."

"Oh, yes," she said. "Growing up with a loving family on a farm was so difficult for you."

"There's more opportunity in a city, that's for sure. Now, let's just do what we came here to do."

He risked putting his hand on her back. She didn't fight it as he guided her toward Tayvada's house.

"Now, when we get in, let me do the haggling," Whitney said. "I know these types. They're vultures in gentlemen's clothing, traders. The moment you think you're their friend is the moment they bend you ov…" The words trailed off as Whitney remembered what had happened on the road with that lecherous dwarf. He winced ahead of time, expecting to feel Sora's scorn, but she didn't hear him.

"Seriously?" Sora asked after taking one disgusted look at Tayvada's house. "This is the city you talk so highly of. The place so accepting of all peoples and cultures?"

"A lot of people got displaced by war," Whitney said. "They needed homes quick, and they lost so…"

"I get why we need to leave, but you're really defending this?"

"No, I'm just saying that not everything is so black and white. Look at me." He grinned. "I don't even have a home."

"Would you stop comparing yourself to these people?"

"I compare myself to everyone. You know that." He gave her

a friendly nudge, but she wasn't having it. Her whole face had been stuck scowling since the moment they crossed the canal.

"I don't want to talk about this anymore," she said. "Let's just speak with Tayvada and get out of here."

"Fine by me," Whitney replied, relieved.

He approached the man's door and slammed on the knocker while shouting his name. A thin line of flickering light came from beneath the door, but nobody came. He tried again. Still nothing. A stray cat hissed and leaped out from the browning bushes, giving them both a scare. The thing set Tayvada's front gate squeaking on its rusty hinges. Whitney couldn't help but notice his was the only home on the whole street with a perimeter fence and gate.

"He's probably asleep," Sora said.

"Let's go find out," Whitney decided.

"We're just going to go in uninvited?"

"Uh… thief, remember?"

"You're supposed to be acting like a noble, if that's possible for you."

Whitney tried the door and found that it was unlocked. He shot a smile at Sora and pushed it open. "I am. We found the door ajar, and like any good citizens, wanted to check if everything was all right. The richest man in a place like this?"

"Somehow, you're going to make an enemy out of the only man who can help."

"C'mon." Whitney peered through the opening. A single candle burned on the mantle, nearly down to the wick. He waved for Sora to follow.

"Tayvada!" Whitney called. "You home?"

There was a thud upstairs, then Aquira came screeching down a flight of a dozen or so stairs. Whitney was up on the dining table, daggers drawn before he knew what happened.

Sora jumped in front of the door before the wyvern could escape.

"What's wrong, girl?" she asked, kneeling down. Aquira hid behind her leg and hissed at the staircase. Whitney thought he saw a speckling of embers spew from her mouth like spit, a failed remnant of the majestic, extinct dragons it devolved from.

"The sound came from upstairs," Whitney said, pointing with a wavy blade.

"Well, are you going to get down from there and check it out?" Sora asked.

"I'm pretty sure he's not home."

Sora released an exasperated sigh, then removed her fancy glove, pulled out her knife, and drew a line of blood across her palm. She crept toward the stairs and started climbing. Aquira, however, didn't go further than the first step.

"Smart girl," Whitney said to the wyvern before reluctantly following Sora.

As they climbed, the dim light from the candle burning downstairs became even dimmer and was replaced by the orange glow of Celeste's light gushing in through open windows.

They split up at the top, Whitney going to the left, toward where the sound might have originated. Sora went right.

Whitney found nothing but rooms, empty of life but packed with valuables. He could almost see gold autlas dancing before his eyes, but his visions were abruptly ended by the sound of Sora's scream. He turned and took off down the hall. If anyone was in the house, they were now fully aware of his and Sora's presence.

Clearing the threshold of what was clearly Tayvada's bedroom, Whitney saw what had frightened Sora. Hanging from the ceiling like a butterfly's cocoon, was what remained of a Panpingese man. Blood stained the body all the way down from a slash on his neck, still dripping from his jet-black hair, pooling across the floor, and seeping through the planks in the wood.

"Shog in a barrel," Whitney whispered.

"Is that…" Sora could barely get the words out.

"Yeah, it's him."

Whitney sheathed his daggers and moved in for a closer look, covering his mouth and nose with the collar of his shirt to ward against any potential smell. People about to die tended to make a mess of themselves. Those who did die always did.

Tayvada's skin was whiter than snow, the veins on his neck like blue spider webs. He hung upside down from a rope looped around a crossbeam. His body had been drained of blood like butcher's meat.

"Watch the door. Whoever did this might still be around." Whitney closed his eyes before shoving a hand into Tayvada's doublet.

"What are you doing?" Sora asked, terse.

"We came here to find passage. His papers can get us that."

"Do you ever steal from anyone who's still alive? You're going to get us cursed!"

Whitney rooted around and found a small envelope in the man's front pocket. It was exactly what they needed—a temporary trader's export license issued by Prefect Calhoun of Winde Port.

"Mumbo jumbo," he said. "Trust me, if I'm not cursed yet, I never will be."

"How did you know that was in there?"

"At Tum Tum's, he said it was always on him, remember? Lesson four hundred twelve—always pay attention. Now let's get out of here."

"You're just going to leave him like that? This is barbaric."

"Welcome to Winde Port, home of deals gone sour," Whitney whispered.

"Whitney," Sora said, stern, "we can't leave him."

"Sometimes it's best to stay out of bad business. Besides, nobody knows we're here. Nobody saw us."

"Oh, but I did," spoke a voice from within the darkness of the room.

Whitney spun toward the sound and watched as a man emerged from the shadows. He wore boiled leathers with an absurd number of buckles and clasps over his torso, each of them holding sharp looking knives. Long, white hair fell far below his shoulders, but the man didn't look anywhere near old enough to be so gray.

"It is funny how the fish can sense the hook but cannot deny the bait," he said as he strolled forward. His thick, bold accent informed Whitney that the color of his hair wasn't due to age but was indicative of the people from the northeastern land of Brek-liodad. "Its allure surpasses the wisdom of even the brightest of creatures."

"Look fellow, I don't know who you are or what you're talking about, but you'd better turn around," Whitney said. He drew his daggers and took a step back to get his footing before realizing his back was against the rickety wall. Sora was beside him, and the mysterious intruder stood between them and the room's only window and door.

"How can you not see how outmatched you are, pathetic little man?" The white-haired devil stopped beside Tayvada's hanging body, ran a single finger through the man's bloody neck and marveled at the shiny red liquid, smearing it between his fore-finger and thumb.

"You murdered him!" Sora shouted.

The mysterious man shrugged. "Bait is bait."

"Bait for wha—" Whitney didn't have time to finish before he heard the familiar wincing sound of Sora cutting her already bleeding hand even deeper, fueled by rage. Ever since they arrived in Winde Port, he could see her affinity with her race growing, and seeing one hanging out to dry had put a look in her eye unlike any he'd seen there before.

She thrust her hand forward, fire erupting from the tips of her fingers. It struck the white-haired man in the chest and exploded with a blinding flash. It temporarily blinded Whitney, but when he could see again, the man was enveloped by smoke and flurrying embers. The expulsion of such energy left Sora doubled over, panting.

Whitney saw motion in the cloud and expected to see a body topple over. Instead, when the smoke cleared, the man rose from a crouch and rolled his shoulders like it was nothing. The only visible damage was a small scorch in his armor. The blades of his many daggers glowed red hot, and his dark, thin lips curled into a nightmarish grin.

"I knew I was right about you," he said to Sora, who was as shocked as Whitney. "So much untapped potential. So much raw... power."

"Sora, run!" Whitney charged at the man, swinging one of his daggers. The man moved so swiftly it was like swiping at air. Whitney staggered, then came whipping around with his second dagger. For a moment it looked like he'd catch the man's stomach. But again, it was almost as if the man disappeared into nothingness. Whitney tripped over a loose floorboard and scrambled for the door.

Sora and Whitney reached the door at the same time, but two knives stabbed into it right in front of their faces, the force of the throw causing it to slam shut. They looked back and saw the white-haired man holding more knives, fanned out like cards in a game of gems.

"Now, now, don't run," he said. "Things are just starting to get fun."

"Stay away from us!" Sora screamed. She raised her hands

and released fire again, only she was so drained from last time, it came out as little more than a sputter. The man spun out of the way, flames catching the end of his cloak, then dropping to the floor. The dry wooden planks beneath him caught fast, but the man removed his cloak and snapped it, extinguished the fire in one smooth motion. He shook it out and calmly placed it back over his shoulders.

"Our friend here is no good to anyone cooked," he said, slapping Tayvada's corpse on the arm. "

"Whitney..." Sora whispered as if he had any answers.

He was lucky he could even hold his weapons his hands were so sweaty and shaky. His heart raced so fast he could no longer feel it beating, just a steady rock in his throat. "If you wanted us dead we would be, so j...just tell us what you want," he managed to say.

"You small, insignificant fool. You could not comprehend what I want in one hundred lifetimes."

"Try me," Whitney replied, finding his last bit of courage. He found himself thinking the oddest thought, wishing Torsten were there. But the man chuckled and stole Whitney's focus back to the moment.

The Breklian darted at them. It all happened so fast, Whitney wasn't sure whether he actually tried to defend himself or simply closed his eyes. When they opened again, the man was gone. A breeze wafted in through the now-open window, curtains flapping in the wind. All that was left in the room was the lingering sound of the man's haunting laugh.

"Who the yig was that?" Whitney asked after a moment. He turned to Sora, only to find that she too was gone.

Three hard raps on the front door startled him.

"Whitney Blisslayer, we know you're in there!" someone called up from the street. "Surrender in the name of the King!"

"No, no, no," he said. He peeked out of the window and saw

at least a dozen Glass soldiers spread out in front of the home. A crowd of ghetto locals gathered to watch as if they'd never seen soldiers in their district before.

The townhouse was so narrow, there was no way out through any upstairs window except the one they'd clearly see him leaving. Whitney sheathed his weapons and swept out into the hall and downstairs, searching for a side door, back door, anything— even a basement. Nothing. The Panping Ghetto was contained, its row homes facing straight onto the streets, backs of the homes butting up to the back of others on the adjacent street. His back was literally against the wall.

He patted his clothes and found Tayvada's trading papers before also realizing he still had his half of the Glass Crown hidden beneath his cloak. Swearing, he removed both, wrapped the papers around the circlet, and ran to the hearth. The soldiers knocked again as he shoved his hand up the flue. He found a bit of loose stone and hung the Crown from the ledge along with the papers.

The front door flew open.

Whitney leaped upright and raised his hands in surrender as the soldiers poured in, spears and swords drawn and aimed at his throat. Out of the corner of his eye, he saw Aquira zipping out the front door behind them.

Lucky little... he cursed inward. Then he grinned. "Hey fellows," he said. "I think I saw who you're looking for upstairs."

XI

THE KNIGHT

"I am, hear me," Torsten whispered. He clutched his holy pendant—the same one given to him by King Liam, nearly lost only weeks ago—against his chest while looking upward. The great Vigilant Eye towered in the apse of the Yarrington Cathedral. The holy symbol was cast in gold with a pupil of glass that, when looked at from the east, framed Mount Lister in all her glory.

Light poured in through stained-glass windows above and behind it. They depicted the story of the God Feud and Autla Nothhelm, the First King of Glass, the one for whom their currency was named. In the depiction, he was being anointed on the flattened summit of Mount Lister by Iam himself thousands of years ago after the Feud ended, given the task to spread His light to all creatures.

Torsten imagined that King Liam, young and healthy, once kneeled in this very spot gazing upon the legends of old before deciding to bring an end to the incestuous squabbling that had, for so long, confined the Glass Kingdom to its own little corner of Pantego. Now, their sphere of influence extended from Latiapur in the South to far east Panping, well beyond Yaolin City, and up to Winter's Thumb at the foot of Drav Cra. Pi had only been king for a month, yet already he was following in his father's footsteps by bringing Redstar's people into the fold.

It just felt so… different this time.

"A trickster and heathen has been invited within these very walls," Torsten said to Iam. "Only ruin follows in his wake. Never has Your light led me astray, but please, help me understand why he should be counted amongst Your holy kingdom. Show me, oh, Vigilant Eye, what am I missing?"

"Something troubling you, Wearer?"

Torsten turned to see Wren the Holy shuffling toward him. His cane clacked across the marble floor, echoing down the cathedral's soaring nave as he navigated the room. He looked more weary than usual, even considering his age. Dark rings wrapped his eye-sockets, scorched from taking the vow of sightlessness. Heavy white robes and the clunky necklace of interlocking Eyes of Iam around his neck seemed to weigh him down.

Pi's resurrection had left the cathedral inundated with worshippers, come to see the place where he had been reborn and where, long ago, Iam ended the God Feud and took man under His sheltering wing. They came to hear the words of Wren, the mouthpiece of Iam in Pantego. The High Priest's voice usually carried with vim and vigor, but today, it was raspy from his many sermons.

Torsten had come at sunrise to try and give the old man time to rest before the doors opened to the public, but Wren was ever vigilant.

"It's nothing, Your Holiness," he said. Torsten went to stand, but Wren lay a hand on his shoulder. His aim was true despite having no use of his eyes.

"Please. I have been around long enough to know when a man is feeling exceedingly… mortal." His thin lips creased into a smile. In a kingdom where war had left so many children orphans, perhaps his greatest gift of all was a fatherly smile. Of course, Torsten's father was a lecherous cur who'd never served, but there was still something about Wren that made him feel at home.

Torsten sighed and lifted himself onto the front pew before the altar. Wren sat beside him, his old knees popping.

"We leave to quell the Shesaitju rebellion today," Torsten said.

"So I have heard."

"Then you also know who the young king has invited to march at our side?"

Wren nodded.

"Then please, Your Holiness, tell me how I can march beside a heathen like that?"

"My son, when Liam sought to bring all of Pantego under a single banner, he knew he could not force the people beyond this realm to see the light of Iam. He could only show them the way; they had to do the rest. Now the world is a brighter place for his many efforts."

"I don't question anything Liam did."

"But you fought alongside him for a long, long time. Beside allies old and new, men and dwarves from different corners of our world. Not all of whom believed Iam to be the source of light in their soul. Yet you fought with them nonetheless."

"Redstar is different. I know it may be a sin to think, but I don't believe his soul is redeemable."

"Every soul is redeemable."

"What about all the fallen gods who have been banished from this realm. What about Nesilia and Bliss?" Wren's brow furrowed at the name of the latter. "The One Who Remained," Torsten corrected. That was the name people were familiar with when speaking of her. Torsten realized then that Redstar was the one who claimed Bliss and the One Who remained were one and the same, that Bliss had defeated Nesilia, the Buried Goddess before the feud ended. And that Iam had then punished her by transforming her into a beast and condemning her to that foul place, a vindictive act against the very nature of the God whom Torsten loved.

Redstar also claimed that Nesilia and Iam had been lovers, not mortal enemies and that everything he knew about the God Feud was a lie.

More of his lies and games.

Bliss was likely a demonic creature of Elsewhere, similar to any other. All Redstar's talk of serving the Buried Goddess by slaying her; in the end, he was clearly just trying to keep Torsten away from Yarrington while Oleander suffered from the wicked curse placed upon Pi. All a part of Redstar's plot to get Torsten killed so that, in her grief, Oleander would lead the Glass Kingdom, which left him behind and forgot him, into ruin.

As Torsten's darkening thoughts twisted his features, Wren's smile deepened.

"All *mortal* souls are redeemable," he said. "We are all the children of Iam, and His word is mercy. His word is peace. I cannot say why He has brought Redstar to us, just how I cannot say why He saw fit to afflict Liam with so wretched an ailment though his hair had only just begun to gray. But to say it wasn't his time is folly."

"Can His enemies not upset His designs? Redstar poisoned King Pi's mind and led him to suicide."

"Yet, he lives again by the Hand of Iam." Wren groaned as he used his cane to rise from the pew. "They can certainly try, Sir Unger, but so long as we faithful remain, they cannot shake us."

Torsten turned from the High Priest of Iam to regard the massive eye set before him. He ran his fingers around his own eye sockets in prayer, then stood.

"Thank you, Your Holiness, for helping show me the way."

Wren shook his head. "I am only an oracle of Iam. The path of light is always within you." He tapped Torsten's chest with his cane.

"I hope I don't lose it. You'll look after King Pi while we're gone? I worry about him, up in that castle. He barely left his quarters as a boy. Even those few on the Council who remain from serving his father are strangers to him."

"Always. In these times of peril, it will help the young king to turn to his holy studies."

"Thank you, Great Father." Torsten bowed and traced his eyes again.

"Thank Him," Wren said, gesturing to the gargantuan Eye of Iam. He needed no sight to find it. "I am but a vessel."

Torsten turned to leave the cathedral, suddenly feeling lighter. It still didn't feel right, what he had to do, but Wren and the lofty cathedral had a way of calming him, of making him realize he was but a small part of Iam's plan.

He pushed open the massive front doors, two hunks of iron with patterned rifts cut out and filled with frosted glass. Crisp, cold air greeted him, even though the sun shone brightly that morning, making him long for summer.

A small cohort of King's Shieldsmen awaited him, though he had come to the cathedral alone. He was about to ask why they weren't at their posts or with the rest of the army outside the city walls when Oleander hopped down from her beloved white horse and ran to him, wearing tall, spiked heels despite the cobblestone streets of the Royal Avenue.

"Torsten." She threw her arms around him before he could say a word.

He got caught halfway between embracing her in return and pushing her away. He wasn't sure when their relationship had become so informal, and he could see the prying eyes of his men over her shoulder, struggling to stay at attention as they likely thought the same thing.

"Is everything all right, Your Grace?" Torsten asked. He peeled her off him, and Torsten started walking, so they didn't linger. The Queen Mother out on the streets was a rare thing indeed. He saw no need to inform the whole city of her presence. She hadn't made many friends, and he wasn't sure who might seek retribution.

"Is everything all right?" Her expression soured. "I had to beg my newly brazen son to let me out of my room. It's as if he has forgotten who was really in charge after Liam forgot how to speak."

"He spent that time in a cloud of horrid visions, Your Grace."

"Yes, yes. Put there by that bastard I call 'Brother.'"

"I don't like the way you're treated any more than you, but Pi is King now. Would you prefer him unconscious and clinging to life again?"

"Of course not!" Her raised voice brought the attention of a few passersby.

Any other month, the end of the Royal Avenue, the grand plaza in Old Yarrington within which the Cathedral of Yarrington stood, would be full of flowering trees, but now it was barren. Instead, pilgrims from afar filled it with tents, waiting for their chance to hear a sermon from Wren the Holy.

A young man, the father of several, pointed back at the Cathedral, his wife and children smiling. Torsten stopped and followed his finger to the snow-covered summit of Mount Lister, visible through Iam's Eye, standing proudly at the peak of the roof. The pupil was made from glass similar to the one at the altar, but this one was segmented, like a cut diamond. As the sun rose over the mountain, the prism cast a rainbow across the plaza. The pilgrims flocked to the vibrant strips of light, praising Iam, kissing the very street upon which His light touched.

"It's been a difficult year, hasn't it?" Torsten said.

Yet there was Iam's light, still shining bright—an arm of warmth against the bitter onslaught of cold.

"Torsten," Oleander said, clearly irritated. She shook his arm.

"Yes, Your Grace?" Torsten replied.

"Did you hear a word I said?"

"I'm so sorry, Your Grace. I must have missed it. My mind is on the forthcoming battle."

Oleander groaned. "Is there a man in this world that isn't just like my husband?"

"There is no man like him."

"Hey, careful with her or I'll have your hands!" she snapped at the stablehand who had taken the reins of her horse to walk her behind them. She slapped the young man's hands, then ran her fingers through the horse's mane. Torsten couldn't remember the last time she let her favorite horse out of the royal stables where she kept her locked up and safe like a piece of jewelry.

"I… I'm so sorry, Your Grace," the young man stuttered.

"A light touch, and grace. If I hear a whinny from you pulling her…"

"You won't. My apologies."

Oleander rolled her eyes and returned to Torsten's side. "The age of great men is clearly over."

Torsten forced a chuckle but didn't respond. He'd been on the receiving end of her seemingly senseless scorn enough times to know how it felt. He snuck the stable hand a nod of approval before they continued down the Royal Avenue, flanked by Shieldsmen. Mansions belonging to Yarrington's noblest families stood, nearly all of them for generations, the stone of their foundations hewn from Mount Lister itself. The newest belonged to the reinstated Master of Coin, Yuri Darkings. It was at the end of the row, still partially under construction but even more magnificent than the others.

Yuri came from a family of no-names who rose up the ranks

of the Winde Traders Guild until he was running the accounts. That was the greatness of Liam, he looked beyond established houses to raise men like Yuri and Torsten beyond their station. Now, Yuri had a crew of human laborers constructing the newest wing of his Old Yarrington home, including a giant for a foreman who was busy hefting a wood column as thick as the trunks in the Webbed Woods.

A giant, yet the Crown could barely entice an experienced group of dwarves to repair the Royal Crypt. He blamed Oleander's wrath for their lack of respect, but the truth was, it would've happened anyway. The people didn't know all the real reasons behind why she had so many loyal servants hanged and most would fear their rulers regardless. Kings and Queens across Pantego had done far worse and been feared far more.

Pi had been revived by a miracle of Iam and was greatly revered in the weeks leading up to a coronation barely anyone of worth showed up for. Nothing really changed. In the end, the people were thankful to Iam, not a child-king they barely knew. Oleander could have been the most beloved queen in history, and still, nothing would have changed. Because neither of them was Liam.

"Forgive me if it is not my place to ask, but do you ever miss him?" Torsten said.

"Who?" Oleander replied.

"Liam. I know he didn't always make your life easy, but…"

"Of course, I do. Is there a reason you are so interested in my relationship with my late husband?"

"It's only that… I was there… at his funeral. The kingdom wept, yet you didn't even shed a tear."

"Do you know how long I spent feeding him? Changing him once he fell ill—probably thanks to one of his dirty, foreign whores? How many times I watched Tessa clean him after he…" She drew a deep, solemn breath, and Torsten wasn't sure if it was because she was finally stricken by what she'd done to her former handmaiden, or over the memory of Liam. He hoped both.

"I was waiting for him to die and was relieved when he did," she went on. "I bid farewell to that man long before his kingdom did."

Torsten's head hung a little lower.

"I never cared that he took me from my home and my people when I was but a girl because I had never seen a man so mighty," she said. "It was as if Iam Himself had come to the Drav Cra in the form of a man."

"I remember thinking the same thing when I saw him down on the docks as a boy," Torsten replied. "With his white armor shimmering, wondering how we could both possibly be counted among men. He was like a god."

"I hated seeing him so weak. I would miss the way he scolded me for not presenting myself appropriately for an audience or when I failed to produce a worthy heir for so long. By the end, I couldn't bear to look at him. All I cared about was Pi and him getting healthy again, helping him become even a fraction of the man Liam was."

"He seems to be finding his footing."

Oleander frowned. "Yes...."

"My Queen, I know you're concerned for him; I am too. First, leaving no option but war without even consulting his Council, then allying with Redstar and warlocks. Whatever happened after his body died, it's as if he feels he is all alone."

"It's the Drav Cra in him," Oleander said. "In the far North, a boy his age is sent out into the wilderness to survive on his own. To battle the wolves and bitter cold."

"He's half Liam too. I didn't know our great King at that age —I wasn't even born—though I'm sure it took him some time to find his way, too. Pi can't do it alone. You need to try to get through to him while I'm gone."

"His father would have broken his neck if he'd talked to him the way he does me."

Her horse neighed, and she shot a look back at the stablehand so fierce it could've frozen the air between them.

"May I speak frankly, My Queen?"

Oleander eyed him from head to toe, then nodded.

"Don't push him away," Torsten said. "Endure his insults. Show him how much you love him. I've seen it firsthand the lengths you're willing to go for the slightest chance at helping him."

They were in front of the castle fortifications now. Torsten made sure not to let his gaze stray toward the ramparts, where less than a Dawning ago, the Queen had strung so many up to die.

Hers, on the other hand, flitted there, and just for the briefest moment, Torsten thought he saw a wave of regret pass like a shadow across her face. A sight he thought impossible.

"Get him to open up, My Queen," Torsten said, "so that we may begin to understand what he went through and what's now going on inside him. If there is one strength within you to which even Liam paled in comparison, it is your undying love for your son. Show him that."

Oleander's features grew hard as she folded her arms. "Do you have no fear, Wearer? Speaking so openly to the Queen Mother?"

"I have many fears, but there is not one of them I wouldn't face for this kingdom."

Oleander stalked forward, her smoldering blue eyes enough to make a man feel small. Not to mention that with her heels on she was taller even than Torsten.

"Even me?" she asked. She lay both her hands on his shoulders, her nails clacking against his armor.

"Anything," he said, voice shaky. His mind took him back to

the night in his chambers when she threw herself at him. To even think of Oleander in that manner made him feel ill, dirty.

"Then do something for me, my honest Wearer." She leaned in, her warm breath tickling his ear. "Slaughter those rebels in the name of your king and remind Pantego who his father was. And when you're finished with him, see to it that Redstar never returns here. I care not how."

Torsten backed away, incredulous. "Your Grace?"

"You know what must be done, so do it. And when you return victorious and free of this blight, I'll see to it that ours is the only advice my precious boy will care to hear." She grabbed him by the back and pulled him close. Then, she kissed him on the cheek. "Good luck, my knight."

She whipped around, her long, cerulean dress kicking up the powdered snow. "Come boy!" She clapped her hands, and the stablehand allowed her horse to trot to her side. She stroked the magnificent creature's mane as she sauntered back behind the walls of the Glass Castle. Her guard went with her, not daring look at him or mutter under their breath about how close the Queen Mother was with the Wearer of White.

It confused Torsten as well. When last he left Yarrington, he had been exiled by Oleander in her unchecked fury. When he returned, she was shattered mind and spirit until Pi came back to her. Now, he left in her good graces, somehow knowing that of anyone in the castle with Pi's ear, she was perhaps the one he could trust the most, the one with the most honest of intentions—protecting him.

Yet there was no denying what she'd just asked of him. Stabbing Redstar in the back was less than the man deserved but to do so was to betray the will of his king.

Torsten looked at the statue of Liam in the castle's entry bailey and remembered how simple things were with him alive. His eyes moved down the line of statues: Remy the Revealer,

Tarvin the Fair-Handed, and even King Autla the First. He wondered if any one of them acted as rashly as King Pi had.

Then the castle gates closed.

"Your horse, Sir Unger?" the stablehand offered, returning from the bailey.

Torsten nodded and waited for the young man to return with his horse, then he rode down through the heart of Yarrington. Wardric met him in the markets, which were simultaneously more crowded and quiet than usual.

"Did you find what you were looking for in the cathedral?" Wardric asked.

"Always… and never," Torsten replied.

"Sounds about right." Wardric laughed, then grew stern. "I went to the kid's home to see if he'd march with us, just like you asked. Sister didn't even let me through the door."

"She's tough, that woman."

"Aren't they all? At least Rand's got a better chance of surviving here."

Torsten surveyed the market. The people were roused, but none haggled, hawked wares, or exchanged autlas. Instead, they watched as soldiers flocked through open city gates. Mothers embraced their conscripted sons, father's their wives and young children. They begged Iam for protection and for victory.

Torsten, like Wardric, knew how many of them would never return. How many would die in the name of Iam and His chosen kingdom?

"I never thought I'd live to see another war," Wardric said.

"Let's hope this one ends quickly so we can rid our castle of unwanted guests," Torsten said.

"I wonder, do you mean the Caleef or them?" He nodded toward the gate. Redstar leaned against the stone in the opening, biting a chunk off a loaf of bread. Beyond him, a group of Drav Cra warriors knelt around the warlock Freydis, her breasts exposed. Her body was covered in white paint, chipped and cracked from the cold. Her head was black except for two streaks of blood under her eyes which dripped down her cheeks and neck. A circle of blood, bright against the snow, was painted over the frozen farmland and in its center stood a goat. Freydis held a knife to its throat; a sacrifice to their Buried Goddess in the name of victory.

Redstar glanced back, noticed Torsten and Wardric, and smiled while he waved with his bread. Not a care in the world.

XII

THE MYSTIC

Sora gasped awake, her heart racing as she scanned her dark surroundings. The air stank of mildew. Light from the moons filtered in through a circular panel of stained glass, a film of dust covering most of the imagery. She could just barely make out the Iam's Eye sprawling across it in gold.

A church?

She'd only been in Troborough's chapel, but she recognized the stone walls and glass windows when she saw them. Cobwebs glistened in the faint light, draping from every corner. The memory of the giant spiders in the Webbed Woods gave her a shudder.

She tried to get a better look around but felt something tight against her wrists. Her arms were stretched taut above her head and spread apart, her feet dangling. She hung from two chains running down from a structure beneath the hipped roof clearly meant to hold a bell. When she stretched her neck to look behind her, she noticed it, a cracked bell on the floor, infested by spiders.

She whimpered softly.

She was in a church steeple, abandoned by the look of it. She felt so exposed under the blurred Eye of Iam, still wearing her glittering evening gown, arms and legs bare. She still had the coin purses they'd earned from selling that trader's silks, which meant whoever did this to her had no interest in money.

"Help!" she screamed. "Help!"

"Nobody will ever hear you way up here." It was the voice of the white-haired man from Tayvada's house. The harsh accent could only be Breklian, far in the northern portion of the continent, beyond even the Dragon's Tail and Brotlebir. Traders from the area had passed through Troborough very rarely, but their kind were hard to forget.

Sora's head whipped toward him, her skin crawling with fear. He wasn't there.

"I've waited so very long for you to wake," he said.

She felt a hand stroke her back, a cold finger tracing the line of her spine. She shuddered but didn't give him the benefit of hearing her scream. But she wanted to. More than ever before, she wanted to.

His voice was bad enough, very harsh consonants hanging in the air like the hiss of a serpent. But his touch... it was like what she felt every time she called upon the powers of Elsewhere, like there was some great evil trying to take her over.

"Get away from me," she spat.

He chuckled. "You will learn to appreciate me." His tongue ran up the side of her jaw. She wanted to crawl out of her skin.

"You're a monster."

"That very well may be true." The man backed away and sat across from her on a moldy barrel. He removed two knives from his bandolier, one being Sora's. Sora flinched, but he merely set them against each other as if preparing to carve roast duck.

Sora closed her eyes and focused on Elsewhere, on that haunting feeling she knew so well. The man was right about power coursing through her, just as her old master Wetzel had been, and with all her willpower she begged for it to come to the surface.

But the wound she'd earlier traced across her hand was sealed and freshly bandaged. Whoever the man was, he knew how to block her.

"What do you want from me?" she asked.

"Everything." Sparks flew out from Sora's blade as he used the other to start sharpening it. Sora wished more than anything she could summon sparks of her own and burn the floor out from under him.

"Is this about Whitney?"

"There you are, mystic. Smart and powerful. When that grotesque little man hired me to kill the thief, he severely under-estimated you."

"Darkings," she realized, all her fears coming true. She was right to be afraid of that vengeful wretch. Whitney had calmed her back at the Traders Guild, but she was right. "Is Whitney..." She couldn't even bring herself to say it.

"Not until sunrise, unfortunately for me. Darkings wants to make a public show of it, fool that he is, and until the kill is made I cannot touch my quarry. I may ignore many of my order's doctrines, but the blood pact is sacred. I may neither eat, drink, nor... play, until his life on this plane is over."

"Well, you're wrong. I'm no mystic."

"I think I'll keep this." He raised Sora's knif, spun it, then grinned as he stowed it. In the faint light filtering through the stained glass, Sora could see now how young he was despite his white hair, how handsome. Yet beneath all his striking features was menace unlike any she'd seen before. Not even Bliss, with her eight eyes and eight legs, could compare.

"You are so much more than you know," he said. "Your blood radiates energy only so few of your people are born with. I could smell it across the city, not like any blood mage or Drav Cra warlock who can't so much as make a spark without gashing themselves. Tainting themselves."

"That's exactly what I am."

"No, you are raw, unfocused power—with a master who either did not see so or was, himself, too weak to properly instruct you."

"How do you know about him?" she questioned. The idea of him digging through her mind had her wriggling, desperate to shake free. But her struggle only seemed to entertain him.

"Relax, my dear. I'm capable of many things but reading minds is not one of them. However, I have walked this plane for a long, long time. I know what it is to see wasted potential."

She shook again. "When Whitney breaks free he's going to kill you!"

"Kill me? I am beyond life and death, but your friend? He will die. There is no escaping it. Because I must have you."

"Please, no. You can take every autla on me and leave, I won't tell a soul. It's...it's enough to buy a ship."

"I already have one." In an instant he was before her, dark eyes piercing her soul. His hands grasped her waist, and he slowly leaned in toward her neck. She turned her head away, but there was nowhere to go.

"His death is the only way," he said. Then, hovering there beside her neck, he exhaled into her flesh, his breath cold as freshly fallen snow.

He backed away, closed his eyes and shivered. His eyelids flickered as if just the scent of her was enough to give him a rush. He licked his lips, and as he did, she noticed fangs as sharp as any dire wolf.

"What are you?"

He drew a deep breath to calm himself. "I am Kazimir."

"What..."

"My kind have been called many things throughout the ages. You may know us as fangs, vampires, even some call us undead.

I prefer upyr, the name Brekliodad gives us. Call me sentimental."

Sora swallowed the lump forming in her throat. Wetzel's text mentioned the upyr from time to time. Men and women trapped between Pantego and Elsewhere, unable to die, yet not truly alive, thirsting for the blood of man lest they lose their tether to the mortal realm and go insane.

Most books thought them a myth—or extinct. The terrible feeling in her gut told her he spoke truthfully.

"You look horrified," Kazimir said, a trace of disappointment passing across his face. "You have no reason to be afraid. Your blood is too precious for me to waste. For centuries upyr took the mystics as wives, using their blood so they may cross the light at will."

"You want me to marry you?" She spat at his feet. "I'd rather die!"

Rage twisted his features. The dark of his eyes grew darker still and his fangs extended. He glared up at her, and at that moment, she knew she was alive only because he needed her for more than a rush. She didn't understand exactly why, but it was clear he could devour her at any time.

His icy breath upon her ear, he whispered, "As I said, you will learn to appreciate me. Together we can do great things."

Kazimir took one last euphoric whiff of her, then backed away. His monstrous face softened once again to the preternaturally handsome Breklian he'd been just moments ago. He turned and peered through the stained glass, where the amber light of the sun filtered through and a purplish glow of dawn washed over the room.

"But for now," he said, looking back at her. "I have an execution to attend."

The thought of Whitney's neck snapping filled her thoughts even more than her captor's horrifyingly pale face. "Please," Sora said, her voice now brittle from unrelenting fear. "Please spare him."

"It doesn't work that way."

"It can. Please, Kazimir, I'm begging you. I'll... I'll try to be whatever you want."

"You will. After his life is given."

"No, please, no!"

"We will see each other soon, my lady." He grinned and bowed, then vanished through a door into the stairwell leading down from the steeple.

Sora shook again, as hard as she could.

"Help!" She screamed at the top of her voice, but by now, she'd realized she was in the abandoned church at the edge of the Panping Ghetto—where her cries for help would be lost amongst the beggars, even if anyone could hear her through stone and glass.

"No, no, no..." If she couldn't break free, they were both doomed. Whitney would be hanged, and she would be forced to marry an upyr for whatever dreadful reasons Kazimir desired.

She searched the room for anything within reach of her feet that might help her. Nothing. Then she noticed the scars on her hands.

Blood for power...

Her captor may not have meant to, but he'd given her an idea. She twisted her neck to try and reach her arm so that she could bite into it. She wasn't sure if she'd be able to clamp down hard enough to draw blood, but she had to try.

She stretched and wrenched her body, but it was no use. The chains cuffing her wrists had her arms spread too far apart to get the right angle.

Her heart sank, and her gut roiled. She bit her lower lip and fought back tears, and then had another idea. The very thought had her wanting to vomit, but she bit down harder on her lip until the taste of copper filled her mouth. Then, she looked inward, reaching out with invisible arms for the vast well of power contained in Elsewhere.

She reached into that dark place which both scared and astounded her. Warmth tickled the tips of her fingers... but nothing more. The sacrifice wasn't enough. She stuck her tongue between her teeth instead. Biting off the tip might be enough, but she couldn't bring herself to do it.

A tear ran down her cheek. She freed her tongue and gasped for air. The upyr was wrong about one thing—she was no better than the warlocks of the Drav Cra drawing on blood. No more powerful.

"Help!" she screamed again. It was all she could do.

XIII

THE THIEF

Whitney was beginning to get used to the feeling of having his wrists squeezed by rope. Ever since his triumphant return to Troborough, he'd found himself bound more often than he changed undergarments.

"I'm sure we can work out this little misunderstanding," he said to one of the Glass soldiers. "This isn't what it appears to be." They held him outside Tayvada's house while they ransacked the place. He crossed his fingers in hopes that they wouldn't shove their heads up the chimney.

"It appears like you were standing just downstairs from the drained corpse of a respected member of the Winde Traders Guild."

"I found him that way."

"Aye," said another soldier walking behind him, "and my wife's half-gray son really *is* mine!"

Whitney would've usually been able to think of some snappy remark, but the face of his and Sora's white-haired assailant flashed through his mind. Those dark, soulless eyes, that nightmarish grin.

"All right, move it."

Whitney felt a shove on his back and stumbled forward. "I swear it though, I didn't do it," he pled. Another push came, this time harder.

"Shut your thieving, murdering mouth, or I'll shut it for you."

Whitney believed the man. He'd been wanted for many things and been placed in far more precarious situations, such as battling a goddess with Torsten in the Webbed Woods but never before was he accused of murder.

The guards finished up inside, then dragged him down the dark streets of the Panping Ghetto. He wondered where they were taking him, but he dared not ask. He simply walked, trying hard not to think about what might have happened to Sora.

Whitney didn't know who that man she'd disappeared with was. He only knew where he was from. And if he had to guess at his occupation, hired blade was a good start considering he was covered in them. But what was he after? Whitney had seen all kinds of men in his life, but never one with eyes like his. They were... soulless.

Poor Sora, he thought. And then, *Poor me.*

He looked around the streets he thought he knew so well as they emerged from the Panping Ghetto. The Shesaitju rebellion had the whole city on their toes. Unlike more normal times, the blue and white of the Glass Kingdom actually seemed to mean something, which meant he'd be under stricter watch and escaping would be even more difficult.

"Shog in a barrel," Whitney said out loud. He received a hard shove for it.

As they approached the barracks, Whitney noted how it paled in comparison to Yarrington—or even Westvale. He'd seen more of their insides than he cared to admit.

"I hope you're ready for the gallows, murderer," one guard said.

"I'm all for new experiences," Whitney replied.

"The guy was just a *knife-ear*, why does anyone care?" the other guard said, low to keep Whitney from hearing. But he heard. He also heard the response, which made his intestines clench.

"Lord Darkings cares, and I heard his father is Master of Coin for the whole kingdom again. He'll probably be prefect of Winde Port as soon as old Calhoun kicks the bucket, so you'd best be caring too."

Darkings Cares?

Whitney recalled how the bastard spoke to Sora—like she was a stain on Pantego. That meant one thing. *This was a setup...*

The realization that he'd been played bounced around like daggers in Whitney's skull. Fantasies of killing Darkings were washed away only by the fantasy that Sora's fire would have devoured him back in Bridleton. That quickly had Whitney wondering why that white-haired Breklian devil took Sora and not him.

"Hey, where are we going?" Whitney asked as they led him right by the barracks. "Aren't you going to throw me in a cell for the night? I'll break out, and you'll spend the next week wondering how I did it."

"Not today, scag."

"That's okay," Whitney said. "I've seen nicer barracks in Fessix."

"Move."

"So where are we going?" Whitney was shoved hard into a barrel. He toppled over, hitting his head on the rim, then rolled off onto the stone. He didn't even have time to breathe before being hoisted back up and moved along.

"You know, I'm not resisting," Whitney groaned.

"Try it. Make my night."

"Your mother said something similar last evening."

Whitney winced, expecting a cudgel to the gut, but none came. Instead, they silently walked him toward the northern sector. He'd already worn into them so much they were growing numb.

Step one.

There was always a calm before the storm. Now he just had to figure out how to push their buttons enough for one of them to snap, try to release all that pent-up rage, and make a mistake.

They steered away from the wharf, instead, climbing up the hill toward the wealthiest district in the city, positioned at the height of its northern bluff, overlooking all of Trader's Bay. Whitney spent his younger days pilfering the area, but after a few occasions in Winde Port, he found the challenge wasn't there. There were too many distractions in the city and unlike presently, spotting a Glass Soldier or guard used to be a rarity.

They dragged him up a gravel path which turned to brick at the top. The haphazard nature of the city gave way to a neighborhood reminding him of Old Yarrington. Stone and wood mansions, heavy on ornament, only here many of them had balconies sticking out over the bluff, challenging nature to do its worst.

He was led to the biggest home of all, the door bearing the Darkings family crest. The constable's place in Bridleton belonged in the Panping Ghetto by comparison. Whitney cursed himself for not looking deeper into the man's history. He remembered wondering how Darkings came to such power in that little town and now he knew.

His family was in power everywhere.

Half a dozen of Darkings' private guards stood out front, one of which Whitney recognized.

"Oi! Scar-Face!" Whitney called, unable to help himself.

The one-eyed guard he and Sora had escaped in Bridleton

growled like a bear. His knuckles turned white around the shaft of a spear.

"Count yourself lucky the constable... former constable... wants you alive," he said.

"I always count myself lu—"

The butt of the spear whipped across Whitney's chin with bone-crunching speed. He spit out a mouthful of blood, glad no teeth came with it.

"He said nothing about your quality of life." The one-eyed guard cackled. "Can't wait to watch you squirm." He raised his free hand to his throat, stuck his tongue out and forced his eye wide, then laughed some more.

He went to take Whitney, but the Glass soldier holding him positioned himself between them. "I believe your boss owed us something for bringing him straight here."

"Aren't you men of the Glath thupposed thu be honorable?" Whitney said, mouth still filling with blood.

"Not for free."

The one-eyed guard grunted under his breath. He reached back and was handed a plump coin-purse. The Glassmen took a peek inside, then handed Whitney over, saying, "Give Darkings my regards."

"You thure you don't wanth thu join uth?"

He was flung through the entry of the house. Somehow, this mansion was more elaborate yet just as sparsely decorated as Darkings' former home in Bridleton. Probably because it was double the size. What hadn't changed was the giant portrait of Darkings hanging front and center. Only, it wasn't *this* Darkings in the painting.

"My father, Yuri," former Constable Darkings said, once again showing up as if from thin air from a side entry. "He is quite a handsome man. I'm told I got his good looks."

Good looks was a stretch, but it was true, they could have

passed for twins. If not twins, it was obvious they were father and son. Both had bellies that hung well over their belts. Darkings the younger's new mustache was an obvious homage to Yuri, his father, as well.

"Father was so kind as to lend me his winter home since mine was *burned to the ground.*" His tone bore such venom Whitney expected to be hit. "Somebody get him a towel," Darkings ordered instead. "He's bleeding all over the marble."

A moment later, a young Panpingese boy returned with a hot towel. Begging for coins on the corner of the Panping Ghetto seemed preferable to having to heed the beck and call of such a wretch. The one-eyed guard took the towel and forcefully wiped Whitney's face. Whitney spat on the floor when he was finished.

Darkings clicked his tongue and shook his head. "Always the rebel."

"You knew I wath gonna go afther Thavatha," Whitney lisped. "You killed him and thet me up, didn'th you?"

"Please stop. You sound like a fool." Darkings snapped again, and another servant arrived with two cups of wine. He offered one to Whitney.

"Don't be proud," he said. "This will clean out your mouth."

"Like you care," Whitney said. He took it with both his cuffed hands and lifted it to his lips anyway. It burned his cut gums on the way in, then quickly began to numb the pain.

Darkings pulled down on his collar to get a look at his chest.

"Whoa," Whitney protested. "I'm sure you like seeing me cuffed and all, but at least gimme a meal first."

The wine was helping, but now his mouth was beginning to swell.

"Where is the necklace you stole from me?" Darkings asked.

"Sold it for a horse back in… I forgot what town."

"You sold that priceless artifact for a horse?"

"Two horses, actually. But they were shorthairs so, really—"

"Shut up!" Darkings shouted.

Whitney rolled his shoulders. "My legs were tired," he whispered under his breath.

Darkings raised the back of his hand, stopping himself right before smacking Whitney across the face. His whole arm quaked. "Tell me, did you think you'd get away with it?" he asked.

"I wouldn't have done it if I thought otherwise."

"I have been watching you since you entered my city," Darkings said. "You and your little pet. Where is she now?"

"You tell me. She disappeared along with that white-haired killer who I assume you hired to come after me."

"Ah yes, Kazimir. I must say, when I employed him, I didn't imagine how excessively thorough he would be."

Whitney pictured the man again, that awful, nightmarish grin. "What are you doing with her?"

"What he does with your *knife-ear* is none of my concern. I offered more wealth than you could imagine for him to track you down, yet the moment he knew of her, she was the only prize he wanted."

"Prize?" Whitney scoffed. "He's in for a rough night."

"Heavens no! You think he's that sort of hired blade?" Darkings chortled. He strutted over to a seat by the stairs, right below his father's portrait. It may as well have been a throne.

"Well, you hired him. I just have to figure he's scum."

Darkings took a long sip of wine, grinning impishly as he licked his lips. "Have you ever heard of the Dom Nohzi?"

Just hearing the name had Whitney swallowing the lump in his throat.

He nodded.

Anyone who'd been to the big cities of the world had, though most thought them a myth. But Whitney had been to Brekliodad, and he'd seen their work first-hand. The Dom Nohzi were an order of assassins whose work was legalized amongst their people by blood pact. If one went to them and provided a case of why a man should die, and some deities they called the Sanguine Lords accepted, that was the end. It was all heaped in layers of mystery but what was known was that upon being employed, their order was ruthless, calculating, and apparently, now operating this far south.

"I'm sure you would have, being the worldly thief you are," Darkings went on. "It was only when I got here and looked through father's ledgers that I found a contact there. The business of coin can be so cutthroat after all."

"And people insult *my* profession," Whitney scoffed.

"Swindling people is a fool's profession. And fools die."

"Yet here I am," Whitney said, "alive and breathing."

That was the thing about the Dom Nohzi, if you were unlucky enough to be chosen as one of their targets, it was said you never saw them coming. One night you were carousing at a tavern, and then the tip of a knife found its way into the back of your skull.

Burning down a man's house after robbing him was certainly enough to get their gods to approve the blood pact, yet, somehow, Whitney lived. And it was then that he realized; he hadn't burned down the house. That was Sora.

"All right, all right, Darkings, you got me." He clapped his hands, chain jingling as he did. "So why don't you let Sora go. The whole her-burning-the-house-down thing? It was an accident." He released a nervous chuckle. "Seriously, you should have seen her face after."

"You think I don't know that you were the ringleader of that little escapade? As I said, what Kazimir does with your knife-ear girlfriend is not up to me. Though I can only imagine what use his order might have for a blood mage with no family to care about her."

Before Whitney could think better of it, his eyes shot open with horror. Darkings had challenged him to that game of gems, and Whitney's bluff was already shot. After looking into Kazimir's horrible face, he couldn't imagine. He didn't want to.

"Darkings, look—"

"It is Lord Bartholomew Darkings to you!" he roared, springing up from his seat. He slammed his drink down on a table and approached Whitney. "I want you to hear me, boy," he said. "I own you. I *own* you."

He squeezed Whitney's puffy jaw tight between his fingers. Whitney winced, feeling like a barrel of pins had burst in his mouth. "You're still here because that is how I want it."

"Just… let… Sora… go," Whitney forced out.

"I wouldn't even if I could. She is a perversion, a taint of Elsewhere that we loyal followers of Iam cannot abide."

"Now… you're so… pious?"

"You'll never see her again. The blood pact on your head is complete. She is payment and now, your death is going to earn me the trust of the entire Panping citizenship."

He released Whitney's jaw and sauntered back to his seat, grabbing his wine on the way. The one-eyed guard promptly grabbed Whitney and shoved him to his knees.

"To think," Darkings said as he sat back down. "I simply wanted to destroy you. I wanted to sully the name of Whitney Fierstown, or whatever you call yourself. Now, I get to drag two of your names through the mud, watch you hang, and further my foothold in this city." He took another sip of wine, savoring every last drop. "You are the most useful pile of shog I've ever come across."

"And you're the ugliest."

The comment earned Whitney a right hook across his already injured jaw from the one-eyed lackey. He would have gone down, but the other guards forced him upright.

"We hang him at dawn for the murder of Tayvada Bokeo," Darkings ordered. "Such a sad city these days. They will revel in the entertainment. Throw him in a cell and tie all his limbs. We don't want any miraculous escapes."

Whitney spat out another gob of blood. "Then you captured the wrong man. Miraculous escapes are my specialt—" A cudgel to the back of the head had him on his knees and seeing bright lights. By the time he could see clearly again, Darkings was crouched in front of him.

"You're nothing, boy." He reached into Whitney's jacket and removed the letters patent presented to him by Torsten and sealed by the Crown itself. On it, was proof of his noble name and house: Blisslayer. To his horror, Whitney remembered that in the chaos created by Queen Mother Oleander, there was no time for the newly named Master of Rolls to add a copy to the archives.

It was just a name and a worthless piece of paper, yet as Darkings raised it to one of the candles mounted on the wall, Whitney felt his heart sink. Fire caught the corner and spread, the ink melting away as it flaked into ember and ash.

"You will die as nothing," Darkings said as he dropped the papers to the floor to finish burning. Then a second blow to the head sent Whitney face first into cold marble, and his whole world went black.

XIV

THE KNIGHT

It was two days marching before the stone of Fort Marimount shone under the light of the moons against a sea of darkness. It was said that the natural portion had been excavated by dwarves and used as a foothold for hunting the ancient dragons that stalked the region. The fortress itself was built across a shallow valley, half-sunken into the rock with a stone stronghold rising from its edges. The Glass Road, running north and south, led right through it like an armored bridge with a gate on either side. The farmland they passed on the west side helped feed the capital, and on the east was the Haskwood Thicket where Muskigo's men were said to be waiting.

The valley didn't cut across all the Southern Reach like the Jarein Gorge did up north, but Torsten knew Muskigo wasn't foolish enough to go around it. He'd looked into the afhem's eyes after all.

Marimount guarded the Southern Reach, the last bastion of defense before Yarrington. Muskigo had already ambushed many of the surrounding villages when the Glass was distracted by Liam's death. Taking the Fort would make it easy for him to invade the heart of the realm without risk of being surrounded, to impede trade routes from the south and east, then put Yarrington under siege and to starve them out.

Redstar zipped up a nearby hill on his black horse, two gray dire wolves flanking him along with a Drav Cra dradinengor and the warlock, Freydis. Torsten felt like he was stuck in a nightmare every time he saw the man, still dressed in robes like a heathen instead of being armored properly like a Glassman off to war ought to be. Flame wrapped his hand for light. A torch would have been easier, would've required no drawn blood, but Redstar seemed intent on unsettling Torsten's men with his dark magic… or perhaps he thought he was impressing them.

"Torsten," Redstar said. "I bring news from the valley."

"Nobody asked you to," Wardric grumbled.

The dradinengor led his horse in a circle around Wardric. He didn't speak, only stared. The man had a beard so thick it was hard to tell where it ended and the furs draped over his shoulders began. Torsten recognized him. He was Drad Mak the Mountain-ous, leader of the southernmost Fyortentek clan. Torsten didn't know many of their kind by name, but this one was larger even than Torsten and had led so many successful raids against the towns surrounding Crowfall over the years that, as Wearer, Torsten had been forced to help bolster defenses.

Now they marched together.

"I prefer to rely on scouts that know the land, Shieldsman," Redstar said. "Not fools with eyes."

"Just spit it out," Torsten said.

Redstar said something to Mak in Drav Crava.

"Yes, Drad Redstar," the dradinengor grunted in response, then sneered at Wardric before riding to their people. Redstar then fell in beside Torsten.

"I had my followers in that ruin—you remember it, don't you Torsten?" Redstar said.

"I remember the face you wore."

Redstar referred to the dwarven ruins southwest of their current position where, not too long ago, Torsten had been deceived into believing Redstar was his long-lost mentor, Uriah Davies.

"Ah yes. You know, I always did dream of being some great knight after King Liam stole my sister. I always imagined what it would have been like if he took me too."

"Perhaps you should have thought of that before trying to stop him with blood magic," Wardric bristled.

"Stop him?" Redstar snickered. "Liam invaded in the name of his *peaceful* god and stole a young daughter from the hands of her father… yet, somehow you paint me the villain? I swear, the hypocritical nature of you people never ceases to astound me."

"You're welcome to leave at any time," Torsten said. "Now what did you want to tell me?"

"You won't like it."

"Spit it out, I said!"

"My followers called on the Buried Goddess to listen. To hear the rumblings through the earth. They tell me that Marimount is not the Shesaitju's only target."

"And where else might they attack?" Torsten asked.

"Nesilia does not reveal all, only glimpses from so deep below. She speaks of grating mud, of river water sloshing beneath the feet of great beasts."

"I thought you said your work in bringing your goddess back was complete?"

"I am her vessel, I only do as she asks."

"What would you do then?" Torsten asked.

"The only logical targets for the afhem and his afhemate are here and Winde Port. I suggest you send a portion of your army east to the port city just in case. My men can go if you'd like?"

"And miss the battle?" Wardric said. "You truly are a worm, Redstar. Are you that frightened at the thought of fighting?"

"The armies of mortals are nothing compared to the goddess we slew in the woods. I am merely trying to help my nephew."

"How quick your loyalties turn," Torsten said. "Now, are you finished?"

He nodded.

"*My* scouts inform me that Muskigo's army gathers before the fortress and he, himself is in the lead. Siege towers and catapults are preparing to breach the walls, and Prefect Calhoun of Winde Port sent word by galler, just this morning, that the only ships in Trader's Bay are anchored merchants and our fleet."

"And what does Iam tell you?" Redstar asked.

"He tells me that the sick feeling in my stomach is from being next to you, not doubt in our strategy. As we speak, Commander Citravan of the Winde Port guard rides this way. We will surround Muskigo here at Marimount, and we will end this rebellion before all the Black Sands decide to fall in with him in the name of their Caleef."

"You shifted forces from the east?" Redstar asked, incredulous. "Why was I not informed about this?"

"Because you're not the leader of this army, heathen," Wardric said. "You're here to do what Sir Unger tells you, then go home to your ice."

Redstar slowly drew his dagger and held it over his lap. "Torsten, I would advise your man not to speak to me in such a manner, lest he experience pain no mortal should know."

"You dare threaten a member of the King's Shield?" Wardric reached for his sword.

Torsten raised his hand. "Enough. None of this is up for debate. The King placed me in command. Redstar, you will take the Drav Cra west around the fortress and through the valley. When the flaming arrow hits the sky tonight, our cohort from

Winde Port will charge from the east and you from the west. With the enemy surrounded, we will flood out of Marimount, surround them, and end this."

"You have a fortress, yet you want to initiate the attack?" Redstar asked

"This victory must be swift if our new king is to appear strong. Muskigo will expect us to dig in, but he will not be expecting Drav Cra allies. We'll catch them preparing for a siege."

"And this is what Iam tells you to do?"

"It is what Liam would have done."

Redstar chuckled. "Of course. Bold and unexpected Liam. Well, you may be a fool, Torsten, but at least you're not a coward. We'll follow your plan for now, but I hope, for your sake, it works. You may hold the ear of the Queen Mother, but her son's remains open." He lowered his voice to a whisper. "And you can't sleep with him."

Torsten's arm shot out and wrapped Redstar's throat. Choking him was becoming like second nature. It took every ounce of his being not to fulfill Oleander's desires.

"Just do what you're asked to," he said, seething. "Fire a flaming arrow into the sky when you're in position."

"I think I'll just use my hand." He purposefully sliced his thumb on the way to stowing his dagger, and a flurry of embers formed in his palm. "My Wearer."

He bowed his head low, then muttered something in Drav Crava to Freydis. A horde of warriors and more warlocks branched away from the Glassmen, their heathen tokens rattling, furs billowing in the wind. As they vanished into the darkness of the valley, it was impossible to tell them apart from the dire wolves they ran with.

"Circling wolves," Torsten muttered.

"What was that, sir?" Wardric asked.

"Nothing. Just something Uriah used to say."

"Would that he were here. It would make him sick knowing we are fighting beside these savages."

"You have no idea."

"Well, I don't trust any of them," Wardric grumbled. "If Redstar's trying to curry favor with King Pi, who knows what he might try."

"Save your eyes for the Shesaitju. I'll keep the corner of mine on Redstar."

"I know, you're right," Wardric said, lowering his head. "It took me long enough, but I do trust the man Uriah trained to take his place."

"Trust in Iam, my friend. We're just here to do his work."

Torsten kicked the sides of his horse and spurred it on ahead. The northern gate of Marimount clanked open to greet him. Soldiers ran out to help the traveling army with supplies. Lord Eveliss, Duke of Marimount, rode out to greet them. Gentry Eveliss came from a distinguished house of Yarrington who presided over the southern reach. His father and his father's father had served the Kings of Glass for generations.

Eveliss himself, on the other hand, was about as green as they come. Barely able to grow a beard, he reminded Torsten of Rand.

"Sir Unger," Eveliss saluted. "Everything is prepared to your specifications."

"What of Black Sands?" Torsten asked.

"They remain out of range behind the tree line, preparing their siege engines. The man you described as Afhem Muskigo is in their lead."

"Excellent," Torsten said. "Wardric, ready the first legion at the southern gate. At my command, we charge their camp and end this."

Wardric saluted and continued on ahead with Eveliss to prepare. Torsten dismounted and headed up onto the ramparts.

Archers used pulleys to haul wood buckets of arrows up from the courtyard. Others carried food and water stores up from Marimount Keep. Torsten had no intention of withstanding a long siege but learned long ago it was always better to be prepared.

He climbed the watchtower, the highest point in the southern reach. From there beside the gate, he looked upon what was to be his canvas for battle. On a clear day, he might be able to see all the way to the mists of the Fellwater and along the coast of Trader's Bay, but presently, the sight was even more ominous.

The greenish glow of nigh'jel lanterns stole away the darkness. Thousands of them—creatures born in the vastness of the Boiling Waters now confined to small, glass and bone lanterns—stretching across a vast swathe of forest. There seemed like even more than when Torsten had stumbled upon the Shesaitju camp in the swamp.

In their light, he could see the charcoal-colored wooden planks of siege towers—that unmistakable wood from the palm trees littering the black, sandy, Shesaitju coast. Massive stones were being loaded into catapults.

"Lord Eveliss could have lent more urgency to his words," Torsten said to the archers posted around him as if any of them were listening. The siege wasn't just being prepared. From what Torsten could see, Muskigo appeared to be planning to unleash the fury of his forces that very night.

There was no time to waste.

Torsten leaned out over the ramparts. "Muskigo!" he bellowed. It carried across the cold night air, and at the sound of his voice, all his men stopped what they were doing. It grew so quiet he felt he could even hear snow flurries bouncing about on the light breeze.

Torsten saw motion behind the cover of the thicket. He kept his peripherals on the alert, waiting for the other units to get in position.

A thunderous rumble was the first indication that Muskigo had answered the call. He rode out alone into the clearing. His zhulong mount let out a roar that, combined with its heavy footsteps, shook earth and sky. Gold plating wrapped its tusks, but it wore no armor. Its thick, rust-colored scales and rock-hard hide were all the protection it needed.

Muskigo himself wielded a long glaive, staff made of blackened wood and a flawless emerald set in the curved blade. It caught the light of the nigh'jel hanging from the post on the back of his mount, which made it glow as if there were some great power sealed within the gem.

Even from so far, Torsten recognized the afhem. He could never forget that intense glare. The Shesaitju were from a place where winter never brought snow, yet Muskigo barely wore a hint of armor, tattoo-covered body bare against the cold.

But Torsten had seen the man fight in the Fellwater Swamp, and there was no better way to measure a man. He was a true showman who would freeze to death if it meant intimidating his enemies.

"Muskigo!" Torsten roared again. "Surrender now, and you alone will be tried for your crimes. Spare your men!"

Muskigo didn't answer. He moved closer still, until he was so near a single arrow could easily end it all. Now Torsten's men atop Marimount's walls could see, in detail, the great zhulong and the man's corded muscles. Torsten heard some of the archers already beginning to mutter about how he didn't need armor.

"Stop this!" Torsten shouted. "No one need die here today. We can all find peace in the light of Iam."

Finally, Muskigo stopped and looked up at Torsten, his eyes boring through him.

"The time of the Glass is over," he said. His voice was calm, like the rising of a wave carrying with it the threat of devastation.

"Caleef Rakun swore fealty to the Nothhelm's in perpetuity.

Stand down, and he will not be harmed. We will continue in the prosperity of King Liam that has helped both our lands flourish."

"It is too late for that. Your child-king thinks he can insult the mighty Sidar Rakun? His flesh, borne from the Black Sands—our beaches themselves. His blood, fused from the waters of the Boiling Waters. You've sealed your fate; all afhems will stand with me now. We will carve through you, straight to the capital, and free our great Caleef ourselves."

"In the name of Iam and *your* king, you will lower your arms and surrender. This is your final warning."

"The boy is no king of mine! I will string him up in the Boiling Keep and bleed him over the waters as his father did to mine so long ago. Pray to your god, Glassman. You will see him soon."

Muskigo snapped on the reins of his zhulong and raced back toward the forest, leaving Torsten with a hundred different responses on the tip of his tongue. He hadn't expected diplomacy to be an option—not with the size of Muskigo's army—but he didn't expect such coarseness either.

He looked to the sky, his blood boiling. A flaming arrow arced across the inky darkness to the west.

Commander Citravan.

The green lanterns in the forest suddenly drew back his attention. All at once they began to stir, their bearers falling into formation. As they spread apart, the numbers seemed to swell, ranks stretching across the breadth of Fort Marimount, extending deep into the thicket.

There was some shouting in Saitjuese, then a crank and a loud *snap*.

"Hold ranks!" Torsten yelled. He grabbed onto the parapet as Celeste illuminated two chunks of rock soaring through the air. They slammed into the walls, chewing out stone, and causing the entire keep to buckle.

"It doesn't appear catching them napping is still an option!" Wardric called up from the bailey.

"Hold!" Torsten answered.

He looked back to the eastern sky and braced himself for another round of catapult fire. One of the boulders smashed into the base of the tower on which he stood. He reeled with the impact, feeling the vibrations in his glaruium armor and his bones. In the forest, the siege towers begin to budge, and through the two in the center, a pair of zhulong charged, a massive battering ram being hauled between them.

Time was running out. If the Shesaitju advanced, they'd trap his forces within the keep. Their only route of escape would be funneling through the South Gate straight into Muskigo's hands while he held off the smaller forces to the east and west.

"Redstar!" Torsten screamed, and just as he finished the word, a ball of fire traced across the sky like a shooting star. He never thought he'd be so relieved to see magic.

His head rang from the crashing of stone, but he gathered himself and raced downstairs to the South Gate where Wardric waited with his horse. The rest of the King's Shieldsmen sat atop their own horses at the front of the mass of Glass soldiers—their mighty cavalry.

"Open the gate!" Wardric shouted. "Archers, loose!"

Torsten caught Lord Eveliss' attention. "My Lord, barricade yourself and your most loyal guards in the keep. If we fail, hold them off as long as you can."

He glanced between Torsten and the slowly rising gate. Another bang of rock on stone sent Eveliss into to a crouch. Torsten hoisted him back up by his fanciful collar and shoved him toward the keep, then turned to take his position at the head of the army, claymore drawn.

Green tinted dust swirled about in front of the gate as it rattled, colored that way by the distant nigh'jels. All he could hear was the chattering of armor and rapid breathing as some of the less experienced soldiers behind him shivered in fear.

Torsten, however, was calm, his hand steady. It had been a long time since he saw battle but there was nowhere else where he truly felt at home. The simplicity soothed him. Kill or be killed, in the name of God and Crown.

"Men of the Glass!" he yelled. "The Vigilant Eye falls upon us today, forgiving of what we must do. Our enemies pillage and raze. They would slaughter our women and children, destroy our very way of life. But their master is only mortal, as our great King Liam proved so many moons ago.

"I beg you now, find the strength of light in your heart, for we are the sword of peace. Let us show now that the Glass will neither bow nor break. Our lives for Iam!"

"Our lives for Iam!" Wardric repeated along with the entire army. Nervous as so many of them might have been, together the boom of their voices shook the walls. Torsten didn't wait for the echo to quiet. He snapped on his reins and charged forward, the thundering sound of pounding hooves and footsteps just behind him.

A volley of Glassmen arrows momentarily blotted out the light of the moons before they went stabbing into the forest to a chorus of screams. Then came the *snap-hiss* of another round being loosed from atop the keep. Torsten closed the distance on the tree line and could now see the silhouette of men within the green glow.

His gaze was fixed on only one: Muskigo atop his beast. The afhem barked orders in Saitjuese, sounding panicked, clearly having expected a long siege and not to fully unleash his army so soon.

Suddenly, a cluster of trees straight ahead went up in flames. Their naked boughs were too powdered with snow for it to spread but it was enough to burn the bark fast and hot and coat the forest in a thick fog of smoke.

Whale oil, Torsten realized.

"They're trying to split us!" he shouted. "Forward. Charge through with all your might Glassmen, and let Iam's light shield you!"

The red radiance of flames coalescing with that of the nigh'-jels made it seem as though he were charging into Elsewhere itself. But he didn't slow. His horse leaped over a tendril of flame and into the Shesaitju ranks.

His claymore arced down, gashing one of the battering-ram-pulling zhulongs across its thick hide. He swept it to the other side, expecting to find a soldier, but it was only a silhouette in the smoke. His men rushed through the blaze at his rear. Torsten whipped his horse around, trampled another Shesaitju soldier, but again, wasn't able to quickly find a second target.

He spun, searching the smoke, expecting to hear the clash of metal and the unforgettable shrieks of death as two great forces collided but the cries were scattered, drowned out by the sound of feet on earth as the unit from Winde Port and the Drav Cra converged from the east and west.

Something was strange. The last Shesaitju he slew had a post sticking up from his back, but that wasn't it. That was normal. They hung their lanterns from tall poles attached to their rear armor at night so that their hands would be free—but this one was positioned horizontally in a way that would make it difficult to traverse the dense woods and impossible to fight effectively. A half-dozen lanterns hung from it alone, each filled with a nigh'jel hanging at different heights, tentacles pulsing green.

"Torsten!"

Wardric dove from his horse and tackled a Shesaitju drawing back a bowstring. The man's arrow sped over Torsten's shoulder, and the thought of having to remove another of their barbed projectiles stopped his heart. He watched it stab into a burning tree, then noticed more of the lanterns strung up between boughs.

His men raced by, plowing through only a handful of enemy soldiers who had abandoned their posts at catapults to take down as many Glassmen as they could before dying.

"Torsten, where are they?" Wardric asked. He unsheathed his sword from a gray chest and stood.

A Drav Cra horn sounded, followed promptly by fur-clad warriors swarming the forest. From horseback, Torsten could see, but down in the fog of smoke, everyone was a shadow.

"Stand down!" Torsten ordered! "Fall back. It's a trap! Fall back!"

Wardric echoed his command and Torsten spurred his horse out of the woods. He coughed as he emerged on the plains, smoke filling his lungs.

"Drad Redstar, where are the enemies?" Freydis said, her hair wild as the fires.

"What is the meaning of this?" Redstar questioned as he approached.

All Torsten could manage was to shake his head.

"Must I do everything?" Redstar moaned. He hopped down from his horse and advanced toward the burning trees. Glassmen and Drav Cra poured past him in full retreat. He stopped, removed his dagger, and drew a deep cut across his hand. Blood dribbled onto the snow-covered grass.

He whispered something, then swiped his wounded hand to the side. In an instant, all the fire was snuffed out, and the smoke swirled out to either side. Then, a soft light bloomed in his palm as if holding a star. Murmurs of confusion broke out across both armies until Redstar laughed.

Torsten jumped down and ran to his side. With the smoke and fire cleared, Redstar's illumination spell revealed the entirety of Muskigo's camp amongst the trees.

A single boulder sat by two operational catapults, and all the rest were simple planks of wood balanced to appear like weapons. The siege towers were hollow, with wheels that barely worked. The battering ram didn't even have a ram under its cover. Thousands of nigh'jel lanterns were strung up everywhere as well as littering the ground by corpses.

There were no supplies alongside their tents. No food or water, none of the essentials needed to man a successful siege. And amidst it all, were the bodies of no more than one hundred Shesaitju warriors and a handful of Glassmen.

That was all.

"What sorcery is this?" Torsten snapped at Redstar. "What have you done!"

"What have *you* done, Shieldsman?" he replied. "It appears to me that Muskigo's army is not here."

"You think I can't see that!" He whipped around. "Wardric, send scouts out in every direction. Find where they went. We won't be caught out here in the open. Everyone, return to Marimount!" He went to take a step, but Redstar stopped him.

"What of the men you summoned from Winde Port?" he asked. "I see no new faces among these men."

"He signaled his approach. They're likely still in the for…" The words got lost in his throat when one of his men shouted and pointed east. Sitting on his zhulong, atop the hill, moons at his back, was Muskigo. He fired a flaming arrow straight up into the sky, then disappeared over the peak.

"That treasonous scag," Torsten swore. He rushed back to his horse and took off toward the afhem.

"Sir, it could be a trap!" Wardric called.

"Don't follow," he called back. "Get them all back to the keep!" He snapped his reins as hard as he could.

A horse appeared next to him carrying Redstar. Two dire wolves dashed at his sides.

"I said don't follow!"

"You're not the king," he answered.

They crossed the hilltop and Torsten could hear the echoing snorts of the zhulong long before he saw them. A full regiment of mounted Shesaitju raced across the plains, so far now they were only shadows. Muskigo was chasing after them, all headed east toward Winde Port.

Between Torsten and Redstar and the Black Sands riders, was the unit of a thousand men he'd summoned from Winde Port to surround Muskigo. They looked like they'd been hit by an avalanche, trampled and broken, groaning and in need of physicians.

Massacred.

Commander Citravan was at the front, his helmet caved into his skull.

Torsten wasn't sure how they didn't hear it happen until he remembered the chaos in the smoking forest, his men screaming in the heat of battle as they fought to kill barely a hundred men— Shesaitju warriors who had sacrificed their lives to be a distraction.

Marimount was never the target at all.

Torsten glanced at Redstar, speechless. The Arch Warlock looked back. He didn't smile like usual, but he wasn't mournful either. In fact, he didn't look surprised at all.

"The eye far above is blinder than the one beneath our feet," he said, calmly. "May She save us all."

XV

THE THIEF

"Oh, One-Eye?" Whitney called out.

Darkings' scarred lackey ignored him like he had during Whitney's previous twenty attempts at gaining his attention.

"Buried a bit north of here and to the east, there is a ring so precious you've likely never seen its equal," Whitney went on. "Let me out, and it's yours. You'll never work in a shoghole like this again."

He considered bringing up the broken crown stuffed into a chimney in the middle of the Panping Ghetto but hated the idea of giving up his greatest prize. Even in half, it once sat upon the head of Liam the Conqueror.

"Shut your mouth!" the guard finally grunted from his seat down the hall. "Ah, yigging shog, look at what you made me do." He threw down a deck of cards and the guard across from him plucked a few autlas off the table.

Whitney poked his head as far through the bars as he could, pulling the chains on his wrists and ankles tight.

"Don't blame me. You threw an anvil down against the

archer? You need that ring if you're expecting not to lose all your money in gems."

"Enough, thief. Pray to whoever you think'll care and eat your last meal. Dawn is coming, and it'll be the last one you see."

Whitney stared longingly back into his cell. "That slop is my last meal? I thought I'd at least get chicken. Looks more like what the chicken ate for supper."

He turned and climbed up a bench to peer through the tiny window slot at the back. It was dark as pitch outside, which would only mean one thing; dawn was about to break. Never before had Whitney been so sure he was going to die. He'd always had a plan, but right now, he had nothing and no allies to speak of. He could usually get guards to come around and take a bribe, but these guys weren't biting. Probably because they worked for Darkings and not the Crown, and that meant they were well paid.

C'mon Whitney, think! But nothing came. All he could imagine was that Sora... poor Sora... was in the hands of a ruthless assassin while he was left to hang.

He found himself subconsciously grabbing at his throat, swallowing hard.

"The ring and the Splintering Staff," he said. "I have them both hidden nearby. I can take you there right now. They're yours. Worth more than you'll make in a lifetime. Just let me out." He emphasized those last words, shaking the cell door.

The guard rose and silently began unlocking the cell.

"Oh, thank you," Whitney said. "Thank you. You won't regret this. I will—"

"Shut it, thief!" the guard said. He reached through the bars, grabbed Whitney by the scruff of his neck, and pulled him hard into the bars. Whitney's head cracked against the metal before he staggered backward.

"You ain't going nowhere but to your death," the guard growled.

His gems partner arrived as well, along with another of Darkings' goons. They unlocked Whitney's chained limbs and dragged him along. He tried to fight, but he could barely stand, his head was ringing so loud. Plus, each act of resistance only furthered their resolve to injure him more. By the time they'd hauled him out of Darkings' basement, down the street, and to the upper wharf where the gallows had been set up, he had been kicked, punched, and otherwise beaten more than a dozen times.

A gathering had amassed. Word about hangings always traveled quickly within big cities. Nothing roused the common-folk more than watching one of their own flail at the end of a rope. Usually, it was cultists, leaders of rebellions, bandit crews, or— apparently murderous folk. Or in Whitney's case, men set up to look like one.

Through swollen eyes, Whitney saw people of all shapes and sizes, most of them poor, and most Panpingese. Light, bronzish skin, pointed ears, and expressions of profound sadness.

"All right, last chance," Whitney said to Darkings' lackey. "I'll get you the ring, the staff, and... I can't believe I'm saying this... the Glass Crown of Liam Nothhelm."

"I'm going to enjoy watching your neck snap, scag."

Whitney was handed off to the city guard, proudly donning the blue and white of the Glass Kingdom. He was promptly shoved through the growing crowd. The looks of sorrow among the Panpingese quickly transitioned to rage as vegetables and hard chunks of bread slammed into his body from every direction. What appeared to be a turnip clipped his ear and even drew blood. The soldiers made as little effort to shield him as was physically possible.

Everyone with pointed ears wanted to take a shot at the bastard who killed Tayvada, even if it meant spoiling much-needed food. It appeared Tayvada was loved dearly. He was probably the pride of their community, using the wealth of the Traders Guild to provide food and other necessities. For the first time since finding his drained corpse, Whitney felt a hint of remorse over the man himself. None of them realized they blamed the wrong guy. From their viewpoint, he agreed.

The soldiers walked him up a small flight of stairs and tossed him down on the wooden planks. Raising his head, he watched as many of the onlookers spit toward him. Whitney never cared whether he was liked before, but now he knew he hated being so reviled. Thieves who meet their end usually did so rotting in a cell or falling from a rooftop. Public execution was never what Whitney expected, or deserved.

He watched Bartholomew Darkings ascend the steps from the opposite side of the platform, donning his best formal silks. He licked his lips beneath thick mustache and edged toward Whitney and his detainers. A hush fell upon the gathering mass as the former constable of Bridleton and son of the Master of Coin positioned himself at the front of the platform.

"Nice shirt," Whitney remarked. Darkings didn't even pay him a passing glance. "Did your mother sew that—" He lost his train of thought when, out of the corner of his vision, he saw someone familiar watching from the shadows. Standing under the pitched roof of a bell tower was the white-haired assassin who'd taken Sora. He leaned against a column, grinning.

"Good people of Winde Port," Darkings announced. "Especially the fine folks of the Panping Ghe…" He cleared his throat. "District"

"Welcome!" he shouted.

Thunderous applause rained down on him.

"Yes, yes," he continued, motioning for the crowd to quiet. "My name is Bartholomew Darkings, beloved son of our great Master of Coin. My family helped build Winde Port centuries ago, and so I stand here today, a man of the merchant city just like each of you."

Yeah, minus the fact that you live in a mansion on a hill the whole ghetto could fit into. Whitney scoffed internally.

"I hope for today to be more than the execution of one worthless whelp," Darkings continued. "I hope it to be a day of eternal memory. One we can look back upon as the beginning of a new era. For too long, you've been forced into obscurity. This fact accented by the death of one of the greatest men in all of Winde Port being brutally murdered in a place where, with even the slightest presence of city guards, it could have been prevented."

Murmurs of agreement carried across the crowd. Whitney would've rolled his eyes if they weren't so fixated on the assassin. Never in his life had just seeing a man made his throat clench. All the hope that his good luck would get him out of this drained away.

"Had it not been for my personal guards receiving a tip about this… scoundrel being in our fine city, Tayvada Bokeo's death may have gone days without notice."

"I didn't even do it!" Whitney finally drew enough focus to shout. The last word came out as a grunt, one of the guard's boots finding his ribcage.

"But no more!" Darkings shouted, inviting an uproar from the crowd. "The Darkings have returned to Winde Port. Returned home. And we will fight to make our city safer for everyone!"

Darkings turned to face Whitney, eclipsing the menace watching from a distance, and winked.

"It all starts now," he said. He raised his hand, and the soldiers roughly pulled Whitney to his feet. They gave him a shove toward the center of the gallows where a noose hung.

"This man is a fraud!" Whitney shouted, but no one could hear him over the cheers. Without the dark eyes of Kazimir upon him, he felt like himself again.

Darkings came close and said, "No one cares about you, thief. Your name means nothing. You will go down in history only as the man who sealed my hold on Winde Port. And nobody but I will ever know."

Darkings turned back to his captive audience and waved his arms for them to quiet. "Ladies and gentlemen, I give you the man who stole Tayvada Bokeo's life in cold blood. Whitney Blisslayer!"

The crowd cursed his name. The executioner wrapped a coarse rope around his neck, then stepped back to a lever, ready to plunge Whitney into Elsewhere. Things got so crazy it sounded like a riot until a lone, gruff voice cried out.

"Stop!" Whitney couldn't find its owner in the crowd. "Ye ain't got the right to hang a noble at these gallows."

The people parted, revealing Tum Tum. The rotund dwarf stood tall, however short he was.

"He deserves to stand before the prefect for his actions and defend himself, aye?" Tum Tum said, looking around for support.

To Whitney's shock, a few of the wealthier onlookers in their posh outfits agreed.

"And who might you be to question a Darkings?" Bartholomew said.

"I be the true voice of the people, standing up to those who think themselves above the law because their daddy's a big shot in Yarrington."

Bartholomew laughed humorlessly, then his face contorted into a scowl.

"I assure you, my bearded friend, that the prefect is busy securing the region against possible rebellion and has vested in me the power to take this unfortunate matter into my own hands. Tayvada was..." He closed his eyes and feigned sincerity, "...a dear friend."

"Tayvada fed my children when we had nothing!" a Panpingese man hollered from the back.

"Hang the bastard!" A cacophony of onlookers voiced their agreement.

"And someone will pay for his death!" Tum Tum said. "But, I've known Whitney for years, and the man be gentle as they come."

"Hey, I'm not that..." Whitney said, before realizing how stupid it would be to argue that. "Yeah, he's right! I can't even hurt a spider."

"This man was found in Tayvada's very home," Bartholomew shouted, "blood on his hands."

"Yeah, so I hear. So ye say he slit the poor bloke's throat—let the blood drain from him. The Whitney I know retches at the sight of a cut." Tum Tum hopped—or, rather, rolled—up onto the stand. A kind onlooker even rushed to help him to his feet after watching his struggle. "My Panpingese brothers and sisters, I know ye are angry, and why shouldn't ye be? But is this really Winde Port justice?"

"Maybe the dwarf has a point," that same highborn in front said. Whitney thought he recognized him from the Guild Hall. "Should we not hear the accused's defense before he is sent from this world?"

"Yeah, what he said!" Whitney cried out. "I'm weak and harmless. But maybe there's someone else who gets something out of painting a new villain. Maybe he's right here among us."

A mixture of approval and distaste spewed forth from the non-Panpingese members of the crowd. Bartholomew leaned in close to his one-eyed guard. "Kill the dwarf as soon as we're gone," he whispered so only Whitney could hear.

He turned back to address Tum Tum.

"Your complaints are duly noted, Dwarf," he said. "But this decree has already been made and signed by Prefect Mortimer

Calhoun." He unfurled a piece of paper from the folds of his jacket. Whitney couldn't see it, but he could see Tum Tum's features darken and knew his fate was sealed. And even worse, he could once again see the grin on the assassin's face now that Bartholomew had moved, teeth and hair white against the shadow.

"Today," Bartholomew pronounced with renewed vigor. "The murderer, Whitney Blisslayer die—"

A sudden scream rang out. "In the bay!"

Whitney turned toward the water. A flaming rock crashed into one of the Glass Kingdom warships floating in the bay. Then, suddenly, an arrow exploded through the chest of the noble that had taken Whitney's side. For a moment, Whitney thought someone was coming to spring him, but then he realized... only a Shesaitju barbed arrow could tear through a man with such force.

A frenzy broke out as more arrows trickled down, men and women tripping over one another. Even the Glass soldiers overseeing the execution dispersed.

Whitney saw his opening. The executioner no longer stood on the platform, and Bartholomew's guards were otherwise occupied. Just as Whitney began to duck out of the noose, one of the lumbering brutes bumped into him. In turn, he bumped another guard, who bumped into Bartholomew, and finally, the man's fat ass struck the lever. In an instant, the floor fell out beneath him and Whitney was hanging.

He gurgled and strained. As he struggled, he wondered why his neck hadn't snapped, though he wasn't complaining.

His vision grew blurry, blood rushing to his eyeballs. He could feel drool against his cheek before he went lightheaded. His ears rang, but he heard a loud *crack-boom,* and suddenly, he was falling again.

It took a moment for him to figure out what happened. A shower of wood fragments rained down on him as, somehow, he lay safely on the ground. He stood beneath the gallows, sides broken but for a few supporting struts. Beyond the structure where the crowd had just been, was an open marketplace. Everyone was busy running for their lives.

The Shesaitju are attacking again?

Whitney didn't wait around for an answer. He went to run, but Bartholomew grabbed his ankle and sent him sprawling.

"You won't escape me again!" Bartholomew hissed.

"You're right, I won't." Whitney kicked him across the jaw. Then he rolled over and jumped on the man. He used the rope that still bound his hands and pulled it taut against Darkings' neck. "Where is she!"

"Unhand him!" The loyal, one-eyed guard grabbed Whitney and flung him off.

Before either could make a move, another volley of arrows rained down. The guard raised a chunk of broken wood and kept an arrow from shredding Bartholomew's head. Another landed in the dirt, right between Whitney's legs.

He stared at it, frozen by fear. He knew firsthand what the barbed arrows could do. All the while, Bartholomew's men lugged their master away while he vowed revenge again and again.

With them gone, the sight of Kazimir standing through an open doorway across the plaza finally stirred Whitney. While everyone fled for their lives, the Breklian assassin stayed in the darkness, calmly juggling one of his many knives.

Whitney rolled and hopped to his feet, then ran, arms bound and severed noose flapping behind him. He saw the source of his salvation in a massive ball of stone that had apparently been catapulted into the city. There was no time to celebrate his renowned luck. He needed to get out of the target zone, lest another boulder or arrow come crashing down.

Kazimir was now nowhere to be seen, and none of the city

guards paid any attention to the escaping prisoner. Whitney sprinted as fast as he could and only stopped once he knew he was free of the threat of discovery. Ducking into an alley, he slid the noose from his neck and worked the rope until his hands were untied.

He rubbed his neck. Knowing there'd be a mark, he pulled his collar up tight against his ears. Only then did he finally allow himself to catch his breath. Once he had his fill of the precious, life-giving air, he peered around the corner toward the bay. From the morning fog along the shore, emerged hundreds of dark rowboats cracking through the ice toward Winder's Wharf. Each of them carried gray-skinned rowers by the dozens, so many that some were even hanging off into the freezing cold water.

On the back of each, stood an archer, loosing arrow after arrow into the city. Glass soldiers fired back and formed along the wharf, but boulders from catapults soared out of the fog. They came from the direction of the coast as if somehow an entire army had snuck right onto Winde Port's doorstep overnight.

The Shesaitju mounted the wharf, descending upon the shields of the Glassmen like a tsunami.

Bells tolled from all around him. Whitney felt the breath catch in his lungs. This was no mere raiding party with a lust for bloodshed. It was an army. The biggest Whitney had ever seen. And once again he was in the wrong place while they were attacking.

He backed away and as he did, noticed Kazimir on a sunken balcony on a neighboring building, staring out at the bay. The assassin was enraptured by the sight of the invaders, same as he was. Whitney used the man's distraction and sunk all the way back into the alley. He found a sewer cover nested at the base of a building and weaseled his way in.

Darkings, Panping—they could all wait. He had to find Sora before the whole city burned down around them... or Kazimir killed them both.

XVI

THE MYSTIC

By the time sunlight filtered in through the stained glass, Sora's throat felt like tree bark.

"Help!" she grated. She thrashed her body and clenched the muscles in her stomach until they finally gave out and she hung slack.

Multi-colored light painted the cobwebs like splintered diamonds hanging from rotting beams in the otherwise empty room that would be her grave. A spider flitted across one. It was tiny, but it still brought her back to the Webbed Woods and the last time she thought she was going to die.

She tried to force herself to think about the same things she had when Redstar was killing her—when she lost control and the energy of Elsewhere coursed through her like a hot spring. About all the places in the world she'd missed out on seeing while hiding beneath a shack. She considered every scar. How Wetzel used to cut her mercilessly, bidding the darkness within her to rise up.

She begged her body to bring that power back to bear.

But it never came.

"At least I'll die in a church," she groaned, sardonic.

She'd never been religious. Wetzel didn't care for anything but his studies and his potions. But as a child, she'd gone with Whitney and his family to the Troborough church house. Her first few visits, everyone stared at her. Whitney's mother told her it was because she was "just so cute." But his father's eyes shot daggers sharper than her ears.

But she'd watch the other families leave service, their eyes circled by luminous white paint once a year during the Dawning, when the moons blotched out the sun, and the people of the Glass were forced to look inward for Iam's light. Tears speckled her eyes as she recalled how they smiled and caroused, mothers hugging their daughters, fathers tussling their sons' hair.

She'd always longed for that. One year, Whitney's parents even took him to Yarrington for the ceremony led by Wren the Holy at Yarrington Cathedral. She remembered being the loneliest she'd ever been in her life, sitting by the stream staring at the empty Troborough chapel while Wetzel called for her to help with his potions.

No matter how many times Whitney told her what a load of shog it all was, she always wanted to belong. Wetzel cared for her the best he knew how, but he wasn't her real father.

She hung her head and closed her eyes. Wetzel didn't believe in any Gate of Light, didn't believe that the dead would be delivered into the waiting arms of Iam. Like her ancestors, he believed that after death, the spirit went to Elsewhere. To linger without purpose, watching until the essence of one's soul would one day be returned to the world of the living. She wondered if she might find her true parents on that eldritch plane.

In truth, she only hoped death would bring relief from painful memories. That when her eyes shut for the last time, she would no longer have to remember the pain of abandonment, the shame of her heritage, or the brutality she'd experienced at the hands of men like Kazimir.

She swore. There were no men like Kazimir.

The steeple door creaked open.

"I won't go with you," she said. She opened her eyes and expected to see Kazimir, only the entry was empty. She searched from side to side, trying to keep her heart from beating through her rib cage. She'd seen him move like this, like a shadow. "You might as well kill me because I won't come with you."

A faint clicking noise drew her gaze to the floor, and there, sniffing her dangling feet was a wyvern.

"Aquira?" she said, incredulous. "What are you..."

The creature blinked. She stood up on her hind legs and stuck her forked tongue at Sora's feet.

"You need to leave right now before he returns. You need to go home..." The words trailed off as she realized that, like her, Aquira had no home to return to. Her master had been murdered for merely being in the wrong place at the wrong time. Just like Sora's own parents.

"I'm so sorry girl," Sora said. "You didn't deserve any of this. Neither of us did."

Sora stretched her foot to pat the wyvern on the head. Aquira's frills rippled as she closed her eyes, purring softly in a series of rhythmic clicks. Sora could feel the heat radiating off the creature, even through her heels.

The corners of her mouth rose.

"Aquira," she said. "Do you want to help me out of here?"

The wyvern merely stared up at her and blinked again.

"The chains. Can you melt them?" Sora shook her arms, and in doing so, her entire body. Aquira scurried away, and Sora cursed under her breath.

"Why don't I speak wyvern?" she groaned. Aquira stopped a few paces away and turned to look back at her. Sora inhaled slowly and remembered one of Wetzel's lessons about ancient Panping mystics who learned how to dominate the minds of lesser beings. Sora couldn't do that but the birds her old master always tested his concoctions on always favored her.

"Aquira," she whispered. "I know you can't understand me, but if you don't break me free, I'll lose everything."

A chorus of distant screams echoed, then a loud crash outside kicked dust off the ceiling and made Aquira dart for the door.

"Aquira!" Sora shouted. "Please, stop!"

The creature stopped in the entry near the stairs and turned.

Another crash, louder than the first, made the entire steeple rumble. Aquira tilted her head and before Sora could say another word, rushed back to her.

She flew up onto Sora's leg, claws poking into her.

"Good girl," Sora said, gritting her teeth. "You can do this." Aquira's needle-like claws wound their way up her body until she was sitting on Sora's shoulder.

Sora shook her right arm, so the chain holding her bound to the ceiling rattled.

"Right here," she said.

Aquira's strange, yellow eyes blinked in Sora's face, then she growled and turned to the cuff.

"Yes!" Sora exclaimed. "That's right."

Aquira's scaly tail wrapped the back of Sora's neck for balance. It was like wearing a campfire for a coat the wyvern was so warm. Then, she flapped her wings to hover just overhead. The weight made Sora's already sore shoulder feel like it was going to tear from the joint.

Sora squeezed her eyelids shut to stifle the groan festering in her throat, not wanting to scare her reptilian savior again. A sweltering brush of air wrapped her forearm. Fire spewed from Aquira's mouth, bright and hot. It was aimed at the chains, but Sora's hand blistered anyway.

The metal wilted like the wax of a candle. Even Sora's magic couldn't compare. When half her body swung free, Aquira used the momentum to leap up onto the other chain. In an instant, the second was reduced to molten slag as well.

Sora crashed to the floor, one of her heels driving a hole in the old wood plank. She gasped for air. She hadn't quite been crucified, but with both arms stretched she hadn't realized just how labored her breathing had become until she had a lungful. She clutched her chest. Against her cheek, she felt a dry, coarse tongue.

She threw her arms around Aquira. The wyvern didn't fight it, just nuzzled against Sora's neck, frills tickling her chin. More screams and banging noises sounded from outside, but Sora couldn't bring herself to let go. She squeezed harder and Aquira's purring intensified.

Before she knew it, she was sobbing. Her tears trickled down onto Aquira's scales and turned to mist. Her whole body, inside and out, grew warm from holding the wyvern but she didn't care. Her life had been so chaotic since the Black Sands took everything away from her that she hadn't even really had time to stop and let it all out.

Wetzel. Troborough. Seeing Whitney again and dealing with his 'jobs'—tears over all of it poured from her eyes like a dam had been broken. It took all her effort to pull away and momentarily focus her blurry vision on the lizard-like face of her unexpected rescuer.

"I promise, you'll never be without a home again," she sniveled.

Aquira went to lick her again when the bang of the church doors slamming shut downstairs made her heart sink. She waited for the loud thumping of boots against the stairs, same as she'd heard when Kazimir left her earlier.

"C'mon," she said, scrambling to her feet. Her legs were

numb from hanging, but she didn't let that stop her. She ran to the stained glass window, she wrapped her fist with the hem of her dress, then bashed on it as hard as she could. The glass vibrated but didn't break. If there was one thing for which the Glass Kingdom was proficient, it was hardened, stained-glass panels.

Sora struck it again and again until Aquira released a snarl that raised the hairs on her arms. She turned around, and in the entryway, saw the white hair and dark, callous eyes of her captor. Her hand fell toward a knife she didn't have—a knife Kazimir had stolen from her.

He strolled forward calmly, clicking his tongue in disapproval. He purposefully avoided the beam of sunlight flooding in through the high window, but as he turned, she noticed that, unlike before, he was now covered in grime. His hair was unkempt, and a few of his knives were missing from his bandolier.

"Where are you going, my dear?" he asked. "We were just starting to get along." The sound of his voice made her spine tingle, but she also noticed something new in it. For once, he seemed flustered.

"I'm not going anywhere with you," she said.

"You are going to help me find your friend and honor my pact."

He's alive?

Hoping Kazimir wouldn't see the relief on her face, she looked down as she unwrapped her hand from her dress and balled it into a tight fist. Aquira snarled at Kazimir. Only a spark came out of her mouth, clearly drained from melting the chains.

"And who is this adorable, new friend?" Kazimir asked. "I swear, today is just full of surprises."

"Stay away from us!" Sora screamed. She drew back her bare hand and punched through the glass. It was only a small hole, but when her hand recoiled, it was sliced all over.

Bleeding.

Now she felt it, that dark, unexplainable power inside. All at once, she was unstoppable and vulnerable, as if she, herself, were walking the planes of Elsewhere. Fire erupted from her injured hand and blew the entire window open just before Kazimir was able to grab her.

Wind howled, and light flooded the steeple. Kazimir leaped backward into the shadows, wincing as if in pain. It was then that Sora remembered another of the lessons in one of Wetzel's old books. The upyr were fearsome, but immortality came with draw-backs... the insatiable need for blood, and a horrible allergy to sunlight which turned their skin to ash.

Sora grabbed Aquira and backed away slowly. The lust in Kazimir's eyes was replaced by terrible rage. She lifted her leg over the sill and stepped out onto the slanted roof, her eye never leaving her captor.

The racket in the city was deafening. Metal clashing, screams of agony and war—death all around her. Out of her peripheries, she saw the low palisade wall on the landlocked side of the city. Gray-skinned Shesaitju from the detainment camp swarmed over it like ants from a nest.

The image of Troborough burning at the hands of the Black Sands flashed through her mind. She tripped on a loose tile and rolled to the roof-ledge. Aquira flew from her arms, but Sora caught her by the tail.

As Sora struggled to pull the squirming, squealing wyvern back up, she stared through the steeple's broken window. Kazimir stood in the light, his skin flaking away, smoking like parchment under the heat of flame. He clenched his jaw but never made a sound. Instead, he knelt, scraped his knife along the ground to coat it with Sora's blood, and lifted it to his lips.

Sora felt a nibble on her finger and looked to see Aquira flut-tering below. She let go, and the wyvern drifted downward.

She quickly returned her attention to her assailant. His eyelids flickered as he licked off every last drop. His skin seemed to shift a to a lighter shade. The sun's blisters slowly faded as he stood and rolled his neck with a series of pops.

"Your blood is like a storm," he said with renewed vigor. "Come, my dear. We have so much to accomplish together."

Sora panicked. She looked down, then back up at the monster bearing down on her. The sunlight dried and cracked his skin, but the marks healed faster than they could form.

Sora didn't think. She pushed off the wall of the church with her feet and let go. Air rushed up around her as her heart sank into her stomach. The fall ended abruptly as she crashed onto the flat roof of a Panping Ghetto home. Her ankle banged off something, a sharp line of pain streaking up her leg. Her back felt like it had broken in two. She thanked the gods she'd crashed through a galler bird cage and into in a pile of feed. It wasn't soft, but it was better than the unforgiving ground. Groaning, she flipped over and noticed Aquira had already taken to stalking one of the freed birds.

She wanted to lay there forever, exhaustion tempting her to close her eyes and pass out, but one look back at the broken-down church and she saw Kazimir preparing to make the leap.

"C'mon!" She grabbed Aquira and swung her up onto her shoulder just as the wyvern went to snap at her unsuspecting prey.

Behind them, Kazimir made the jump like it was as easy as walking. He stretched his arms out wide, like a bird in flight, and then at the last moment, flipped head over heels, landing with the grace of a prince.

Sora's ankle burned, but she pushed her legs as fast as they could go. Blood coated her hand from the glass shards digging in, and she flung a ball of flame back over her shoulder. Kazimir spun out of the way and kept moving. She'd never seen anyone move like him.

She jumped between two flats. Where only the day before she

found herself cursing how the Glass Kingdom had crammed together the houses of her ancestors, now she was grateful for it. From roof to roof she went, not daring to look back. Kazimir's footsteps—if they even made a sound—were drowned out by the unseen chaos overtaking the streets of the city.

"Running is futile," Kazimir said, not even panting as he chased her. "With me, you'll be so much more than some thief's plaything."

Sora glanced back, and her foot crashed through a tarp covering a devastated structure at the edge of the ghetto. She crashed through wooden beams, then through a flimsy floor. Aquira slipped from her shoulder, but not before one of her claws ripped off a small chunk of skin.

By the time Sora stopped falling she was at street level, covered in dust and bits of wood. Her dress was torn at the seams, half her scratched torso exposed, one sleeve missing.

"Aquira?" she moaned. Her vision was spotty at best, but she didn't see her new friend anywhere.

"Alva shueth!" someone barked in Saitjuese. Before she could see where it came from, a gray hand pulled her from the rubble. Her gaze met those of a Shesaitju soldier wearing scaled leather armor and a waist-coil of black wooden plates.

Sora was in so much pain she couldn't think straight. She knew she had to keep moving, but the sight of a Shesaitju again transported her weary mind back to that fateful day Troborough burned.

"Get off me!" she snapped, tearing free of the soldier and igniting a fire around her hand. There was so much blood it enveloped nearly her whole arm, burning hot and bright. A second soldier aimed a spear at her neck and cursed her in Saitjuese.

Before any of them could make a move, a knife sliced across each of their necks. Blood squirted as they fell to their knees, pawing at their throats.

"Nobody but I will ever touch you again," Kazimir said.

Sora spun and fell backward, her magic abandoning her. The white-haired devil emerged from the ruined structure, mindlessly flipping a throwing knife by the blade.

"G... get away from me," Sora stammered. She reached inward for that well of power she so often relied on but was too petrified.

"I—" Kazimir was cut off when Aquira appeared on his shoulder and dug her teeth into his neck. He howled and fell to one knee, smoke sizzling out of the wound as if the wyvern's teeth themselves were made of fire.

Kazimir ripped her off him and held the flailing creature by its neck. Rage contorted his features. His fangs extending like swords. He drew another knife and raised it to Aquira's throat.

"Enough!" he roared. "I tire of chasing you, mystic. Perhaps killing your friend here will show you that I will not be denied."

"Please don't!" Sora begged. "Don't hurt her. I'll... I'll do anyth..." She didn't finish because she noticed that while the marks from Aquira's bite were healing, Kazimir's flesh was beginning to flake away again from the sunlight. His hand crackled, allowing Aquira to squirm free and hide between Sora's legs.

"Just leave us alone!" The chance to fight back energized her. Sora raised both bloody hands, and a pillar of flame exploded from them. It struck Kazimir on the hip and sent him flying back into the rubble.

Smoke and embers danced, but he didn't stay down. He flung a plank off his body and hopped back to his feet. Now, from the shadows, he watched her.

Before she could catch herself, Sora's eyes lowered toward a stain on the floor. His followed, and what he saw made him grin.

He knelt down to the tiny pool of Sora's blood gathering around his boots. Sora looked deep into herself. Her whole body was numb from pain, but she drew on all her worst memories. She knew summoning another flame so soon might make her pass out. Elsewhere sapped her body like it'd spent a week harvesting barley every time she did it.

But she had no choice. Fire swirled around her hands once more as Kazimir raised her blood to his lips.

She heard another voice behind her, sharp and sudden. She glanced back, just for a moment, and saw a cluster of Shesaitju warriors staring at her, clad in golden armor and faces were covered by masks in the visage of snakes. At their center stood a breathtaking warrior unlike any she'd ever seen. Despite the chill in the air, he was shirtless, his gray skin covered head to toe in white tattoos.

When she turned back, Kazimir was gone.

Sora scanned the shattered remains of what appeared to be a home in the middle of the Panping Ghetto. Fear had her crippled, both physically and magically. She turned back toward the impressive Shesaitju man.

"Who are you?" she asked.

"I could ask the same of you?" His gaze wandered momentarily toward her exposed midriff before he caught himself.

"I... I..." Between sheer exhaustion, relief that Kazimir was gone, and the overwhelming presence of the man standing before her, she could hardly speak.

The man looked down at the two dead Shesaitju warriors, then to the smoldering wake left behind by her magic where Kazimir had stood only moments before. Some cloth smoked amongst the embers as if she'd completely vaporized another attacker.

"You did this?" he asked.

Sora hesitated. If she said no, she'd need to tell them about Kazimir. Who would believe there was an upyr chasing her through the streets of Winde Port? If she said yes, they might lash out and kill her on the spot. Again, she was rendered silent.

"Very impressive," he said. "My people were ordered not to

touch a single dwarf or Panpingese. They clearly deserved their fate. Am I right men?" The soldiers flanking him said nothing. They stood silent beneath terrifying, golden, serpentine masks.

"Our people have no qualms with you or yours, mystic," the man continued. He went to touch her shoulder, but, instinctively, she recoiled. However impressive he seemed, she couldn't ignore the rage growing inside of her. His was the gray skin of the people who had senselessly slaughtered Troborough.

"You deny me, mystic?" he questioned, his features hardening.

She was about to correct him—to tell him she was no mystic and he was responsible for burning down the town she called home. She was also about to summon fire to the tips of her fingers and burn him to a crisp. Then she remembered Whitney and the man after them.

"No, my head is just fuzzy from the fight," she lied. If she tried anything rash, she'd die with him. Which meant Whitney, wherever he was hiding, would be left alone against Darkings, Kazimir, and an army of Shesaitju who wanted all Glassmen dead.

"Well, I assure you, I will have word spread that any of my men caught harming one of your people will be punished in kind." He lay his hand upon the dilapidated wall and closed his eyes in deep thought. "This place… it is a graveyard for your people. A cesspool of filth and no place for one of such stunning beauty to dwell."

Just then, Aquira skittered out from behind a pile of rubble. The snake-faced warriors moved to attack.

"No, stop!" Sora shouted. "She's mine."

"Yours?" the man said, raising his hand for his men to obey. "No one can own a dragon."

"She is my companion," Sora corrected. "But she is also no

dragon. She's a wyvern. I know as well as anyone, dragons are no longer with us on this plane."

"In that, I'd argue you are wrong, mystic. My people believe there are plenty of dragons who remain, but like so many in Pantego, they've retreated into solitude in response to the heavy hand of the evil, vile, King Liam and his ilk."

"Is that what this is?" she asked. "A battle for freedom?"

"That is how it began." He took a step toward her. "But then the Child-King Pi dared imprison our great Caleef. His unprovoked attack—"

"Unprovoked?" Sora interrupted. "Your people burned towns to the ground. Homes and businesses—destroyed people's lives."

"How dare you speak to Afhem Muskigo with that insolent tone!" One of the snake-faced men moved toward her, readying the back of his hand to strike her.

"Stop," Muskigo demanded. The soldier froze immediately. Never had Sora seen a man command such respect. His baritone voice even raised the hairs on her arms. "She is right."

Sora wasn't sure who was more surprised at the response, her or his men.

"War makes villains of us all" Muskigo said. "I'm not proud of that which must be done."

"What must be done?" She recognized the name Muskigo from so many rumors on the road to Winde Port. He was the rebel who caused it all. Again, the rage built in her, the storm now crashing upon the shores, tearing trees at the roots and foundations from the earth. She could feel Elsewhere reaching through her very pores, the energy desperate to explode out of her and claim vengeance for Wetzel and so many others.

And then Muskigo spoke again. "You saw those villages?"

Sora thought carefully about how she would answer, and as she did, she noticed the unmistakable pangs of sorrow in his eyes. She didn't know many people throughout her secluded life, but she'd seen that same look every time after Wetzel used to scold her.

"No, but we hear horrible things here at the center of the world," she said, trying to fight back the surge of energy in her fingertips. If she told Muskigo she was in one of those villages, he might know that she was as unimportant as the folks living in the Panping Ghetto. But she still wore her fine dress from the guild, tattered as it was. And he'd seen her with a wyvern, using magic like a true mystic of old—he didn't have to know it took leaking blood for her wounded body to summon it.

Use my assets, she thought.

Suddenly Whitney's lessons didn't seem quite so asinine. She remembered the way Muskigo had eyed her figure when he first saw her. The same way the boorish mercenaries in the caravan by the gorge did. If Whitney—the most cynical and sacrilegious man she'd ever known—could pretend he was a priest of Iam, she could pretend she was more than a girl from Troborough. Until the time was right.

"But I suppose you're right..." Sora said, edging closer and standing up straight, no longer cowering. "They've held us down for far too long. There are likely many of my people in this city who are grateful for your... interference. I would count myself among the lucky for my powers to be put to use against the petulant King and his crazed Queen Mother."

Muskigo exhaled. "It is good to see someone with reason. May I ask, are you from this city? I don't mean to presume, but... a wyvern... practicing magic, you don't—"

"I am not," Sora interrupted. She knelt and extended her arm toward Aquira. The wyvern quickly slithering into the crest of her arm, terrified. "I'm from Yaolin City, but I moved here with my husband, Tayvada Bokeo when we joined the Winde Traders Guild." She hated using poor Tayvada's name like this, but at least it may help her stay alive long enough to get vengeance on the man who murdered him.

"The Traders Guild?" Muskigo said. "I hadn't realized they took on people of your descent. You and your husband must have great influence in your homeland with the Order of Mystics dissolved."

"Late husband," Sora blurted, almost forgetting to hang her head in sadness.

Stupid, Sora. Remember what Whitney would do—keep the subject of your lie wanting.

Despite her mistake, the word "late" put a sparkle in Muskigo's eye which he couldn't mask even if he'd tried.

"I'm so sorry to hear that," he said. "I hope it wasn't due to this unfortunate fighting?"

"No, he was murdered. Some time back. But he lives on in Elsewhere, always waiting until the day I may return to him." A bit of truth never hurt the illusion. She wasn't sure if Whitney had told her that, but was sure she'd learned it from watching him. Tayvada was indeed murdered, and from her studies, she knew that her ancestors didn't fear Elsewhere—the spirit realm—the way the children of Iam and other gods did. To them, it was merely the next step in the soul's journey reflective of a life lived on Pantego.

"I hope that day is long from now," Muskigo said. The sincerity in his voice was unmistakable. "We came here to strike the heart of the Glass Kingdom. Yet seeing how your people are forced to live beneath them, the glory of your ancestors thrown aside, forced into churches of a God in which you don't believe, forced to ignore the flicker of power so many of you are blessed with—I see now that perhaps we have come here for more people than my own."

Sora stuck her chest out and stated, "Or have you merely come here for more allies?" She felt ridiculous, the way she fully annunciated each syllable like the men and women she'd seen in the guild that night. Like she'd grown up in some fancy mansion on the right side of town and not in a basement below a dilapidated shack.

Muskigo's cheeks went a darker shade of gray. "You see right through me…"

"Sora," she said, bowing slightly.

Muskigo returned the bow. "Beautiful name. Though it doesn't sound Panpingese? And your speech; even I can hear you have not the slightest hint of your home in your voice."

Sora's heart raced as she somehow maintained a stoic façade. She knew her chances of survival were slim if she didn't play her cards right. Maybe the Shesaitju were sparing her kind, but not those who try to trick their ahfem. Especially not those who wanted him to pay for his crimes.

"My parents were worldly, or rather… they had to be after the Glass Kingdom disbanded the Order."

Muskigo's dark eyes lit with wonder. "They were Council Mystics?"

Sora nodded and cursed herself inwardly. *Stop spiraling further!* All Whitney's dumb lessons were garbled around in her head, but she knew that the more layers she added to her lie the easier it'd be to slip up. *Simple is better.*

"What surprising things we find here at the edge of despair." Muskigo went to wrap his arm around her waist, earned a growl from Aquira, then lightly took her arm instead. Even the way he stepped was not so brazen anymore, which meant Sora had him intrigued… she hoped. The noblest man she'd ever met was Torsten Unger, and he was impossible to read.

Muskigo regarded her arm, sliced and bleeding in more than one location. "My men did this to you?"

She lowered her head. "They were not so kind as their leader."

"Again, I cannot express how sorry I am. What can a simple afhem do for a true daughter of the mystics to make amends?"

"I... I could use a good meal and some rest."

"Of course, where are my manners? If you waited any longer, you might mistake me for a Glassman. The men of the Black Sands treat our women as we treat the palms..."

His words trailed off there as if he expected her to finish. She tilted her head, then regarded Aquira, who was now starting to get more relaxed.

A crooked smile formed on Muskigo's face.

Is he nervous?

"...We never shake them."

"Now," he continued, "join us within the prefect's estate, and you'll have all the food and rest you need. And I'll ensure one of our physicians examines and cleans your injuries immediately. In fact, all Panpingese men and women are invited to share in the festivities while we will finish the work we've begun; bringing Yarrington to its knees."

Without so much as another thought, Sora took a step forward, and Muskigo's men parted, inviting her into the inner circle. They led her through the city, past the carnage of their wake. She'd missed it from the rooftops of the ghetto because Muskigo wasn't lying, his people didn't seem interested in that place. And her people probably barred their doors shut and closed the shutters like they did every time there was a ruckus in the better parts of town.

Glass soldiers littered the ground like trash. But not just them, civilians too. Merchants, chimney sweeps, anyone born west of the Great Ravine who got caught in a wave of Shesaitju warriors. A few of their ashen bodies stained the ground, but more of them stood. Hundreds, everywhere, being forced to stack the bodies of the dead on carts to wheel them off to Iam knows where. Sora couldn't help but scan every single one for Whitney's ridiculous

Traders Guild outfit.

"So many dead," she muttered. The air felt trapped in her lungs. She squeezed Aquira for comfort without meaning to, but the warm creature didn't seem to mind. Suddenly, Troborough felt so small and far away, and all Muskigo's talk of heroics, which actually had her questioning her dark desires, melted away.

"A forgettable foundation of blood for a brighter future," Muskigo replied.

"Are the lives of these people so frivolous?"

"That is an unfair word. Their deaths will be with me forever. It is the weight I bear, so others don't have to. But it is not only the lives of my enemies who mar these streets and will stain them further tomorrow."

Muskigo stopped and knelt beside a Shesaitju warrior, writhing on the ground, a spear through his gut. He extended his palm and one of his men handed him their sword. He leaned in, cupped the dying warrior's neck, and whispered something into his ear.

Sora knew what was coming. She fought her best intentions to stay quiet. With enough of a blood sacrifice, she knew she could heal him. It would drain her so much she'd probably pass out, but she could. However, it would show Muskigo that she was little more than a blood mage. Plus, why him and not another?

While indecision wracked her mind, Muskigo plunged the blade into the man's heart. Sora had to look away as the life fled his eyes.

"You see?" Muskigo said as he wiped the blade on his skirt and returned it to his guard. "You may look away, for only I need wield the blade that brings their end."

He rose, and they began walking again.

"You could have not brought them here in the first place," Sora said.

"They've pledged their lives to this cause and were all too eager to fall for the glory of our Caleef."

"It must be nice to be so devoted to one man."

Muskigo stopped and in doing so, brought their whole company to a halt.

"Caleef Sidar Rakun is no mere man," he said. "He, like all those who came before him, was birthed from the depths of the Boiling Waters and the churning sand. He is the embodiment of god."

"Which god might that be?" she asked. She knew she might be pushing her luck but couldn't help herself. As much as she hated him for what he'd done, as much as she wanted to give in to the power begging to leap from her body... so too did she hope to understand why her home had to be destroyed, and everyone she knew had to die. "I've heard of many so-called gods, but none of them have lived up to the hype."

Muskigo's dark eyes fell upon her. For a moment, she thought the man would lash out at her, bringing a swift end to her the way Kazimir had to her attackers. Instead, he laughed. "That does not surprise me, Sora of Yaolin City. You have not seen the likes of the God of Sand and Sea."

"I thought your Caleef is your god?"

"He is, and he is so much more. He does not hide behind a name or scripture like Iam, but instead, walks amongst us.

They started moving again over Winde Port's grand, central canal. She ignored the Glass Soldier lying face down on the frozen water but then, she saw worse. All down Merchants Row, the palisade wall surrounding the city was visible. The heads of soldiers dotted the stakes, overlooking where she and Whitney ate on their first day in the city. Her stomach did a spin.

"Speak your mind, Sora of Yaolin City," Muskigo said. Apparently, she hadn't been as proficient at concealing her disgust as she'd hoped.

"It's just…"

"Yes?"

"These people… what did they do to deserve this? The towns you burned. Those were lives, families, people like you and me."

They stopped again, and Muskigo placed his hands upon Sora's shoulders. She winced.

"This is war, mystic. You should know as well as any the consequences of battle. Are you too young to remember the Third Panping War?"

She wondered the same of him. His beard was dark and thick, and his skin was smooth—signs of youth—but his eyes held great depths within. Having lived in Troborough most of her life, she didn't have tremendous experience with Shesaitju. Did they age slower? She wasn't sure if Afhem Muskigo was twice her age or less… or more.

"My parents fled after the war, but I was so young I remember very little of it," she said, allowing herself to look up at the heads.

Crumbs of truth.

She didn't remember a thing of her true parents, but she had a single memory of her ancestral lands. Chaos and screaming… It was why she never cared to go back until her memories of Troborough were forced to be the same.

Muskigo finally decided to wrap his arm all the way around her. Aquira grumbled in disapproval, glare fixed upon the afhem's hand as if daring him to try hurting her. Sora again flinched at his touch, but she didn't fight it as he guided her away and continued their walk toward the palace.

"My father died at the hands of that wretched killer, Liam. To his people, Liam was the great conqueror—uniting Pantego under the banner of his God. In *peace.*" The word left Muskigo's mouth as if it were poison. "But what about us? Did we ask to worship Iam?"

"I suppose not," Sora admitted.

"And now they've imprisoned our Caleef. Would the Glass not have done worse to get their own king back? What would their crazed queen do?"

Sora remembered the bodies hanging from the Yarrington walls in the Queen's mad quest to save her son. It was her first, and she hoped only impression of the Glass Castle.

Before she had a chance to respond, they stopped in front of a beautiful two-story estate. Marble columns supported a balcony that jutted from the upper story. Vast, green, gardens were visible in the courtyard through the lower floors arcade—lush despite the bitter cold.

"Welcome," he said, spreading his arms. "My new home belongs to you. It belongs to all who have long suffered under a Glass boot."

The inside of the palace was as grand and luxurious as the exterior. In the center of the lofty greeting hall was a great hearth set in stone. Shesaitju soldiers sat around the blaze, drinking and laughing as if it were any other day. As if there weren't dead bodies littering the streets of a foreign city just outside the door.

Muskigo snapped and a handmaiden, dressed in clothing more appropriate for a desert than the land north of the beaches, approached them. He whispered something in her ear, and she bowed. Her face was covered by a shawl, but the skin around her eyes was creased with age.

"Now, I have business to attend to preparing our defenses," Muskigo said. "Shavi will take care of anything you need. We shall speak soon, Sora of Yaolin City."

He fell in with a group of gold-armored guards and left the estate. Sora was too overwhelmed by the majesty of the place to muster more than a faint curtsy to bid him farewell.

"Come, dear," the old handmaiden named Shavi said, leading Sora deeper into the place.

Sora followed along. She wasn't excited about the prospect of temporarily sharing the home of an enemy, but she knew it was her best chance at finding Whitney—her best chance because it was the only option that seemed to promise her life. With all the soldiers around, and the daylight filtering in through the great arches of the courtyard, Kazimir wouldn't be able to touch her.

She glanced down at Aquira, who looked up at her. Sora was no expert on wyverns or their facial twitches. Her frills undulated, and her mouth was crooked, with one sharp fang hanging out over her lip. She didn't appear overly nervous, and Sora couldn't blame her.

"Can't be worse than being drained by an upyr," she whispered to the wyvern. Then they entered.

XVII

THE KNIGHT

"By Iam," Torsten said. It was all he could manage as Winde Port appeared on the horizon. It didn't take long leading his army along Muskigo's tracks for him to realize he'd underestimated his enemy. A mass of refugees swarmed the hill. Traders and civilians, guards and dockworkers —anyone who could escape the port city before the wrath of the Black Sands fell upon it. Some were bloodied, many crying, others being carried with Shesaitju arrows protruding from their backs or limbs.

Torsten reached down from his perch atop his horse and grabbed a fleeing city guard by the shoulder. The man looked petrified, hands shaking and sweat pouring from his brow. "Soldier, what happened?"

"The Black Sands... th-they... they..." the man stuttered.

"Spit it out," Wardric grunted.

"They came from the f-fog... thousands of them." He finally seemed to remember the world around him and grabbed Torsten's leg. "My brother. He's still in there. You have to save them."

"We will," Torsten said.

"Only Nesilia can save them now," Redstar remarked.

Torsten glared back at the scourge of his life, then spurred his horse ahead of his army to get a better view. Every thud of his mount's hooves made the refugees shudder. He hadn't seen such frightened people since the Third Panping War, after their great mystics were vanquished and the people were left to clean up their dead.

He rode his horse up a promontory and stared down at the city. Words failed him at the sight. The late King Liam had once called Winde Port 'the key to Pantego,' the fulcrum upon which the East and West swung. It wasn't heavily fortified, even with the defensive measures taken after Torsten returned to Yarrington with news of Muskigo's betrayal more than a month ago. Wooden palisade walls now wrapped the city where it met land, though they remained unfinished at the city's north.

It wasn't anything insurmountable, and that was half the reason Torsten never expected Muskigo to center his invasion of the Glass heartland on it. But he had forgotten the Shesaitju of his youth—the ruthless, godless warlords whom it took every ounce of Liam's brilliance to defeat.

Glass Soldiers were hung by their necks over the palisade walls in the very same manner Oleander had used, some still squirming and alive. The heads of more soldiers crowned many of the pointed stakes comprising the wall itself, and piled in front of it were the decapitated bodies, fortifying defenses with a layer of flesh. Muskigo's savagery made Oleander's killing spurt seem like child's play. Blood rushed to Torsten's head. It was almost as if the afhem mocked her.

And yet, of all of it, that wasn't the worst. From his vantage, Torsten could see a fenced area protruding from the wall, surrounded by spiked barriers. Thousands of Glass civilians were packed inside a camp that appeared as though it had been ransacked. Innocent people tied together by chain and rope like cattle on their way to the slaughterhouse. Gray-skinned Shesaitju warriors stood guard like shepherds over sheep.

Or worse, like butchers.

Not warriors, Torsten realized. They wore little more than tattered rags, and every one of them wielded weapons stolen from the Glass Soldiers. The young King had issued an edict to detain any Shesaitju civilian west of the Walled Lake, and in an instant, Torsten knew that these were those people, spurred to revolt by Muskigo's invasion and making it even easier for them to gain ground.

The King's edict, meant for protection, had collected all those potential enemies in one place. With that, and Torsten falling for the deception of Marimount as the primary target, they'd handed over Winde Port on a silver platter.

"I tried to tell you not everything was as it seemed," Redstar said from behind him. Just the sound of his voice had Torsten clenching his jaw. "Nesilia is many things, but a liar she is not."

"I'm getting tired of hearing about her," Torsten growled, not bothering to look back.

"And I suppose your men will quickly grow tired of a commander who lost a battle without even being present. Where was the all-seeing Eye of Iam when Winde Port needed him?"

"Distracted by snakes in our ranks."

Redstar laughed. "Blame me all you want, but it was your scouts who missed this." He rode up beside Torsten and pointed to the coast of Trader's Bay, south of the city. A light mist loomed over it as it always had in this region. And within that veil of white, tremendous shadows loomed. "That is their fleet, dragged up the coast in the cover of night and fog by their beasts."

He was right. One by one they were being turned by zhulong and heaved into the water, completely blocking off the bay. That was how nobody noticed their fleet sailing in from the south because they hadn't sailed at all. They'd exhausted their beasts hauling their ships, siege weapons and supplies up the oft-rocky, and always foggy coast.

"Whispers. Rebellion. Spiders," Redstar said. Torsten turned back and saw him, calm as could be despite the horrors arrayed before them. "It is what lurks in the darkness that we fear more than anything, isn't it?"

"This is what you hoped for all along; to watch us fail, all because King Liam took your sister and gave her a life worth living in a place worth living in. Do you know why he and Uriah left you behind?"

"Because I committed the awful sin of seeking power that is freely available for those willing to grasp it."

"Because you were a wretched boy, more interested in playing blood magic than caring for your sister. It was your fault. She needed you in a strange new world, and you couldn't shut your mouth, keep your weapon down, and help her."

"Playing?" Redstar sniggered. "Tell me, Torsten Unger... King Liam died of a long, terrible sickness. I wore the skin of Uriah Davies, his Wearer of White after the Goddess Bliss drained the blood from his body. Does that sound like a game to you?"

"Are you admitting to regicide?"

"Heavens no. But *my* goddess is just." He patted his horse's neck like their conversation was nothing more than talk amongst friends. "You were there that fateful day when your 'great' king stole a girl from her home and made her a wicked woman, hanging her own from the parapets. I wonder what will happen to you next?"

Redstar sidled his horse close and laid his hand on Torsten's shoulder. His other hand pointed with the flat edge of a dagger toward the bodies piled and staked before the walls of Winde Port. "How poetic would it be for you to join them?"

Torsten hoisted his claymore off his back scabbard and held it at Redstar's neck. "I could kill you right now for your words."

"I'd be careful if I were you, Sir Unger," Redstar said calmly. "My people are fiercely loyal."

"Are you two ever going to stop bickering?"

Torsten and Redstar whipped around to see Wardric. Behind him, the front ranks of the army stared intently. The Drav Cra warriors squeezed the handles of spiked clubs and spears. The eyes of the Glassmen darted nervously from side to side.

Redstar lowered his blade first. "Not bickering," he said. "Merely discussing strategy."

"Well, tell your savages to back off," Wardric demanded.

"Of course." He bowed his head. "The true enemy is behind those walls, after all." He shot Torsten a smirk, then led his horse back toward his forces.

Torsten could feel the tension in the air like a thick paste, and he realized the mistake he'd made. Driving a wedge further between their combined forces after allowing himself to be fooled was the last thing he needed. He wasn't ignorant to the whispers as they marched through the bodies of Citravan's slaughtered legion from Winde Port. Redstar's people, saying how Nesilia predicted this, his own, fearing that Iam had abandoned them.

"Wardric," he said.

"Yes, sir?"

"Set up camp on this hillside," Torsten said. "I will ride into the city."

"For what?" Wardric asked, clearly perturbed by the idea.

"I plan to speak with the rebel."

"You've already heard all he had to say at Marimount. Look at the wall. This man has no honor. If he gets the chance, he will string you up with the rest of them."

"Then the Shield will be left in your capable hands."

"Sir, it is the King's decision who serves as his Wearer of

White." He shot a sidelong glare Redstar's way. "If you are lost, there is no saying who would replace you."

Torsten brought his horse right before Wardric's and leaned in close. "Barely a man outside the King's Shield has fought in a war. Even fewer of them against the Shesaitju, and already, we have lost a battle."

"That was barely a battle, it was a sacrifice."

"We lost to one hundred ghosts in the fog. What do you think is running through their minds, seeing that city overrun? It's exactly what Muskigo wants."

"How do you know?" Wardric asked.

"Because it's what Liam would have done—sewn fear until our army sees them as more than men. It started when they burned down villages during the sacred cycle of mourning. Lights in the trees. Fire. We only lost a handful of soldiers yet half of those remaining shiver in fear."

"Losing you won't help."

"No," Torsten agreed, "but it will show them that one of us Glassmen isn't afraid. Now, follow your orders." He sped off toward Winde Port before he could be dissuaded. Unclasping his cape as he rode, he raised it in the air as he headed straight for the gate.

A westerly breeze blew out from the bay, making the hanging bodies swing and bang against the wall like bamboo wind chimes. It also carried with it the fresh stench of chaos and death. Screams still echoed from the city as the Shesaitju's conquering of Winde Port was made complete.

Torsten instinctually reached for his necklace and squeezed the Eye of Iam hanging from it, the gift from his former king which he'd only once removed—never again.

And he prayed.

He prayed for all the poor souls hanging because he shifted all his cards toward Marimount. He prayed for his kingdom, King, and Queen Mother. And mostly, he prayed for himself. He brought his horse to a halt at the gate and swung his legs down, then removed his helmet, leaving his sword sheathed in its back scabbard. Approaching the gate with his hands raised in front of him, he heard bow strings creak and tighten in the hands of the Shesaitju glaring down at him from atop the wall. Chains of their new captives rattled from the detainment camp, the sound of whips ringing across the foul air any time one of them tried to speak.

"Muskigo!" he bellowed. "This is over." How recently had the situation been reversed? It had only been a matter of hours when Muskigo arrived at the base of Marimount threatening to bring the Glass Kingdom to its knees. Now, Torsten stood, the one looking up at walls—only these were far from a dwarven fortress. Winde Port's construction was slapdash, barely reinforced but for the corpses stacked before them.

The heavy iron grated open and the doors swung wide. It was only then Torsten saw that the Winde Port cathedral was defaced. The golden Eye of Iam atop its roof was shattered and all its intricate stained-glass windows just a latticework of shards.

Heathen monsters.

A dozen Serpent Guards, all clad in gold filed out, scimitars in hand, faces covered as if they were scaled demons from Elsewhere. From between them, rode Muskigo atop his prodigious zhulong.

His bare, tattooed torso was covered in gooseflesh from the cold winds and the blood of his enemies. And now that Torsten could see the man's dark eyes, he remembered how intense they were, like a storm brewing over the Torrential Sea.

"Do you like what I've done with the place?" Muskigo asked. "I took some inspiration from your queen, but the rest was me. Just one last finishing touch." His hands came out from behind his back, revealing the two severed heads he gripped.

Torsten recognized them.

One belonged to Winde Port's Prefect, Mortimer Calhoun, a distant cousin of the Nothhelms who'd presided over the city for many decades. The other was the city's priest. Torsten regretted not knowing the man's name, but the cloth covering his brow made his position unmistakable.

He raised them both by their gray hair. "I couldn't decide which would look better hanging from the gates."

Torsten stared at the gaping mouth of the priest and couldn't help but trace his own eyes in prayer for the poor soul. Muskigo shrugged and rolled them both across the mud and snow.

"So, I took both."

"You will pay for this," Torsten said.

"And here I thought you came to debate the finer points of decor. My lights in the forest were a nice touch, I thought."

"You won't last in there, Muskigo. This is our land. You'll starve and freeze until your own people would rather hand you over than keep fighting this futile rebellion."

"I don't think so, Wearer. See, news of your weakness spreads like wildfire across the Black Sands. Soon, all will throw off their shackles and join us. So long as we own the bay, we will eat like caleefs. And I may only just be getting acquainted with this city, but I've found the old prefect's estate quite hospitable."

Torsten bit his lip in frustration. "This doesn't end with you surviving, you must know that."

"Our ancestors believed that death in the glory of combat was the only way to reach the shores of paradise. If that is my fate, I will not blink an eye. Will you? Will your Iam forgive you all this bloodshed?"

"If it means stopping a monster?"

"Monster?" He raised his arms to gesture to all the swaying and decapitated bodies. "A monster stands beside your throne, and Iam rewards her by breathing life back into her son. I hear he whispers to himself in the night as if he's lost his mind."

"Enough, Muskigo," Torsten snapped. "It's time we end this. Let all those innocent people go. Face me, on that field, the right hands of our respective kings."

"You dare mention my Caleef whom you hold captive within your walls?" Muskigo swung his legs off his zhulong and approached. He too wielded no weapon. In stature, he was a head shorter than Torsten, but his entire frame was laced with muscle. And now that Torsten saw him even closer, he noticed more scars than he could count speckled amongst the white tattoos.

The arms of the Shesaitju archers, still holding arrows at the ready, shook as their leader stepped into their aim. He didn't stop until Torsten could feel the warmth of his breath.

"Long ago, Liam Nothhelm issued my father the same challenge," Muskigo said. "I was just a child then, you probably no more than a squire. And do you know what happened?"

Torsten's hands balled into tight fists within his glaruium gauntlets. He could reach out and break the man's neck if arrows didn't shred him first. Instead, he stood, unspeaking. Defiant.

"My father was foolish enough to accept," Muskigo continued. "He died that day, his afhemate fell, and the Glass Kingdom crept ever nearer to the Caleef's sacred seat in Latiapur, which, of course, was conquered as well."

"At least he had the honor to spare your people," Torsten said.

"The heads of the afhems were hung from the palms like so many coconuts. Our wives were cast into exile—likely raped by your savages. My mother took her own life in shame. All my father did was help grow the legend of Liam the *Coward.*" He spit.

Torsten ignored the insult.

"Then defeat me," he said. "Prove you're better."

"There is not a doubt in my mind I would slice your throat

open before you could even cry in protest. But you are not Liam Nothhelm. You are not even Uriah Davies, who, as Wearer, earned so many victories in the name of king and God. You are a disgrace to that helm. Nobody. Less than nobody—the hand of a murderous shrew."

Torsten reached for his claymore. The Serpent Guards unsheathed theirs in unison. The archers, whose grip had slackened, drew their strings back farther.

"Do it," Muskigo whispered, smiling. "Do. It."

More than anything, Torsten wanted to oblige him. His hand shook with rage. Sweat poured down his neck only to be kissed by the bitter wind. The entire city went quiet watching, waiting until finally, he lowered his hand.

Muskigo shook his head. "How far the Glass has fallen. Return to your people, Torsten Unger. Tell them they can bring Drav Cra, Panpingese, even the damnable dwarves... you will all die together." He turned to walk back to his zhulong.

"Do not turn your back on me, heathen!" Torsten ordered.

"Go back to your people and pray to your God," Muskigo said, hand upon the saddle of his terrifying beast. Raising one arm toward his throng of chained captives, he shouted, "Because the moment you try and retake this city, every single one of them will help me finish decorating this wall."

He led his zhulong through the gates, never turning to face Torsten. He did, however, snap his fingers and arrows zipped into the ground at Torsten's feet, purposely missing but forcing him back to his horse before it fled. As he pulled himself onto the saddle, thousands of captives were whipped and forced to move, bound together in bunches, and one by one sent to spread across the length of Winde Port's palisade walls—to sit upon the piled corpses of soldiers.

A human barrier.

Torsten could charge, his army could surmount the clumsy

walls, but doing so would mean sacrificing his own people. And it was then, as his horse backed away, he understood just how long a game Muskigo was playing.

If Torsten brought his army east over the Jarein Gorge to maintain control over the Shesaitju lands, the Glass heartland would be exposed. If he stayed, Muskigo would dig in and sew unrest throughout the Shesaitju cities until the Crown's control over his conquered people eroded.

They were at an impasse. Muskigo denied his challenge because he knew that as well as Torsten did. There was only one clear choice for Torsten, impossible as it may have been. He had to do whatever it took to cut the head off the serpent. To kill Muskigo.

XVIII

THE MYSTIC

Sora stared down into the warm water of a bath in one of the prefect's estate's many luxurious chambers. Afhem Muskigo's handmaidens drew it for her, giving her no choice but to try it. Before she knew what was happening, she was spinning out of her tattered dress and covering her privates with her hands and forearms, simultaneously hiding the countless scars on them.

She did her best not to protest. A woman of wealth and circumstance like she'd claimed to be would have experience with warm baths. In reality, she'd never cleaned off with anything but running river water.

Aquira had no problem getting comfortable. She was as calm as Sora had seen her since the moment they met. She lay, her long, scaled body sprawled out along the rim of the opposite side of the bath. Her eyes were closed, tail and one wing hanging down, swishing through the water. Thin lines of smoke escaped her thin nostrils every time she snored.

"Go on, dear," Shavi said.

Sora sighed, then stepped in one leg at a time. The water stung the many wounds striping her body as she lowered herself. She gritted her teeth, the pain didn't last long and after it dissipated, was well worth it. The warm water was like a healing salve now that her adrenaline wasn't pumping and she realized how beaten and bruised her body was from fleeing Kazimir. She could draw on her own power and sacrifice to heal others, but she'd never been able to do the same for herself.

Kazimir...

Her eyes flitted toward the window behind Aquira. Sora had ordered them not to be covered by the cascading, velvet drapes. He was somewhere out there, hunting. The only thing that allowed her to try and stay calm was the fact that she was now in probably the safest place in all of the city. Wherever Muskigo was, those gold-clad protectors were with him.

She sunk back further until her entire head was submerged and the window was just a pale light beneath the rippling water. All the sounds of the world were drowned out. It was like she was weightless. She tried to close her eyes, but every time she did, all she could see was Kazimir's devilish grin.

So, from beneath the water, she screamed. She screamed at the top of her lungs until face was surrounded by bubbles. When she returned to the surface, it was like a weight being lifted off her shoulders. She could finally relax and enjoy a luxury she never imagined she'd know.

Shavi knelt behind her, grabbed a clump of her now wet hair, and ran a comb through it.

"Your hair is knotted like I've never seen, my dear," she said, ignoring the scream. Her voice rattled with age.

"I travel too much," Sora replied softly.

"A woman like you shouldn't have to."

Sora turned to face her so Shavi would stop brushing, startling the old women. "Does the afhem treat all of his guests like this?"

"I could lie and say yes."

"I just... it seems so wrong being in here bathing while people are suffering out there."

"People are suffering everywhere, at all times, my dear—"

"Sora."

Shavi's shawl lifted revealing a soft smile. "Sora," she said as if in wonder of the name. "Take every rare chance at reprieve you can. Trust me, I've been around a few years."

"As a servant," Sora remarked, then immediately regretted it.

"I am no servant. I could walk through that door anytime I wish, and not a soul would touch me. I've willingly served the family of Muskigo Ayerabi since I was as young and pretty as you are."

"I... thank you. I meant no offense."

"I take none." Shavi took Sora's hair and again began brushing it. "We women of the Black Sands may not be warriors, but the depths of the sea are not unreachable. Our men die in battle to please the God of Sand and Sea, but we bring those men into this plane through womb and water. We feed them. Ensure their houses do not fall. And a life lived in service to our people is as worthy as one lived in war."

"I'm sorry, I don't know much about your people," Sora said. In fact, the only thing she really did know is that their warlords like Muskigo were renowned and that his men slaughtered Troborough and all those other innocent villages, seemingly without a second thought.

"There is more to us than war, my de—Sora."

"It seems like that's all there is to anybody these days."

"It comes in tides like the rising of the sea. Men are born, they fight, they die, and we are left to make the ruin in their wake shine. And people say us women are powerless." She leaned forward and winked. "We're all that really matters."

"Talking another girl's ear off, Shavi?" Muskigo asked from the doorway. Now that they were out of public sight, he had furs over his bare shoulders. His scimitar hung from his hip, harmless.

Shavi wasn't alarmed in the slightest by the sight of him, but Sora threw her arms over her body as if she could even be seen over the gold-trimmed rim of the tub. Aquira sprung awake, flipping over and nearly slipping into the water. Her frills went back, and she showed her teeth at the uninvited guest.

"You should know better than to interrupt a woman's bath, Muskigo," Shavi scolded. No titles, no proper names or bowing. She talked to the afhem as if she was his mother.

"My apologies." Muskigo raised a bowl. "I came to offer our esteemed guest a proper meal before it runs out."

Shavi stood, walked over to him to take the bowl, and returned to Sora. She didn't even bow or offer thanks.

"Here you go, dear," she said to Sora.

Sora glanced back at the afhem before taking it. He didn't smile, but he watched with an anxious look on his face. His features only seemed to relax when she grabbed it as quick as possible so her arm wouldn't be visible above the water long.

"What is it?" she asked.

"A Latiapur delicacy. It was my mother's recipe."

"You cooked this?"

Shavi laughed. "That boy hasn't made a meal in his entire life."

"Enough, Shavi," Muskigo said. "Let her eat."

Sora took another look at the afhem. He still stood in the doorway, but she couldn't believe how eager he seemed. He, the rebel who had ordered the destruction of her home, who had sacked Winde Port and staked the heads of his enemies at the gates, was waiting on her... to see if she liked his food.

Sora cursed herself inwardly for feeling such pride over that fact. Her chin was held high as she raised the bowl to her lips and took a sip of the chunky stew. An involuntary moan of pleasure escaped her lips as the broth hit her tongue.

"Good, no?" Muskigo asked.

"Deli—" she cleared her throat. "It's not bad," she said, a bit of the stuff spilling over her bottom lip and down her chin. Out of the corner of her eyes, she noticed that he'd crept further into the room.

"You're a terrible liar, Sora of Yaolin City." He chuckled.

She looked back. He took another step forward but Aquira objected, soaring over the tub and up onto Sora's shoulder. Sora had to quickly lift the bowl to keep it from spilling. The wyvern's sharp claws dug into her skin, drawing pinpoints of red. Her body was so used to being cut she barely felt it.

"And your friend needn't be so protective," Muskigo added.

"She's been through a lot," Sora said. "We both have."

"I only sought to help clean your mouth with a meal that *wasn't bad.*"

He pointed to his chin. Sora did the same and realize a chunk of stew was stuck there. Her face grew hot—first, because she was blushing, then from anger because she realized she was blushing.

Keep it together. You're not a little girl playing princess. This man is a murderer.

But who was she to talk? Did she not recently trick a caravan full of men into aiding her and then rob them of everything they had? She considered the men in the caravan. It was the Shesaitju among those brutes who treated her with respect, just as Muskigo was now. But she also remembered what Whitney told her—how they were at the attack on Troborough ordered by Muskigo and did nothing to help.

They deserved it, she thought.

"Leave her be, Muskigo," Shavi said, continuing to brush Sora's hair. "Women are permitted to eat however they please."

"Of course, Shavi," Muskigo said. "I would never think otherwise. I simply want to be sure the lady enjoys some of the finer things our people have to offer."

"Well, *be sure* over there." Shavi pointed to the door. "How did I help raise such a man who would pry on a stranger in a bath?"

Now it was Muskigo's turn to blush.

Aquira crept down from Sora's shoulder as he backed away, but she didn't go far, and she kept her piercing yellow eyes on him. Sora took another sip of her meal. The stew wasn't quite like anything she'd ever tasted, and Wetzel had been no stranger to whipping together random concoctions for her to try. His famous rabbit foot soup could make a pig vomit, and his herb mixes, which he said would help her "unlock her powers," were even worse.

"What is this anyway?" Sora asked.

"Zhulong stew," Shavi answered.

"It's so tender though," she exclaimed. "I would expect zhulong to be tough." They were dirty, smelly, scary beasts. Not the kind of animal she was used to eating.

"You will find it is not only the zhulong whose outward appearance is a poor reflection of what lies inward," Muskigo said with a smile, lips crooked, all the confidence oozing off him as his commanding façade faded.

Sora nearly choked on her next mouthful. She wasn't sure if Muskigo was just being kind to her because he thought she had worthwhile connections in Panping, but now she knew it was much more than that. The way he regarded her wasn't lecherous like drunks in a tavern either. It was the same way someone else looked at her in those rare moments of vulnerability… Whitney.

"Anyway, I'm glad to see you are satisfied," Muskigo said, breaking her train of thought. "When you're finished, Shavi will find proper clothing and somewhere you'll be able to sleep."

Sora glanced up from the bowl.

"Nothing nefarious, you have my word. There's not a man within these walls who would trifle with you now that we are friends."

This time she actually did choke. She had to hit her chest to get the piece of zhulong to tumble down her throat.

Friends.

Playing this role was all fine and good for survival's sake, but hearing him call her that had rage mounting within her again. She could feel the water around her begin to boil.

"Sora?" Muskigo said.

She hadn't realized he'd been speaking, so caught up in her thoughts as she was. "Oh, sorry..." she muttered.

"I have more planning to attend to with my commanders, but I'm glad to see you cleaned up. Tomorrow, if you are ready, I hope we may discuss plans for inviting your people to this fight for freedom. I have been in need of a liaison with the ability to reach out to Panping, and I believe I may have found that in you. Sleep well."

"Of course," Sora said softly. "I'm looking forward to it."

He smiled again, that same reticent look that spoke of many more intentions than wanting an ally. Then he turned to walk away, a host of faceless warriors in the hall falling in around him.

"He's more bark than bite," Shavi said once he was gone.

"The headless bodies outside might not think so," Sora snapped before she could stop herself. "Sorry, it's just... seeing all of that... I remember what happened to my people."

"No need to apologize, dear. Sometimes when I look at him, I still see the young boy I cared for while his father was out fighting King Liam. He's not that anymore, is he?" She laughed, and Sora couldn't help but smirk.

"Not at all."

"No, but he is a better man than the horror you see outside.

Now, lay back. I'll get your hair so cleaned out you won't have to worry about it for years."

Sora did as she asked. While Shavi went to work, her gaze listed back toward the window where the occasional scream of pain rang out thanks to the war outside. Perhaps Muskigo wasn't the horrible monster deserving death who she'd been imagining since the day she left Troborough behind, but just because he wasn't Kazimir didn't mean Whitney's views on people like him were wrong.

Lords and ladies always appear impressive, but they don't care a lick for the people they step on to get what they want—no matter how much they claimed to. Whether in the name of gods or freedom, the ends were always the same... and only the people suffered for them.

Even if Sora could never bring herself to be the one to drive a knife into his heart, she'd never help him. And she'd certainly never sit at his royal side and become a person like him. No matter how much of his wealth, wiles, or charms he threw at her.

XIX

THE KNIGHT

Torsten tested the ropes on a newly-erected tent. They were loose, the fabric flapping in the wind. What better could he expect from an army that had never set camp before? Untried. Untested.

He lay his hand on the arm of a soldier. "Stake those in deeper," he said. "Or you'll be sleeping in the cold."

"Yes, sir," the young man saluted.

"And you," Torsten pointed to another, "get a fire started. Staying warm is the difference between life and death."

"Wouldn't want the puny Glassmen getting cold," murmured Drad Mak as he strolled by, a cracked battle axe propped against his shoulder.

"Ignore them," Torsten said. "Out here, the Black Sands aren't our enemy. The elements are. The Shesaitju aren't used to being so far north. With Iam on our side, we'll outlast them."

"A weak god, for a weak people. You should hear their villagers squeal and run when my warriors arrive to take their crops. Not a man among them." Mak laughed again.

Torsten paid him no mind. He couldn't, even as arguing broke out between them and some nearby Glassmen. If he stopped every time one of Redstar's men insulted one of his own he'd be busy for days.

The men remained shaken by what happened at Marimount. The bodies dangling from the walls of Winde Port didn't help either. Nor did the biting cold.

Torsten sighed and pulled his cloak a bit tighter. He remembered something King Liam used to say to former Wearer Uriah, "War has no schedule, no fixed times of meeting. The better prepared army always wins, and it is a leader's job to have his men ready for anything, at any time."

Like most of Liam's lessons, it was quite simple, at least until panic settled in. And fear of loss and life. Uriah, however, was never rattled. He'd walk the camp before battle, and just the sight of him in his pearl-white armor was enough for Torsten to know they couldn't fail.

As Torsten strolled by, offering nods of encouragement to different groups of soldiers, he wondered if he instilled that same courage.

How could I after Marimount?

Riding fearlessly to meet with Muskigo at the gates might have helped, but until they defeated him in battle, Torsten knew he was no Uriah. Not even close.

"Hang the traitor!" a voice cracked through the nervous din of preparations. Torsten turned and saw a bit of commotion. He expected to see another brawl between Drav Cra and Glassmen but realized that a few of them stood side by side, yelling at something together. He hurried over.

"What is the meaning of this?" he asked, pushing some men aside.

"Look what we found, sir," a Glass soldier said. He had a Shesaitju on his knees and kicked him in the back so hard the man hit the dirt. "A raincloud sneaking about."

"One of Muskigo's spies, no doubt," said another.

"I do not know what you are talking about!" the Shesaitju man protested, earning another boot to his spine. He had the look of a fighter—strong jaw, hard body, only he wore furs and boiled leather armor that looked western in origin. His black lips trembled with real fear.

"And who are they?" Torsten asked. Also kneeling in the mud behind the Shesaitju were two identical-looking men in unmarked armor who were unquestionably mercenaries, a stocky, red-bearded dwarf, and an old man dressed in silks that appeared to have at one point been of excellent craftsmanship. Now his clothing was tattered and his features just as ragged, with all the others not faring much better.

"We be silk traders ye no-good, flower pickin—" The dwarf's rant was interrupted as Mak the Mountainous arrived to spit on him.

"Go crawl back underground, dirtmonger." Mak said as he walked by and went to punch him but Torsten caught his arm. He knew there was no love lost between the two peoples. Their lands shared a border in the north, and even though the dwarves lived beneath the mountains, that didn't mean their riches were any less sought after.

"Enough," Torsten said. Drad Mak turned, daggers in his eyes. Torsten didn't flinch.

The men halted their barrage on the odd group of travelers but kept them on the ground—especially, the dwarf, who thrashed and cursed in ways Torsten didn't think were possible.

Torsten approached the old man and knelt. "Who are you?"

"I…I'm a simple merchant," he stammered.

"He's helping the spy!" someone shouted from the quickly growing crowd. Torsten glared back at him, then turned his attention back to the merchant.

"I swear in the name of Iam! These men are my protection, Grint Strongiron's company."

"Who is that?" Torsten asked.

"Me ye dolt!" the wobbly-eyed dwarf barked. "Finest company west of the lake."

"A merchant?" Torsten asked. The man nodded emphatically. "Where are your goods?"

"We were on our way to Winde Port to meet with the Traders Guild when we were set upon by bandits. They stole our caravan, my wares, everything. We hoped to find them in the city, but then this…"

"Finest company, yet you were taken by a couple of bandits?"

"Wouldn't have happened if anybody listened to me," the dwarf grumbled. "Never stop on the road to help a pretty woman, I tell ye. Especially not a knife-ear witch."

Torsten's brow furrowed. "Did you say Panpingese witch?"

"I said *knife-ear*. Her pretty boy mate stole the caravan while we tried to help her. By Meungor's axe, that's what we get for trying to be good citizens."

"Keep telling yourself that Grint," the Shesaitju said.

"She wasn't no witch," another one said.

"Might as well've been, the way she conned ye," the dwarf said.

"Conned you, too."

"Not another word out of you, spy!" the soldier restraining him snapped and shoved him back into the dirt.

Torsten looked into the terror-stricken eyes of the old trader, then couldn't help but smirk. It wasn't that he endorsed thieving, but he had a feeling he knew exactly who was behind what happened. It was Whitney, the newly minted noble, and Sora, the Panpingese blood mage who Iam saw fit to use as his vessel back in the Webbed Woods, saving them from Redstar's wrath.

"All right, everyone off them," Torsten ordered. "They're telling the truth."

His own men looked at him, perplexed. Mak the Mountainous scoffed.

"The gray man stays," he grizzled. "By edict of *your* king."

"Don't you see what happened to Winde Port because of that?" Torsten said. "We're safer with him far away from here."

"I promise, we will go far... very far..." the Shesaitju mercenary stammered.

"Safer still with him dead!" Mak shouted to a chorus of agreement from all those present. "Why should we listen to you anyway? It wasn't the King's choice to go to Marimount, I hear."

Torsten kept his head high. "No, but that doesn't mean locking every Shesaitju behind a wall is right."

Mak laughed and turned to a crowd of his people. A warlock stood, emotionless, amongst fur-clad warriors. Torsten wasn't sure he'd fully realized how much of his army wasn't his own until then. How many weren't even faithful to Iam.

"So now the Wearer doubts his own king, the beloved nephew of Arch Warlock Redstar!" Mak announced. "Yet we're supposed to follow him into battle, bells on our ears?"

"He'll let the gray men slaughter us!" shouted another. "I say kill the spy!"

Mak brandished his axe while others held the trading crew down. Grint's company writhed and shouted in protest. The axe went up, but before it fell, Torsten swung his giant claymore to stop it.

"Enough!" Torsten's thunderous roar combined with the clang of metal brought an abrupt end to the fighting. "We are together in this fight, whether any of you likes it or not. King Pi shares the blood of both our peoples. Can we not work together to bring glory to his name?"

Everyone watched in silence. Drad Mak didn't let off his axe or soften his glare. The Shesaitju warrior scurried away through the dirt toward his crew.

"We'll play nice when you get on your knees, kiss the ground, and thank the goddess for your existence," Mak said, seething.

"How dare you speak to our Wearer that way!" the Glass soldier holding the dwarf yelled.

"He is nothing to me."

Both sides erupted. Punches were thrown. Someone tackled someone, and Torsten couldn't see much more in the cloud of dust and snow that formed as a scrum broke out. All he was sure to do was shove the dwarf, trader, and the mercenary crew out of the way.

"Winde Port is under occupation," he told them. "I suggest you head back the way you came." He regarded the Shesaitju man who was clearly shaken. Torsten was smart enough to know the man had nothing to do with this rebellion. Lost on the road without a wagon thanks to Whitney, they probably didn't have any idea there even *was* a rebellion. "And I'd suggest keeping him out of any taverns."

"Flower picking humans," the dwarf groaned. "This is why I prefer the Dragon's Tail. Let's go, boys. Leave the knights to their foolish quarrels." He gave the old trader a nudge, shocking the man who was busy staring at the brawl.

Torsten watched them leave, then squeezed the grip of his sword. The sounds of fighting and cursing were deafening. He went to turn, to demand order when a familiar voice stayed his hand.

"Better off letting them vent, sir," Wardric said, approaching on horseback from the side.

"They'll kill each other before we get anywhere," Torsten replied.

"They won't," Wardric assured him. "I've been thinking— yeah, I do that from time to time—if we lose, Redstar loses. The

Black Sands will wipe him out as well and whatever influence he plans on gaining over the Crown will die with him."

"Is it wrong that a part of me thinks that might be preferable?" Torsten looked across the field to Redstar who was barely fazed by the chaos. He sat in a circle beside Freydis and a group of Drav Cra warlocks all covered head to toe in furs and small, heathen tokens and bones. A dire wolf lay at his back, sleeping. They had candles arrayed in a circle between them, lines of blood crossing between them.

"I fear that man's devotion to his goddess above any army in this land," Torsten said.

"I'm with you sir, but if we face all our enemies at the same time—"

"They'll pick us off like wolves, I know. Which is why I hope not to fight a battle here."

"But starving Muskigo out won't work."

Torsten looked up the hill they were camped on. A group of horses clomped in from the northwest along with a gold-trimmed carriage. They flew the blue of the Glass Kingdom, but flying proudly above the carriage was another standard—a family crest, a ship with a coin.

"Right on schedule," Torsten said. "Come with me, I have a plan."

They returned to the center of the camp where several tents stood in a defensive position. The King's Shield tents were more lavish than the rest, but Torsten was beginning to appreciate why. Most of the men of his order had spent years training. They needed to stay warm and well-fed if there was any chance of defeating Muskigo's rebellion.

A map of the Winde Port region was unfurled atop a small,

round table. There was no need for figurines to show where Muskigo was. He owned the entire city, from Merchants Row to Trader's Bay.

"You invited me?" Redstar said as he approached, a gray dire wolf at his side. The giant creature weaved in and out of a line of King's Shieldsmen, making each of them quiver.

"The time to decide our next move has come," Torsten said.

"For someone so loyal to Iam, you spend an awful lot of time believing you have any control over our next move."

"A man who walks no path cannot be steered to a new one."

"A convenient sentiment." Redstar clapped his hands, then plopped down on the seat at the end of the table. A seat reserved for Torsten during war meetings. "Now, I can't wait to hear this plan."

Wardric scowled at him. Torsten raised a calming hand. A seat was no more than a seat so long as they all worked in concert.

"Muskigo is everything," Torsten said. "His ruse has inspired his followers to believe they can win even though they lost more than we at Marimount. He thinks he can dig in here and hold us while more Shesaitju rebellions spring up across the southern peninsula. And he's right."

"Sir?" Wardric asked, incredulous.

A flicker of interest showed on Redstar's birthmarked face. He leaned forward and started twirling the tip of his dagger on the table.

"To attack head on is to sacrifice the lives of his captives and a vast portion of our combined army," Torsten said. "I won't allow the King's people to die in chains."

"How very unlike your benefactors," Redstar remarked. "Liam would've trampled them himself if it meant victory. And my sister... well... we've all seen firsthand how she feels about her subjects."

"That's enough out of you!" Wardric growled. "If you have nothing to add, you might as well leave."

"Shall I take my people with me?"

Wardric bit his lip. "Just show some damn respect to your Wearer."

"My apologies." Redstar pointed his dagger with a limp wrist. "Proceed, my Lord."

Torsten caught himself staring at Redstar. Normally, one with such a grotesque birthmark covering half his face, making the eyebrow scraggily and gray, wouldn't have been so confident. Torsten had been waiting since the moment they departed Yarrington for him to drop his smirk, yet it seemed permanently affixed.

"Yes," Torsten sighed, tearing his gaze away. He pointed to a spot on the map: the heart of the city. "The prefect of... late prefect of Winde Port... lived on this estate. Our scouts on the ridge tell me that Muskigo's Serpent Guards stand outside as he makes himself comfortable within."

"A conqueror with taste," Redstar remarked, back to spinning his dagger. "I like him already."

"We have a chance to end this before it escalates, to kill Muskigo and persuade the Caleef to sign a new treaty aimed to spare his people the same fate."

"Sir, that estate is old as the Glass itself," Wardric said, "in the most well-defended portion of the entire city along Merchant Canal."

"And that's why we will come from beneath," a new voice said.

Yuri Darkings entered the tent and lowered his hood. His finely embroidered leather jacket could be confused for armor, but Torsten knew it was all for show. Just one of the puffy sleeves could feed South Corner for half a year.

The longtime Master of Coin was back where he belonged.

No longer hiding from the wrath of the Queen, he was every bit the picture of the wealth the Glass Kingdom brought with it to the lands it touched. His gray hair was perfectly combed, mustache trimmed above his lip. But more importantly, he had the tanned skinned of a man from Winde Port where the sun shone but for a few months of winter and when the morning fog rolled through.

"Lord Darkings, I'm glad you could finally join us." Torsten bowed.

"Apologies for the wait, Wearer," he replied. "I didn't stop even for a bite to eat after receiving your message." He turned to Redstar. "Ah, and the royal uncle. I hear you are the one I should thank for talking sense into our young king and getting me my old post back."

"I have an eye for men of value," Redstar said. He nodded, but for a moment Torsten thought he could see a flicker of surprise in the man's features—as if Yuri's arrival wasn't something he'd calculated into his plans.

"Yes, well, Lord Darkings is from Winde Port," Torsten said. "In fact, before Liam named him Master of Coin for the whole kingdom, he served as such for Prefect Calhoun."

"How is the old badger?"

Torsten hung his head. "He is with Iam now." He decided it best not to elaborate on how Muskigo had rolled the man's head across the ground like no more than a worthless piece of trash.

Yuri traced his eyes in prayer. "I'm sorry I couldn't be here sooner."

"There is nothing anyone could have done. The man now enjoying the comfort of his halls is a monster bent on vengeance."

"And now, so am I." Yuri bent over the map and scanned it intently. He ran his finger back and forth, then stopped at a bluff a short way north of the city on the western side of the Winder's River. "Here," he said.

"What is it?" Wardric said.

"There is an old tunnel that leads out here, branching off the sewer lines. Merchants once used it to smuggle contraband before the Winde Traders Guild took control."

Redstar chuckled, purposefully loud.

"What?" Torsten questioned.

"Nothing. I'm simply amused by his use of the word contraband. You Glass folk are so terrified to admit what you truly are, it's maddening."

"And what is that?" Wardric said.

Redstar grinned. "The same as everybody else."

"Are you finished?" Yuri said before anybody could respond, a harsh edge to his tone. "I don't care what you are to the King, or what recommendations you stole from Sir Unger and claim as your own. In regards to me, you have no title, and you will not interrupt a member of the Royal Council again."

Torsten coughed in shock. Redstar's dagger spun too far and fell off the table.

"Now, if I may continue." Yuri cleared his throat. "These tunnels lead beneath Winder's Wharf and tie into the sewers leading directly beneath the prefect's estate. The Shesaitju haven't the luxury of building atop dwarven ruins. The sands do not permit sewers, leaving their... filth to be funneled through an aboveground system. They will not be mindful of the tunnels beneath them."

The man had a gravitas which even Redstar seemed to respect. Torsten had never seen him speak out much while Liam was alive, but that was no longer the case. Now, he was the oldest on the Royal Council by decades, old enough to remember when the Glass Kingdom only comprised a small corner of Pantego. When even Winde Port was a lawless, free-trading city without a Crown.

"Precisely," Torsten said. "Yuri has a contact in the city who will lead me and a small cohort of our finest men beneath the estate. We will end Muskigo's reign of terror before they know what hits them."

"And if you fail?" Redstar said.

"We won't."

Redstar stood and circled the table, his glare fixed on Yuri. "The city teems with gray skins. If any spots your torches before you make it, they'll be on top of you in seconds. Are you really going to hand me lead over this great army so easily?"

"No, because you and your wolves and your finest men are going to come with us. They will help Yuri's men navigate the dark without need of torches, and I've seen what you are capable of. If we're unable to take Muskigo down by blade, you'll bring the entire estate down around us."

"My, my, Sir Unger, now you're so willing to abuse my unholy gifts?"

"Countless lives are at stake. I have to believe Iam brought you to our side for a reason. But with our finest warriors working together, I have no doubt we will succeed."

"So, let me get this straight. You want me to sacrifice my best people for this impulsive plan, and if things go wrong, which knowing you they no doubt will, give my life for the Glass?" Redstar chuckled.

"If it's meant to be."

"My apologies, Sir Unger. But I must reject this plan."

"You don't get to."

Redstar chuckled again. "You see, Wearer, that is where you are wrong. I've beseeched my goddess for guidance, and hers are the only orders I will heed. She warned me you would send us on a suicide mission. She tells me that if we wait and pray, we will know the time to strike when the cold is driven away by wind and flame."

"You would cower back here until spring?" Wardric said.

"If the goddess wills it. Or do you forget the last time we ignored her warning and allowed Torsten here to lead us astray."

Torsten's anger was cooled only by noticing a few of the King's Shieldsmen surrounding the tent, watching. "The cryptic messages you concoct aren't a warning, Redstar. They are an excuse for cowardice. We were all deceived, and now is our chance to make it right. We need our best men to carry this out, yours and mine. That is an order."

"Unfortunately, I still must decline."

"That is treason," Yuri said. "You're worse than your sister."

"Careful, my Lord. Saying that, I might accuse you of the same."

Torsten looked down and realized he'd been squeezing his fists so tight his palms were sore. He stepped in front of Redstar but didn't draw his dagger. Instead, he stared into the man's eyes —the man who'd tried to murder him in the Webbed Woods, and had hurt so many countless others.

"Redstar, I know we don't trust each other, but this is our chance," he said. "Do it for your sister or your nephew. By Iam, do it for yourself. Even if we die killing him, you'll be remembered as more than the uncle who cursed a child. You'll be a legend, remembered forever for saving the lives of thousands."

"Just as Nesilia was remembered for giving her life so Iam may end the God Feud?" he said. "Excuse me if I have a hard time believing you."

"Forget gods," Torsten said, unable to believe his own words. He took Redstar by the shoulders. "Do this, and I will forgive you for everything you have done. I might even begin to trust you."

Redstar closed his eyes. His lips twitched at the corners as if he were picturing what it might be like to experience a triumphant return to Yarrington. Torsten thought he finally got to him until he opened his mouth again.

"Whilst I'm touched by your sentiment," he mused. "I cannot so easily throw aside the will of my goddess."

"Damnit Redstar!" Torsten released him and slapped aside a group of tankards sitting on the table. "What must I do to get you to fight beside us? Every minute, one of your people starts a brawl and you do nothing. You're a member of the royal family, and if you would just demonstrate the worth of this alliance, we could return peace to the kingdom."

Redstar backed away and strolled around the table. He stopped behind Yuri and massaged the man's shoulders before being promptly shrugged away. "It has been made plainly apparent that neither I nor my goddess are your equal," he said. "But my army is to yours, and they will follow me no matter what. We will not risk fighting again. I must obey my goddess."

"Then you are a coward!" Wardric slammed on the table.

"The King will hear of this upon my return," Yuri said. "You have my word."

"I'm sure he will," Redstar said. "Right after you tell him of my future victory. Now, you must excuse me, my Lords. We must continue praying to the one below so we do not fail again." He bowed absurdly low while leveling his gaze upon Torsten. It reminded him of the sarcastic way the thief Whitney used to acknowledge him, only this wasn't playful. There was something curious in the gesture—as if it were meant to be the last bow he ever gave. Then, he walked away.

"How dare you turn your back on your Lords!" Yuri hollered.

"Forget him," Torsten said. "If he wants to hide, then we're better off without him. I was wrong to stake our chance at victory on the foul powers he calls upon by blood and sacrifice."

"Agreed," Wardric grumbled.

Torsten turned to Yuri. "Can your man quickly lead us through the dark alone?"

"Nobody knows these tunnels better," Yuri said. He was stuck staring at Redstar until he became just another fur amongst the ranks of his people.

"Then take us to the passage. I will lead a cohort of Shield-smen beneath the city and end this."

"No," Wardric said. "I will lead them."

"Wardric, I refuse to argue with someone else about this," Torsten said.

"Then don't. Redstar is a bastard, but he's right about one thing. This may well be a suicide mission. It's not like riding to the walls under the banner of peace. You are our Wearer, and I cannot in good conscience allow you to take on this burden."

"That is why it must be me."

Wardric pulled Torsten aside and lowered his voice. "This is exactly what he wants, don't you see? He's gambling that you will die on this mission and he can step into command. By Else-where, he might burn the entire city to the ground while you're in there just to do it."

"I know what he wants."

"Then don't risk it! I have served the King's Shield for decades—far longer than you. Now, I may not be the same warrior, but I knew Uriah and King Liam just as well. I never wanted to be Wearer, I only wanted to serve my kingdom. But now I'm asking you... use me for this. Stay behind with the army."

Torsten swallowed the lump forming in his throat. To think, he once worried old Wardric would be a thorn in his side when he took on the mantle. Now, he wished he had an army of the man.

"It has to be me, Wardric," Torsten said. "If you fail, Redstar will use it to contest my leadership either way. He wants the King's favor more than anything. He thinks me dying will make him Wearer but he's wrong. If I fail, it will be you who takes over... I know it."

"You know that's not true. Like we said, it is the King's dec—"

"What do you think I spent my time doing while you two were gone?" Yuri interceded. "The young King will heed my counsel. If Torsten fails, I will tell him who deserves to wear the white."

"And if I don't, even his own people will learn to respect us," Torsten said. "You've been to Drav Cra. They respect only strength, nothing else. They'll see Redstar for the coward he is when his beloved goddess is wrong."

Wardric looked to the ground. Tears welled in the corner of his eyes but he slowly began to nod. "Don't fail, sir," he said softly. "Don't fail."

"I don't plan to. Iam hasn't forsaken us. Not yet." Torsten pounded his chestplate in salute. Wardric returned the gesture.

And then, they embraced.

"I don't care what anyone says," Wardric said after they released, "you're as brave as Uriah was."

"And twice as stupid." Torsten grinned. "Look after the men while I'm gone?"

"Oh, I plan to. And if my sword accidentally finds it's way into Redstar's back, I'll say it was an accident."

"And I'll support you in that as well," Yuri added.

"Try to keep him alive," Torsten said. "I can't wait to see his ugly face when I return with Muskigo's head."

"I'll try," Wardric chuckled.

"Now, you know the men even better than I. Send me one hundred of the most experienced Shieldsmen we have, but leave some for yourself. No wolves. No dark magic." He shook the pommel of his sword, sculpted into the form of Iam's Eye. "Iam will guide us beneath the rebel, and we will bring him swift justice."

XX

THE THIEF

Whitney gagged as his feet splashed up shog and piss. The Winde Port sewers reminded him of the Fellwater Swamp... and he hated the Fellwater Swamp. A thin beam of light slashed in from the small hole above and the sounds of battle echoed through the tunnel. He couldn't help but laugh.

Did I really almost finally get hanged?

Of all the adventures he'd had since leaving the homestead, his last couple of months were the craziest. He'd been purposely imprisoned after accepting the world's stupidest challenge to steal the Glass Crown off the head of a dying king. A challenge in which he'd succeeded.

He'd been at the wrong place at the wrong time when the same enemy that now attacked Winde Port laid waste to his hometown of Troborough. He narrowly escaped but only thanks to yet another capture at the hands of Glass soldiers.

He'd been commissioned by the Wearer of White to journey into certain death where he was captured—again—by cultists before finding himself face to face with a Spider Queen goddess.

He was spun up in her web, fought giant man-eating spiders… and somehow survived.

Now, he thought all that was behind him until the one part of the adventure that felt just like every other caught up to him—a spoiled, entitled, good-for-nothing, has-been constable named Bartholomew Darkings and his hired assassin from some mysterious land in the North.

Whitney peered upward at the slime-coated, moldy, dripping ceiling.

"Gods and yigging monsters! What have I done to deserve this?" he shouted. His voice boomed, his words echoing, returning to him again and again. He kicked the wall.

"Shog in a barrel." Now his foot hurt on top of everything else.

As he trudged through what resembled dwarven-dug channels, Whitney found himself wishing he really was far up north in the Dragon's Tail, gulping down tankards of ale. Those dwarves knew how to drink.

He glanced down at the ropes still binding his wrists together. They were tight, and it wasn't until that moment he realized pins and needles were running up and down his arms. He heard the squeaking of a rat, and straining his eyes, spotted the little critter gnawing on what appeared to be leather.

Whitney was proud, but not too proud to admit when he saw a good idea. Raising his wrists to his mouth, he began to bite at the ropes. By the time they unraveled, his teeth were in agony, but otherwise, he was no worse for the wear, and his arms were free of pain and restraint. He silently thanked the rat and sludged on.

There was so much going on in the city above that Whitney couldn't prioritize his own thoughts. Sora was missing. A hired assassin was loose with his knives trained on him, and the Shesaitju were overrunning the place.

Way to defend your cities, Torsten.

He'd missed being able to blame the once-and-present Wearer of White for his bad luck. Against all odds, it actually helped him feel like things were normal. And normal helped him realize that he was standing in the one place in the whole city that could likely get him out alive. The sewers had to run somewhere probably straight into the bay. And since no good city planner would allow the muck he presently stood in to filter out too close to the city, he might actually find himself on his pathway to true freedom.

He closed his eyes and felt his chin sink into his chest. There was no way he could abandon Sora—even if there was a good chance she was already dead.

"Being heroic is a pain," Whitney sighed to another rat hunched over in a corner. He had made a decision to take on a partner when she found him in the western forest. Her training on thievery and the ways of the world wasn't done yet, he realized, ignoring the second thought that popped into his head about how perfect "On Thievery and the Ways of the World," would be for the name of a book on his life.

He resolved to not leave Winde Port without Sora. And to someday write a book.

He had no idea where to find her, but if she was in the city, he had two ideas. She was still in the Panping Ghetto, either captured by Kazimir, or she was able to escape in the chaos and knew that would be the best place to disappear. In a district where others looked like her, and where the fighting would be minimal she'd find rest. There were no soldiers or guards for the Black Sands to fight there.

His other thought was that Darkings had her somewhere in his mansion, waiting to sell her off to Kazimir as some sick gift after Whitney kicked the bucket... only he was still alive, which meant the blood pact was open and Sora remained Bartholomew's offering.

With newfound gumption and faith that she remained alive, he set off down the tunnels. At a fork, he turned against the slow current of the muck, toward where the smell was fouler and not diminished by the salt of the bay. He had to hold his nose. This was far from his first foray into city sewers, but the people of Winde Port who could afford it were known for revelry. Which made for smellier garbage.

He kept going until he reached a wider tunnel with a trough down the middle connected to one of Winde Port's many canals. He couldn't see which one, only that it wasn't grand enough to be the Merchant Canal running through the heart of the city. Shouting echoed from beyond it in too many languages for him to discern a word.

Whitney hopped across the trough and made his way to the canal. An arched opening led out to the frozen surface, and since from so low all he could see were stone walls, he decided it was time to figure out where in the city he was. He'd already been circling the sewers for Iam knows how long.

He lay back and pulled himself through the opening along the ice. Cold stung his back through his sodden shirt, but the fresh air was a welcome reprieve. He kept his legs spread wide to form a sturdy base on the ice, then leaped up and grabbed a loose stone on the canal wall. A drain pipe leaked icicles, and jutted out. From there, he was able to grab onto the lip of the canal and slowly pull himself up to peer over the edge.

He was at the opposite side of the square where he'd faced execution.

He stole a glance toward the coast. Even on the small portion of the wharf visible from so far, there were dozens of rowboats bearing the tan and black standard of the Shesaitju army. Hundreds of gray men lined up, marching down the streets, fauchards and spears erect. Dead and dying Winde Port citizens and soldiers were scattered throughout the plaza. The battle for

Winde Port was already finished, and the Black Sands were in complete control.

A loud *thwack* drew his attention to a barbed arrow still trembling in a wooden docking post to his right. His eyes went wide as he spotted a cluster of Shesaitju warriors on their own, bearing down on him. Probably performing clean up duty while they secured their new city.

Whitney ducked just before another arrow zipped overhead. He leaped along the wall to another pole, then looked down. A fall from up so high might send him plunging through the ice to a watery doom. And if it didn't, he'd been leading the blood-thirsty soldiers right into the sewers after him. So, he did the unexpected, didn't overthink it because a second guess about rolling up into the open and he wouldn't have done it. An arrow slashed through his sleeve, drawing a thin line of red once he was up. He sprinted straight at the soldiers who emerged from the nearest alley.

A spear whipped over his head as he slid.

Just like running from angry Yarrington guards, he told himself. Only these ones had the intent to kill.

He planted his foot against the wall and shoved off. A scimitar clanged right behind him. Reaching the wall opposite he did the same, and again, back and forth until he'd scaled up to the tile roof.

The warriors chattered in Saitjuese, several pointing upward.

"Sorry to disappoint," Whitney shouted, "but I've a meeting to attend. Good luck with the whole invasion thing!"

As he cleared the lip of the rooftop, a spear careened through the air right in front of his nose. He rolled onto the flat of his back, taking a moment to catch his breath and keep his heart from bursting. Then, he peered off to his right and realized his mistake. Beyond the square, the army amassed, and it would only be seconds before he was spotted by one of the thousands. Or even worse... Kazimir. In all the insanity, he'd forgotten about the wretch hunting him.

He stood, backed up enough to gather some speed and then leaped across the chasm to the adjacent rooftop. Below, he heard armor clattering. He peered back over the ledge. The Shesaitju group had done precisely as expected, rounding the corner of the building Whitney had climbed to wait for him on the other side. He quickly slid down a balcony, dropped to the plaza, and darted back for the canal behind their backs.

He slid down the first docking pole he saw, earning a couple of splinters on the way. His feet tapped lightly against the ice. Enough to cause some shallow cracks. Whitney didn't bother to be careful the rest of the way. He clambered through the porthole back into the sewers, his feet digging out chunks of ice in his wake.

Darkness returned, and the awful smell returned with force. "Better than being skewered by Black Sands arrows," he panted, sitting in the stale water and happy to be there. Now that he knew how thoroughly Winde Port had been conquered, he knew there was no more surfacing to figure out where he was.

He'd have to endure the warren of tunnels and troughs criss-crossing beneath the city. He'd figure out landmarks—a misplaced stone here, a chunk of moss there, and rely on looking straight up through grates to find his bearings. His foray into the plaza had him all spun around, so he decided he'd head for the Darkings' mansion first. It was closer than the Ghetto, straight to the north, somewhere where it looked down upon the wharf with the rest of the city's high nobility.

Whitney set off. The deeper he delved, the colder it got. The ends of his sleeves were literally starting to freeze. He had to hold his hands tight against his chest to keep from shivering.

The smell grew worse too, like death and decay now. The corpses dotting the surface surely didn't help, nor the blood tricking through grates here and there. His eyes were fully adjusted now, able to distinguish between grime and blood. His sense of hearing was heightened as well as he listened for which direction the wind was coming from, which direction the bay was.

He'd always prided himself on his senses and their ability to get him out of a jam. When he was just a boy, he and his family had traveled to Yarrington to witness the Dawning at Yarrington Cathedral with a view of the sun over Mount Lister. It was one of the few times they'd left Troborough. At the turning of every new year, Pantego's two moons drifted side by side in front of the sun, blotting out its light like two eyelid's closing over the world.

His father made them get there early to attend the ceremony led by Wren the Holy himself. At the end, the High Priest made them focus their senses inward. That was what the Dawning was all about, a test at each passing year when, for a short while, Iam's light was blocked, and humanity was left to look inward to find it.

With their eyesight all but stolen from them, Whitney found he could hear snails inching along the wet ground, or the grass grow. Wren explained it all with his mumbo jumbo about faith, but to Whitney, it always felt like a magical power.

Then, he met real mystics and blood mages and realized it was nothing like magic.

The thought of Sora picked up his pace. He ignored the swishing of human excrement beneath his boots and tickling the hem of his pants. He'd been walking for what could have been minutes or hours.

As he shivered, he caught himself daydreaming of a warm bed and a blazing hearth. Without even being aware of it, he'd been imagining the Twilight Manor, the tavern and inn located in the middle of Troborough. Or at least, it had been there before the gods-damned Shesaitju came in and razed it to the ground.

Whitney's desire to drive a dagger into the skull of every gray-skinned bastard in Winde Port and avenge Sora grew.

Torsten would be proud. "For Iam!" he would yell before hefting his absurdly large claymore high above his equally oversized head.

Something weird was happening, something Whitney wasn't used to. He found himself caring about people in a way he never had. Sora was a given—they'd grown up together. But with the occupation of the city above, he couldn't help wonder if the Wearer of White would arrive in time to save the day.

He laughed and shrugged the thought away.

Then, a sound not unlike an earthquake rumbled through the sewer and focused his wandering mind. Several screams replaced it when it stopped. Against his better judgment, Whitney bolted in the direction from which it had issued.

You're not a hero, you fool! Stop acting like one.

"I helped kill a goddess," Whitney said to no one but himself, then ran faster.

The amber light flickered up ahead, reminding Whitney of Sora's fire. As he rounded the corner, he saw the back of a Panpingese woman with long black hair, with the exact same stature as Sora. His eyes bulged until she turned around. He couldn't deny his disappointment. She was a bit older than Sora, and the man beside her was older still.

"Please," she begged. "Help my son. Help us!"

She shifted her weight, and the movement revealed a little boy, barely ten years old. He looked strangely familiar, but he could have been any number of beggar children Whitney had seen since entering the city.

The man Whitney presumed was the father was working hard to extract the boy from a large pile of crumbled stone. Whitney glanced up. The source of the noise was revealed in the gaping hole in the ceiling and the mound of stones beneath.

"What happened?" Whitney asked as he rushed to the man's side and began removing large hunks of rock.

"Cave-in," he said. "Must have been the catapults. By Iam, I hoped I'd never see another war."

"Then you don't know much about kings and queens."

Whitney kneeled before the mound of debris to better appraise the situation. "We're going to get you out of there, kid."

By the looks of the situation, he couldn't help feeling like he was lying.

The boy moaned—deep and agonizing.

"What are you doing down here?" Whitney asked his parents.

"Those tunnels lead out of the city," the woman said, pointing toward a crude opening in some loosely stacked stones. Beyond it, was a tunnel that no longer looked to be a part of the circular sewer-ways, but instead, rough and carved through rock.

"Our master is a cruel man. We thought we could escape," the woman continued. She bent over to do as much as she could to help remove the stones, but they were too heavy.

"You're slaves?"

She shook her head. "No slaves this far in the heartland, but we may as well be the way he pays us. That very passage was created to smuggle our peoples in and out of Winde Port after the Third War of Glass."

Whitney recalled that was how the Panping people referred to the Panping Wars. It made sense. In their eyes, Liam and the Glass were just foreign invaders come to take yet another land that didn't belong to them. They'd always made the excuse they were fulfilling the will of Iam—free them from their unholy mystic rulers—hog shog.

How many lives across Pantego had been taken in the name of some unseen god or goddess? Whitney had almost been one of them, fighting to find some cursed doll for a mad prince. Well, this wasn't going to be just another casualty added to a long list.

"You're coming out of there," Whitney said, even though he knew he should've just tucked tailed and run. "You hear?"

Whitney fought every ounce of his survival instincts, bent his knees, and grabbed a particularly large boulder. As he pulled, more dirt settled and the pile shifted, threatening to come down on all of them.

"Fate is determined to kill you, Whitney Fierstown," said a pitchy voice from behind him. "And you? My best servants. So sad it had to come to this… your boy always was my favorite. Never spilled a drop of brandy."

Whitney glanced over his shoulder to see Bartholomew Darkings, then back at the boy.

That's how I know him! He'd brought them wine after Whitney was forcefully escorted to the mansion somewhere above them.

"It's not the time for this," Whitney growled, continuing working to help free the boy. During his quick glance, he'd seen Bartholomew's one-eyed lackey. Whitney huffed a curse but didn't let it stop him.

"Fenton," Darkings addressed his man. "Mr. Fierstown needs to finally learn his place."

"*Fenton?*" Whitney laughed. "How proper. I think I'll stick with One-Eye."

Whitney heard shuffling behind him and fully expected to feel the clammy hands of One-Eyed-Fenton on him at any moment, but it never came. Instead, he heard a scream as the guard seized hold of the boy's mother and dragged her toward Bartholomew. He removed a hunting knife from his boot and held it to her throat.

"Turn to face me, or we make this father and son watch as Fenton does to her what he likely already does to her every night," Bartholomew said, eliciting a chuckle from Fenton.

Whitney didn't know if he'd ever hated anyone more than he did Bartholomew Darkings. The woman's husband wiped tears from his eyes and spun on Darkings.

"Don't worry about me!" the mother cried. "Save Ton'kai!"

Her husband didn't listen. He stomped toward Bartholomew, but before he'd come within a meter of them, Fenton's fist hit his stomach with such force he crumpled to the ground like his legs had disappeared.

"That's enough *Barty*!" Whitney shouted. "This kid is going to die if we don't get him out of there."

Bartholomew stuck a fat finger out toward Whitney. "I *own* that boy! If I want him to die, that is my choice."

The boy's mother was sobbing now and the boy, Ton'kai, had stopped making noise altogether. His pale Panpingese skin was even paler, and Whitney feared they'd already lost him until he saw a finger twitch.

"Fenton," Bartholomew said, "bring the thief to me. He'll die in these tunnels like so many of his whore-girl's ancestors."

Whitney clenched his teeth as he hauled off a couple more rocks, finally seeing the boy's legs, crushed and bloody. He bided his time, waiting until the perfect moment. Listening to Fenton's footsteps, he counted under his breath...

Three...

Two...

One...

He spun around, gripping a heavy stone with both hands. It connected with the side of Fenton's face with a bone-crunching crash. His knife flew from his hands, and Whitney snagged it out of the air as Fenton hit the stone floor. He wasn't dead, but he was definitely no longer an immediate threat. Bartholomew stood staring, incredulous.

"Whitney," he stammered. "Just calm down. We can work this out. Let's help the boy out, together."

"Lord Blisslayer, to you," he said, pointing the knife his way. "You're lucky I don't carve up your pudgy little face." He looked to the boy and then to his blubbering parents. "But we need all the hands we can get."

"You can't expect me to—"

"Help him!" Whitney brought the knife toward Darkings' face, stopping only inches away.

The worthless wretch looked like he'd pissed himself.

"I won't ask again," Whitney said, seething. He grabbed him by the collar with the other hand and shoved him toward the pile.

All four went to work. There were a couple of close calls, clouds of dust spilling down from the loose ceiling, but they managed to avoid catastrophe. When the final hindrance was removed, Whitney pulled Ton'kai out. His father grabbed him immediately and cradled him tightly. His mother sobbed louder when she saw the state of his legs. One was crushed and bruised. The other was bent backward at the knee, clinging on by a thread of skin with a bone sticking out.

Whitney turned his head to hide his retching. Out of the corner of his eyes, he noticed Bartholomew doing the same. The big tough man who treats his servants like proper slaves didn't even have the stomach to watch them suffer.

Whitney shoved him. "Lead the way," he demanded.

Bartholomew glanced at him, then at the suffering family. His lips curled into a wicked grin. "Your heart is going to get you killed."

A small stone whacked Whitney in the side of the head before he could react. It wasn't enough to knock him out—not with Bartholomew's flabby arms—but it sent him sprawling as the former constable took off into the smuggling tunnels.

"You said that about my tongue," Whitney groaned, rubbing his head. "Follow him!" he called to the family. "Save the kid."

The father passed Whitney, chasing Bartholomew, Ton'kai draped across his arms. His mother tried to keep up but fell behind, losing so much of her strength to tears. Whitney gathered his wits and gave chase, knife in hand.

Bartholomew maintained a healthy lead. Whitney was amazed that the man could keep up the pace for so long with all his excessive weight. He seemed as determined as any to escape the city before the Shesaitju killed them all.

After a multitude of turns, they followed him around a corner, the amber light of Celeste reflecting off the river outside. Bartholomew was the first one through but stopped the moment he emerged. Whitney soon found out why. Before him, stood a host of King's Shieldsmen. At their helm was one familiar face Whitney wasn't sure he wanted to see. Torsten Unger, the Wearer of White.

The first thing Whitney thought to do was grab Bartholomew and raised the knife to his throat. "Of all the smuggling tunnels in all the world," he said. "Here you are."

XXI

THE KNIGHT

"Get them to the camp and wrap his wound!" Torsten picked out two Glass soldiers escorting his company of King's Shieldsmen. They got to quick work, grabbing the injured Panpingese boy who'd emerged from the tunnels and rushing him up the hill. His parents followed close, faces streaked with tears.

"Now, Whitney, drop the dagger," Torsten demanded. Of everyone he'd have been glad to see emerge from their secret path into Winde Port, there wasn't anyone lower on the list. The thief held a dagger to the throat of a middle-aged man. He looked familiar to Torsten, but he couldn't place him. He wore the clothing of a noble… had the gut for it, too.

Whitney's eyes darted nervously at all of the armed King's Shieldsmen surrounding them.

"I don't think so," Whitney said, sliding the blade closer along his captive's throat. It was so quiet Torsten could hear the metal scraping across the man's stubble. "By the way, it's nice to see you, too."

"Bartholomew Shelley Darkings, what have you gotten your-self into?" Yuri asked before Torsten could respond.

Both Torsten and Whitney snapped toward him. Whitney stifled a laugh. Torsten's head cocked, his mind racing over how strange a reunion this was. Almost as if there were another, greater hand at play.

"You've been in the capital too long, Father," Bartholomew said. "This is the filth infesting our city now."

"So, this is your big, famous Pa?" Whitney said. "Kind sir, I mean this with all due respect, but where in Iam's name did you go wrong raising him?"

"How dare you speak to him like—"

"Quiet boy!" Yuri bristled. "You were supposed to meet us here to let us know whether or not the tunnels are clear. Why am I not surprised you somehow managed to find trouble doing even that?"

"Your son is the contact?" Torsten asked. He didn't know much about Yuri's family beside how fabulously wealthy they'd grown under Liam's rule. In fact, he didn't know much about many of the Royal Council, old and new. His focus, since the day he took the white helm, had been Oleander, her dying husband, and her cursed son. He made mental note to study those closest to Pi, should he survive the coming battle.

"Unfortunately, it wasn't enough that you allowed my favorite house in Bridleton to burn, was it?" Yuri said.

"I thought that was *your* house?" Whitney asked Bartholomew, barely able to contain himself.

"I swear, thief. When this is over, I'm going to revel in watching you suffer," Bartholomew said. "I'll boil your tongue."

"Pretty foolish thing to say to the man with a knife at your throat," Yuri reprimanded.

"Whitney, I know you're barely sane, but are you really going to murder a Darkings?" Torsten said. "In front of the Wearer of White, no less?"

"This one I might," Whitney replied.

Torsten sighed. He'd forgotten what it was like to deal with the intolerable thief Whitney Fierstown, now Blisslayer. "After all we went through, you haven't changed a bit, have you?"

"Why mess with perfection?"

"Whitney, for Iam's sake, just put down the knife."

"What, so he can stab me the moment I do?"

"He won't."

"Trust me, Shieldsman," Bartholomew said. "I would."

"You two are standing in the way of a royal operation." Torsten lifted his hand to graze the pommel of his claymore. "You will stand down, or you will both find yourselves occupying dungeons in the Glass Castle!"

"Relax, Sir Unger," Yuri said, extending his arm. He calmly paced before Whitney and his son, hands clasped behind his back. "What sort of mess did you get yourself into Bartholomew?"

Bartholomew went to speak, but Whitney angled the blade just under his chin.

"C'mon, Barty," Whitney said. "Tell him."

"If you insist. This whelp masqueraded as a blind priest of Iam before burning down the Bridleton estate."

Torsten's jaw dropped when he heard that. He knew Whitney was no favored son of Iam, but posing as a priest?

"Then, he stole my mother's—your wife's—favorite necklace, and who knows what else," Bartholomew continued. "Is that not enough?"

"Okay, I admit that sounds bad," Whitney said, "but burning down the house was an accident."

"An accident carried out by a Panpingese witch illegally practicing blood magic!"

"A priest?" Torsten mouthed, barely able to get the word out.

"That's the part you…" Whitney caught himself. "Look, none of it was my finest moment, but we were desperate."

"To steal from my dead mother!" Bartholomew bellowed. He turned his head to get a glimpse of Whitney, ignoring the knife as it drew a thin line of red across his neck.

"I can promise you that pendant saved everyone's life in the Webbed Woods when we…" Whitney turned to Torsten. "Am I allowed to say, or…"

"These are high crimes, Whitney Fiersto—" Torsten's glare shut him up halfway through correcting the name. "And that's besides me wanting no explanation of why you were deceiving the people of Bridleton when we were on a sworn quest to find the Queen's brother! You should be hanged, not thrown in a cell."

"Trust me, I tried," Bartholomew sneered.

"Quiet you," Whitney said, wrenching the man's head back into place.

Yuri held up both hands to silence everyone before the yelling continued. Torsten had plenty more he wanted to say, considering Whitney had abandoned him in their quest to play thief in Bridleton for a time.

"Are you referring to the pendant I gave your mother on her half-century? The piece of heartstone hewn from Brike's Passage in the Dragon Tail?"

Bartholomew nodded.

"Then you should have guarded it better!"

"Father I—" Bartholomew stammered, smug smile disappearing.

"Don't speak," Yuri cut his son off. "Do not speak. We are Darkings men. We don't stoop to the level of thieves and brigands, yet here he is with a knife at your throat rather than running from your justice. So I'm going to ask once because I have no idea… what have you been up to in my city? And do not lie."

Whitney actually felt a lump bobbing in Bartholomew's

throat. "I've been trying to track this man down so I may return mother's necklace."

"Really?" Whitney asked. "Because for all your dungeon-throwing, gallows-hanging, and speech-giving, this is the first I've heard of it."

"Because who knows what a monster like you would have done with it if you knew it meant something."

"I don't care about a necklace!" Yuri roared.

Torsten felt the hair on the back of his neck stand. He had no idea a man with hair so gray could have a voice that carried so thunderously. Even the eyes of the other King's Shieldsmen watching went wide.

"Tell me, thief, what slight did my hopeless son offer you?" Yuri asked. "We must all move on and focus on this war."

"Lord Darkings, I know this man," Torsten whispered in Yuri's ear. "I'm sure your son has good reason."

Yuri's only response was to hold up a finger before turning back to Whitney and Bartholomew. Torsten wasn't used to being dismissed like that by anyone but the Queen, however, he allowed Yuri this one. He had no son, so he didn't know what it was like to be disappointed in one.

But he did know Whitney. The thief was a man capable of instilling an endless well of disappointment.

"Well, for starters, he treats his servants like common kitchen trash," Whitney said. "Oh, and he hired a Dom Nohzi to kill me in exchange for Sora. So there's that."

Yuri took a hard step forward and raised his hand with the intention of collaring his son. Whitney reeled them back and further angled his blade.

"You went to the Dom Nohzi?" Yuri asked, face flush with unbridled rage.

"The assassins from Brekliodad?" Torsten asked. He'd never dealt with the order of legal killers, as their lands were beyond the realm of Glass, but he knew of them. It was said they were richer than any kingdom or guild after centuries of killing. That they had toppled kings of old without a soul knowing.

"I told you about this runt," Bartholomew said. "You were too busy to listen, so I took things into my own hands. This man assaulted our family."

"The Dom Nohzi are animals!" Yuri shouted. "We deal in gold, not blood, favors and whatever else they ask for. Do you know what it means to hand them your blood? If you do not hold up your end of the pact, even if it isn't your fault, they can find you anywhere in Pantego and make things even. You will have tied my hands!"

"And you promised him Sora?" Whitney said. He chuckled. "If I know her, she's probably already slipped him, and now he'll be coming for you."

Torsten saw a flicker of doubt on Whitney's face even as he tried to act brashly. It'd always been evident that he cared for the blood mage—as much as a thief could care for anything—which meant there was no question of how much danger she was in.

"Whitney," Torsten said. Three sets of eyes darted to face him as if he'd set off an explosion. "Maybe we can all find a way out of this."

"I can't imagine where this is going." He rolled his eyes.

"Sora is still in the city?"

Whitney nodded. "Wherever that killer is keeping her."

"Where is that, Bartholomew?" Yuri demanded.

"You think I know?" Bartholomew answered. "The Dom Nohzi find you or invite you, they don't get dropped in on, and they're always on the move."

"He can't have her until I'm dead, or something," Whitney said. "So he can't run even if he wants to. That's how their deals work, right?"

Bartholomew kept his mouth shut.

"Answer him!" Yuri hissed.

"Yes, that's how it works," Bartholomew hissed. "This one is loose with the rules though. He probably already had his way with her and tossed her in the bay."

"How many stories did I tell you about the Dom Nohzi growing up boy?" Yuri hissed.

"Too many," Bartholomew said. "How do you think I found him?"

"Then you know, until he kills the promised target, he would not dare."

"You're sure she's alive?" Whitney asked, eyes glinting.

"I'm sure that my son is an idiot. But they are as strict as they are exacting. The man will hunt you to the ends of the known world to fulfill the blood pact."

"Can it be rescinded?" Torsten asked.

"Once the pact is made? I don't know. You are among a very lucky few. The Dom Nohzi typically act swifter than a man can reconsider and are usually not interrupted by war."

"Bartholomew?"

"I don't know," he grumbled.

"You will draft a writ immediately, informing them that the deal is annulled," Torsten said. "You will offer to compensate them for time lost, and Whitney and his friend are to live."

"After everything he's done? I'd rather die."

"This is not a debate!" Torsten thundered. "The Dom Nohzi are killers, but from what I've read, they are honorable. The blood pact is over by command of King Pi's Royal Council, and they will obey it."

"I knew I liked this guy," Whitney remarked.

"I'm not finished. Burning the home of a noble and robbing him of his mother's heirloom? Posing as a priest? When I had the Master of Rolls ennoble you, I was unaware of these unspeakable atrocities."

"About that," Whitney said with a sly grin. "Any chance the Master of Rolls can draft up a new one? *Someone* burned what was apparently the only copy."

"I can't say you didn't deserve it," Torsten said. "But no son of Iam deserves to die without fair trial. And so, as punishment, you will help us in our quest to end this war. You will lead us back through these tunnels and create a distraction like I know only you are capable of. Cover our ambush."

Torsten looked to Yuri. "This is our best chance at Muskigo, and the more men drawn from his side, the more exposed he'll be."

"You expect me to go back in there?" Whitney asked.

"I do. Sora is still in there, and if you do this, I will ensure that when we retake the city, we search for her, and present the assassin with Bartholomew Darkings' resignation."

"And if I say no?"

"Then you will be arrested for high crimes, nobleman or not. I'm growing tired of seeing you in a cell, but I will make sure the next is one you won't escape from."

"You can't be serious," Bartholomew groaned. "This man can't be trusted! Father, it was my duty to lead them through these tunnels. I've played in them since I was a child, nobody knows them better than I."

"Played?" Whitney said. "Did you push children in front of collapsing walls back then, too?"

"Enough Whitney," Torsten said.

"I'm just saying. I've seen how this guy likes to pla—"

"I said, enough! If Lord Darkings agrees, that is how this is going to go. You've insulted the wrong family, Whitney, but here is a chance, once again, to show that you're out for more than yourself."

"I agree," Yuri said. "Clearly I can't let my son out of my sight for even a minute. If you think the thief can lead you back through and under the prefect's estate, then I won't stand in the way."

Torsten stared into Whitney's eyes. They were full of terror no matter how hard he tried to mask it. Torsten wasn't sure why he trusted Whitney wouldn't lead them astray, yet he did. Reuniting with him like this, with everything in the balance… it really did feel like something—someone—greater was at work.

"Sure, I can," Whitney said. "But are you really sure you want to go back in there? I've seen it Torsten. It's a war zone."

"I have no choice," Torsten said. "But you do. If you won't help to serve your kingdom, then at least do it for her. I've seen the way you look at her, Iam knows why. If we don't retake Winde Port, there isn't a soul in there that'll be safe."

"You have to be kidding me," Bartholomew said. "Father, you're really going to leave this in the hands of this scoundrel?"

Yuri didn't even bother to respond.

Whitney started to let up on his grip of the man, his dagger sliding down to around his shoulder. "You promise you'll help me look for Sora?"

"To any extent I can, *after* we handle Muskigo," Torsten said.

"No, you have to swear on him. Swear to Iam, and I'll give you the best yigging distraction anyone's ever seen."

"My word is my bond," Torsten said.

"You bond needs to be stronger if I'm going back into that shoghole."

"You're not in a place to bargain, thief."

Whitney slowly brought the dagger back to Bartholomew's throat.

Torsten growled. "Forgive me, Iam." He fell to a knee and traced his eyes with his fingers. "I swear to Iam, beneath the Vigilant Eye. Help me, and you have my word."

Whitney's gaze arced across the faces of all the King's Shieldsmen, then to Yuri, and back to Torsten. His hand momentarily tensed, then he chuckled and pushed Bartholomew away.

"You son of a—" Bartholomew whipped around but was promptly seized by his father. Yuri took him by the ear like he was a petulant child and drove him to his knees.

"My son will draft the annulment at once," Yuri said, twisting further.

Whitney watched gleefully as Bartholomew moaned in pain, slapping the ground.

"With my seal upon it," he continued, "the Dom Nohzi are more likely to acquiesce. You've placed me in a precarious situation, boy. We can only hope they don't ask anything of me in exchange, or for your worthless life."

"Thank you, Lord Darkings," Torsten said. "For everything."

"I live to serve the Crown, my Wearer. Thank you for suffering through this family matter."

Torsten strode forward and took Whitney by the arm. It almost felt a dream that the thief was back in his life until he touched him. The Webbed Woods, Bliss… it had only been a month, but it all seemed like eons ago considering how much had changed since then. Again, Torsten was placing the kingdom's future in the hands of a thief, but he was never one to ignore the silent hand of Iam at work.

"Are you ready for another quest in the name of the Glass, Blisslayer?" Torsten asked. As the words left his lips, he couldn't even believe how accepting he was of the notion.

Whitney shrugged. He was still busy marveling as Bartholomew received the punishment he so deserved. "Just let me enjoy this for a few more minutes," he said, "then we can go be heroes again."

XXII

THE THIEF

"So, this is what it feels like to lead an army," Whitney said, glancing back at the line of King's Shieldsmen. It was impossibly dark, but a few pricks of light filtering in through cracks above allowed him to see their gleaming armor. Torsten wore his white helm, face guard open, which meant things were serious.

"Feels good," Whitney continued. "Maybe if you die up there…"

"You're lucky to not be living out the rest of your days in a cell, thief," Torsten replied. The word came out with extra venom as he stepped over a lumpy pile of something in the narrow passage. All that he could be sure of was it didn't smell good.

"Oh, c'mon, we've got to be on a first name basis by now."

Torsten gave him a grunt, nothing more. Whitney knew the big lug was glad to see him though. There was no reason the King's Shield needed Whitney to lead them through these secret passages when a Darkings could do it, which meant Torsten must have trusted him more.

The thought had him grinning.

"Think you could get me on royal retainer?" he said. "You know, for whenever you need my special skills?"

Torsten scowled but didn't answer.

Whitney led them further through the warren of smuggling tunnels, trying to remember the path he'd taken following Bartholomew. He was nearly at the point of praying he'd led them the right way through the stifling darkness when they reached a break.

Rock turned to carved stone, buried tunnels intended for sneaking horrible things became sewers intended for shipping shog. A false wall of stone blocks lay dislodged and around the corner. Whitney raised a hand. The troop stopped behind him. He craned his neck to hear better. Something was wheezing just on the other side.

"What is it?" Torsten asked.

"Wait here."

He hurried through the opening. What sounded like wind weeping through cracks was really Fenton on his hands and knees trying to gather his bearings. A few thin lines of light seeped in through a ruptured portion of the ceiling above. He saw the wet spot of blood where Ton'kai nearly died. Whitney couldn't help but hope Kazimir would decide to end that fat slob Bartholomew when he caught wind of the proposed annulment.

He patted his pocket to make sure the papers hadn't fallen out into the muck below.

Fenton looked up at him, eye lulling, blood coating the side of his head. "You... it's—"

Whitney kicked him hard in the head. His body flopped over onto the collapsed rock, unconscious again.

"The first one was for them," Whitney said, shaking out his foot, "but that was for me."

"Who was that?" Torsten questioned. He appeared behind Whitney, sword in hand.

"Nobody now."

"Whitney."

"Just one of Darkings' boys who deserved way worse."

Torsten grabbed Whitney by the arm and forced him back to the front of the line. "No more games, Whitney. I want you in front at all times. Is that clear?"

"Fine, fine. I got it out of my system anyway." He pointed to the right, into the sewer tunnels, toward where the air smelled fouler. "This way is the city sewer system. I don't think any gray skins saw me go down here but we should be on the lookout."

"I wouldn't worry about that," Torsten said. "The invasion is complete. As far as they or anyone else knows, the sewers are confined to the city limits and empty into the bay, which they control. They'll be covering exits, but no longer the tunnels themselves."

"How do you know that?"

"Their focus is defense. They're digging in to wait out the winter."

"Just be on the lookout."

Torsten regarded the King's Shieldsmen at his back. "These are the finest warriors the Glass has to offer. *If* we see anyone, they won't live long enough to bring word to a soul."

"It's your funeral. We run into trouble, I'll be swimming across the bay."

They continued, now wading through slosh. Whitney was more accustomed to the smell this time, but behind him, he heard a few of the King's Shieldsmen gag. Torsten, however, was barely affected.

Maybe he really did grow up in South Corner.

"I just don't understand, Whitney," Torsten said after a while.

"What's that?"

"You proved yourself worthy of a new name. You helped save

so many people from Redstar and that beast. How could you so quickly return to your shystering ways?"

"'Once a thief, always a thief.' You know the saying."

"Enough of your foolish jokes. I am your Wearer, and I'm being serious."

"As am I, Shieldsman. You may have been born in the shog, but you've been living pretty for most of your life. I'm not ashamed of who I am. Made a name for myself and it's my name to do what I want with."

"Do not presume to know a thing about how I've lived," Torsten said.

"All I'm saying is I'm going to do what's right for me."

"All sin can be traced back to selfishness," Torsten said.

Whitney spread his arms and looked toward the ceiling. "Then Iam strike me down."

Torsten slapped his hands down. "He might. You posed as a priest. What greater sin could you commit?"

"I could think of a few." He sighed. "I do what I must to survive. You weren't too concerned about my practices when it benefited you and the Crown back there in the Webbed Woods. And you don't seem too concerned now, sneaking through hidden tunnels toward the prefect's estate, not even concerned about how I know my way there."

"I do what I must for my kingdom," Torsten countered. "If that means placing my trust in you, then I can only walk the path Iam puts before me."

"I'll tell you this, if there is an Iam, and I'm not saying I believe in any of that mumbo-jumbo, he's got a great sense of humor because he keeps bringing us together."

"Indeed."

"I mean, here I thought I'd never get to see your dour face ever again, and there you are, right in front of me when I'm about to exact my vengeance on old Bart Darkings."

"There is no road back from murder, Whitney. If I stopped you from crossing that line, then I too am glad we had to be reunited."

"Aww, touching sentiment," Whitney reached back and rubbed Torsten's pauldron. He earned a glare that sent his stomach sinking into his ass. "Wouldn't be my first time killing. I took a few of these gray men down back in Troborough. I'm not sure if your men told you the stories before they captured me."

"They left out the details." What followed was a sound Whitney couldn't quite place.

"Is that a chuckle I hear?"

"No," he said, stern. "Besides, that's not the same. That was battle. Kill or be killed. But to slit the throat of an unarmed man... it's something you can't undo."

Whitney looked back, met by Torsten's thousand-meter stare.

"You say that like you have experience," Whitney said.

"There are many things I've had to do in the name of king and Crown. Not all of them bring joy to think of. Not all of them make me proud. All I can hope is that when Iam receives me at the Gate of Light, he sees my intentions were pure."

"If you don't wind up in Elsewhere," Whitney offered.

"If I do, I'll spend the rest of eternity haunting you. And maybe one day, I'll make you into a decent man."

"I don't think eternity is long enough for that."

This time, Whitney was confident he heard a chuckle. He wasn't sure why he felt so proud at that. Maybe because it'd never once happened during their quest to the Webbed Woods. Or perhaps it was that he knew, as well as Torsten, that beneath all their bickering, there was a bond. The kind only a team who had battled a giant spider goddess together could forge.

"Giant spider goddess," Whitney said under his breath with a laugh.

"What's that?" Torsten asked.

"Nothing."

Whitney stopped when they reached the widest tunnel yet. A flowing trough ran down its center, flanked by branching tunnels. If the Shesaitju were anywhere in the sewers, this was where they'd be. But there was nothing except scurrying rats hiding from the cold.

Short bridges led over the stream of water and shog which emptied out through a porthole into Winde Port's largest canal along Merchants Row. Whitney stared through the barred opening. He could see the many gray legs of an army marching by on the walkway above. It was only then he realized if a single soldier spotted them, they'd be slaughtered.

"We're in the heart of the city now," Whitney said. He pointed to the porthole. "That's the Merchants Canal. If you follow that, the prefect's estate should be up a ways, somewhere on the north side."

"You're sure?" Torsten asked.

"Chasing Darkings down here wasn't my first run through the Winde Port sewers. I've been getting into trouble here since before you were Wearer."

"That's only been a year."

"Then way before. See how experienced I am?"

Torsten exhaled through his teeth. "How far up do we go?"

"Without being able to pop my head through that grate? Beats me."

Torsten gave him an encouraging look and nodded his head toward the opening.

"No way, not again," Whitney said, shaking his head. "I got you here without a hitch. You can check all the offshoots until you're under the courtyard. You've probably been there, so you'll recognize it. Lowly thieves aren't usually invited to meet prefects."

"Fine."

"Then this is where we split up. The wharf is down that way, and I have a plan that'll get every eye in Winde Port on them."

"Just don't destroy the city."

"When Whitney Blisslayer gets hired to make a distraction, he goes all out. You don't get to hold me back now." Whitney turned to walk away and felt a heavy gauntlet on his shoulder.

"Iam willing, we will meet up after the fighting is through." Torsten's tone was solemn, heartfelt. Whitney was sure it was the first time he'd ever spoken to him that way. "Do not die, thief."

"Let me worry about dying. I have a great plan for when that day arrives, and it isn't today. Just wait for my signal."

"How will I know?"

Whitney sighed. "Haven't you ever done this before? The answer is always, 'you'll just know.' I take distractions seriously."

"I'm sure you do." Torsten went to turn, and this time Whitney grabbed him.

"But remember, I'm not doing this for free. Sora is up there somewhere, and you gave your word that you'll help me find her after you end Muskigo."

"And I stand by it. I know you're not doing this for the Crown, but maybe you're not so selfish after all."

Whitney pulled away. "Don't go getting soft on me."

"Just do me a favor? When we find her again, stop being a fool for once."

The lumbering Shieldsman turned to his men and raised his voice just above a heavy whisper. "All right, the prefect's estate is down this trough. I want a man on every grate. We know what we're looking for."

Whitney watched the Wearer of White get to work.

Did he just tell me to make a move on a Panpingese blood mage?

He thought he might have been dreaming considering the way he'd treated her on their last adventure.

"Yep, he's definitely gone soft."

Whitney sighed. It couldn't be a dream because only the real world could smell so awful. He regarded the stubborn Shieldsman one more time, then turned to continue down the shog-covered sewers toward the wharf.

He couldn't tell Torsten what to look for because he honestly had no idea how he was supposed to distract an entire army. Genius usually struck for him in the heat of the moment, so he decided to turn off his brain and allow instinct to take over.

Before long he was standing at a large, barred opening at the bay. The smell of salty air greeted him along with a freezing gust of wind. It smelled like freedom, but he knew it couldn't be. Even if he'd decided to bail on Torsten and take his chances with Kazimir, Sora was still somewhere within the city, and he refused to leave without his apprentice.

He took inventory of the area. From the opening, he could see the wharf, lined with trader's ships. They swayed to and fro as a heady wind blew, battering the docks with small waves of water cold enough to stop a man's heart. Lonely chunks of ice floated, broken by the churning bay.

The Shesaitju rowboats littered the sandy coast south of the wharf. And further down, massive galleons made of black wood, with bowing, triangular sails floated menacingly. Some still had catapults on their decks, stuck in launch position. A herd of zhulong traipsed around in the mud where they were moored under the watch of stablemen.

Whitney squeezed through the bars and pulled his body up so he could see atop the wharf. He moved slowly, quietly, unable to escape the sinking feeling that the moment his head popped up he'd be target practice again. Only now, at least, he had the cover of night.

Several Shesaitju warriors stood guard along the coast, but since none of the hiding Winde Port citizens would dare attempt an escape, they weren't paying much attention. Many of them were engaged in some kind of game under the green light of a cluster of nigh'jel lanterns. It involved a large sheet of zhulong skin and throwing spears.

Merchant ships and personal vessels lined the wharf, packed in tight like a deck of cards due to the grounding of ships. He watched them rock back and forth, the ropes holding them going loose and taut in rhythm with nature's song. An idea popped into his head as he watched them. It was insane, but thinking twice was a thief's worst enemy.

He pulled himself up onto the wharf and slinked down the edge. The heavy winds coming from the west made such a racket of water and creaking wood that nobody would ever hear him. However, if any one of the hundred Shesaitju soldiers posted decided to look in his direction, they'd no doubt see a scruffy thief climbing aboard one of the ships under the light of the moons.

He chose the largest vessel, a western galley big enough to transport a herd of cattle and with sails the size of the Darkings mansion. Tall deck walls kept Whitney mostly hidden as he crouched and ran toward the bow. His plan was as simple as it was crazy, but he hoped it would be effective.

"Pssst."

Whitney whipped around, saw no one. He heard it again and spun in the direction it had come. A stout but muscular dwarf with a dark, patchy beard popped up from a corner behind a spool of rope.

"Tum Tum!" Whitney nearly exclaimed before he caught himself. "What are you doing?"

"Got stuck between a rock and a hard place, I did," he replied. "Yiggin gray men have been keepin watch all afternoon. And after what they did to me bar, I ain't for takin no chances."

"You mean the Winder's Dwarf is..."

"Infested." Tum Tum pointed across the way to his bar. The front windows were bashed in, and Shesaitju were everywhere. They had full run of the place, but not one of them drank. The Black Sandsmen did so hate enjoying life.

*All that wasted ale...*Whitney frowned. "These Black Sandsmen are intent on ruining everything, aren't they?"

"Aye. They barged in askin if the dwarf who owned the place would support the fall of the Glass. O'course, I told em to stop botherin me customers and blades started takin away all the Glassmen. What good be a tavern without downtrodden men to drink at em?"

"Oh, Tum Tum, silly dwarf. You always say 'yes.' War makes even the best men drinkers and peacetime... well, that's even worse."

"I know, I know. But I was drunk when they asked," he chortled.

"Of course, you were," Whitney said. "Well, since you're here, wanna help me win the war and get your place back?"

"Me fightin days are long gone, me Lord," Tum Tum replied. "Ain't for sayin I can't be tossin some fists round, but I'd be doubtin we could handle hunerds of them gray men."

"I've got a plan, and we shouldn't even have to ball our fists." He leaned in to whisper. "I'm working with the King's Shield again."

"By the sharp axe of Meungor!"

"Keep your voice down," Whitney scolded. "Now, gather up all that rope and tie it around the mast."

"What's the plan?"

"You'll see."

Whitney looked out over the rails at the city he used to love. Suppertime along the wharf was usually the most fun place one could be in all of Pantego. It wasn't just Winder's Wharf, but bar after bar, packed with people ready to spend. There were some of the finest restaurants, including the Winde Traders Guild at the end of the row. Now, anywhere that wasn't swarming with Shesaitju invaders was empty. Not a drink being poured.

Unable to bear the sight anymore, Whitney turned to look down the wharf. The ships were tightly packed between pilings and floating walkways ramping down from the wharf. From the vessel they were on, there were ten more docked down to the sandy shores where the zhulong and Shesaitju rowboats occupied. Enough to make a racket even the gods might hear.

"Done yet?" Whitney asked after some time had passed.

"Me legs ain't as long as yers be," Tum Tum groaned in response. "Hold yer saddle…" Then, a few minutes later, "There, done."

"Okay. You sit tight and stay low."

"Ain't no other way I can be." Tum Tum laughed, and his belly rolled.

Whitney placed a finger against his lips to shush him.

"When I give the signal, raise the sails, then get your ass to the sewers, or inside. Anywhere but the docks."

"Aye, aye, Cap'n."

Whitney sighed in relief. Tum Tum was no thief, but he'd helped Whitney try and woo a fair share of pretty women in the Winder's Dwarf over the years. Enough time to know that when Whitney offered a signal, it was best to wait and see what that might be.

Torsten could learn a thing or two.

The spool Tum Tum had used for a hiding place was nearly all they would need for this ship. Whitney took the free end, tied it to a bucket, and threw it to the ship docked in the next slip. He winced, expecting to hear clanging metal that might alert the guards, but the wind was causing such a ruckus, even he couldn't hear it.

"Wish me luck," Whitney said to the dwarf.

"With what?"

Whitney ignored him and leaped from deck to deck. He found the bucket, removed the rope, and tied the end around the ship's mast. Then, he found another spare rope and affixed it to the mast as well before using the same bucket to fling it to the next ship. He continued on down the line of ten ships to the one nearest the southern coastline where the zhulong grazed.

Just as Celeste and Loutis reached their climax in the night sky, he tied his last knot. Sweat poured down his forehead despite the cold. All that jumping and crouching... thieving was a younger man's game. Not even three decades, he was already on the decline.

He peered over the railing and saw a couple of gray-skins doing rounds down the length of the wharf. He waited for them to pass, then slung the end of the rope not affixed to the mast over the side of the ship. He slid down it onto a floating walkway and shimmied toward the wharf. Miraculously, the Shesaitju were still unaware of his presence, and he hoped to keep it that way. When his feet hit the wharf, they were already running.

He hopped down to the muddy shores and toward the zhulong herd. In the darkness, the Shesaitju were easy to spot with their green, glowing nigh'jels. There were a few care-keepers scattered about, but Whitney made sure to steer clear of them.

"All right," he said out loud to no one. "They're just big pigs. Nothing to worry about—just big pigs with spiked tails and massive tusks."

As he got closer, he realized they were far bigger than he remembered. He was actually quaking now, his knees weak. Sweat still poured off him, threatening to freeze on his face.

"Shogging exile, Whitney," he cursed. "Get a yigging grip."

He sidled up to an exceptionally large male—he could tell by the length of its tusks—and patted its side. Its head turned, eyeballs the size of Whitney's fist, maybe bigger. It leaned down to sniff Whitney's pants, shog-stained from the sewers.

"Hey, boy, think you could help me with something?" Whitney stammered. "Yeah, attaboy."

Whitney grabbed the reins hanging from a bit in its mouth and gave them a soft tug. The beast thrashed its head in protest, causing Whitney to back away, arms in the air. The zhulong followed him, stuck out its short, coarse tongue, and licked his calf.

"More pig than dragon, eh?" Whitney said.

He strode a few meters, then turned and noticed the zhulong following him, its massive snout huffing.

The patrolling warriors were on the opposite side of the wharf, so the time was right to get to work.

"Stay," he said to the zhulong. It didn't listen. As he went to climb back up, it hooked him with a tusk to get at his pants.

"How come only ugly beasts want to get in my pants?" he groaned. It made a deep rumbling noise. "Okay! You're not ugly. I'm sorry." He weaseled out of its clutches, then reached down and tore off a strip off his sodden pants. He tried to imagine they were only wet with water as he raised the cloth.

The beast grabbed it from him and started chewing.

"Good boy." Whitney shrugged and made his way back beside the nearest ship. He found the loose end of the rope he'd slid down and carried it to the zhulong. It was still busy chomping on his pants when he knotted it to its saddle.

Just then, he heard shouting. A Shesaitju warrior fell off the side of the ship Tum Tum was supposed to be hiding on, splashing into the ice-cold water. A contingent of warriors sprung into action and headed for the ship. Before Whitney could even make a move, he saw the towering sails go up, accompanied by a cacophony of Saitjuese cursing.

"Tum Tum!" Whitney shouted.

He had to think fast. He ripped the stained piece of fabric from the zhulong's mouth and tossed it down the beach. The zhulong's giant nostrils flared with rage, and Whitney had to summon all the courage he had to give it a slap on the hindquarters like he was playing. He closed his eyes, half-expecting to be gored, but the mighty beast turned and ran toward the cloth.

Mission accomplished.

It tugged on the rope, which was bound to the mast of the nearest ship, which was connected to the one adjacent, and so on until the compromised galley.

The sails Tum Tum had raised caught the strong westerly winds, and with the zhulong also pulling with its substantial strength, the row of ships tipped, slamming into one another. There was a series of cracks, loud as thunder, and the zhulong herd went frantic. The rope on Whitney's friend snapped free, whipping across and taking out Whitney's legs.

They stampeded toward the city, throwing sharp, hooked tusks as they charged. Whitney had to roll back and forth to avoid being trampled. Giant, clawed paws smashed into the mud all around him, and when he finally was able to look up, he saw a mass of Shesaitju along the docks, half staring, aghast, at the toppled ships and others trying to calm the zhulong.

Whitney kept waiting to hear shouting about a dwarf but heard nothing. He dug himself deeper into the mud to hide. All he could do was hope Tum Tum had abandoned ship and hid before it was too late. Used to the deep cold of the northern mountains, dwarves were resilient, maybe enough to survive that water for a few minutes.

What was certain, however, was that Whitney's distraction had worked. His service to the Crown was complete, with exceptional success if he had to say so. Now it was up to Torsten to handle his end so they can get started trying to find Sora and the monster who held her.

XXIII

THE MYSTIC

Shavi didn't have to give Sora any clothes after she dried off. Her chamber in the prefect's estate was already full of them. The old handmaiden quietly finished cleaning and straightening her hair, told her to rest while she could, and left the room—but not without first asking countless times if Sora needed anything. She was warm and welcoming like a mother should be... not that Sora knew much about mothers. Wetzel was called many things back in Troborough, matronly not numbered with them.

Sora watched her leave, then dug through a wardrobe for something appropriate to wear. As she did, she couldn't help but wonder who the countless clothes belonged to and what had happened to her.

It wasn't hard to discern the answer. Winde Port's prefect was gone, probably a head on the city walls. There wasn't a soul with pink skin or round eyes from the heart of the Glass Kingdom to be found. No servants, or wives, or children.

Sora ruffled through more exquisite clothing than she'd ever seen in one place until she found the plainest dress available. It was tree bark brown and barely hugged her figure. There was no finery along the seams of tan, threaded trim. It wasn't servant attire or anything, but she was tired of playing the role of a fancy royal. She strapped the fat coin purse she and Whitney got from selling the silk trader's goods to her thigh underneath the folds, then, she found a pair of long, satin gloves to pull up all the way over her forearms to hide her scars.

She turned and saw the luxurious bed waiting for her opposite the bath, begging her to get lost in the impossibly soft sheets. Aquira was already curled up in a ball on one of the pillows. Sora didn't dare join her. Not even for a moment, knowing that if she hit the cushion, she'd be passed out for hours. And she couldn't do that.

The sun was falling, its protection against Kazimir with it. Whitney was still somewhere out there, and as soon as the light was gone, he'd be in more trouble.

Maybe he fled, Sora thought. *Maybe he left me behind just like when he ran from home.*

It was a thought that would have usually pained her, but now, all she did was hope he was as bad a man as he sometimes seemed—worse even. She hoped he'd stolen a ship in the chaos and was already sailing the Boiling Waters on another mad adventure.

Then she remembered Kazimir's terrible grin and what he'd said about the sacred nature of a blood pact. He'd hunt Whitney to the ends of Pantego if it meant getting her. Yet still, she had no idea why. There had to be countless other Panpingese magic-users hiding around the world. Her people were supposed to share the closest affinity with Elsewhere, whether through blood or otherwise.

No more hiding. I need to find him.

"Aquira, let's go," she said. The wyvern raised her head and blinked wearily in her direction. "C'mon girl. He may be a pain, but he's all I've got." Aquira stood and stretched, arching her spine and looping her tail around to brush her neck frills. A puff of smoke poured from her mouth as she coughed, then she hopped down and followed behind Sora.

It was a short walk down the hall to a huge anteroom, arched windows along the side looking out upon the bay. Dusk was made even darker by a thick layer of clouds and snow flurries.

Sora stopped in the entry when she realized Muskigo wasn't lying. The hall was filled with homeless Panpingese men, women, and children wrapped in blankets. A few Shesaitju guards stood silently at the entries but kept to their own.

It was an odd sight; the room, so luxurious and lavish, and a people so much the opposite. Velvet covered chairs were parked before intricately marked tables upon which were myriad varieties of food and drink. Maybe the people didn't have a warm bath or hearth to stay warm, but even a roof overhead was a far cry from how so many of them were living in the ghetto.

She stepped in and immediately recognized two children sleeping on their mother as the ones she'd tossed coins to back in the Panping District. Her hand instinctually fell to the purse beneath her dress, filled with more gold then anybody in this room had seen in a lifetime combined.

"You need something?" the mother asked.

Sora shook her head, not even realizing she had been staring. "No sorry, I recognized your sons," she said.

"Ah, you must be 'beautiful angel' that gived that gold autla."

"I...uh... yeah. They looked like they could use it."

"Could have used more." The woman wore a glare for a few seconds, then her features softened and she said, "Thank you."

Her skin creased like leather as she smiled, even though she didn't seem very old. Within her dark, almond-shaped eyes, Sora saw peace. It was strange for anyone to seem peaceful during these times, but as she looked around the room, at the other Panpingese refugees, it was a common attribute.

"That is Tayvada's wyvern," the women stated.

Sora glanced down and saw the wyvern calmly sitting at her heels. Her heart sunk, but she nodded. "You knew him?"

"Every Panpingese in Winde Port knowed him. He didn't go around tossing out gold, but did what he could to feed us."

Sora eyed the Shesaitju guards to make sure they weren't listening to her. She was supposed to be Tayvada's widow after all. "I wish I had a chance to know him better, but Aquira found me in the chaos and won't leave my side."

"You must be a decent one then. She was his pride and joy, and she has eye for troublemaker. Always growled at these two for causing ruckus." She shook her children a bit and laughed.

"Ouch, momma," one of them groaned. He rolled over and rubbed a cut on his arm. It wasn't deep, but Sora knew cuts better than anybody. It was the kind that stung but wasn't bad enough for anyone to heal. Sora recalled many times when Wetzel scolded her for being a weakling. This mother did the same.

"Oh, quiet," she said. "It just a scratch. You're lucky that's all we got in the fighting."

Sora knelt in front of them then sliced her thumb on her shoe buckle and ran the blood gently over his wound. A bit of blue smoke rose, and the boy's cut began to seal until all that was left was a line of irritated skin. Sora released a mouthful of air and panted a few times. Healing took more out of her than anything, but the wound was so minor she recovered quickly.

The boy was too tired to notice what had happened, having fallen asleep almost immediately after changing positions. The mother, on the other hand, gawked at her like she was from another world.

"Are you a—"

"Mystic," Sora finished for her, keeping her voice low so as not to wake the children or earn more attention. "No, I just learned a few tricks with blood magic in the west."

"Tricks, eh? Think you can get my leg to stop aching? Knee pops every time I stand." She grabbed her knee cap and wiggled it around more than was natural.

Gross as it was, Sora couldn't help but chuckle. "I don't think so."

The woman waved her hand in dismissal. "Bah, what good are you?"

"Still figuring that out." Sora smiled and sat, legs folded in front of her. Now that the woman had warmed up to her, she figured she might be able to get some real information. "So, you have lived here in Winde Port your whole life?" she asked.

"Born and raised in ghetto. Never been anywhere."

It explained her accent and broken way of speech. Sora imagined most of the district dwellers stayed among their own.

"Why do you call it that?" Sora asked, her eyes narrowing. "It's such an awful word."

"What more is there to call it?" an old man leaning against the wall beside them spoke up, suddenly paying attention. "We count ourselves lucky to even have a place of our own. So many of us died after the Third War of Glass… better here in Winde Port than in Elsewhere."

He spoke with elegance. More like Tayvada than the others.

"Or some backwater village," added another. "Here we get to see world, even if only through eyes of travelers."

"Or invaders," Sora muttered.

Everyone looked to the gray men lining the entries. They all wore weapons, but none were drawn. Several just laughed with one another, shoulders against the walls.

"They've treated us better than others has," the mother said, shrugging, almost apathetic as if the slaughtering of so many outside meant nothing.

"Aye," said the old man. "These warriors have spared us, given us food and shelter in a place bigger than the whole Ghetto. They are no enemies of mine. If the mystics would stop hiding, maybe we could join them."

The mother slapped the man's arm. "That is enough, Nijo. Council is gone, and every time they're bringed up I have to explain it to my children."

"Good. They should learn exactly why we're here kissing boots." The old man stood, huffing. His bony legs shook for a moment before he decided to sit back down and continue enjoying his free meal.

"Sorry about him," the mother said. "Talk of war stirs up rotten memories."

"I don't remember it, really…" Sora said. "Well, I have one memory actually."

"That is enough for lifetime."

"It's of my mother." Sora wasn't sure why she started explaining. She'd never told anybody about the memory; not Wetzel, or Whitney. Nobody. But she'd never been amongst so many people that didn't look at her like she was misplaced, or delicate.

"I can't recall my father, but her," Sora continued. "I can almost picture her face. I think I look like her except my eyes; those must have been my dad's. Maybe it's just a dream, but she cradles me and tells me she loves me. She's crying. I think I am too. She kisses me on the forehead. Then she's gone."

Sora could feel her eyes starting to well up. The woman, however, barely seemed moved. "Sometimes, it is better to barely remember," she said.

"It's always better," Nijo scoffed. "My wife was burned for using magic. My daughter, chained up and sold. Last I saw she was being dragged away by her hair and I was too broken to help them."

"It's not competition, Nijo." The woman took Sora's hand. "It is beautiful memory, dear. But that's all it is. We here now, eating, thanks to these people. What more is there to ask?"

"These people destroyed my home," Sora said, softly.

"Welcome to the club," Nijo groaned

Sora bit her lip upon realizing how foolish she sounded. She couldn't expect any of these people to feel bad for her. She was delivered to a home after the war. It wasn't perfect, but Wetzel looked after her, fed her, gave her shelter. And she had a friend who helped her through so many hard and lonely times. He may have abandoned her for a while, but he was back now. Whitney was counting on her, and she'd wasted enough time on her own curiosity over her people's living situation.

"You say you knew Tayvada?" Sora said. The woman nodded. "The man they said murdered him, Whitney Fierstown. Did you see what happened to him?"

"I was not there," she said.

"I was," Nijo said. "Bastard escaped when the gray men attacked. Slipped right into the sewers."

Of course! Sewers.

They were a thief's best friend according to one of his lessons if she remembered correctly. The one place in the world where Whitney could hide and never be found. Probably not even by Kazimir. But the upyr couldn't summon a fire that never dwindled in a place that wet. And he didn't have a Wyvern who'd met Whitney and could no doubt sniff him out.

"Thank you," Sora said. She stood and bowed. "Thank both of you."

"Don't think I've ever been bowed to befo—"

Nijo was interrupted when the grand, central doors to the anteroom swung open. Muskigo appeared, flanked by his gold-clad guards. Gone was the look of calm Sora had seen on his face since they first met.

"All civilians must vacate the estate at once," he commanded.

All the Panpingese folk glanced up at him, then returned to their meals. "Now!

His men flowed in, ripping the people from their meals and shoving them toward the exits. All around the room, soldiers did the same. Nijo's chair was kicked out from under him. The mother's children awoke, startled.

Sora stormed toward the afhem. Aquira caught her leg on the way and used it to get a boost up to her shoulder. "What is the meaning of this?" she questioned. "These people aren't hurting anybody."

"Sora, I don't have time," Muskigo responded. He wouldn't even look at her, too busy watching his men bully the homeless.

"You promised these people shelter."

"I don't have time!" he thundered. Now he stared straight at her and in his pale gray eyes, she saw storm clouds. He drew a deep breath. "It is no longer safe here. The Glassmen are coming."

"It's safer here, protected, then out there if battle is coming."

"I don't have time to explain. Take them back to their district and stay inside."

"I don't lead them."

"Someone needs to. Now go, Sora of Yaolin City. Our conversation will have to wait." He turned to leave without even a second glance, but it was what he clutched in his hands that drew her attention. It was a letter bearing the unmistakable seal of the Darkings Family—a ship and a coin. She recognized it from the ring Darkings wore, and from the door of his house in Bridleton.

"Was this all just to impress me?" she shouted as more of her people were shoved by.

Muskigo stopped but didn't look back. "No, this is war."

Sora watched as he hurried to the railing around the courtyard and looked down. She watched as armed guards pushed her people around no matter how young or frail they were. Only a moment before they felt safe for once in their lives, and now, children were crying.

A hand fell upon Sora's shoulder. She looked left and saw Shavi.

"You must listen to him, Sora," she said. "If he believes danger is coming, it is. Fighting. It's all he's ever trained for."

"Apparently," Sora replied. "Go, I'll be right there."

"Trust him." She went to leave, stopped to help an elderly man up, and they continued out of the room.

"I don't," Sora muttered. She turned and spotted the mother and her children hurrying to gather their blankets. Sora ran to them, reached under her dress, and shoved the coin purse into the woman's chest.

She stared down, eyes wide with confusion.

"I don't need it anymore," Sora said. It was true. There were no merchant ships left to charter. And even if Whitney was right that she couldn't make a difference in these people's lives by handing out gold, she was done not trying.

"Take it. Be the new Tayvada, or give it out. There's enough there to fill a dozen flats with new beds and more."

"I… I don't…" The woman fumbled over a response until there was a booming crash. It was like thunder, only the sound repeated a few times and was immediately followed by shouting in Saitjuese.

Sora grabbed the woman and guided her toward the exit. "Just go!"

Her eyes darted between her children, Sora, and the money. Then she ran. She ran with enough gold to buy a ship.

Whitney won't mind, Sora told herself. And she also told herself that he wouldn't mind one more detour before she went after him. She glanced back up at Muskigo, still staring down into the courtyard. The sight had the rage she'd been holding down bubbling back to the surface.

Whatever that bang was, it signaled war. More killing. Muskigo forcing the Glass Kingdom to attack. Her people may have survived their surprise invasion, but nobody would survive an all-out war in the city.

All his talk of fighting for freedom, yet he was clearly working with Darkings, a man wicked enough to turn to the upyr and blood pacts. Sora suddenly realized how foolish she was to believe there was more to Muskigo. They were royals, helping each other, and the people be damned.

The series of crashes had drawn all the soldiers' attention to the courtyard. All the refugees and handmaidens were cleared out.

Sora was alone.

She picked up a shard of a broken clay plate which must have fallen in the chaos. Aquira dug into her shoulder and growled as if she could read Sora's mind. Then, they headed straight for Muskigo.

Sora knew now that she could help her people. She could end the looming war and keep what happened to Troborough from happening again. Maybe not forever, as there would always be greedy lords and ladies wanting more, but at least enough to make fewer orphans and refugees.

She could end the fighting.

XXIV

THE KNIGHT

Torsten raised a hand, stopping the legion—one hundred of his finest King's Shieldsmen at his back. They had been trained during Uriah Davies' reign as Wearer, by Wardric as the eldest in the order, and by Torsten himself, after he took on the mantle. Not since King Liam turned the entire army of Glass into a hammer of faith had the Shield led an operation like this.

Yet, perhaps the most astounding thing about where they now stood was that Whitney, the damnable thief without a filter hadn't failed in leading them.

Torsten looked up through the grille of a gold-clad grate and into the courtyard of the prefect's estate. He placed a finger over his mouth as a pair of gray legs passed, then regarded his men. He knew a few of their names—Mulliner, Reginald, Nikserof—but he wished he knew them all. He wished he'd been forced to spend less time at Oleander's side or watching to make sure Liam wasn't taken advantage of after he'd grown too ill to speak. In fact, he longed for the days when he had been one of them—an anonymous face in the great order, following a worthy Wearer whose accomplishments were so vast he'd never be contested by a murderous, Drav Cra Arch Warlock.

This will change everything, he told himself.

"Muskigo is somewhere above us," he said aloud, voice low, but carrying down the narrow passage. The dwarves, although small in stature, developed spacious tunnels to accommodate men and even some giants. Torsten was thankful for that as he traveled through the main lines, but now that they were within the estate's infrastructure, things were tight. They were forced into a long line, no more than two men crammed across, and the ceiling so low he had to crouch. A pain in his neck now but it would help them swarm into the courtyard when the time was right.

"We are with you until the end, Wearer," the man nearest him said. "Or let Iam strike me down."

He was young but hardened. Three lines of scars ran across a chin like an anvil. His eyes glinted with a healthy blend of fear and resolve, proving he was not a man driven by bloodlust but a true warrior. Torsten recognized him but wasn't sure of his name.

No more heeling like a dog at the feet of royals. This is your order. These are your men.

"What's your name, Soldier?" Torsten asked.

"Xander Corsocova, Sir," he saluted.

"Where are you from?"

"I… Westvale, Sir. Born and bred. Trained by Sir Wardric Jolly under the command of Sir Uriah Davies a few Dawnings back."

"It's an honor to be here beside you, son. Can you do something for me?"

"Anything, sir."

"Ask the name of the man on either side of you, who trained them, where they're from. Then, tell them to do the same." He knew some of them might already know each other, but these were the finest, selected by Wardric. That meant they were posted all across the western half of the kingdom.

"Sir, the—"

"There's time. We await a signal from Winder's Wharf to move. It's an order. Here we stand, ready to die in Iam's name, I would like to better know the brave men at my side."

Xander nodded and turned to Nikserof, the Shieldsman beside him, to ask the same questions. Then on and on down the line. Torsten listened to the answers of those nearest and watched the rest. Some were calm like Xander, others more visibly taken by fear. But, as a few men joked in their answers and earned low laughs, the terror began to dissipate.

Liam's armies were a unit. Thousands of men unified in resolve and their trust in him. Uriah's King's Shield was an extension of that. No single member mattered, only the unit as a whole. Alone, they were only drops of rain, but together, a great hurricane.

But the time of great and famous men was over. Torsten had led for a single battle and been deceived. He had to argue with a heathen imposter for every move, under the orders of a king whose voice had yet to lower, in the shadow of a Queen Mother now best known for killing her own people.

"What about you, sir?" Xander asked while the rest continued.

"Excuse me?"

"Sorry, sir. If I overstep…"

Torsten looked up into the courtyard, flakes of snow danced by, melting just beyond the grate. Then, he turned his gaze down upon the sewer and the layer of muddy water running past his feet. He remembered why the stench and darkness of such a place barely affected him.

"South Corner, Yarrington," Torsten said finally, eyes closed. "Born to a no-name father and a streetwalking mother. Iam saw fit to lead me into the arms of Liam Nothhelm and never once have I looked back."

He regarded Xander, who stared at him in disbelief.

"We are all Iam's children," Torsten said. "No matter where we come from." He reached out, took the man by his pauldron and shook. "Now we are ready."

A crash echoed in the distance, followed by a bell, and shouting in Saitjuese. Dust trickled off the ceiling as footsteps pounded across the ground above.

Torsten grinned. "Maybe there is still hope for the boy," he whispered to himself and above. Not only had Whitney led them successfully but his distraction appeared to be working as well.

Torsten positioned himself below the grille. His fingers twirled the Eye of Iam hanging from his neck. "Forgive me Iam, for what we must do. Watch over us, but do not judge, for in the name of peace we take up arms against those who trespass against Your light."

As he prayed under his breath, so too did his men, each in their own way. Some mouths moved silently while others took a knee, speaking to the inside of their eyelids. He let them all finish in their own time, and when he saw the whites of all their eyes, he traced his own.

"We are the armor of Your holy kingdom," he said, raising his voice enough for his men to hear. They quietly echoed every word —the words of the King's Shield, which Torsten couldn't remember the last time he'd had the opportunity to recite.

"Our lives," he continued, "are given freely under the sight of your Vigilant Eye so Your children may thrive in this world You have blessed us with."

Torsten raised his hand to the sewer grille, then raised his voice even louder. His men did so as well. "We are the right hand of Iam. The sword of His justice, and the Shield that guards the light of this world."

He shoved the grille with all his might and jarred it from its setting. Xander gave him a boost and his feet fell upon the snow-filled courtyard, the first of all his men—as it should be. If Liam had taught him anything of war, it was that no leader inspires his men like one willing to head the charge.

The rest flowed in after him, men with long swords and heater shields at the front, spears and pikes at the back—the wedge and hammer.

Torsten spun to study the yard wrapped on four sides, at two levels by an arcade utterly devoid of Shesaitju. Bells rang louder in the distance, accompanied by a series of crashes. Whatever Whitney had done, it cleared the entire place.

Torsten signaled to Xander. "Secure the front door," he ordered. "Muskigo is somewhere in here. We take him now, or we die trying."

Xander saluted, then led a smaller unit toward the palace doors. Torsten surveyed the courtyard again, trying to decide the next move. And that was when he heard a scream of agony too near to be Whitney's doing. He drew his claymore and swung back to face the direction it'd come from.

A bar of spikes had swung across the Arcade's central passage from one side. Xander screamed and flailed, trying to free himself from the bar which had him pinned against the wall. The sound of Saitjuese orders cracked the air, the voice familiar. Standing on the walkway right above where Xander met his fate was Afhem Muskigo, arms crossed, eyes fixed on Torsten.

The moment he saw him, Torsten knew Redstar's betrayal was complete. He had warned Muskigo, sending any and all competition for command of the Glass Army to their doom.

Muskigo barked something and archers flooded in from surrounding rooms. They lined the second-floor balconies over-looking the courtyard as well as the roof.

"Ambush!" Torsten shouted. "Form up. Form up!"

King's Shield armor was durable, laced with the glaruium of Mt Lister herself, but it was not impregnable. At the right angle, the Shesaitju's barbed arrows could pierce it, as Torsten knew too well. And now his men would learn too.

Arrows zipped around the courtyard from every direction like angry hornets in a stirred nest. They stabbed at angles, stung shields. The Shieldsman right in front of Torsten took one to the weak, flexible mail around his throat as they all closed rank. Another arrow glanced off Torsten's white helm, sending him staggering and knocking the helmet off his head.

"Wearer!" one of his men shouted. Whoever it was grabbed him and raised a shield, but was stung from behind by another projectile. Torsten went to pull him back and received a mouthful of innards as another arrow erupted through the man's stomach.

He wiped blood and bits of flesh from his eyes. Metal clanked all around him as the King's Shield formed a circle of shields.

"Shields…" Torsten coughed, the tang of copper heavy on his tongue. A wave of frantic bodies crushed him in the center of the circle, pressing against his chest, stampeding his feet. He could hardly breathe.

Of all the battles he fought under Liam, he'd never felt so… hopeless.

Every arrow clashing against their shield wall stole a bit more breath from his lungs. And those were the ones that didn't sneak through the cracks, shredding flesh and sinew of one of the men he'd foolishly led to their dooms.

He pawed at his chest for the pendant of Iam—something to squeeze as he prayed for a miracle. But his arm was pinned between two of his men jockeying for position under the umbrella of shields being slowly picked apart. He was able to loop a finger around the necklace when someone banged into his side and caused the chain to snap off his neck. The pendant cracked as it hit the ground, then shattered beneath a boot.

Torsten fell to a knee, finally able to gasp for air. He pawed at the shards, and in the reflection of the largest piece, he caught a glimpse up into the balcony. All the breath he'd only just regained fled his lungs at the sight of Muskigo standing there.

The gray man watched like a galler bird, eyes set upon floundering prey, so focused that he didn't see what was coming up behind him.

The blood mage—from a village razed at his very command—walked up behind him, something sharp in hand. A strange, scaled creature, which looked like it could be a newborn zhulong sat perched on her shoulder.

Iam is still with us!

Anger contorted her features just as it had in the Webbed Woods when Redstar pushed her to the brink of death. Torsten watched her weapon sink into Muskigo's shoulder blade, and then his mass of soldiers shifted and obscured Torsten's view. Swimming through the mess of legs and armor, Torsten clambered for a better view. Arrows battered the metal on the other side, but he lifted his head regardless.

Now he saw Muskigo hulking over Sora, sword to her throat as she crawled back across the floor.

"Muskigo!" Torsten roared. "Come down here and face me like a man!" The barb of an arrow slashed his cheek on its way by. His men pawed at his shoulders in an attempt to drag him back to safety.

He stood strong.

Muskigo momentarily turned his attention from Sora to meet Torsten's glare. The girl grabbed the sword by either side of the blade with her bare hands. Blood leaked from her palms as she squeezed and fire swirled around her. The scaly creature on her shoulder leaped at Muskigo and dug sharp fangs into his shoulder. The afhem released a roar, sword slipping from his grasp.

The attempt to kill their afhem had some of his men

distracted, but others rallied. Arrows flew at Sora, flaking to ash before they reached her flame-covered body. Another charged her from behind and swung a curved sword, but a flick of her finger sent fire hurtling into the man's face.

Muskigo ripped the creature from his flesh and threw it back at Sora. It screamed loud enough to be heard over the din of battle as it skidded to a stop. Muskigo backed away slowly, lowering into a Black Fist fighting stance.

"This is for my master," Sora said. "This is for my home!"

Fire exploded from her hands. At the same time, it shot forth from the scaly creature's mouth. Both streams merged together.

Muskigo spun out of the way, but a part of the blast caught his side and sent him flying backward so hard he broke through a wooden post. The rest hit the structure of the roof and courtyard, igniting the wood rafters and melting the stone columns of the arcade as if they were iron under the smelter.

The entire half of the building sagged, then began to crumble away. The devastation rippled across the entire building, wood catching everywhere. Torsten and Sora's eyes met for but a moment before the ceiling caved in around her. She grabbed her scaly friend and vanished.

"We're not alone!" Torsten hollered. He could feel the energy flooding his muscles, his despair fading beneath the blinding glow of fire. "Fight toward the exit. Push!"

Half of Muskigo's men surged across the crumbling upper walkway to dig him out of the rubble. The others continued the assault, but Torsten's men seemed reinvigorated by the spreading inferno.

The mass of shields and armor shuffled out of the courtyard and into the entry hall. Walls collapsed around them, and the ceiling fell away. Torsten never felt such incredible heat, but he took comfort knowing the Shesaitju hadn't either. They preferred their nigh'jels to fire, and this fire was unnatural. Its arms licked and spread as if fueled by the rage of the very girl who ignited it.

Shesaitju soldiers fell upon them as they reached cover. "Shift!" Torsten ordered. The men at the edges of the formation turned their shields and those behind thrust spears through the openings.

"Wall!" Torsten said, the shield closing once more with a thunderous clap.

"Push!" They pressed forward toward the front entry as if one unit. Less than half the men he'd come with remained, but in the King's Shield, that counted for hundreds.

A large portion of the ceiling crashed down, breaking their formation. Torsten didn't wait for Shesaitju to flood the gap. He leaped over the bodies, his claymore carving a bloody arc across the chests of his enemies. He parried a spear, then ducked under another. A Shieldsman—Sir Nikserof Pasic—jumped forward, blocked an attack from his flank and pulled him back to cover.

Another chunk of the ceiling gave way ahead of them, crushing a mass of Shesaitju warriors. Torsten, seeing an opening, waved his men onward, over the smoldering rubble. He lowered his shoulder, and cold air filled his lungs as he broke through the estate doors, finally feeling like he was able to breathe. Icy snow and burning embers met in a macabre dance, sweeping across the entry. Dark clouds swirled in the darkening sky, bringing with them a robust and west-blowing gale that felt like daggers upon his bleeding cheek. The prefect's estate was wholly consumed, but it wasn't alone.

The strong wind rapidly carried flames across the city. At the same time, a strange voice echoed through the air. The words were long and trailed off, but it sounded like Drav Crava, as if he could hear Redstar chanting across the battlefield.

The wind allowed the inferno to bridge Winde Port's canals

like forest wildfire. Building after building caught, even though it was snowing—an unstoppable force of nature's wrath.

Torsten turned his attention to the streets. They were out of the cauldron, but Muskigo's army still filled the city. A cluster of unmanned zhulong stampeded through the streets, throwing massive tusks in every direction.

"We are the right hand of Iam!" Torsten shouted as his men formed rank again. "The sword of His justice and the shield that guards the light of this world!" The zhulong crashed into them, throwing Nikserof aside like a rag doll. Another couldn't dodge the pack, taking a long tusk through his abdomen.

"Fight toward the gate!" Torsten ordered after the beasts passed. "We shall make it out of here alive, men. Iam is with us!"

Torsten emerged from the shield wall and brought his claymore down upon a Shesaitju warrior's skull. He heaved Nikserof to his feet by the forearm, and they fell back into cover. In and out of the formation he and others went, taking five with them for every Shieldsman that died.

But they were dying.

Torsten knew they wouldn't last long surrounded by enemies and fire, but now he wasn't afraid.

Just like in the estate, their formation slowly ebbed west through the overwhelming force. The finest men the Glass had to offer would only die if they took hundreds more with them. The further west they edged, the louder Torsten could hear Redstar's voice, as if the warlock was directly beside him.

The wind grew stronger as well, and Torsten saw the fire hopping across the rooftops. The distraction helped give them breadth through the army, and now it was beginning to catch the palisade wall surrounding the city.

Torsten's giant hands snapped the neck of a Shesaitju, cracking like a branch underfoot, then he spun, pulling his sword free and bringing it down through the shoulder of another. A blade slashed his thigh, but his armor dulled the blow. He grabbed the man by the neck, and as he raised him, a ram's horn filled the air. One long blow.

'We will know the time to strike when the cold is driven away by wind and flame.' The words Redstar had spoken before he left suddenly filled Torsten's mind. That horn belonged to the Drav Cra, and suddenly, all around them, Torsten's men were no longer the Shesaitju army's target.

Shouting echoed all over in common and Saitjuese. Torsten could make out the meaning of some, like 'wall' and 'charging"— enough to know that Redstar was about to do whatever it took to be the hero while Torsten and his men failed, damned be to the innocent citizens being used to shield the city.

Redstar would claim it was Nesilia who sparked the fire that took the walls even though Torsten knew it was Sora. He knew Iam was working through the girl though he knew not why. As a blood mage and descendant of mystics, she was everything Iam's scripture preached against, but he knew it to be so.

He crushed the throat of the man in his grip. His men cheered as the horns of reinforcement sounded and Shesaitju warriors flowed by to meet the army at the burning wall. Torsten's heart, on the other hand, sank again. He looked back toward the estate and searched.

Muskigo was being helped out of the crumbling building and led toward a zhulong. He shook one of his Serpent Guards off and hopped up. Half his chest was seared, his usually-gray skin bubbling, exposing the pink of muscle and sinew.

"To the wall!" Torsten shouted. He helped Sir Nikserof take down a Shesaitju soldier, then pushed him in the direction of the walls. "Go!"

He and the rest of his men rushed by. Torsten stayed put. He leveled his sword, its tip pointing down the street at Muskigo.

"Muskigo!" he bellowed. The afhem's dark eyes spotted him through the smoke and embers. "Will you cower from me again?"

One of his Serpent Guards threaded a bow, but Muskigo raised a hand to stop him. He slid his scimitar out of his sheath and pointed it back at Torsten. "Defend the city," he ordered. "The Wearer is mine!"

XXV

THE THIEF

From his perch atop the tilted mast of the black galleon, the reality of Winde Port's fate was all too clear. The hundreds of buildings and businesses lining Merchants Row were being destroyed. Fire raged along the road as the wind blew, hopping the city canals and burning both sides. The strong western wind fanned it along so it couldn't spread to the wharf, but it rapidly pushed toward the city walls. It was as if the gods themselves were blowing upon it and Whitney thought he could hear eldritch chanting in the air.

The Shesaitju army stormed toward the palisades to defend their captured city, vanishing in the smoke. War cries and battle drums were all Whitney needed to hear to know what was happening. The Glass Army was charging.

"Torsten," he said under his breath. The inferno spread fast, but Whitney was sure it began at the prefect's estate where Torsten was making his ambush.

He ran down from the boat and onto the quay. The Shesaitju remaining were so distracted trying to saddle the dozens of zhulong roaming the streets, they didn't even see Whitney as he bolted passed them.

As he reached the place where Winder's Dwarf used to stand, he thought about Tum Tum. The look on the dwarf's face as they watched his livelihood be overrun would stay with Whitney forever. Tum Tum had always been a good friend. If Whitney believed in life after all this chaos, he'd hope to be wherever Tum Tum ended up—even if it meant the Great Hall of Meungor.

"For you, good buddy."

He stopped at the turn onto Merchants Row. Fire licked at the streets from all sides, but the wind kept Whitney's face free of smoke. That was when he realized he had no idea what to do next. He could barrel into the burning prefect's estate and find Torsten, his best chance at standing up to Kazimir. Or he could continue searching for Sora in the most logical places he could think of—the Panping Ghetto and the Darkings Mansion.

Both were on the north side of the city, beyond where the fire was spreading. But the Darkings Mansion was atop a hill and mostly stone. The Ghetto was down at the base, and if a single ember reached those shoddy, wooden flats, the place would go up like a bonfire.

Torsten can handle himself, he decided. If starting this fire was part of his plan to ambush Muskigo, he'd have a lot to answer for to Iam.

Whitney went to cross the canal when, from the direction of the prefect's estate, a mob of Panpingese men and women raced toward him through the smoke.

Whitney turned and pushed through into the heat and smoke. "Sora?" he questioned. In all the smog, half the women looked just like her. He coughed and called for her again. His eyes were burning now, tears streaming down his face.

"Sora!" He stopped, placed his hands on his knees, and tried to take a breath as the crowd fully passed him by. Instead, he just made himself cough even more. He watched them, unsure what to make of the exodus. He wasn't even sure why he imagined Sora might be with them. He'd spent the whole trip trying to prove to her that it didn't matter what she looked like, that the only *people* she had were the ones she chose to stand with.

Wetzel and himself, namely. Half the reason Whitney was so okay with taking her to her ancestral homeland was so she could see that it had nothing to do with her. It was just a place with a name and similar looking people. It also had a great deal of strange and magical treasure to steal, especially if they stumbled upon any underground mystic covens. But that was beside the point.

He sighed, pulled his shirt up over his mouth, and backed up out of the smoke.

Focus Whitney. You'll find her.

He went to turn and continue back on his path across the canal when he heard a low growl.

"Aquira?" he said. The little wyvern stood on the ash-and-snow-covered street blinking its big, yellow eyes at him. Whitney fell to his knees in front of her.

"Aquira!" He went to pick her up but she growled even louder, and he wisely redrew his hand. "Aquira? Where is Sora? So-ra." He pronounced both syllables. "You remember her, right?"

He patted himself down, searching for anything he had that might contain her scent. There was nothing. A month together and he realized he had nothing of hers. If she died in the city or was already dead, he'd have nothing to…

A woman burst through the gathering smoke and fell to the ground. She hacked and coughed, sounds that would have made Whitney vomit if not for realizing the mouth they came out of.

"Sora?" he said softly. His eyes went wide. He scrambled over and pulled her further out of the smoke so she could catch her breath.

"Whit," she rasped. She threw her arms around him and he her. They held each other there in the middle of the street as the city came undone around them. Whitney went to pull away so they could get moving, but she squeezed tighter.

"We need to move," he said.

A group of Shesaitju warriors rumbled by, half of which were mounted on zhulong. They must not have seen Whitney or Sora as enough of a threat to stop.

"C'mon, Sora." Whitney forced them apart, took her hand and led her over the canal to the side where the fire was less rampant. Aquira flew up and dashed along the railing in pursuit.

Whitney leaned Sora against the side of one of the few buildings still standing in that district. He coughed and breathed, and then, again.

"Are you okay?" he asked. Now that she was in front of him, he realized tears were streaming down her face. And not just from the heat of the fire. Her shoulders bobbed like she was trying not to weep.

"Me?" She wiped her eyes. "Are *you* okay?"

"I'm fine, just breathed in too much smoke. Wasn't my first time. There was that time with the dragon—wait a second."

"What now?"

"Why were you coming from the prefect's estate?"

One corner of her lips pulled slightly into a smirk. It was a half-hearted attempt, one that couldn't mask a deeper layer of sorrow, but it was there. Whitney looked up at the flame devouring all the buildings up Merchants Row ahead of them.

You fool, Whitney!

He wasn't sure how he missed it. There was no mistaking her distinct brand. It wasn't like an ordinary flame that billowed and grew gradually. Hers was like a tsunami, chewing through wood and stone like parchment.

"This was you, wasn't it?"

She glanced at Aquira. "I had some help. We found the man who destroyed Troborough. Who killed Wetzel."

"Iam's Light, Sora. Did you forget that this isn't his home to get revenge on?"

"I… I lost control." She hung her head.

Whitney took her by the shoulders and smiled. "Merchants Row needed remodeling anyway. Oldest part of Winde Port and it shows."

Sora looked up with only her eyes.

"So, is he dead?" Whitney asked.

"I'm not sure."

"Well, Torsten will finish the job. He was headed there too."

"I know." A genuine grin finally broke out on her face. "I saved his life," she said, and then a second later, "again."

"Oh, he won't like that at all."

"No, I wouldn't think so," she said.

"If Muskigo is still around—"

"Don't forget the assassin after us."

"Ah, yes, how could I?" He laughed. "Shogging exile, I think it's time we get the yig out of here."

"Remember when you said I'd love it here?"

Whitney rolled his eyes. "Well, the gates are burning, thanks to you. So now both armies are killing each other. I'd rather avoid that, so, same plan as ever?"

"Which is?"

"Steal a ship," Whitney said, matter of factly. "There are a few smaller ones docked on the northern wharf that I didn't knock over. Just gotta get our papers and we can be on our way."

"Papers? Seriously? You think anyone is going to be concerned with papers at a time like this?"

"The law is the law, Sora." He winked.

"Everyone's a bit preoccupied right now. I doubt anyone is going to be stopping us to see our papers."

"It's not for here. We'll be crossing Shesaitju waters, and if you haven't noticed, they're in the middle of a rebellion. The Winde Traders Guild isn't going anywhere, however much their home city is hurting. They have pull."

"I don't know," she said. "We are in this mess over those stupid papers."

"Did I mention pirates? Only the worst ones will hit a member of the Guild. Which reminds me, do you still have our gold?"

"I... uh." Her gaze flitted toward the burning cinder that was the prefect's mansion lost in a cloud of smoke across the canal. "Lost it while uh... running from Kazimir."

"Shog in a barrel," he said. Then, he clapped his hands together, smiled and said, "Then we really need those papers. Give a pirate enough gold, and they'll leave you alone. Give them nothing, they'll take your ship and leave you for sharks."

"They can do that even if we have papers."

"But they're less likely to. Trust me, they are in a safe place. We'll be in and out."

"Where?"

"Tayvada's house."

Whitney saw a wave of fear wash over her face.

"What's wrong?" he asked.

"It's nothing..."

"Sure, doesn't look like nothing," he said. "What's going on? Oh, him."

He was ashamed he'd so quickly forgotten their last experience at the guild member's home. He could only imagine what horrors she'd suffered at Kazimir's hand.

"It's fine," Sora said. "Let's go get some yigging papers."

"There's my girl!" Whitney took her hand again, and they took off.

The further from Merchants Row they got, the less forgiving the chill in the air became. Lucky for the city, the fire seemed contained to that avenue, the strong wind keeping it focused. Merchant fronts and governmental buildings, the places the owners could afford to rebuild.

The more residential districts were left mostly untouched, baring the arrows and spears stuck in their walls—and the haphazardly discarded corpses littering the ground from the fighting. Smoke, fog, and snow mixed to create a thick haze at street level. It was like a ghost town.

"How did you escape Kazimir?" Whitney asked as they ran.

"He went to watch you be executed," she answered.

"As if that were possible."

"Then, Aquira showed up and freed me." The wyvern screeched from her perch on Sora's shoulder. "Kazimir chased me until I found Muskigo."

"And you decided to go after revenge instead of finding me?"

"I...I..."

Whitney laughed, then stopped walking and looked her in the eyes. They stood on the opposite side of the canal leading into the Panping Ghetto now.

"I'm kidding. You were trying to survive, and you did, which means my lessons really are working."

"Don't flatter yourself."

"I am glad you didn't kill Muskigo though. I had the chance to take down Darkings too, but embarrassing him was way better. Torsten told me there's no coming back from murder, and for once, I think he might be right."

"That self-righteous oaf?"

"I know, right?"

"He'll take care of Muskigo," she said. "They'll all hang for what they did. The ones who deserve it."

"Your mouth to Iam's ears." Whitney bowed with a flourish and beckoned Sora over the canal toward the run-down church on the edge of the ghetto. "My lady."

Sora didn't move. She stared in the direction of the church and the dilapidated homes of her people, and Whitney thought he noticed her legs start to tremble.

"You want to wait here?" he asked.

"Shogging exile, no."

"Don't worry about Muskigo." He patted his pocket, feeling the writ issued to Kazimir and the Dom Nohzi requesting they rescind the blood pact in the name of Yuri Darkings. "Darkings' father called them off, so I think old Barty is in more danger from Kazimir than us."

"Bartholomew?"

"Right? That's his name. I know, ridiculous. Anyway, I've got the papers right here. If Kazimir shows up, we flash them, and we'll be fine."

"More papers?"

He stuck out his chest. "It's the way of greater men."

"Well, let's be quick anyway."

The Ghetto was nearly untouched by battle but for a couple of homes near the front, across from the church. Their roofs were caved in, probably just due to shoddy craftsmanship. For once, the streets were empty of the homeless. There wasn't a lighted candle or even a sound.

The door to Tayvada's remained ajar, so they pushed their way in. Whitney's own memories flooded back so he could only imagine what Sora would be thinking. Tayvada swinging, dripping blood. Kazimir's nightmarish grin as he emerged from the shadows and made their lives living exile.

"I hid it over there," he said, pointing to the chimney.

He reached up and pulled down the makeshift package—the crown wrapped in the trading papers. Opening it, his eyes gleamed like he'd won the pot in a game of gems. In a way, he sort of had.

He felt a hard fist against his shoulder.

"Are you *kidding* me?" Sora shouted. "That's what this is really about!"

He heard a hiss and nearly toppled over when Aquira popped up over Sora's shoulder, a flicker of fire in her open mouth.

"Call off your dragon!" He smiled.

"This isn't a joke, Whitney Fierstown. You dragged us back here to this… place… just so you could get your beloved crown?"

"No, it's not like that. I swear. Happy accident. We just needed the papers and I happened to leave them with the crown."

Sora folded her arms and huffed. Whitney went to place his hand on her shoulder, but Aquira hissed again.

"I promise, Sora," Whitney said. He extended his hand with the crown. "You can trash the crown if that'll prove it to you."

"Okay," she reached for the crown, but he swiftly reeled it back.

"Come on, is that necessary?"

"You just said—"

"Fine, it was a little about the crown, but it was more than that. We have no autlas now, and we're sailing war-ravaged waters. We need a bargaining chip in case of—"

"Shesaitju ships, I know."

"Or pirates." He sighed. "And I wanted you to come back here. Look." He took her by the hand and led her outside. To his surprise, she let him. He pointed to all the dilapidated buildings. "I think you should burn it to the ground. The whole place. Make sure no one ever has to live under these conditions ever again."

Sora just stared.

"You said it yourself," he continued "'No one should have to live like this.'"

He could see wheels turning in Sora's mind.

"No," she said, finally. "Let's just go get a ship."

"Wait, what do you mean? Yesterday you were ready to do whatever it took to make sure these people didn't live this way. I thought…"

"I don't want to talk about it," she said and started walking.

"Sora."

She spun around. "Fine, if you need to know. I followed every one of your dumb lessons. I used my 'assets' to get into Muskigo's inner circle. I pretended to be Tayvada's wife, and he bought it."

It was now Whitney's turn to stare.

"While I was with him," she continued, "I saw so many of my people being treated with far more respect by them than I ever have by the Glass. But even so…it was just a ploy by Muskigo to get more allies so more can die in this war."

"War is what forced my kind here," she said. "This isn't their realm. This is foreign territory. Same as when I came to Troborough. I lived in a basement below a shack, Whit. But you know what? That was leagues better than not having any home at all. What if I burned this place down and the Glass didn't care? Actually, they won't care. This isn't Merchants Row."

"But Sora—"

"But nothing. Muskigo burned down my little shack, and now I have no home. What would make this any different?"

Whitney tilted his head, looked back into Tayvada's empty home and said, "Fine, it's the gesture that counts, then. Let's go."

"One second." Sora returned to Tayvada's door and knelt before it. Whitney couldn't help but listen in. She set Aquira down in front of the house. "You deserve a chance to say goodbye, girl."

The wyvern trotted up to the door and gave it a whiff—enough, Whitney assumed, to remember the scent of her former master forever. She let out a squeal and looked back at Sora with her big, yellow eyes.

"I know, girl," Sora said. "This place will miss him, too. But things will get better, I know it. Now, c'mon." She extended her arm, and Aquira darted back onto her shoulder. Sora closed the door, then drew a deep breath.

"All right, what are you waiting for?" she said, turning to Whitney. "We've got a ship to steal."

"You have no idea how proud I am to hear those words," Whitney said. "And Muskigo's inner circle? By Iam, I demand to know every detail of that story and how you used your *assets*."

"Is that jealousy?" she asked.

"Professional curiosity."

"Shut up." She chuckled and punched him in the arm again. He had no idea he could miss a sore spot so much.

XXVI

THE KNIGHT

Torsten shifted his stance. Despite the heat beating down on his body from all around, the street was slick with melting ice. His fingers tightened around the grip of his claymore until it felt like an extension of his arm. He drew slow, steady breaths, the air thick with smoke. He wasn't afraid. So much of his world had become a mystery but this, he understood. Battle. And as he watched Muskigo's zhulong charging him, gold-clad tusks thrashing, he was both there and at the beginning. His mind recalled when he was but an armiger, and those first few bouts training under Uriah Davies. He remembered the sting of the wooden sword upon his back. Being slammed to the dirt over and over. And of course, he remembered the first time he landed a strike on the then-Wearer.

Kings, queens, and ancient feuds were one thing, but this he understood. This was kill or be killed.

He waited until the last possible moment, then shifted to the right and swung his sword wide, low to high. The side of a tusk smashed him in the ribs just as the tip of his claymore cut through the zhulong rear haunch. Any ordinary sword wouldn't have pierced its thick, scaly hide, but the glaruium of Mount Lister was strong and its sharpness never dulled.

Torsten caught himself before hitting the ground and turned, half-crouched. His chestplate had a dent the size of a fist, the pain of the blow pulling at his entire left side. The zhulong, on the other hand, went down hard. Muskigo flew from its back, rolled across the street and found his footing in one smooth motion.

"I'll give it to you, Shieldsman," he said as he flicked snow off his scimitar. "You are brave as you are foolish." His left half was horribly burned, and blood oozed out of the wound in the back of his other shoulder where Sora stabbed him. If the pain affected him, he didn't show it.

"I am a vessel," Torsten said, having to growl just to cover for the fact that every breath he drew made his ribcage feel like it was going to pop through his skin. "Now, you will see the power of faith."

Another plangent moan of a Drav Cra horn sounded, and with it, the din of battle escalated. Every clash of metal like thunder creeping ever-closer. Footsteps like raindrops pounding on stone. The coming of a storm.

"Do you hear that?" Muskigo said. "It's the sound of your army failing. And when they do, I will bring everything I have crashing upon Yarrington."

"Not if you are dead."

"Spoken like a true follower of Iam. Peace?" he scoffed. "Your god is a bringer of death. So come, vessel, and do what he does best!"

Muskigo brandished his sword, and Torsten charged. Torsten was larger, as was his weapon, but even with his many injuries, Muskigo was impossibly fast. He ducked right, then spun out of the way of a furious swipe. Torsten immediately recognized the Black Fist style. Muskigo never let the full brunt of Torsten's claymore land upon his sword, but deflected blow after blow downward. He used his scimitar more like a shield than a weapon, and his lack of encumbering armor always had him one step ahead.

That was the essence of the style—to be as unshakable as a balled fist. To wait, absorb, exhaust your enemy until the time was right to land one perfect, deadly punch.

Muskigo caught a thrust between his blade and hip, then slid forward, slicing Torsten across a weak spot of armor behind one knee. Torsten roared and whipped around, his scimitar cracking the street as it barely missed Muskigo.

"You want to know what I learned from my father?" Muskigo asked, pacing out of range, barely breathing heavily. "Patience."

Torsten turned with him, struggling to hide his windedness. Between the bruised rib, exhaustion from the ambush, and the weight of his glaruium armor, his muscles were being pushed to their limits. He vowed, should he make it from Winde Port alive, to train more often and focus less on politics.

"The zhulong is a stubborn beast, you see," Muskigo continued. "When it feels threatened it charges—no matter what. But the sand serpents that inhabit the beaches outside Latiapur, you would barely know they were there, even if you were staring right at them."

"Are you going to keep talking? I've been looking forward to this since the moment I saw you in the Fellwater."

Torsten took a hard step and swung low at Muskigo's shins. The afhem's agile body allowed him to hurdle the sword. He landed, and before Torsten could bring his sword back around, the man had darted forward and sliced his elbow.

It was as if Muskigo's blade were precisely drawn to Torsten's armor joints. He pulled a sharp breath through his teeth.

"The serpent buries itself and waits," Muskigo continued, keeping his distance and circling Torsten like a hunting wolf. "Sometimes for days, sometimes until it starves. It waits for prey to stroll by, unassuming, and then… it strikes like a bolt of lightning." Muskigo feigned attack.

"Fight me!" Torsten bellowed.

"There is honor in charging like the zhulong as my father did but they are clumsy, mindless creatures happy to be ridden. The serpent, on the other hand, won't move a muscle. And by the time you realize it's still alive, its venom is coursing through your veins."

"No!" Torsten said. "Your rebellion ends here, today."

Torsten went at him again, throwing every bit of his remaining energy into every attack. Muskigo didn't even use his sword this time. He dipped and evaded, and as Torsten went high with his claymore, Muskigo's gray fist shot forward and struck in the center of his chest.

Torsten's armor caved, and he careened backward, the sword slipping from his grasp. He looked down when he landed. He had taken hits from battle hammers and not suffered such damage. His time for amazement ended swiftly as Muskigo's scimitar raced toward his head. Torsten did the only thing he could. Used his strength.

He caught it with both hands, the blade driving through the joints of his gauntlets and slicing his hands. He held it there, the edge only inches from cleaving his skull. Now it was Muskigo's turn to look surprised.

Torsten shifted one hand, allowing the scimitar to continue into the ground at the side of his head. With the other he punched Muskigo hard across the face, the spiked knuckles of his gauntlet splitting his lip. A second shot tore chunks of flesh from his cheek.

Muskigo staggered back. Torsten fought the sharp pain racking his limbs as he scrambled to his feet and drove his armored shoulder into the afhem. They tumbled across the slick street, their tangled bodies spinning. They punched and kicked all the way until their bodies slipped over the edge of Merchants Canal.

They landed on their backs. The thick ice covering the water splintered but didn't break. Torsten's ears rang from countless blows to the head. The sounds of battle at his back were louder than ever, as if the armies were now warring within the city itself.

Muskigo didn't seem to be faring much better. And as they both got to their feet, ready to engage again, the ice cracked more.

Half the man's gray face was carved up and drenched in blood like his torso, but Muskigo's confidence never waned. "I wonder which one of us will go through first?" He spread his sandaled feet wide to disperse his weight.

Torsten looked down. Cracks snaked away from his armored feet like the webs of a spider. It didn't matter how he shifted his weight. He reached for the pendant hanging from his neck, only to be reminded it was no longer there.

But he never needed it, not really. Iam was in his heart, always —right there along with the King who helped forge him into the man he was.

"You forget, afhem," he said. "Only one of our deaths matters!"

Torsten darted forward. He could feel the slick surface giving way under his heavy feet, but he kept pushing. Muskigo got his sword around a fraction of a second too late. Torsten's massive body barreled into him, and when they hit the ice, this time it gave way.

Icy water and darkness enveloped Torsten as he clung to Muskigo's waist to try and drag him under. The afhem clawed at the unbroken ice, desperate to stay above the surface. His lack of heavy armor made him fast, but even seconds below the surface might stop his heart.

Torsten could feel it; bitter death seeping through the cracks in his armor. Pushing against his lips to reach his lungs. Yet even with his weight and armor, they didn't sink. Instead, they began to rise through the ice.

His head emerged from the water. Two of Muskigo's Serpent Guards had thrown a rope wrapped to a gondola post to the afhem and were hauling him up.

"Yo—u d—die… here," Torsten said, shivering.

Another warrior, standing at the lip of the canal, threaded his bow. It took every bit of his strength for Torsten to move his head out of the way of an arrow. Muskigo then thrashed and caught Torsten in the face with a foot. His numb arms gave out, and the leader of the rebellion wriggled free.

As he plunged into the water, Torsten watched Muskigo be heaved to the surface and wrapped in leathers. Torsten could hear nothing but the slowing rhythm of his own heart, but he saw the afhem's now-purple lips rasp orders.

Muskigo stared down into the depths of the canal for a moment. He didn't seem proud or satisfied, just bowed his head in respect as he was escorted away.

It was Torsten's last clear sight before the cold started to blur his vision. His entire body went numb, toes to skull. Even his heart was silent. And as the water closed in around him, he couldn't help but feel this was his path to Elsewhere. He had dedicated his life to the light of Iam, and here he would die, weightless in the dark. A failure.

A spear stabbed through the surface. Torsten couldn't feel his fingers, but he was able to get a few around the staff. Then the tip of another spear hooked around the back of his armor. Before he knew it, the reddish glow of fire filled his vision. A dozen hands grabbed at him, rolling him up onto the surface.

He couldn't speak, couldn't even move. He could do nothing but shiver as the world came into view again. Shesaitju forces were in a full retreat, pursued by the combined army of Glassmen and Drav Cra. The fire, which had carved a path of destruction all the way to the walls was dwindling as snow fell harder.

A familiar face leaned down over him, pale and half-covered by a spiky, red birthmark. Redstar spoke, but Torsten couldn't hear a thing. He could only watch as Redstar extended his hand for the warlock Freydis to slice. He placed his bloody palm against Torsten's chest and began to mutter under his breath until the hand glowed red. His eyes were shut, lids flickering.

Warmth built within Torsten's heart. He could feel it spread through his veins like a tree laying roots. First, his fingers and toes thawed, then the limbs themselves, and then he gasped for air. Water spewed out, literally steaming thanks to Redstar's blood magic.

Redstar withdrew his hand. "There you are," he said. "Breathe. Nesilia tells me it is not yet your time."

Torsten brushed him aside and rolled over. He still couldn't find the ability to speak, but he leaned back on perched elbows and stared down toward the docks. The Shesaitju were fleeing to their ships and rowboats, abandoning Winde Port. And now the streets were filled with Torsten's own people... and the Drav Cra.

They beat their chests and cheered, and on the lips of both peoples, Torsten heard a name that had a part of him wishing he'd drowned.

"Redstar, Redstar, Redstar..."

XXVII

THE THIEF

As Whitney, Sora, and Aquira crested the hill of mansions overlooking Winder's Wharf and the rest of the city, Whitney was sure of one thing—Winde Port would never be the same. That free-loving, gold-flipping place he'd loved had seen the wrath of war. Not just the fire that burned its finest shops and most stately buildings, but a terror would hover over the place that would change it.

Whitney felt it in Panping any time he was there—this weight, as if the spirits of the dead were constantly whispering to the survivors of Liam's war that they were left behind.

War would ruin another place he loved, but as he looked down upon the battle-filled streets at the walls and heart of the city, he couldn't help but feel a bit of pride that he'd helped the winning side. It was difficult to see through the lingering smoke in the night, but the Shesaitju were clearly starting to retreat, eyes set on their rowboats and ships moored on the southern beaches. The Glass Army charged through the city walls like a nail through a ship's hull.

"He did it," Whitney said, not even trying to hide his joy. "He really yigging did it!" The war was stupid, a pointless squabble between rich lords over land and forgotten slights. But Torsten, his friend, led this battle. And after everything that had happened to the kingdom he loved for whatever Iam-forsaken reason, Whitney knew the Shieldsman deserved a win.

"Praise be," Sora said, her voice dripping with sarcasm. "I suppose he'll give all credit to Iam for saving his hide once again?"

"Oh, you know he will. Never to you... unless... are you Iam and you didn't tell me?"

"If I were, I'd have created you without a mouth. Now let's move before the docks are overrun again." Her fingernails dug into Whitney's forearm as she pulled him down the hill. Aquira looked back and screeched at him as if warning him not to test her.

"Are you sure you don't want to take a moment and knock another mansion off Darkings' board?" Whitney pointed left, at the highest point in the city upon which the homes of Bartholomew and Winde Port's richest families stood. With the glow of dwindling flames so far off, they were drenched in darkness. A corner here or there glowed under whatever slivers of moonlight slipped through the clouds, but not a candle was lit. Snow piled up in front of their heavy doors.

Most of their inhabitants probably got out safely through their own tunnels like the Darkings. Or they threw their slaves at the Shesaitju and ran. Now, the homes stood as great, big gravestones for the city.

"I think we should stop making enemies," Sora said, pulling him harder.

"That's a great lesson," Whitney answered. "Write that down: friends are better."

The road flattened out, and he pulled Sora back against a building on the edge of the wharf. A cohort of Shesaitju ran by, screaming and cursing. Whitney noticed, out of the corner of his eye, they were leaning against the Winde Traders Guild Hall. Through a shattered window, he could see all the velvet-cushioned chairs were overturned and plates of delectables strewn across the floor.

Sora peeked around the corner. "Most of the ships are tipped!" she exclaimed.

"About that…" Whitney said. He stole a look as well. The ships used in his distraction were in rough shape. With the snow picking up, a few of the smaller ones were weighted much too heavily to one side, others were half-sunken in the shallow water from ruptured hulls.

He cursed himself as he looked down toward the beachfront.

The Shesaitju vessels remained in fine condition, awaiting the return of their respective crews out on the bay. It looked like a choreographed dance upon the waters, rowboat oars plunging and pulling in perfect harmony as gray men made their way to freedom. Zhulong and their riders plunged into the ice-cold water, where the hulking beasts proved to be unexpectedly agile swimmers.

A volley of arrows cascaded overhead, then rained down upon the waters, many finding their places buried within the boats and their pilots. The Glassmen were advancing, while brave Shesaitju warriors still on the wharf gave their lives to allow for a thorough retreat.

"What about that one?" Sora pointed toward the small, black corsair vessel at the north end of the dock. It was right next to the one Whitney and Tum Tum had started the chain reaction of devastation upon. Its low stature kept it safe even as the adjacent ship's hull angled up and over it.

"Good enough." The small, nimble ship would be easy to maneuver through the crowded bay, even, hopefully, by a crew of only two. "All right, on my count, we run for it."

Sora regarded the wyvern on her shoulder. "Ready?" Aquira clicked her tongue in response.

"Three...two... one..."

They hurried out onto the quay. Sora's foot slid out on the icy surface, but Whitney was there to catch her. The heaviest fighting was south of them, by Merchants Row and the beach. They made it to the ship without a hitch and climbed up the lowered ramp. It was only when they were onboard that they noticed the four gray men already on the deck.

"This will be our ship we are having!" one of them said in broken speech. They raised their curved blades.

"I've got these," Whitney said, holding out his arm.

"What a gentleman," Sora replied.

Whitney was just about to say something smart when he saw one of their knees snap inward. Tum Tum stood behind him, a giant hammer in hand.

"Not without me ye ain't," Tum Tum shouted.

Whitney charged while they were distracted. He lowered his shoulder, and it connected with one of their stomachs. Luckily, Tum Tum noticed him and dropped to hands and knees at the last moment. The Shesaitju propelled backward, tripped over Tum Tum, and flipped over the railing into the icy waters of the bay.

The remaining two went back to back. One kept their sword trained on Tum Tum and the other on Whitney.

"If ye'd told me your plan it'd saved me a heap of trouble," Tum Tum said.

"But you love trouble," Whitney replied.

The warrior swung at Whitney, who rolled aside and came up wielding the dagger he stole from Fenton. Tum Tum slammed his hammer down on the deck with all his might. The wood planks nearby came unsettled, and Whitney's opponent lost balance when he went to take another swipe.

"Watch the ship! We need it!"

Whitney ducked to the side, then darted forward and delivered a deep slice through his opponent's hamstring. At the same time, Tum Tum raised the handle of his hammer into his target's groin, then flipped him, legs first. His head slammed into the floor, knocking him out cold.

"Uh, Whitney, when you boys are done!" Sora said.

Whitney looked back. Several more Shesaitju were bounding down the wharf toward the ship, desperate for any suitable vessel.

"Tum Tum, hoist the mainsail!" Whitney ordered.

"I won't be able to reach, ye dolt," he said. "This ship was made for taller men."

"Must I do it all?" Whitney groaned. "Fine, just help Sora."

Whitney tossed her his dagger before hurrying to help Tum Tum prep for launch.

Sora drew a cut along her palm, then raised her bloody hand toward the attackers and screamed. No ball or pillar of flame exploded from her hand as Whitney was used to. Only a smattering of pathetic embers spewed out.

Whitney stopped by the mast. "Where's your magic?" he hollered.

"I... I don't know," she said, suddenly sounding faint. "I can't manage even a spark."

Whitney was about to run back to help when Aquira soared off her shoulder. She swept in front of the Shesaitju, blowing a line of fire between the ship and the wharf. She didn't pack much of a punch, but the heat was palpable.

Tum Tum waddled over to the ramp to hold them off. The ramp was securely attached, but the dwarf brought his hammer down on it as one Shesaitju braved the flame. Just then, Whitney unfurled the sails, and they snapped up, catching the heady winds.

The ship pulled away from the dock. The weakened ramp snapped in half, the Shesaitju upon it plummeting into the icy depths. A second later, the vessel jarred to a stop.

"Sora," Whitney shouted. "Forget them, get that rope!" He pointed to the single rope still attached to a cleat on the wharf. The Shesaitju must have untied the rest before they overtook them. Sora nodded her understanding. She panted as she slashed at it twice, sending two frayed ends into the wind. A Shesaitju dove toward the ship and grabbed onto the stern before his fingers met Sora's knife.

"Jolly fine departure everyone!" Whitney exclaimed.

"Whit!" Sora screamed.

Whitney turned quickly to face her as a sword swiped only inches from his head. He heard a hum, felt a sting, then blood sprayed in front of his face. He dropped to his knees and saw a Shesaitju behind him. His knee was a mangled mess, but he stood upright on his good leg. He didn't get his sword back around before the dwarf finished the job, crushing his skull against the deck.

"Whitney," Sora said, running toward him "Are you okay?"

"What?" He placed a hand on the side of his head. It was bleeding profusely, and his head rang.

Tum Tum came around in front of him, holding the top half of Whitney's ear. He lifted it to his mouth and shouted, "Can ye hear me?"

Whitney ripped it out of his hands. He held it to the portion of ear still attached, and only when they touched did he realize how much it really stung.

"My yigging ear!" he shouted.

Sora knelt in front of him. She couldn't mask her concern, but Aquira looked like she wanted to lick up the blood.

"Is it bad?" Whitney said.

"I've seen worse…" she lied.

"Can you fix it?" he asked Sora, holding the ear up.

"Not right now I don't think." She looked down at her bloody hand. "I think I'm completely drained."

346

"Well, you did just light half the city on fire..." His words trailed off. He looked back at Tum Tum, who not only had no idea she could do such magic, but it was his city that burned. If he took offense, he didn't show it. The Black Sands had overtaken the place, regardless.

"So ye be a mystic?" Tum Tum asked.

Sora shrugged. "I'm something. We're going to Yaolin City if we make it out of this bay alive."

"Hello!" Whitney interrupted. "My ear!"

"Oh, quit whinin ye flower picker," Tum Tum said. "It's only a piece." He slapped him in the side of the head. Whitney yelped.

"Here." Sora took the chunk of flesh from Whitney's hands. Then she buried it in a bit of snow piled around the mast. "We'll keep it fresh, and I'll see if I can help after we have some rest."

"Sure, I'll just sail around, earless," Whitney said. He stood and drew a long breath of the chilly air.

"You two dump these bodies off the ship. Tum, I'm guessing you're okay with going to Yaolin? Otherwise, I can drop you off in the Boiling Waters."

The dwarf stood at the rail and stared longingly back at the wharf and his city, glowing red. "Aye. All I gots be gone anyway," he said, sadness heavy in his voice.

"Then I hope you're ready for a fun ride." Whitney grabbed hold of the wheel and spun it. The ship lurched and changed course.

"How do you—" Sora began.

"What part of 'I sailed with Grisham "Gold Grin" Gale' did I not make clear?"

He knew she didn't believe him about half the things he said he'd done—which was probably smart on her part—but this one was the cold, hard truth. He knew how to run a ship, though he was glad to have Tum Tum and Sora onboard to help with things.

Who knows, maybe by the time they reached Yaolin City, Sora would be a right good sailor.

First, they had to weave their way through a number of Shesaitju warships and rowboats. He hoped they were too preoccupied with their escape to worry about a small corsair vessel. Still, he kept their course southeast, so it seemed like they were Shesaitju soldiers part of the retreat. At his first opportunity, he could cut the sails to steer them behind the Breakwaters—a tight clumping of dagger-like stones sticking up from Trader's Bay.

For a large ship, the boulders would be catastrophic, but this corsair would slip right into the strait with no difficulty. Then, it would be off toward the Boiling Waters on the fastest route to Panping.

"We don't want to be spotted, so everyone stay low," Whitney said. "Or, well, Tum Tum, you can just stand."

"Very funny, one ear."

Whitney grinned and steadied the wheel, feeling the weight of the ship and waters fighting back. "I think we finally found my pirate name."

"Too bad you can't grow a beard!" Sora hollered over from the other side of the deck.

Whitney glared back at her, then smiled. He'd never been so happy to see someone sliding a body off the deck of a ship before. He'd never been so happy to see anyone.

XXVIII

THE MYSTIC

"I must say, Sora," Whitney began, "ever since you found me, these have been adventures for the record books. Of all that happened in that gods-forsaken city, being pivotal pieces in a battle for Pantego's soul will be tough to top."

Whitney stared over the starboard side of the deck back to Winde Port. He barely paid attention to the wheel now that they were passed the retreating Shesaitju army and heading for the strait out of the bay. Tum Tum was busy angling the ship's single, triangular sail to catch what little breeze there was. After that focused gust that fed Sora's fire and felt so much like magic, the air was still. The water may as well have been frozen it was so flat, tiny ripples wiggling like glowing snakes under the light of the moons.

"Clearly, I attract trouble," Sora said.

"And rebel afhems," Whitney muttered.

"I knew you were jealous!"

"Just that I missed such an incredible display. I was worried you were too uptight to act." Whitney flinched, clearly expecting her to punch him. When she didn't, he turned and found Aquira leaning over the boom of the sail, glaring down at him. "We're never going to be alone again, are we?"

Sora reached up and stroked her new friend's tail. "Nope. She's part of this scoundreling crew."

"Going with scoundreling, then? Perfect."

For a short while, they quietly watched the retreat. The Shesaitju vessels were already unloading at the docks of a small village on the opposite side of the bay. Back in Winde Port, the Glass army celebrated victory. Or at least, that's what the tiny, shiny dots flitting around the wharf looked like they were doing.

"Do you think Torsten made it out?" Sora asked.

"Of course, he's too stubborn to die. Look." Whitney pointed to the wharf. "That's probably him right there. Of course, it is; no one else has such blinding armor at night. Happy to be of service again, Torsten!" He waved.

"Why were you helping him, anyway?"

"He was supposed to help me find you after Muskigo was eliminated. Clearly, since I found you well enough by myself, he still owes me one."

"That makes two of us. Did I mention I saved him and his men from an ambush in the estate when I started that fire?"

"Yeah?"

"They walked right into it."

Whitney sighed. "What is that man going to do without us?"

"Probably lose a war."

"You're right. We should go back." He pretended to start spinning the wheel.

"Whitney, stop!" Sora laughed.

"What? You're right, we can't leave him behind. He needs us."

"Whit." Her hand fell upon his, and they turned toward each other. She stared at him while he wore that same, goofy grin that hadn't changed since he was a boy. He still couldn't grow a beard, but for a runt from Troborough, he was handsome as a prince. The standards weren't high. The only difference was one of his ears now had a chunk taken off.

"I'm sorry," they said at the same time.

"For what?" they said at the same time again.

They chuckled.

"You first," Whitney said.

"No, you go ahead," Sora replied. "I want to hear this."

Whitney stole a page out of Sora's book and rolled his eyes.

"Fine," he began. "I'm sorry I let you get taken back at Tayvada's place. I'm sorry for dragging you into this life. It's not safe. It's no place for a… lady."

"Hah! A lady? Don't let my tattered clothes fool you. Plus, you didn't *let* me be taken. You couldn't have stopped that heinous creature even if you wanted to. He's a yigging upyr, Whit. You know what tha—"

Whitney held out an arm. He held his stomach like he was going to vomit. "Vampire," Whitney said with a shudder.

"Let me guess, you worked with them a few years back. Cue some ridiculous story."

"No, my dear, Sora. This one will be a first, and one I'm glad to be rid of. No wonder he avoided sunlight."

Sora nodded.

"Yigging gods. If I knew that was what Barty sent after us maybe I would have killed the slob. He didn't want to…"

"Drink my blood?" Sora asked. "He did, but Aquira wouldn't let him."

"Thank the fallen gods for her."

At the mention of her name, Aquira craned her neck down from the sail toward Sora.

"You were scared, weren't you?" Sora scratched the wyvern under her chin. Aquira's wings expanded, and she stuck her head out, the thin flap of skin underneath stretching taut.

"I'm sure it was only her," Whitney remarked.

Sora regarded him and her heart sunk. "I wanted to find you," she said, not looking him in the eye. "But so much happened so fast. I was worried you died, then running from Kazimir, Muskigo, seeing my people. It all—"

He placed a finger over her mouth. "Sora, you don't have to explain a thing to me." He craned his neck and gestured to the red mark ringing his neck. "The gods seem to want me alive no matter what. I think I might be invincible."

"By Iam, Whitney." She pulled him closer and examined the dark red ring around his neck. "I didn't notice that. It looks awful. Kazimir said you survived execution, but he didn't say you were already strung up to die when you did. How did you get out of it?"

"You've got magic, and I've got my own secrets." He puffed out his chest and went to playfully run his hand through his hair. His finger grazed the sliced part of his ear, and he winced.

"Smooth," Sora chuckled. "We're going to have to do something about that soon. It's going to get infected." She reached up toward it. Her thumb hit a piece of his hair, and a thick, wet paste rubbed off. "Ick! Is that, shog?"

"Long story," Whitney said.

"Oh, c'mon, I finally want to hear a story and you're holding out?" When she looked down, she realized how close to him she'd gotten to examine his wounds. She could feel the warmth of his breath. They locked eyes, and on his face, he wore an expression unlike any she'd ever seen him wearing. Her heart started to race, and she didn't know why.

He smiled, but he didn't back away—not even as Aquira growled from up above. Instead, she could feel him slowly growing closer. "Well, we do have plenty of time," he said softly.

"I wouldn't be so sure of that," said a voice from behind them, accent thick as blood.

Sora and Whitney fell apart from each other and whipped around. Kazimir emerged from the shadows of the open captain's quarters. He clicked his tongue in disapproval.

"Did you think I would so easily allow you to leave?" he asked. "After all we've been through together?"

"Who the yig be that!" Tum Tum shouted from the bow.

Aquira flew down to Sora's shoulder and growled. Sora raised her hand. It was still bleeding, but she couldn't feel an ounce of that dark power roiling within her. No matter how she willed on Elsewhere, she felt... empty within.

Whitney's arm extended in front of her as he stepped forward. "No need to burn down the ship." He reached into his pocket and removed a roll.

"Kazimir," he began in diplomatic fashion, "I have a writ signed by Yuri Darkings himself. You are released from your blood pact with Bartholomew Darkings, so we can just all move on."

In the span of a second, Whitney was on his back, and Kazimir straddled him like a mare. Whitney turned away from the man and clenched his eyes tightly. But still, he held up the paper. "You wouldn't want to upset your bosses," he said. "The Master of Coin could be a powerful ally."

"Not a soul will know what happens here."

"Your Sanguine Gods will," Whitney grated.

"*Lords*. And they know that a pact cannot be rescinded. Not even by a king, let alone some Council member. This paper is as worthless as you are." Kazimir ripped it from his hands. His nightmarish grin widened as he released it to the wind.

"Damn that family," Whitney swore under his breath.

"I don't understand, Whit," Sora said. "You said the pact was ended." Her voice shook. Even having Aquira on her shoulder, ready to fiercely protect her, didn't make her feel brave. All she could do was stare at those terrible, soulless eyes, frozen.

"Clearly, father Darkings lied so I wouldn't kill his son. I knew I should have gone with my gut."

Sora's stomach went tight. She knew precisely why Whitney didn't go with his gut. Why he delved back in the city, helped Torsten... everything. For her.

"This is no longer about you, thief," Kazimir snapped. "In time, Bartholomew Darkings will pay for his attempted retraction with his own blood. But I'm here for her."

He regarded Sora, breathed in deep, and released a moan. The way his lower lip trembled made Sora's skin crawl.

"Yes," he said, a twinge of ecstasy lacing the word. "Cut, dash, slice, rend. The smell alone gives me a strength I haven't felt in years."

He leaned down and spoke softly in Whitney's ear—something Sora couldn't hear. Whitney's face lost its color, and he stopped fighting like he was petrified into stone by the gorgons of legend.

"I suggest ye get off him and off our ship," Tum Tum demanded. He stood beside Sora now, hammer in hand.

Kazimir rose but kept a boot on Whitney's chest.

"My ship actually," he said. "An entire night wasted hunting the two of you, and you come right to me." He laughed, then looked back at Sora. "It's almost as if our union were destiny."

"Even still, yer outnumbered. Leave, or I'll make ye."

"Remain where you are, Dwarf! We have no quarrel, and that fact need not change. Besides, do you think your lumbering body is any match for me?"

Again, before Sora could blink, Kazimir changed locations. Aquira hissed and went to bite him, but he slapped the poor wyvern aside and sent her into the wall of the ship.

"Aquira!" Sora gasped.

The wyvern groaned but was still breathing. Sora tried to run to her, but Kazimir wrapped her midriff in a soft caress with one hand and placed the other against her neck.

"Take your hands off me!" she screamed, squirming, but it was no use. He was too strong.

Kazimir's hand slid down from her neck, fingertips tickling her shoulder, then her forearm before finally coming to rest around her wrist. She let out a squeak. She couldn't help it, his strength was unimaginable.

He extended his arm and with it, hers. Then, he licked a line of half-dried blood off her forearm. "We will be so happy together."

Whitney sat up but remained silent. Whatever Kazimir said had to be horrific to still his tongue for so long. Tum Tum stood like a statue, watching in horror as the upyr called Kazimir had his way. A simple tavern owner from Winde Port had likely never seen magic, let alone a man move so impossibly fast.

"I will die before marrying you," Sora said.

That seemed enough to shake Whitney. "Marry?" he asked. "Shogging exile, what are you talking about? This *creature* wants to marry you?"

"Watch your tongue, thief, or I will devour it," Kazimir said.

"Whit, what do I do?" Tum Tum asked quietly.

"Just stay still." The ship was beginning to lilt with nobody at the helm. Whitney slowly stood and wrapped his fingers around the steering wheel. Kazimir squeezed Sora tighter.

"I don't think you understand, Kazzy," Whitney said. "Can I call you that?"

That was when Sora saw that mad glint in his eye when Whitney was about to do something monumentally stupid. *Please don't,* she willed him. *Please.*

"Just weeks ago, we killed an actual goddess," Whitney continued. "She wasn't some two-bit joke wearing leather and silver clasps, flitting around the night like a bat. She was a real yigging goddess, and we gutted her like a fish."

Kazimir chuckled. "If the spirits are correct, it was the dark-skinned Wearer of the Glass and the marked orphan of the Drav Cra who brought doom to Bliss. You were merely a distraction and she… oh, the power within you." Kazimir again took a break from the conversation to take a whiff of Sora's neck. She could feel his fingers fluttering from the joy of it.

Hate welled inside of her. It felt like Elsewhere, yet it wasn't readily at her fingertips. No spark or preternatural heat. She cursed herself, cursed Wetzel for not training her better. In the distance was Winde Port, ravaged by the work of her hand. The fire seemingly fed on her anger and connection to Elsewhere even after it left her fingers. She had nearly won the battle for the Glass Kingdom all on her own, but now, faced with mortal danger, she couldn't even help herself or her closest friend.

"Let them go, and I'll come with you," she said. Her natural instincts screamed at her, but she said it anyway. "Be with you. Whatever you want."

"Sadly, dear, the time for courtesy has passed. You don't need to want to be mine for me to take you."

His breath was hot on her neck now. She could feel him against her back, an animalistic aura pulsating from him. His sharp fangs brushed her neck.

"Stop!" Whitney said. "Take me instead."

"What?" everyone asked at the same time.

"Take me, right? I'm a Lord now, technically… I'm not one for bureaucracies. But that's gotta count for something. The Wearer of White owes me, too. I can give you power, wealth."

"Whitney what are you doing?" Sora asked. "It's my blood he needs."

Kazimir seemed amused. "I rejected a Darkings. What could street filth possibly offer?"

"How about this?" Whitney slowly reached into the folds of his clothing, leaving his other hand raised. Kazimir grew tense until Whitney pulled out the broken half of the Glass Crown. All the precious gems set in its point glimmered even under the dull moonlight. "This here is the Glass Crown worn by Liam Nothhelm himself. Well, half of it."

"Meungor's axe!" Tum Tum exclaimed, stirred from his trance.

Kazimir approached it, dragging Sora along with him. Even his dark, soulless eyes seemed to brighten with wonder. Whitney shot her a subtle wink.

"I stole it right off his head," Whitney said, edging closer. "It broke while I escaped, but still has to be worth a damn fortune." Kazimir went to grab it, but Whitney pulled it back. "Not so fast. You drop this pact and leave us alone, it's yours. You can wear it for all I care."

"Why should I not just take it?"

"Honor?" Whitney audibly swallowed the lump forming in his throat. "Honestly, I was just trying to buy a second or two." Whitney jerked the wheel to the side. "Ah hah!"

The ship lurched a bit, and everyone took a small step to the left, but little else happened.

"Shog in a barrel. I really thought that would have done more."

Sora growled and used the minor distraction to kick Kazimir in the shin and escape his grasp. Whitney tossed her his dagger, and she caught it mid spin and whipped it around to plunge it into Kazimir's chest. Her strike met only air.

"Hands off him, demon," barked Tum Tum, brandishing his hammer.

Sora turned back around to see Kazimir somehow already holding Whitney.

"You children don't seem to understand how this all works!"

the upyr snarled, a knife to Whitney's throat. Sora's knife. "Every single one of you is going to die. The only question now is how fast."

Kazimir pushed down on Whitney's shoulder and with his free hand put pressure on his forehead, stretching the skin of his neck.

"You kill me, and your bosses will be quite mad," Whitney taunted. "There's no blood pact on me anymore. You should be going after Bartholomew."

Kazimir laughed. "The Sanguine Lords didn't request the life of Tayvada Bokeo either, yet he is dead."

Whitney swallowed hard.

"How dare you speak his name after what you did," Sora snapped.

"Do you think anyone controls whom I send to Elsewhere? The Dom Nohzi's days are numbered. Only I can lead them away from the fires of exile. We no longer need to hide in the shadows."

"It's okay, Sora," Whitney said, smiling, trying to stay brave. "Just blow us both away. I know the power is in you. Sail off to your people and see where you came from."

Sora knew what she wanted to say; that he was the only people she ever really had. But she couldn't bring herself to.

"Just leave him alone," she managed. "You've got what you want!"

Kazimir leaned down and licked Whitney's wounded ear. Whitney writhed in pain. The sight made Sora sick. All he'd done for her, and this was how he was going to die. He could have sent her on her way back in the forest all those weeks ago when she found him, but instead, he brought her into his way of life. He promised to show her things she'd never dreamed of. Accepted her. Gave her a purpose, even if she didn't love what it was.

Kazimir tore the crown from Whitney's fingers and shoved it

onto the front of his head so hard it drew lines of blood on his temples.

"I've always wanted to taste the blood of a king," Kazimir whispered. Then, he sunk his fangs into Whitney's shoulder.

"No!" Sora yelled as Whitney cried out.

She felt a sudden rage bubbling again deep within. There was a familiar taste on her tongue—a mingling of iron and ash. She'd tasted it before, felt it before, but something was different this time. It was pure—unbridled.

"Leave him alone!" she bellowed.

She wasn't bleeding any longer, but she raised her hands anyway. She could feel the energy crackling around her fingertips. A blinding light bloomed around her hands—not just her hands, her entire body.

The light intensified and with it, all the strength fled her muscles like Elsewhere was sapping her. It was similar to conjuring a ball of flame or when she healed another's wound, only exponentially more intense. Even when she summoned the blast that stopped Redstar in the Webbed Woods, it paled in comparison.

She almost couldn't continue standing, yet she couldn't fall. Somewhere in the distance, she heard screams. Familiar screams, but altogether preternatural. Her name. Someone was screaming her name, but she could barely hear it over the sound of a rushing wind. Her face hurt like she stood in the middle of a hurricane. But at that moment, she realized she was the hurricane.

A deep rumble shook the deck beneath her. Then, a *crack, boom!*

Her eyes opened, and Tum Tum stood beside her shielding his face with his arm, beard and hair in tangles. The compass beside the ship's wheel spun wildly. Wind flapped the sails even though the bay remained flat as glass.

She fell to her knees, barely able to see, straining her eyes to

359

focus on Whitney, but he was gone. Kazimir was gone. Where they had just been, there was now nothing more than scorched wood, two piles of clothes with her knife laying atop them, and the King's Glass Crown teetering on its edge. Aquira limped over to the spot, sniffing the air as if something were missing.

"Whitney?" Sora whispered. And then she collapsed, accepting sleep like an old friend.

XXIX

THE KNIGHT

Torsten stood on Winder's Wharf, staring out upon the moonlit bay. He wore a wolf pelt over his shoulders for warmth, given to him by Redstar after he was pulled from the canal. Everyone was cheery now that the battle was won even though they were surrounded by death and destruction, Glassmen and Northmen patting each other on the back.

What have we won?

Afhem Muskigo was alive thanks to Torsten's failure. He'd called the retreat early, and now most of his army crossed Trader's Bay to the eastern banks, and there were few ships intact to follow them before they regrouped. Torsten wasn't surprised Whitney's distraction wound up doing almost as much harm than good. All the vessels moored directly in the harbor were tipped onto one another, hulls and masts shredded by a chain of ropes.

A sole Breklian corsair ship headed south apart from Muskigo's army. It was far, but Torsten could see a man waving from the wheel and knew exactly who he had to be. What he didn't expect, however, was how much he hoped Sora, a blood mage, had made it on safely as well. He could only trust Whitney had changed enough to genuinely care about someone other than himself. He owed her that much after saving his life for the second time.

"Smile, Wearer," Redstar said, stepping up beside him. "Muskigo may live, but it is a victory nonetheless."

"Winde Port will never be the same," Torsten said.

"So it is with war. You should know better than any. How many cities did Liam ravage as he reached further across Pantego?"

"That was different. He fought to brighten the world."

"It wasn't different for those he... *brightened*."

"What do you want Redstar?"

"Must I want something to speak with my Wearer?"

"You're here to gloat," Torsten said. "I led my men to their doom while you stole the glory."

"I did nothing. The Buried Goddess showed me the moment to strike, I merely obeyed and called upon her strength."

"You warned Muskigo I'd be coming, didn't you?" Torsten snapped, his hand clutching Redstar by the collar before he could stop himself. Over the man's shoulder, he noticed a handful of men watching, concerned for the Arch Warlock and uncle of the King. More than a few of them were of the Glass.

Redstar lowered his voice. "If I wanted you dead, I wouldn't have fished you out of that canal after *you* failed to kill the only Sandsman whose death mattered."

"I don't know what you want, but saving me was the biggest mistake you'll ever make." Torsten shoved him and stormed away. His men parted for him to pass, though they were too fixated on Redstar to salute.

"Where is Sir Wardric?" he asked.

Nobody had an answer. He'd been searching for the man who'd been left in charge of his army since the fighting stopped. He imagined that he and both Darkings, father and son, were back at the camp. Noblemen like Yuri didn't have a taste for battle.

So, Torsten walked back through the city, now cautious to take a true measure of things. He still felt cold and pulled his pelt tight, but the anomalous warmth in his chest didn't wane. It even dulled the pain of his many wounds.

The prefect's estate was a pile of glowing rubble like coals in a fire that had burned too hot and too long. A line of homes west of it were charred husks of buildings. It would take half the gold in the royal vaults to undo the damage. Bodies filled the streets— Shesaitju, his own army, civilians unfortunate to have been caught in the invasion in the first place.

On his way by, Torsten noticed something white glinting in the wreckage. He trudged through the ash and debris and lifted his own white helm, nearly in perfect shape but for a dent on the side. Pure glaruium was a difficult thing to break. His armor was similar to the other members of the King's Shield, though slightly more ornate, but that helm had been worn by Wearers for decades before even his mentor Uriah. Torsten lifted it, dumped the ash out, then continued on his way with it tucked under his arm.

The densest stacking of corpses was by the palisade walls, or rather, what remained of them. The wind had spread Sora's fire before the snow had time to extinguish it. The dry, wooden walls caught in an instant. Barely a segment still stood, the rest ashes.

"Sir, you're alive!" someone shouted.

Torsten turned and saw Sir Nikserof Pasic, one of the old guard, a member of the King's Shield who'd been in the ambush, sitting on a chunk of burned wood. His steel armor was coated in blood, most of it probably belonging to his own people. A barbed arrow protruded from one arm.

Torsten approached, and the man went to salute, but he stopped him. "You don't need to stand for me."

"Thank you, sir." He winced.

"You should see the physicians."

"I'm in good shape compared to the rest. Can you believe what happened here? They say the King's uncle summoned wind and fire to take the walls. A moment slower, we would have died in that courtyard."

"He didn't summon any fire." That much was true, but Torsten recalled hearing Redstar's incantation echoing in the air after they escaped their ambush, as if he was willing the fire along.

Nikserof's gray brow furrowed. A few more nearby soldiers and Shieldsmen started to eavesdrop. "Then who did?"

Torsten bit his lip. He couldn't say that it was the work of a Panpingese blood mage he knew, even if he believed Iam was working through her—then they would not only think him a failed general, but a madman.

"Iam reached down to save us," Torsten said. "Redstar may have charged at the right time, but at what cost? We were supposed to save those prisoners."

"You haven't heard, sir?" Nikserof asked.

"What?"

"Their bonds were tied to the walls. When they burnt, the people of Winde Port were able to break free, and the gray men couldn't give chase because our army charged. They're all back at camp, mostly. Many of them will need new homes but still… it's a miracle."

Torsten looked closer at the remnants of the wall and all the bodies covered in ash. They were almost entirely soldiers from either side, stacked in twos and even threes where the fighting was fiercest.

"The Buried Goddess is with Drad Redstar," Mak said from nearby. It seemed he was always around to stir up trouble. "Lucky for you, Wearer."

"There is no such thing as luck," Torsten snapped.

"The way I hear it, they had to scoop you out of the canal after you let Muskigo survive. Without Redstar, you'd be an icicle. Sounds lucky."

"Watch your tongue," Nikserof said. "That is your Wearer."

Mak smiled and bowed. "My apologies. What a fine job he's been doing." He laughed and continued on his way. After a few paces, he looked up to the sky. "Where's your light now!" he shouted, laughing some more.

"Ignore him," Nikserof said. "If we didn't distract Muskigo, they wouldn't have accomplished a thing."

The truth was, Torsten knew that wasn't true. Perhaps with Muskigo able to lead his army in the defense, they would have lasted longer, but they still would have lost because there was no accounting for a fire like what Sora caused. More of them might have even perished instead of calling an early retreat to fight another day.

No, Torsten's distraction helped with nothing. Sora still would have tried to kill the man she blamed for destroying her home. She still would have failed in the face of a mighty warrior like Muskigo and been forced to use magic. And the fire still would have spread on Redstar's otherworldly, west-faring wind.

Torsten merely answered with a grunt and a nod.

"Have you seen Wardric?" he asked.

Nikserof shook his head. "Can't bring myself to climb the hill. I've lost a lot of blood, as have many. I think Sir Austun Mulliner headed up there though."

Torsten left him, wading through the piled bodies, careful to show the proper respect. Then, turning his head to the sky, he whispered, "Where *is* your light now?"

He caught a whiff of something foul and glanced back down. A pile of dead Drav Cra warriors was being burned across the field while the warlock Freydis stood before them chanting. Her words were as foreign as the rattling of her tokens.

Priests of Iam would arrive soon to help lay the fallen Glassmen to rest as well, as they did after every battle so the dead may be committed to the Gate of Light. But all the soldiers and refugees standing atop the hill overlooking a victorious battlefield would first see the warlocks of the Buried Goddess staining it. Torsten could barely look without thinking impure thoughts; however, as he went by, he noticed a silvery sheen amongst the corpses.

A King's Shieldsman?

"Stop this!" he barked as he ran over. He shoved Freydis out of the way. A few warriors pulled their weapons on him before they realized he was kneeling by one of his own.

"How did this man wind up in here?" he questioned.

The shaggy-haired warlock seemed as confused as he was. The black paint on her brow cracked as it furrowed "An accident, I suspect," Freydis said. "There are so many bodies."

"This was no accident." Torsten reached through the fire and grabbed the body by the arm. He tried to pull, but it wouldn't budge. A fur-clad hand fell upon his shoulder.

"It is too late," a warrior said. "His ashes will join the others in the dirt as his soul is passed to Skorravik, where he may spend eternity in glorious battle."

"He is a soldier of Iam." Torsten went to pull him out again, but this time, the warrior wasn't so gentle, grabbing Torsten and pushing him away. Torsten reached for his sword before he realized it was at the bottom of a Winde Port canal. A gathering of Northerners glared at him, knuckles whitening on the grips of their axes.

Torsten backed away slowly, then returned on his path to the camp. His blood was boiling with rage. A few more warlocks were burning their dead. Ashes into the dirt. Torsten tried only to look at the ground. If he saw one more of his people caught up in their heathenistic ways, he wasn't sure what he would do.

Iam's followers were buried in death so their mortal vessels would be hidden from the sight of the Vigilant Eye while their souls rose to Iam's waiting arms. The process was longer, and with all these bodies, it would take a new graveyard to do, but his people deserved eternal rest for sacrificing their lives. Redstar, his followers—all they wanted was to take the easy way.

Civilians filled the camp, both refugees and the thousands who had escaped thanks to Sora's fire. Only one name was on their tongues being praised: Redstar. Torsten could even hear it over the screams echoing from the hospital tent where the wounded were being treated and amputated. He never thought he'd prefer that terrible sound over anything.

He made his way up to the Shieldsmen's camp. A few soldiers recognized him along the way and offered a salute. Most were too busy commending heathens to notice.

"Wardric!" Torsten called. "Wardric!"

He found the main tent where they'd planned their attack. A few younger Shieldsmen sat inside, sharing a drink and laughing like they were common soldiers and not the best the Glass Kingdom had to offer.

"Where are Sir Wardric and Yuri Darkings?" Torsten asked the only one he somewhat recognized, a blonde with a crooked nose. He wasn't sure of his name with his head so fuzzy, but he was a young Shieldsman too green to be dragged along on Torsten's ill-fated ambush. Torsten was sure he had overseen a few sessions of the man's training before he took the vows.

"Sir?" the blonde Shieldsman scrambled to come to attention, spilling his drink in the process. "You made it."

"A surprise to everyone it seems."

"I—with the fire—we—"

"It's not important," Torsten said. "Where are they?"

"I haven't seen them since they got back from leading you to the tunnels, sir."

367

"Any of you?"

The other two Shieldsmen shook their heads.

"He was temporary commander of the King's Shield," Torsten said. "You charged without orders from him?"

"It all happened so fast," the blonde Shieldsman said. "One moment, Redstar and all those crazy warlocks were lined up in the field, kneeling and chanting and cutting themselves. The next, the walls took to flames, and the King's uncle called the charge. If we didn't listen, all of the civilians fleeing the gray men would have died."

"You don't have to explain yourself to me. You men made the right decision for those people. But the battle is done. I need to find Sir Wardric so we can discuss the next move. Muskigo remains at large, and now he is east of the ravine, near the ancestral lands of his people and ready to spread his uprising."

"I swear, sir, none of us have seen him."

Torsten's gaze turned to their drinks, then back to the blonde Shieldsman's eyes. "Keep an eye out, all of you. If you find him, send for me."

"Yes, sir," said all.

Torsten thought he heard a snicker as he walked away but ignored it. Members of the King's Shield, drinking and carousing as if one battle ended a war? Torsten wondered if he was still in the freezing depths of the canal, dreaming before his body gave out. Or perhaps death had taken him to another plane entirely.

Is this Elsewhere? Is this my eternal exile?

He left the white helm in his tent, then swept through the other tents of his order, searching for Wardric but only finding more of his men celebrating victory. It was as if his army had raided the abandoned taverns of Winde Port for all their ale.

He stopped and spun a tight circle, unable to stop hearing the whispers of praise for Redstar. His breathing picked up. The warmth in his chest was dissipating now, so he felt the chill of the air once more. He was near ready to drop to a knee and give up when he noticed the luxurious carriage Yuri Darkings had arrived in. The reins for its two horses were sliced, the animals nowhere to be seen. But Torsten's eyes were drawn somewhere else, to a small smattering of red on the entry's frame.

One of his men said something to him from behind, but Torsten ignored it and approached the carriage. His legs were still incredibly sore, one of them gashed deep. He fought the pain and pushed forward. The door wasn't locked, which he found odd considering the wealth and importance of the man who owned it. He swiped his hand over the red spots. *Dry.*

He slowly pushed the door in and what he saw made his stomach turn over. This time he fell to his knees and had to fight with all his willpower not to retch. Wardric lay on the lush, silk bed—or rather, his body did. His throat was slit end to end, blood so dark it looked like pitch stained the sheets and pooled across the wooden floor.

Torsten's fingers slid through the liquid on his way to investigate the body. He wasn't sure why he needed to check if Wardric was alive. Maybe instinct. Maybe he was hoping for a miracle. But it was clear from the moment he entered, his friend was dead.

Torsten crawled backward. He was breathing so fast it felt like his lungs were going to pop.

"Iam guide me," he rasped. "Iam guide me..." He repeated that over and over as he clutched at his chest. His armor was there, stained red and still tight against his frame. He had to unstrap his chestplate just to feel like he could draw air. A few of his men saw him floundering in the snow and ran over. Their faces were blurs, their words, muted.

All he could focus on was the man blithely strolling across the battlefield. His crimson robes flapped in the wind. His pale skin blended with the snow, the mark on his face like a bloodspot.

Torsten went blind to everything else in the world. He rose, threw off his chest plate and stormed at the man.

"Sir Unger," Redstar said as he approached. "You should see one of my healers. They'll sew you up in no time."

"You killed him!" Torsten thundered. He seized Redstar and slammed him to the ground. The Arch Warlock went for his dagger, but Torsten ripped it away from him and held it at his throat.

"What are you talking about?" Redstar grated.

"Wardric. I found him, Redstar. I found him slaughtered like swine so that you could lead the charge."

Redstar closed his eyes and let his head fall back into the snow. He looked exhausted but not afraid, which only propelled Torsten to press the edge of the blade tighter against his skin.

"Deny it!" Torsten shouted.

Redstar tilted his head and looked toward the ground. "He doesn't know."

"Don't talk to her," Torsten snapped, yanking Redstar's head back straight. "This is between me and you."

"This is between you and you, Sir Unger. Look around. I have just taken Winde Port back, and all you want to do is drive us away because we don't follow your god."

"What do you want, Redstar? The King forced you at my side. Is that not enough?"

"Torsten, I suggest you get off me." His eyes signaled for Torsten to look around. A crowd had gathered around them. Drav Cra and Glassmen, King's Shieldsmen and warlocks of Nesilia. Drad Mak stood amongst a group of fur-clad warriors, each one more tremendous than the next, but none more than him. He gripped his axe in two hands. Freydis and two other warlocks held their daggers to their palms, black face paint making their eyes bright with rage

"You think I'm afraid of them?" Torsten looked up but never

let the knife shift. "This man killed Sir Wardric Jolly! He left his body to rot in that carriage!"

Nobody answered.

"Reach into my pocket," Redstar said.

"What?"

"Wardric was nothing but a lap dog. Why would I kill him? Now, reach into my pocket and find the answers you already know."

Torsten pressed against Redstar's throat with his elbow and did as instructed. He removed a stack of letters.

"What is this?" Torsten said. "What are these."

"Correspondence between Yuri Darkings and the rebel afhem. A lot of yammering about the Glass Kingdom's fortunes fading and the unworthy heirs of Liam the Conqueror. Riveting stuff really, but I'll let you decide."

Torsten leafed through them with one hand. Some were written in ink on parchment, the seal of the Darkings house at the top. Others were etched into dark gray sheets of paper made from the black palms of the Shesaitju beaches, signed by Afhem Muskigo. Page after page. He spotted instructions that Torsten was planning to head to Marimount, ways to avoid Glass scouts as his armies were moved into position.

"Sir Wardric caught Yuri and his son sending a galler bird into Winde Port. He wasn't able to stop them warning Muskigo of your ambush, but he detained them and sent for me. When I got there, I found his body and them fleeing."

"And you just let them run?"

"I sent my wolves after them, but they haven't yet returned. I had to make a choice. The traitors, or take advantage of our summoned wind and flame and charge on Winde Port."

"A blessing called upon from Nesilia herself by the hero of Winde Port," a Drav Cra warrior said.

"What did you say?" Torsten said. He yanked Redstar upright

and stood, knife still at his neck. "This man is no hero!" He looked to his own men, whose faces were twisted by concern— even the King's Shieldsmen watching. "He turns to dark arts and fallen gods. His every breath is an insult to Iam."

"Torsten, put down the weapon," Redstar said.

"Don't you all see? Every word out of his mouth is a lie! These letters, forgeries meant to spoil a house that has loyally served the Glass for decades so he may deceive us all; just as he wore the face of Uriah Davies to fool me." He flung the letters onto the ground.

"Wore a face?" Redstar laughed. "I am one with the magic of Elsewhere, but even I cannot *wear* a face."

"Lies! Shieldsmen, I want you to arrest this traitor for the murder of Sir Wardric Jolly."

The men of his order looked to each other, but not a soul moved. Torsten searched the faces for a familiar one. Sir Nikserof Pasic or any of the most celebrated Shieldsmen he'd led into the ambush, but there were none present. They were all dead or injured. And all that remained were men he hadn't yet fought beside and whom he'd barely been a part of training.

"That is an order from your Wearer!" Torsten said.

"Control yourself, Torsten," Redstar whispered. "Look to your God."

"Look to my God? *Look to my God?* I'm going to do something I should have done back in the Webbed Woods. It's time this kingdom is free of—"

Redstar slid his head forward, catching the side of his neck on the dagger. Blood leaked out, but the slice didn't catch anything vital. As Redstar collapsed, Torsten knew what was coming, but he was too slow. The Arch Warlock whipped around, extended a hand, and all Torsten's muscles became paralyzed. Redstar tore the blade out of his hand with a thought and Torsten couldn't do a thing.

Northerners ran to Redstar to stop the bleeding. He pushed them away. The more blood, the stronger his hold on Torsten would be.

"I took Winde Port!" Redstar shouted, the rage in his voice making the very air vibrate. "With this power and faith you eschew, I took it. Perhaps, Sir Unger, you too have been swayed by Muskigo to betrayal. Perhaps that is why the rebel Afhem still lives."

"I…" Torsten opened his mouth to speak, but Redstar closed his fingers, and with it, Torsten's lips went rigid as stone.

"Do not speak." Redstar turned to the crowd. "This is the man who you would follow as Wearer? A man who would kill your King's unarmed uncle just because he's too frightened to accept help from a goddess who loves all of you just as she loved Iam? How many lives among you did she just save!"

Redstar swiped his arm down and forced Torsten to his knees. He begged his muscles to move, but even trying made his entire body burn.

"Shieldsmen," Redstar went on. "You charged with me. Clearly, your Wearer is broken. If I release him, he will kill me. So, I ask you, as the royal uncle and the only man who can lead this army effectively, arrest him. We will drag him before the King, and there, he shall be weighed justly for his actions. Perhaps even he can be saved of whatever it is that haunts him."

His men seemed petrified as they looked to each other, none willing to make the first move. Then, finally, the blonde Shieldsman Torsten had scolded for drinking back at camp stepped forward. He was emboldened by alcohol, and Torsten dug through his mind to find a name with which to beg. He couldn't.

So instead, he just struggled to squeeze a single word through his magically sealed lips, "P… please."

The Shieldsman took Torsten by the arms. Redstar released

those limbs of his magic so they could be wrenched behind Torsten's back.

"I'm sorry, Sir," the Shieldsman said, "but he's right. He saved this city while you were gone. You aren't thinking clearly."

Redstar smirked. "Thank you, Sir Mulliner," he addressed the Shieldsman.

The sense of pride in Redstar's voice as he spoke the name Torsten couldn't find made Torsten feel ill. Never in his life had he wanted to kill someone so badly. Even Muskigo he respected for his prowess, but Redstar was a trickster demon in human form. Whether or not anything he said about Wardric was true, he could have told Torsten on the docks about what happened with the Darkings. He could have revealed the truth then, but instead, allowed Torsten to make this spectacle.

"I'm sorry it had to come to this, Torsten," Redstar said. "But you are in need of help. He leaned down, his breath hot on Torsten's ear. "Pi may breathe now thanks to the Buried Goddess, but it seems Iam favors me now, too," he whispered. He turned to walk away, releasing his mystical hold of Torsten's body.

Torsten had been waiting for that exact moment. "I'll kill you!" he roared. Sir Mulliner tried to restrain him, but Torsten used his massive body to tear free. Another of the Shieldsmen who'd been drinking with Sir Mulliner grabbed him, but Torsten tossed him aside like a doll. The man's face smashed against a rock.

Sir Mulliner ran to his friend, and Torsten tore the sheathed longsword off the Mulliner's belt while he was distracted and sprung at Redstar. He didn't get far. The pommel of a sword bashed against the back of his head and knocked him face first into the snow and dirt. The last thing he realized before he spun into oblivion was who had taken him down like the raving lunatic Redstar made him seem.

One of his own men. A King's Shieldsman, but not Sir

Mulliner or another relative stranger. It was Nikserof, a man of the old guard with whom Torsten had endured a crucible of blood, barely able to stand from his wounds. Nikserof watched in horror, and as Torsten's vision began to go fuzzy, he knew that he'd given him no choice.

XXX

THE THIEF

Gray mist swirled around Whitney as he was jarred back to consciousness. There was no telling how long he'd been out, but nothing looked as it had just moments ago. Where there were night skies, there was now a vibrant red expanse, as if fire filled the heavens. Strangely, the sound of waves was still there, though he no longer felt wood beneath him. Instead, dry chalk billowed with each movement as he coaxed himself to rise.

Before him, the shore of an endless ocean stretched out to the horizon. The fog rolled along it like the wheels of a chariot. But something about the water was... off. It was black—the color of old blood.

"Where the..." Whitney exhaled.

"How did we?"

Whitney spun toward the accented voice behind him.

"You!" he shouted, then lunged at Kazimir with abandon. "This is your fault!"

Somehow, he tackled the impossibly fast upyr and brought

him down. Whitney mounted him and was able to drive one fist into his nose. Kazimir caught his next punch, and while he waited for his hand to be crushed, Whitney noticed the blood pouring from Kazimir's nose. Whitney was so stunned to see it, he allowed Kazimir to push him off.

The upyr wiped his nose with the back of his hand. The look on his face would have given Whitney enough joy to sustain him for a lifetime, had he known where the yig he was.

"No, this isn't possible," Kazimir said. "Not again."

"All things are possible here," said another voice.

Whitney whipped around again toward the voice. It was frail and withering.

"Oh great," Whitney said. "Who the yigging exile are you, now?"

The man was nearly doubled in half he was so hunched over. A robe hung down, whipping back and forth in the black waters along the shore. He stood beside a tiny rowboat that somehow didn't float away despite not being moored. A hood covered his head, casting a deep shadow over his face. If he even had a face.

"You may call me the Ferryman," the stranger said.

"Right, and I'm the world's greatest thief," Whitney replied.

"I know exactly who you are, Mr. Fierstown."

Whitney took a step back, eyes wide. "Then you'll know that's not my name anymore."

"A man cannot escape who he is. I've been waiting for you... both of you."

The mysterious new presence nearly made Whitney forget the upyr behind him.

"Yeah? Then who is he?" Whitney said, pointing to Kazimir.

"Who is he... that is a question with a far longer answer," the Ferryman said.

Whitney shot a glance at Kazimir. The upyr's gaze drifted downward.

"He has gone by many names," the Ferryman continued. "Haven't you?"

"What do you want, old man?" Kazimir asked.

Whitney stepped forward and threw open his arms. "Can everyone take a deep breath and explain what the yig-and-shog is going on? Where is Sora? Where is Tum Tum? Where is—"

"Whatever your mystic friend did has sent us to Elsewhere, you fool," Kazimir said. "The world between worlds."

"We're…" Whitney paused to take a deep breath. "Dead?"

"Some would say so. Some would say not. Much like him." The Ferryman stepped up onto the tiny boat and lifted a long oar just like the ones gondolas used to navigate the canals of Winde Port.

"Now join me," the Ferryman said. "The Sea of Lost Souls is no place to linger."

Kazimir approached without a fuss. "You didn't keep me here last time, spirit," he grumbled as he climbed up. "You won't this time, either."

"Give me one good reason for getting in that boat with him," Whitney said.

The Ferryman raised his hand. Spectral arms reached up through the shallow water, dozens of them, pawing at Whitney's ankles. They passed through his flesh and bone, yet he could feel a chill with every one.

Whitney was on the boat so fast he wasn't even sure how he got there.

"Well put," Whitney said.

"Let's make this quick," Kazimir said.

"No need to rush," the Ferryman said as he pushed his oar through the water. "We have eternity."

The sea lapped against the sides of the boat as they moved forward. Specters teemed beneath the surface, their moans like broken lutes playing on a loop.

"Shog in a barrel," Whitney said as fog enveloped them like a shroud of death.

THANK YOU!

Thank you for reading *Winds of War,* book two in The Buried Goddess Saga.

Being the new kids on the block is difficult and we could really benefit from your honest reviews on Amazon. It'll only take you a minute but it'll affect the life of this book forever! (Not to mention help feed our families). All you have to do is click **here** and then scroll down and write a review. HUGE thank you in advance for helping making The Buried Goddess Saga a big hit!

FROM THE PUBLISHER

Thank you so much for reading Winds of War by Rhett C. Bruno and Jaime Castle. We hope you enjoyed it as much as we enjoyed bringing it to you. We just wanted to take a moment to encourage you to review the book on Amazon and Goodreads. Every review helps further the author's reach and, ultimately, helps them continue writing fantastic books for us all to enjoy.

If you liked Winds of War, check out the rest of our catalogue at www.aethonbooks.com. To sign up to receive updates regarding all new releases, visit www.aethonbooks.com/sign-up

JOIN THE KING'S SHIELD

Sign up to the *free* and exclusive King's Shield Newsletter to receive updates about sequels, conceptual art that breathes life into Pantego, as well as exclusive access to short stories called "Legends of Pantego." Learn more about the characters and the world you love.

ABOUT THE AUTHORS

Jaime lives in Texas with his wife and two kids. He enjoys anything creative, from graphic arts to painting. His office looks like the Avengers threw up on the walls.

Jaime has been writing since elementary school and is a bit of a grammar officer—here to correct and serve.

Rhett is a Sci-fi/Fantasy author currently living in Stamford, Connecticut. His published works include books in the USA Today Bestselling CIRCUIT SERIES (Published by Diversion Books and Podium Audio), THE BURIED GODDESS SAGA and the BASTARDS OF THE RING SERIES (Audible Studios, coming in 2019). He is also one of the founders of the popular science fiction platform, Sci-Fi Bridge.

SPECIAL THANKS TO:

ADAWIA E. ASAD	EDDIE HALLAHAN	KYLE OATHOUT
BARDE PRESS	JOSH HAYES	LILY OMIDI
CALUM BEAULIEU	PAT HAYES	TROY OSGOOD
BEN	BILL HENDERSON	GEOFF PARKER
BECKY BEWERSDORF	JEFF HOFFMAN	NICHOLAS (BUZ) PENNEY
BHAM	GODFREY HUEN	JASON PENNOCK
TANNER BLOTTER	JOAN QUERALTÓ IBÁÑEZ	THOMAS PETSCHAUER
ALFRED JOSEPH BOHNE IV	JONATHAN JOHNSON	JENNIFER PRIESTER
CHAD BOWDEN	MARCEL DE JONG	RHEL
ERREL BRAUDE	KABRINA	JODY ROBERTS
DAMIEN BROUSSARD	PETRI KANERVA	JOHN BEAR ROSS
CATHERINE BULLINER	ROBERT KARALASH	DONNA SANDERS
JUSTIN BURGESS	VIKTOR KASPERSSON	FABIAN SARAVIA
MATT BURNS	TESLAN KIERINHAWK	TERRY SCHOTT
BERNIE CINKOSKE	ALEXANDER KIMBALL	SCOTT
MARTIN COOK	JIM KOSMICKI	ALLEN SIMMONS
ALISTAIR DILWORTH	FRANKLIN KUZENSKI	KEVIN MICHAEL STEPHENS
JAN DRAKE	MEENAZ LODHI	MICHAEL J. SULLIVAN
BRET DULEY	DAVID MACFARLANE	PAUL SUMMERHAYES
RAY DUNN	JAMIE MCFARLANE	JOHN TREADWELL
ROB EDWARDS	HENRY MARIN	CHRISTOPHER J. VALIN
RICHARD EYRES	CRAIG MARTELLE	PHILIP VAN ITALLIE
MARK FERNANDEZ	THOMAS MARTIN	JAAP VAN POELGEEST
CHARLES T FINCHER	ALAN D. MCDONALD	FRANCK VAQUIER
SYLVIA FOIL	JAMES MCGLINCHEY	VORTEX
GAZELLE OF CAERBANNOG	MICHAEL MCMURRAY	DAVID WALTERS JR
DAVID GEARY	CHRISTIAN MEYER	MIKE A. WEBER
MICHEAL GREEN	SEBASTIAN MÜLLER	PAMELA WICKERT
BRIAN GRIFFIN	MARK NEWMAN	JON WOODALL
	JULIAN NORTH	BRUCE YOUNG

17975946R00229

Printed in Great Britain
by Amazon